# AS THE CROW DIES

by the same author

THE LOST PATENT

DUST NUMBERS

TRANSFERRED

THE MEMORY GARDEN OF MIGUEL CARRANZA

THE CONFUSION OF STONES

MARWAN HASSAN

# AS THE CROW DIES

COMMON REDPOLL BOOKS
OTTAWA

Published by Common Redpoll Books
99 Holmwood Avenue, Ottawa, ON Canada K1S 2P1



Library and Archives Canada Cataloguing in Publication

Hassan, Marwan, 1950-
As the crow dies / Marwan Hassan.

ISBN 0-9734637-3-2

I. Title.

PS8565.A729A9 2005 C813'.54 C2005-905214-7





Printed in Canada

commonredpollbooks@sympatico.ca

1 3 5 4 2

for Qays and Baalqis

# ONE

A crow perched on the bough of the leafy oak. Water dripped off the black feathers of the crow. In a second panel of the Japanese print, there roosted on the branches two lines of crows with shoulders hunched. The crows cawed. In a third panel of the print, a man and a woman kissed. Then the cawing of the crows called me out of the pleasure, and I was wide awake. The birds were on the other side of sleep.

I rolled over and saw a smiling face.

"Good dream?" Lynda grinned.

"You bet."

"I could tell."

The crows again, this time recognizably from outside in the alley. We remained silent, side by side in bed, skin brushing against skin, listening to these shrewd birds tattle-tale.

"Alec, I don't remember quite so many crows. Do you?"

"You wanna know something, I haven't given it any thought. But you could be right. I'm aware of them hanging about during winter and spring. Comic crows."

"But there've been so many this summer. They seem so serious."

Lynda got up and went across the creaking hardwood floor to the window, gazed out at the tall poplar in the ragged back alley of the three-storey apartment building. She had a good form. A dancer's dynamic muscles and balanced movements. Graceful poise. I stared at her sinuous leg muscles as she arched and looked out the window.

"Sounds like a whole crew of crows," I called from the mattress.

"Group name. Alec, you mean murder."

"Right, murder of crows carrying on. Sound kinda cockamamie."

"Décalcomanie, eh?"

"De quelquoi?"

"Décalquer. Papered glass bottles. They're out there on the big poplar next to the oak. Must be near to twenty of 'em."

"Twae and twantie corbies sing a chorus of complaint."

"Not corbie. They are not ravens. They're Canuck crows. Caw caw to you. Nevermore." She craned her neck and grinned at me.

"Quoi quoi. Can you dance like a crow?"

"You know I can. It's elementary, my sweet Knight. Dancing like any bird." She scrunched up and went flapping across the oak floor from the window to the wall, from the wall to the doorway improvising a crow dance. Lynda cawed and I laughed as she glided back to the window. "How's that for Aandek?"

"Come again?"

"Anishnaabe, Ojibwe for crow." She stared out the window again. "Wait. There's one down. Looks like a hurt crow on the grass below the tree. But it's not moving."

I got up, went to the window, and glanced out. "Ask me, it looks kinda dead." It was still. Its compatriots were clustered above on the boughs, their beaks biting the morning light. They now sounded inspectoral and sombre with grief.

"I don't like to see dead birds. It makes me feel creepy tender inside. Here." She touched her belly button. "You should bury it, Alec."

"I'm going to call it in. The health department. Contagious diseases said something about calling in sightings of dead crows and blue jays."

I went to the front room and telephoned. The guy came 'round. The weather was beautiful. The air was soft and warm. As fine a day as could be asked for. Lynda and I stood in the ragged yard while he bagged the crow.

On the way into work, I dropped Lynda off at her place. She was getting ready to leave for Japan. She had got a scholarship to study languages at a university in the north of Japan. On the side, she would teach English. That spring she and I, knowing when we had started hanging out things could only be temporary, had held ourselves a little back. I had not quite got to know her. And I suppose that she had not really gotten to know me. Everything had stayed casual and temporary. Low key. The odd weekend together. Lunch or brunch in the market. An evening movie at the repertory theatres, the Bytown on Rideau or Mayfair on Bank. A ride into the Gatineau Hills for a dip in the cool lakes on the hottest days of summer when both of us could spare the time. We didn't talk much about our families and the past. I knew little about that side of her life. In it for the pleasure, a sensual intimacy sheathed in anonymity seemed just fine, lower the level of attachment. Until I realized she was going away. Crummy detachment. But I said nothing.

I drove over to Bronson Avenue, stopping at Saikely's Lunchroom to have a coffee. Morrison Chang and Cheryl Perron ran Maxwell grind through the drip machine at work, and when I drank a cup, I thought my bladder was in need of work. They jested that this was a sign of snobbery and pretentiousness on my part. There was just an element of truth there. I was fussy about coffee. Which made Saikely's really a strange place because it was not just any old bucket of coffee that they brewed. I preferred espresso but Saikely's had perfect percolated coffee by the vat and they weren't selling the formula to Starbucks.

I expected the mundane at work and flipped through the local rag. With each change of ownership there was less and less news and more and more hype. Each new publisher proclaimed a new regime of candour and honesty. If information is knowledge there was one huge deficit being run up. I turned past the front page headlines, to the local city page: a fight in a bar with one guy stabbed, but he was luckier than a squirrel trapped in a cage and would make it, a city council meeting over expansion of the O-train, a teenage girl missing since the weekend, last seen Friday night on Rideau Street. I flipped through the want ads as I sipped the coffee. Even after the Barrett case Lajoie–Chang did not give me a raise although I got the bonus. I had spent the last several months with the routine, doing a lot of process serving and some skip traces. The biggest thing Lajoie–Chang had sent me out on in the last months had been a background check on a dude who wanted to marry the daughter of a millionaire family. The parents thought their daughter was getting mixed up with a broke money grabber. Heck, the guy didn't even play the slots at the casino. He turned out to be no more than a hard-working guy, an electrician, whose worst crimes were an inability to speak well for himself, a traffic violation for a rattling muffler on his worn down ten-year-old half-ton, and a bad bout of unemployment two years ago. The costs of inarticulateness are high. And unemployment worse. I knew. I'd been there. I felt crappy sniffing round the guy's character, getting photos of the couple in their awkward intimacy. Judging by conversations overheard in coffee shops and cheap restaurants, the guy didn't even know the woman came from money, as far as he was concerned she was a legal secretary working for a living just like himself. He gave her in his own clumsy way an affection that the parents couldn't. Then it didn't matter, the daughter was pregnant and the parents were pissed off in that special way that rich people can be over a pregnancy. I had noticed, working with family lawyers, that some people just resent other people getting laid. Probably what the old got against the young. Reserved wisdom on love tossed out to conceal sexual diminishment. I flipped the page, nothing in the want ads. I wanted a raise, thought I deserved one.

I closed the section and left for the office.

"Morning, Alec. Georges wants to see you."

"Sure Cheryl. Any cheques in the mail for the pillar of the agency?"

"Funny guy. Go see Georges."

"Please no more process serving."

"No. He's got something. Clients in the office waiting."

"Who is it?"

"Couple named Strachan. Up from the luminous city of limestone."

"Kingston clients? What's going down in the town of ten thousand cells?"

"Missing daughter."

"Okay."

I rapped Lajoie's door. Georges opened the door himself. Georges was truly the best person to meet in the morning. Ebullient, he had a durable congeniality that didn't succumb to the PCDs, the enfants terribles triplets of this racket: pessimism, cynicism and defeatism. Unlike Morrison, cool and pragmatic, who could trash the morning hours with the rigours and demands of work and in the afternoon grew calm and quiet. After twelve, I tried to avoid interrupting Morrison, the aura of conscientiousness was overwhelming.

On this Tuesday morning after the Labour Day weekend, Georges looked better groomed than usual, a fine beige linen suit, a sharp red tie, his dark hair smoothed back, defined by a careful part. The art objects in the office seemed more brilliant, the vase and sculptures and that enigmatic photograph on the shelf. A stranger, forty or forty-five. The only photo in the room, a two-thirds image of a man in a dapper suit, tie and open woollen overcoat with a rose in the lapel, a fedora hat in his long fingers. The man was bald, his eyes large, the eyebrows thick, long and arching, and the large but graceful nose I presumed to be a nose in the know. He looked tall and dignified. The photo seemed distant. Possibly it was taken as far back as the nineteen-twenties or thirties. The image had a decorum to it. The man was posed and poised yet there was something public and immediate even spontaneous in the taking of the image. A stylish fellow, a slight tilt to the upper torso, shoulders firm, confident lift to his chin caught just in that instant but he was not reckless and had not been caught unawares, he had had his wits about him and had gazed straight into the camera. The aura of springtime. A stone building lurked in the background. Maybe a courthouse or some other official edifice. That's Montreal stonework, I thought.

The guy in the photo seemed to be staring over Georges Lajoie's shoulder at me. And he seemed a protective spirit of Georges himself. I thought I discerned the faintest resemblance between the two men but then I thought it was projection on my part. I had often been tempted to just ask Georges straight up who the guy was but I knew almost from the first day that if you had your wits about you, you didn't ask Georges Lajoie a direct personal question, he'd sink your brain with some obscurity or circumlocution that obliged you to rummage through your own brain. Lajoie abhorred questions of a personal nature, and his imperturbable manner seemed to imply they were imprudent, impertinent and impudent. Worse yet, in an inquisitor they were a sign of impatience, and worst of all, improper, lacking in investigative wit. But I had to admit that over the years the man in the photograph mystified me, and I wanted to pick up the filigreed metal frame on some casual pretext and glance at the back to see if there was some telltale word or sticker, a clue to who the gentleman was. But I dared not touch anything in Lajoie's vicinity. That was a great rule of office protocol on Bronson Avenue. And I respected it. I would wait dutifully. What the heck, I had waited three years. I could wait yet, even three more. I figured some pretext would in time present itself as it inevitably does with any provocative curiosity.

Yet I did wonder why such a small token should instigate my curiosity so furiously and tempt me to pry for knowledge. Maybe it was the season, the humidity of the Ottawa valley, or just the idleness in the brain brought on by too much process serving, the petty stress associated with skip tracing. Rebarbative moments on the doormat. Barking telephone calls. Maybe I was run-of-the-mill in this racket but I did pride myself on two counts, my patience and my memory. Even Lajoie, a man not lavish in his praise, now and again praised my patience and memory though reproaching me for my youth. Prowess in memory, he remarked, is squandered on the young.

"Alec, I know Frank Strachan a little."

"From where?"

"A real estate embezzlement case about fifteen years ago."

"Who was embezzling from who?"

"Whom. Case endings, Alec, discretion goes with asking the right questions of the right person with the correct grammar. An old rule in the language game. And ask no questions that might allow one word or one sentence answers. Technique."

"Right. Another old rule in an investigation. Good grammar. You and old Mr Wolsey, my Latin teacher, just won't leave me alone."

"Alec, the Strachans are real estate lawyers. And if you know real estate law, it's an assembly line gig. Open file, search title, requisition letter, documents, money into trust account, keys to purchaser, reporting letters, fees and disbursements from trust, close the file. All things considered, whether shuffling for the purchaser or vendor, it's got to be as near as the practice of law will ever get to Fordism."

"You mean Freudianism."

"No, I mean Fordism. Taylorism."

"Right Georges. I saw a dead crow this morning. I reported it."

"That was thoughtful of you. Citizen Knight performing his civic duty."

"The city health guy said West Nile virus is floating north."

"You're alert. More important. Trace time. There are clients waiting. The crows, being scavengers, can take care of themselves. With the digestive tract that bird's got it'll still be around when human beings are extinct." He slid the file folder across the desk.

"I'm going to take this up with Morrison. He'll appreciate the import of this information."

"We'll put it under embargo which means in this town you'll never see it again. Go see Frank and Mary Strachan."

"Sure." I picked up the file folder and my paper cup and left.

"Which conference room, Cheryl?"

"Alec, what are you thinking about? The way you are looking at the doors you'd think it was Christians and lions."

"Cheryl, this morning I saw a dead crow under the poplar behind my apartment building."

"Ugh. Icky feeling. Dead birds give me the willies."

"It's an important death. A death in any species is important."

"Clients, Alec. They're important. They've been waiting fifteen minutes. Strachans are lawyers. You know they run the money meter."

"Alright. But a dead crow is important Cheryl. I called the health department."

"Aren't you a man of civic virtue. Maybe you'll join the Civic Unity Party."

"How come nobody's taking this seriously. We're talking about dead crows. A possible avian plague."

"The mop and pail declares it's hysteria."

"Please no Freudianism this morning."

"Alec, go see the clients will you."

I opened the door and went in.

"Sorry to have kept you waiting, Mr and Ms Strachan." I said it but I didn't mean it. Like a fool I only wanted to fabricate some pretext to talk about Lynda but an investigator can't do that with clients. Impersonal is the key word in this trade. "Mr Lajoie was just briefing me."

Frank and Mary Strachan each offered their hand, we shook. Mr Strachan was every inch a real estate solicitor around the girth. Fat would have been cruel and a rudeness, but corpulent wouldn't have done him an injustice. My grandfather's archaic slang for body parts would have called Strachan's stomach an alderman. Although I also heard him on one occasion use the same word, alderman, more obscurely to refer to a burglar's crowbar, all the littler tools in the burglar's kit were citizens. My paternal grandfather seemed to know such arcane things. As for Frank Strachan, he had the further distinction of going bald, and wore a pressed summer-weight blue pin-striped suit. It looked off-the-rack with nothing in the way of alterations to accommodate his waistline. Although not chintzy linen the tightness made it look halfway to cheap, like the solid blue textured silk tie twisted into a graceless and stingy knot more tangled than deft.

Mary Strachan was fleshy. She deserved that but nothing worse. At fifty-five, beneath the residue of puffiness, I could discern a once extremely good-looking woman, maybe she had once been considered beautiful. But with her middle-age slide into solidity and staidness, her face would be called handsome. Her hair was dark with only a few traces of grey, while her dark blue eyes seemed cautious, conservative, and stern. She wore a dark blue dress made of fine fabric, well cut, even tasteful, except that it was just a little snug. Most people can't wear the clothing they want. When a beautiful woman is deemed handsome and dresses well but on the uncomfortable side, the world is governed by appearance and grown cruel with cynical observation. Time, that thug, waylays rich and poor alike with neither politeness nor kindness. The more you want to look good, the worse you'll appear. My own shabby suit suddenly felt as if it needed to be pressed. The morning was already off to a couture contrast and I really needed a raise.

I sat down at the conference table across from the middle-aged couple.

"Mr Lajoie briefed me but it is important to have details straight from you. Maybe we could go over the situation."

"Certainly." Strachan fidgeted. "Mr Knight, mind if I smoke?"

"I'm sorry Mr Strachan, Lajoie–Chang offices are smoke-free."

"Right. We're here regarding our daughter Elizabeth. Liz. And her disappearance. We don't want to be hasty in impugning the abilities of the police but—"

"Mr Knight," Mary Strachan interrupted, "I'm afraid I have to be blunt. Liz has been missing for a week. The police appear to be sitting on their hands. Time is passing swiftly with no answers. Without any action."

Frank Strachan stared at the floor. Mary Strachan pressed her hand against the table's edge. I thought with relief, better not to be married. I thought of the acrimonious late stages of my parents' marriage. Acrimony. Alienation. And alimony. What my Toronto buddy, Johnny Olive, bundled up as the big D, which comes before the little d, the final detail.

"How so, Ms Strachan?"

"We keep in regular touch. We're a pretty close family. It's not like Liz to go off without letting us know where she'd be going. Even if we might not hear from her for two or three weeks. Say, if she were out of the country on a holiday. Something must have happened. But the police are treating this as a little too routine for my taste."

"Let's get some facts in place first. I think we can get to what the police are doing in due time."

Ms Strachan made a subtle impatient sound with her tongue against her palate. If I hadn't been listening to crows I would have taken it as a rebuke.

"Please, give me some background on your daughter Liz. Where she lives, what she does for a living. When she was possibly last seen. By anyone who knows her. That sort of thing. Let's start with what does your daughter do?"

"Liz is a law student at the University of Ottawa. She did her undergraduate degree there. We wanted her to go to school in Kingston at Queen's but she was determined to go to university out of town. She chose Ottawa because it's bilingual and she wants to maintain her French. And they have a good law school."

"What did she do her undergraduate degree in?"

"Psychology. She was an A student. Very sharp. Our daughter is an exceedingly bright woman."

"I see. What year of law school is she in?"

"This is her second year. The new semester, I mean classes begin today so it makes utterly no sense that she is not around. None whatsoever."

"When was the last time you saw your daughter or spoke with her?"

"Two weeks ago from the past Sunday. We told her if we had time we might come up for a brief visit on Labour Day."

"How were you in touch?"

"On the telephone. She mentioned that she would be going up to the Gatineau with friends for a relaxing few days in the last week of

August before school started. Apparently Liz went to the Gatineau on Wednesday."

"Did she come back?"

"Yes. She returned as far as we know on the Sunday. Her sister—our daughter Brenda lives in town—spoke with Liz on the Sunday. Brenda works in the department of justice."

"Lawyer?"

"Yes. It runs in the family."

"Sure. Do your two daughters live together?"

"No. Brenda has, how shall I put it, a different sensibility than Liz. Brenda's the introvert in the family. If you understand me, Mr Knight. They have quite different lifestyles."

"Then Liz lives alone or shares a place with someone?"

"Liz has her own place. Liz is independent. A true extrovert, Mr Knight. There's nobody who isn't attracted or charmed by Liz. She's charm itself. We don't like to compare our daughters. Brenda has a marvellous intellect. She's so brilliant in the law, the justice department snatched her up right away. But she is a very quiet person. Reserved. A true introvert."

"I see."

"And Liz is so charismatic. Very sociable. She has so much charisma people are just naturally drawn to her."

"When was the last time that your daughter Brenda saw or spoke with her sister Liz?"

"Brenda told us she last spoke with Liz on the last Sunday in August, about a week ago."

"You mentioned the Wednesday that Liz went away. How'd she get to the cottage?"

"Drove up."

"Does your daughter own a car?"

"Yes."

"I'll need the make and licence number."

Frank Strachan scribbled down the info on a pad and slipped me the sheet.

"Where is her car now?"

"It is parked in the underground garage of the apartment building where she lives."

"Did she drive it up to the Gatineau?"

"She didn't use her car. I believe she went with a friend. A woman named Connie Yonge."

"How'd you come by that?"

"Brenda mentioned Connie Yonge as one of the people driving up."

"Where'd they go in the Gatineau?"

"To a cottage near Maniwaki."

"Whose cottage?"

"It's not ours. I don't know who owns it. According to Brenda, Ms Yonge seems to have rented it for the last week of August. And Liz just went up for a few days."

"What do you know of Connie Yonge?"

"I understand she's a neighbour of Liz's in the apartment building. She lives across the hall. I believe she works for an airline. Actually I'm not certain on that point. We've actually never met the woman."

"Does your daughter have someone she goes out with regularly?"

"Not to my knowledge."

"Mary, there was that Al Stanley."

"Frank, you mean Ed Stanley. But he wasn't exactly steady or anything."

"Mr Knight," Frank Strachan started in, "the fellow's a student. A football star on the university team. Fullback. Liz went out with this fellow. We met him a couple of times in passing."

"Frank's right. But Mr Knight, I have the impression Liz lost interest in him. He's a nice enough sort. Good-looking. Congenial. But he really was not compatible with Liz's intellect. Not Liz's calibre if you understand me. Although I'm sure he's a capable enough student."

"I see, Ms Strachan. What alerted you to your daughter's absence?"

"Disappearance, Mr Knight. This is not a casual thing."

I nodded.

"We phoned. We were thinking we'd come up to Ottawa on the long weekend to see the girls. We usually talk to Liz maybe every other weekend. We like to keep in touch with our daughters. And then the landlord phoned on the third of September to say Liz had not paid her rent and that it was overdue. That seemed peculiar. It had been due on the first. We do help her out on occasion, but she usually pays the rent herself."

"The landlord called you?"

"No. Not quite. We called them. Liz gave Brenda and ourselves as contacts. And the landlord's building superintendent had called Brenda first. And on the Thursday Brenda called us to ask whether she should go ahead and pay Liz's rent for September."

"Did Brenda?"

"No. We did. We came up on Friday and gave a cheque to the building superintendent. And that's when he told us he had not seen Liz in a week."

"How big is the apartment building?"

"Eighty, maybe ninety units, I think. Maybe a little bigger. A ten-storey building."

"Is it possible that the superintendent didn't notice Liz coming and going?"

"I suppose. But it hardly seems likely." Mary Strachan paused.

"Mr Knight," said Frank Strachan, "what you say seems plausible until you meet the landlord's man, then it doesn't fit. Don't get me wrong, the guy isn't a bad sort but if you talk to him you'll see right off that he's nosey, a snoop." Frank Strachan gave a grin but it had a slice of grimace in it. "If you know what I mean. He's a bored sort and looks to keep a pretty sharp eye on the tenants."

"Mr Knight, the fellow's a busybody," remarked Mary Strachan.

"What's the superintendent's name?"

"Willett. Pierre Willett."

I wrote down the apartment address and the company that owned the building, Melgund Construction and Management. I recognized the outfit. When it came to security they played strictly with para-police corporations. Melgund was a developer famously infamous, it had slapped up every tenth apartment and condo unit in Bytown, from shoddy to stylish, their rental rates worked the wallets from thin to thick. Except they had taken a managerial oath never to rent to a tenant on welfare or a student on an educational loan. They had supplied a string of two-bit lawyers peddling distinguished nonsense and tinned sardines and backed them for the mayor's office and city council. Such chummy personalities came up mostly as winners in the municipal elections. Melgund's candidates had been more stuffed with the rhetoric of civic responsibility than a Thanksgiving turkey with sweetbreads while their mayoral chums reworked the zoning laws towards corporate congeniality. Its leasing subsidiary was Mellow Realty Corp., where a tenant needed a powerhouse lawyer to decipher the lease. Bottom line for tenants' rights, the double emphatic negative: nil and nihil. Sure, the patrons of Bytown bars jested telling jocular tales as Melgund tenants. The lease of megarealty corporations was part of the reason I was still living in a worn down brown brick apartment block on Somerset West built circa 1900. The block was owned by an old Ottawa family that ran a fruit store established by the grandfather, who had been a pedlar. The old guy had trudged the back counties of the Ottawa valley and had purchased the building in the nineteen-thirties. His descendants wanted nothing more than the rent cheque the first of each month with no questions asked. The rent was stable while the lease, a solitary page, was swift and rudimentary in its principles. Concision itself: you pay, we collect, and please don't telephone with complaints. The upscale options in high–rise apartment buildings instilled vertigo. A new apartment block was like being condemned to a vertical debtor's prison. Tall and new with a view I did not need.

"Well you understand Mr Knight, after speaking with Mr Willett and Ms Yonge on Friday we were perplexed and naturally went to the police. Especially after the superintendent checked Liz's apartment. One of Liz's suitcases was by her bed."

"What did the police do?"

"They went through the apartment. They found a packed suitcase. They checked Liz's car in the garage. But they found nothing unusual or suspicious in the apartment or car. They saw nothing to indicate anything irregular. They stated explicitly they saw no evidence of a crime in the apartment. It all seemed pretty cursory if you care for my opinion. And the officer in charge indicated that the police force would treat the situation at this point as a possible or potentially missing person case. Then they did a preliminary background check of some sort on Liz's acquaintances and associates. Or so they told us. And after, they asked us intrusive questions concerning Liz and who she kept company with, her friends, that sort of thing. But until you're asked such questions as a parent by a police officer, it is not apparent to you how little you know, or at least it is implied that you know next to nothing as a parent concerning your child. I must say, after all, Liz has been living up here in Ottawa for more than five years. We really don't know who she socializes with at university."

"Did you tell the police that?"

"Yes. We have nothing to hide from the authorities."

"What have they done since they searched the apartment and the background check?"

"They put out a notice, a bulletin across the country. And said they would study the situation more carefully over the next week."

"You might want to have the police see this through since it is in the preliminary stages."

"Mr Knight something's not right here. The police are reacting too slowly or too cautiously under the circumstances. I'm not sure how to phrase it. Fact is they have not explicitly said that they consider Liz's disappearance a missing person case. They seem to imply that Liz might have just gone out of town on a trip or a holiday for the weekend and simply did not inform us."

"How's that, Ms Strachan?"

"Oh they didn't phrase it that way, Mr Knight. They were more tactful. But when they came back and spoke with us after their purported background check on Liz they were quite guarded in their statements but also less convinced that Liz was missing. The short and long of it is that they seem to take the view that we don't know our own daughter. And left us with the impression that she is probably just out of town for a brief time with an acquaintance and will shortly return. They base this on the fact that Liz has regularly travelled out of the country. Three or four times a year over the last three years. Furthermore," Mary Strachan paused, almost too frustrated to speak, then her voice became emphatic, "Mr Knight, I felt something when I went into Liz's apartment. I had a terrible feeling. I don't know. I suppose you could call it a presentiment. Yes, a presentiment. Something went wrong in that apartment."

"Did the police find any evidence of a crime?"

"I told you no. Nothing. Or so they told us at this point. In my opinion they didn't exactly seem to go over the apartment carefully. As I would have expected under the circumstances. They kept asking blunt questions. These blunt and vulgar questions about whether our daughter would go off with some man or someone."

"Would she?"

"Mr Knight. Think about it. She's in law school. She's to start classes today. A new semester at law school. Why would she? She has everything."

"She's not a minor."

"So the police keep pointing out to us."

"It's only the first day of classes, many students skip the first couple of days of classes. Has she done this before?"

"What do you mean, Mr Knight?"

"Has Liz ever missed the first few days of class."

They both stared at me with a sort of vengeance. I waited.

"The police detective asked the same thing."

"Well has she?"

"Yes." Mary Strachan said this with some bitterness.

"When?"

"A few years back. But this is entirely different."

"The police have limited resources. If Liz were a young child, a minor, or an older person prone to memory lapses the police would move fairly quickly. They have a scale of alertness, urgency concerning missing person cases. We have to keep in mind that your daughter is legally an adult. She's free to move about as she chooses. The police cannot simply pursue a person's whereabouts—"

"Mr Knight, do not say whim. This is not a whim."

"I didn't Ms Strachan. But it is necessary to understand that the authorities cannot pursue, establish a missing person file on an adult individual because that person's parents ask them to. There are privacy issues. Intrusion. Potentially vexatious actions. I'm not suggesting that in this case but—"

"Mr Knight, that's a little off the mark," Frank Strachan commented.

"Not intended to be. On the other hand if the police found any evidence of violence, a crime scene, I can assure you Mr and Ms Strachan, they would be right on top of the situation. But they haven't. You won't consider the possibility that maybe Liz did take off on the long weekend with some intimate friend that none of her friends, family and acquaintances happen to know? These things do happen. Did you consider such a possibility?"

"Liz is mature. Liz is responsible. I can assure you Liz is not some impulsive silly girl. Do you people want to take this case?"

"Excuse me Ms Strachan. Were the police correct in what they found, that Liz has travelled outside the country three or four times a year over the last three years?"

"Holidays. I understand she did travel on occasion."

"Did you know the details of each trip? When, where and who she travelled with?"

"Georges Lajoie said he would take it and now you're asking some of the same sorts of impertinent questions that the police asked and go nowhere. Lead nowhere. But insinuate unpleasant sort of, oh I don't know, things regarding our daughter. Who happens to be a very mature, very responsible woman."

"Ms Strachan, I understand why you're upset. But I have to get the facts concerning your daughter's circumstances before I can get to her whereabouts. Please be helpful here, could your daughter have taken off with someone? Someone you may not know. It may be material to finding Liz."

Mary Strachan's blue eyes were glacial, the crow's feet a fine lace-work. The lawyer began to turn her head to the left but she did not take her sight off me. Her head came back abruptly, her spine straightened.

"Listen, Mr Knight. I know my daughter. No. That's not possible. If Lajoie–Chang is not interested in finding our daughter, well then, possibly my husband and I should look elsewhere."

"Unhappy questions have to be asked. We need information to pursue a missing person search. Minor details sometimes make the difference in a search. If there are embarrassing details you have reservations about I can assure you that everything at Lajoie–Chang is handled in the strictest confidence."

"I have nothing to be embarrassed about concerning our daughter Liz. However, speaking frankly, we do not know each and every time our daughter travelled. And with whom."

"If you can manage to provide me with the details of her travels that you do know over the last three years that would be a big help."

"We'll do what we can Mr Knight." Mary Strachan flattened her hand on the table top.

"Do you have a photograph of your daughter Liz?"

"Yes." Mr Strachan opened a briefcase and took out three photos. He set them on the desk. I saw a striking young woman with raven hair, blue eyes, sharp high cheek bones matched by a fine forehead. A flawless complexion smooth as translucent porcelain, the lips confident like the eyes, deft masterstrokes on the porcelain surface. In all a lovely, even beautiful face which had not yet been masked by the bloated affluence of a legal career and marriage. Still, the photo gave me a jolt. I could not say why. I took a long look at Liz Strachan's striking features. The eyes some would call intelligent, others might consider knowing, then again others would tilt towards mischievous, but something more ineffably unsettling. The right word eluded me. I gazed up from the photo at the Strachans and saw that they were holding something back. But I said nothing. Mary Strachan appeared sad but angry. I sure hoped not at me. I knew clients who would be submissive with the police but let all their rancour come out on the private investigator. Frank's demeanor had shifted to restrain his emotions, not stoic but as stolid as any city councillor I had ever seen, he momentarily sustained a solicitor's comportment then spoke.

"Mr Knight. You're to understand that money is not an issue."

"Mr and Ms Strachan, you have Mr Lajoie's assurance that Lajoie–Chang will do its very best to locate your daughter as quickly as possible."

# TWO

I followed the Strachans in their Lincoln SUV over to the apartment building. It was near the corner of King Edward and Rideau, within walking distance of the market, the Bytown repertory movie theatre and the University of Ottawa law school. A banal ten-storey high-rise that, in its bureaucratic bleakness, which was Melgund Construction's own designer-brand style, made a kid's Lego model look like a masterpiece of art deco.

Pierre Willett, the building superintendent, was a rake thin man who had a cigarette hanging from a jaw as pointy as an elbow. His yellowish grey eyes had creased tight thin lids. He was a man who didn't want to talk with anybody, a man who looked like he'd be more comfortable painting a wall, tinkering with a bit of plumbing and minding the heating ducts.

"Don't worry, Mr Willett. We're only here concerning our daughter."

"Yeah. I kinda understand. Still, I'm not certain this is alright. On account of the fact, there's always the tenant's rights. And I'm not wanting to get into any ruckus with a tenant. It's a drag. But you paid the rent and the management guys okayed it."

"Mr Willett, we are both lawyers. We understand. But this is an emergency situation." Mary Strachan gestured towards me. "Now Mr Knight here is a private investigator who we have hired. Mr Knight please show this gentleman your ID."

I raised my hand to my inside suit jacket pocket, Willett stared at me as if I was about to yank out a magnum special. I showed Willett nothing more than a provincial licence. He didn't bother to even glance at it. He just stared at Ms Strachan.

"Okay." He unlocked the door, "But don't take anythin' out of the apartment. Ya understan'. 'Cause I'm the first guy they gonna blame if anythin' goes missin'."

The apartment was a neat spacious one-bedroom. The living room–dining room was more plush than most student apartments that I had seen. Nice furniture, tasteful a decorator would have said. Solid. More than one expected from a student. No Ikea here. But I said nothing. After all the Strachans were cruising in a Lincoln SUV, squeezing out ten gallons to the mile and didn't look and sound as if they were sweating over that. With globalism, energy consumption was the new currency to measure the sweat factor. They didn't seem the sort to let money stand between them and their daughter's desires and a comfy education.

Mounted on the wall was the very top of the line CD player. In a substantial mahogany cabinet there was a fine DVD player, top notch TV, and a substantial collection of CDs and DVDs. The plants along the balcony glass doors looked a little sad and lonesome. I checked over all the surfaces and searched the drawers and shelves to see if there were any notepads by the phone or on the tables which might have phone numbers or names scrawled on them. But I found nothing, not a scrap of paper, just a stack of unopened letters. I shuffled through them, mostly bills and junk mail. Scattered here and there, magazines, the New Yorker, Gourmet, Italian magazines on slow food, and a pile of Caribbean holiday mags from travel agencies. We went into the bedroom. It was plush. Deep purple. Dark vermillion. Satin and silk. A CD-player–clock-radio combo, smaller and portable but rock solid, straight out of the New Yorker ad, sat on a side table. I checked the side table drawers, nothing. No random jottings or anything in the drawer but hairclips. A fine mahogany bed, even splendid, with a silk bedspread. A silk kimono was draped across the foot of the bed. A piece of luggage rested by the side of the bed.

I picked up the luggage. I asked Ms Strachan to go through the items. A bathing suit. Towels. Clothing. A make-up kit.

"They all appear to be Liz's." She closed it. I asked Ms Strachan to go through the dresser drawers but there was nothing but garment.

"Do you know where your daughter's address book might be?"

"I'm not certain. She has a BlackBerry and an iBook. I suppose she keeps her contacts in them."

I went through a series of compact disks.

"Mr Willett, did you see Elizabeth Strachan with her BlackBerry or laptop?"

"I saw Liz Strachan with a laptop that Monday."

"It wasn't in the apartment when you first came here?" I asked the Strachans.

"No."

"Did you check her car?"

"It was still locked. But when we gave it a quick check it was not there."

We went back out to the hall to the bath. I went through the wastebasket. Nothing there but a ball of fine dark hair. I lifted the lid of the toilet, checked it. Back in the kitchen, I found nothing but a clean empty plastic waste bag on the rack. In the living room by the desk there was a steel retro wastebasket with sheets of paper dumped in it. I went through it. Possibly something here, I noticed a sheet with scribbles on it but I said nothing.

"Mr Willett, could you check and see if there's any trash in the wastebasket in the bedroom." When Willett and the Strachans went back into the bedroom, I filched the sheet out of the trash and stuffed it in my jacket pocket. They came back in the living room.

"Nothing in there."

"Let's go down and take a look at the car."

"I don't know," said Willett. "Maybe I should check with management."

"Mr Willett, for insurance purposes the car's registered in our name," said Ms Strachan.

"Alright. I got things to do anyway."

We went out and he locked the apartment door.

We took the elevator down to the car garage. A Venetian blue Mazda Miata sports coupe stood by a pillar.

Frank Strachan had an extra set of the Miata keys, he opened the car door. I went through the car. I found a BlackBerry secreted under the driver's seat.

"Does this look like Liz's?"

"Yes."

"Please open the trunk, Mr Strachan."

Frank Strachan opened the trunk with the automatic contraption. A laptop computer, an iBook, rested under a woollen Hudson Bay blanket.

"Can I take these back to the office and have one of our people go over them?"

"Certainly. But we don't know the passwords."

"Morrison Chang is good with these sorts of things. He'll give it a crack. Some passwords just need the right mathematical hum. Give Cheryl Perron, the assistant, all your birthdates, full names, anything you think might be special to your daughter that only the family might be in the know about but easy to recall. Pet names. Nicknames. Street addresses. Phone numbers. Good clues, that sort of thing, for opening the computer. People use personal stuff despite all the advice in the world not to. After all, in a world run by numbers, infinite as they are, there are only so many regular number sequences a human being can remember."

"I know what you mean, Mr Knight." Frank Strachan half laughed. "I'm that way. Otherwise, I'd forget."

"You know I once worked on a case with a guy who was a mathematician working out in Kanata. He'd lost his company's files one weekend, had to get them back by the Monday. The guy used his mother's initials and birthdate as the password to everything. Some years ago before the banks changed the sequence of spitting out the money, receipt and bank card, I had a case with an absent-minded pensioner who wrote the PIN for his account on the bank card and forgot the card in the bank machine. Some creep comes after him, finds it and near cleaned out his savings accounts."

"Truly, some horrible people out there, Mr Knight."

"We got him but restitution was another matter."

I told the Strachans to give me a day or two and to let their elder daughter Brenda know that I would be in contact with her later in the afternoon. I wanted to talk alone with Willett and didn't want to talk with Connie Yonge while the Strachans were hanging around. I sent the Strachans back to their hotel on the pretext of having to do the long march through corridors in search of potential tenant information, such performances demand confidentiality. They drove off to the Lord Elgin Hotel while I began checking out the tenants. After a couple of hours of getting zip, I went back to Lajoie–Chang. I laid the electro-goodies out for Morrison to take a crack at. I phoned up Brenda Strachan, but she wasn't in. I left a message to give me a call when she had a chance to discuss the situation regarding her sister. I checked for listings in the Ottawa telephone directory for Yonge, and found a C Yonge listed at the same street address in unit 910.

I drove back to the high-rise. As I scanned the residents' listing, Willett the reed, the superintendent, appeared. He gave me a fishy look and came out to the outer lobby.

"Mr Willett, I was hoping to have a word alone with you if it's alright."

"Whatever."

"Your knowledge of the building might be of assistance in locating Ms Strachan."

"I don't know anything about that Strachan girl. As far as I am concerned she's just a tenant here. I mind my own business."

"I understand. I am sure you respect the tenants' privacy. But you might have seen something in passing. It seemed next to nothing at the time but, who knows, it could help locate Ms Strachan."

Willett said nothing to this. I glanced around the outer lobby and into the interior.

"Mr Willett, I can see you take good care of this apartment building for Mellow and Melgund."

"I do the job I'm hired to do."

"That certainly shows. No doubt you know this building better than anyone else. Probably better than the architect. And the good maintenance of the building indicates it's cared for by an observant person. You look like you keep your wits about you when taking care of this place."

"What's the name again?"

"Knight. Alec Knight." I offered my agency card but he ignored the offering.

A tenant came through, smiled at Willett and excused herself as she slipped through the lobby door. Willett gave a polite nod of acknowledgment. Neither of us spoke until the glass door closed.

"I see what I see. Let's go outside where I can breathe easy and have a smoke."

"Sure."

We went out and sat on a cement garden bench between the building's entrance and a dreary little garden pond surrounded by beleaguered junipers and miniature cedar shrubs. These bedraggled shrubs sure were not harbingers of eavesdropping spirits and spritely mischievous elves. The early September afternoon sunlight, however, was soft and pleasant, a mental relief. I let the sun have its power.

"Gonna smoke. Got to since that new law. Can't even have a beer and smoke at the local tavern anymore. What a drag." I slipped out my street pack of smokes and offered one to Willett. He gazed at the pack of cigarettes for a moment. The temptation too great, the thin man finally took one, but reluctantly, as if he preferred his own trusty brand over the devious freebie offered by a deceitful dervish passing as inquisitive investigator. Proffered freebies tend to instigate psychic conflicts in the skeptical, a mingling of disdain and desire, that's the soul of the information racket. Willett lit up, thin lips narrowing, forming an oval, deep inhalation, the reedy man seemed to go into the smoke rather than the smoke going into him.

"Do you remember when you last saw Liz Strachan?"

"Last week of August on the Wednesday midmorning then again on the Monday, the thirty-first, around noon."

"Was she with anyone?"

"Yeah another woman."

"Do you know the woman?"

"Not exactly."

"Well have you seen this woman on another occasion?"

"Yeah."

"With Ms Strachan?"

"Yeah."

"So she's a friend of Ms Strachan's?"

"Maybe. I don't know. They could be friends."

"So you've seen the two women together in the past more than once?"

"Yeah."

"Is this other woman a tenant in this building?"

"Yeah."

"Do you know her name?"

"Yeah. Connie Yonge."

"What floor does Ms Yonge live on?"

"She lives on the same floor as Liz Strachan, across the hall."

"What does Ms Yonge look like?"

"Blonde. Good-looker, I suppose. One of the other tenants, Mrs Lowe, she's a regular old mouth, told me it's a dye jobby, she said she can tell on account of the brown roots kinda show through sometimes along the part."

"Did you see the two women come or go together?"

"Yeah. They left together."

"Did you happen to notice how they were travelling?"

"Connie Yonge's Firebird." Just then four teenagers rolling along the pavement on skateboards skidded off, scooped them up and cut across the lawn. Willett shouted out, "Hey none of that. Didn't I tell you kids not to cut across the property. Look what you're doing, you're wrecking the grass."

The kids kept on. They said nothing, they didn't even stare back scornfully.

"Don't you little buggers hear me. What's wrong with you kids. Deaf. Hey get off the grass." Willett stood up. Finally one of the kids turned and glanced over his shoulder at Willett. He was a good-looking kid in baggy pants hanging low and a massive T-shirt that read on the front Life is Real Quick and There's No Going Back across the T-shirt's back. He flashed a huge smile. Then off the cut dirt path, the kid set his skateboard down on the pavement and wheeled off smooth, easy, and controlled. Punks have such virtue in their agility. I remembered such skateboarding pleasures, I envied the transitory high.

Willett sat down and swore.

"Them little buggers, willya look at that worn path. Management's on my case about that. Appearances."

"Mr Willett, your position is entirely understandable. They show no respect. It's a drag."

"You don't know. You got no idea. You never worked for Melgund and Mellow."

"Tell me."

"Ah forget it. Isn't worth talking 'bout." He took a deep drag.

"Go ahead."

"Them guys. Management types. Masters ov. Ov. Whatchamacallits. EmBlabBlabAhs or whatever you call 'em."

"Mr Willett, do you mean MBA?"

"Yeah. Master of bullshit and aggravation. Nobody's trying to make a real living anymore doing anything normal. Everybody's trying to pile up money to make a killing on the stock market. It's a racket if you ask me. A rickety racket. Gonna clatter down one day.

Might as well go to the casino." Willett grinned, "A lot more fun and a lot less aggravation."

"Probably right on that score."

"You bet."

"Mr Willett, if you're as conscientious at the casino as here, you must know your stuff."

"I'm not a big player. I play the slots. I set my limit before I go. That's it. Strictly cash. No more than I got in my pocket. I don't fool myself, that's for sure. If there's losing to be done I let others do it. You got to watch a lot of casino action to know when to play. I see a guy slagging a slot machine, bang bang, I wait until he's run his luck. Then I give it a shot. Spend about nine-tenths of the time watching others gamble and lose their shirts."

"That's smart."

"You bet. I keep a steady record of when I lose and when I win. And there's no cheating there. Like so. I write it down nice and neat in my little book." While the cigarette dangled from the corner of his thin lips, smoke curling in the air, Willett feigned with his fingers taking up a pencil and jotting down imaginary numbers upon an invisible notepad. "I don't lie to myself. No way. You take a licking then you take a licking. And if you win a buck you win a buck. It's right there in black and white."

"That's staying on top of the situation rather than letting the situation get on top of you."

Willett said nothing to this but paused and seemed to be thinking about his own wisdom. He smoked less deeply, more meditatively. I waited but he still said nothing. Willett lowered the smoke and stared at it. A long sober stare.

"Mr Willett, do you remember when Liz Strachan and Connie Yonge left?"

"It was that hot stinker of a Wednesday. I figure, let's see ..." He paused. "Last Wednesday in August. Be exactly two weeks ago tomorrow. I envied them going for a cool dip up in the Gatineau. She parked the Firebird out front. I seen them get in the car together. It sure was hot." Willett gave a salacious grin and laughed.

"Yes it was hot. Anybody would have wanted to get out of the city that day."

"That's right."

"How did you know they were heading across the river to Gatineau?"

"I heard them when they come out of the elevator mention where they was going."

Willett took a deep drag on the smoke.

"Did you see the two women return?"

"Naw."

"Did you see Connie Yonge or Liz Strachan after that?"

"Yeah. I've seen Connie Yonge a couple times in the lobby over the past—I think, not sure—days. But recent."

"When?"

"I told you I'm not sure."

"When do you think you might have?"

"Maybe. Maybe on a Sunday. Or Monday."

"And Liz Strachan, did you happen to see her?"

"Maybe. I don't know."

"When and where Mr Willett?"

He looked at me.

"None of this is certain. I see a lot of people every day. Coming and going."

"I understand. Do your best."

"Okay. I was working down in the garage. Maybe it was in the garage that Monday near her car. Maybe she was driving. Just arriving or leaving. Something like that."

"You're certain it was Liz Strachan driving her Mazda Miata?"

"I told you I don't know for certain. But it was her Mazda. Certain on that. Yeah, I figure it was her driving. From a distance it looked like her. Maybe it was, maybe it wasn't." He glanced at his wristwatch.

"Okay. So Sunday the thirtieth or Monday the thirty-first, not Wednesday the twenty-sixth, may have been the last time you might have seen Liz Strachan?"

"Yeah. I suppose. But I'm not saying so."

"And where has her car been parked since then?"

"There's a security company. Guy that does patrol for Melgund four times a day. Why don't you check with him."

I got the name of the company and the phone number.

We said nothing for a moment. I let Willett enjoy his smoke.

"That anti-smoking bylaw is a bugger. When the law's liable to turn everybody into a criminal, it isn't fair. Is it?"

"A law should not only sound fair but actually be fair."

Willett glanced at me.

"Yeah. That sounds right. Sure as hell wouldn't want to be a bartender in this logtown over the next couple of months, gonna be a lot of logjams and lumberjacking."

"Certainly not the job of choice for the month of September."

"Some medical hack dictates how I enjoy my vices. I say vice is nice." Willett laughed hard then coughed even harder. He caught his breath. A bit of tobacco-stained spittle dribbled at the corner of his mouth, he wiped it away.

"Did you notice anyone else visiting the apartment that Liz Strachan lives in? You know, friends. She's a university student. Did other university students drop by? Anyone on a regular basis. That sort of thing."

Willett snickered.

"Student. Let me say this. Maybe she's a student. I don't know. I never splashed in that swimming pool. If she says she's a student I suppose she's a student."

"What do you mean?"

"You seen her apartment. I wouldn't say nothing in front of the girl's parents but she's doing something more than student homework."

"What more?" I rested my hand on the wallet pocket of my suit jacket.

"I don't know. But that Liz Strachan has a regular series of admirers."

"Who?"

"I don't know."

"Students?"

"Naw."

"Then who?"

"I don't know. Some men."

"How often did men drop by to see Liz Strachan?"

Willett shrugged his shoulders.

"Would you recognize any of these men who visited Liz Strachan's unit?"

"Maybe. Maybe not."

"How old are these men?"

"I'm no good with ages. Can't tell."

"You ever catch anyone's name?"

"Not really. I overheard in the lobby one guy referred to as Joe."

"Did you catch a last name?"

"None that I heard."

"Anyone else pass through to visit Liz Strachan?"

"Was a young buck probably early twenties. Muscle type."

"You see him often?"

"I didn't exactly pay close attention when he come round."

"You tell the police this?"

"What I can I told 'em. I can't tell 'em nothing I don't know."

"And how about what they don't ask about but you think might be useful?"

"Look, I can't read minds mister. You need a question to give an answer."

"But you distinguish the tenants and can identify their apartments. And the numbers."

Willett stared at my palm still resting near the wallet pocket of my suit jacket.

"I'm a numbers man. Favourably inclined towards arithmetic. Always was better with numbers. I got a memory for numbers. Words are another thing. Talking tangles me up. Talking is for birds and fools. Interferes with thinking straight. Personally I prefer numbers over letters."

"I can sympathize. Numbers give clear, concise answers."

"Maybe. But lookit, this Strachan woman, she's a tenant. I don't want to get a tenant on my case. She could waltz in here any minute whistling the Maple Leaf Forever. Then, you tell me, where would I be if she found out I was blabbing to the cops all about her? Melgund management people make it plenty clear that a tenant's got a right to privacy." He lit another smoke, one of his own, off the old one.

"You're absolutely right, Mr Willett. Very important to respect a tenant's privacy. In this case I was hired by Ms Strachan's parents. They're trying to protect Ms Strachan's privacy."

Willett said nothing to this. He leaned forward and rested his elbows on his knees cupping the smoke, then taking a drag and staring across the street.

"So you and I, we're in agreement."

"Maybe." Willett straightened up and took a drag.

"Mr Willett, the kind of work you do and the kind of work I do demands respect for other people's privacy. We're of like mind on that point. We're birds of a feather."

"I suppose."

"I can assure you I keep anything told to me confidential. The Strachans want it that way. And being lawyers they fully understand the laws concerning privacy. You can trust us."

"So I suppose I should do what I can to help her folks?"

"And help yourself while still respecting a tenant's rights to privacy."

"Yeah. That's reasonable put that way. Better to be reasonable when dealing with reasonable people. Not everybody is reasonable. What's the name again?"

"Alec Knight."

"Right. Mr Knight, some people with a little power behave mighty unreasonable. High and mighty. But I would never stiff anybody trying to do his job properly."

"Mr Willett, I can't imagine you ever doing that. Especially because you work so hard at your own job. I imagine it isn't easy taking care of this place."

"It's sure no breeze."

"Some people do take the building maintenance for granted." I paused.

"Some people think it's a joke. I can tell you."

"Mr Willet was this man Joe around on the Wednesday, Sunday or Monday?"

"Maybe Sunday, not Wednesday. I saw him with Connie Yonge. He was waiting in a car out front."

"Did you catch the make, model or year?"

"Sport type. Black Porsche. Used but nice vehicle."

"Year?"

"Can't say. Don't keep current with that sort of thing. Way beyond my currency. My car is like fifteen years old. Mellow don't pay enough to keep much more than that on the road."

"You mentioned that older gentlemen visited on a regular basis. How old were they?"

"I told you I'm not certain. Lousy with the age thing. Lousy with names. Maybe one guy looked fifty. The others fifty-five or so. But I don't know."

"And one came more often than the others."

"Yeah. He was a tall fellow over six. Maybe six two. Lean guy. Very well dressed. Very nice car. Money. Real class."

"What kind of car?"

"Can't remember."

"When did you last see him?"

"I don't know, he dropped out of sight some time this year."

"And the other men who came by regularly, do they still visit?"

"Why don't you check with the other tenants on that floor."

Willett pressed out his smoke.

"Is Connie Yonge around now?"

"Couldn't tell you."

"Did you see Ms Yonge today?"

"I saw her this morning. Check her apartment. Maybe she's in, maybe she's not."

"What unit?"

"She's 'cross the hall from Liz Strachan's unit. Nine-ten to nine-oh-nine."

"What does she do for a living?"

"Haven't a clue."

"Does Ms Yonge keep a regular schedule, coming and going?"

"Not really. Uneven. She'll be here for a stretch. Then gone."

"Mr Willett, when did you last see Ms Yonge?"

"This morning."

"Did she mention Liz Strachan?"

"No. But I never ask a tenant that kinda thing. None of my business."

"No. I suppose not. Entirely understandable on your part."

"I tol' you I don't know the woman. She's a tenant. I don't go snooping into tenants' lives."

"I just thought she might mention something concerning Ms Strachan in passing or ask you about her friend Liz."

"No way. I don't get into that sort of talk with the tenants about other tenants."

"I understand Melgund and Mellow management people phoned Brenda Strachan, Liz Strachan's sister. Is that right?"

"I heard something like that."

"How'd that come about?"

"The first come and went and one of the guys from management phoned over with a list of tenants late on the rent. They asked if Liz

Strachan's cheque had been dropped off. I tol' 'em I hadn't seen it. So they told me to check with her. And I tried. But she wasn't around so last Thursday I understand management they called her sister Brenda Strachan. Next thing the folks blow into town on the Friday. Then the girl's parents gimme the rent cheque so everything is proper with Melgund's management. A day later, just this past Saturday on the long weekend, the cops come round checking out the situation. But they didn't do much of anything it seemed. Just done a walk around with the security guy."

"That ever happen before, that Liz Strachan didn't make the rent?"

"Yeah, come to think of it, once or twice before. But it was no big deal. It's not like she tried to skip out on the rent."

"When else did it occur?"

"Maybe once in February. And in April or May. She used to drop off a cheque each month."

"She paid the rent regularly?"

"Yeah."

"Her personal cheques or her parents'?"

"No. Them cheques they weren't issued in her name."

"Whose name?"

"Nobody's name."

"How's that?"

"Numbered company issued the rent cheques for Liz Strachan's apartment."

"You wouldn't recall the number."

"Hey, I love numbers but not that much. My brain's no computer chip." Willett chuckled and lit another smoke. "But I know it."

"Can you retrieve the company's number?"

"Can I?"

"Can you Mr Willett?"

"Depends." He stared at my hand near the pocket.

I fished out a ten and rested it under my palm on the bench.

"I got the info in the office. Couple of 'em came late."

I folded the ten and slipped it in my pocket.

"Come on." Willett got up and very carefully butted out the smoke on the cement bench, opened a pack of smokes and slipped the remainder of the cigarette into the aluminum foil.

We went through the lobby to the superintendent's apartment. The odour of bacon grease and cigarette smoke was layered in the atmosphere, palpable, while the domestic pollutants had larded ceiling and walls with slathers and slabs of grey and yellow. He went to his desk where a bunch of soiled files were piled.

"I keep a photocopy of all the cheques that the tenants give me by hand."

"Why's that?"

"One time a creep tried to burn me. He told the management people that he had given me the rent cheque and made like I had cashed it in one of them funny money joints. Since then I make a copy of any cheque any tenant gives me and keep a record. And record the date I hand it on to the management."

"Impressive, you're a thorough man."

"You bet. I don't like being screwed." He went through a file. He showed me a photocopy of one cheque in May signed by Frank Strachan and another of a company cheque in February. I wrote down the Ontario numbered company's details. The signature was complex and stylized but indecipherable.

"You mentioned this numbered company paid Ms Strachan's rent up until April."

"Yeah. Then her parents paid May, see," he gestured to the other photocopy. "And then she made the next couple of months until this September come due."

"Was Ms Strachan around at the time the rent cheque was late?"

Willett looked at me. I waited.

"I don't know. Seems no. But I might not recall. In February, she showed up late and paid the rent."

"How late?"

"In February I think just one day."

"And the other late cheque?

"Two or three days. I can't remember exactly."

"How did she appear on those occasions?"

"Appear?"

"What was her manner like?"

"I don't know. Like. She said something like, 'Okay here's the cheque Mr Willett. Sorry it's late. Something came up.' That sort of rigamarole. You hear it all the time. Then she said, 'It won't happen again.'"

"But it did. Around April."

"Right."

"What did she say then? What was her mood."

"I don't know. She seemed kinda pissed off. Naw. She was always polite. Never phoney."

"Did it seem as if something was wrong? Or that she might have been upset?"

Willett shook his head. "Okay let's say upset. Whatever that means. We didn't talk about nothing. She gimme her parents' cheque to make up the rent. That was it."

"Liz Strachan didn't offer an explanation?"

"Naw. She just said. 'School's been kinda tough. Focussing on the exams. I forgot about the rent being due.'" Willett motioned to leave.

"Did you believe her?"

"Naw. But who cares, she paid the rent."

"What did you believe?"

"Nothing. You hear all kinds of stories from tenants. No use in going deep into 'em as long as they come through with the rent and don't make no trouble. What's the point of digging around in people's lives. Just digging for trouble."

We went back out to the inner lobby and passed through the front lobby into the courtyard. We sat back down on the bench. I set the ten under my palm. Willett lit the partially smoked cigarette and exhaled. He said nothing for a long moment.

"I want to do some more rounds of the tenants."

"Sure. Be my guest. You don't need to sign a lease." He smiled.

"Mr Willett, you're very helpful."

"I like to co-operate. And I like to smoke."

"Smokes are expensive."

"Smokes? Well, you know what they say in the Cabinet huffing and puffing around the humidor, ne pas cheap." He stared down at my palm and took the ten. "Thanks."

"No problem. If you happen to see any of those men you mentioned come by, could you give me a call?" I gave him my card. Willett took it this time and read it.

"Knight."

"That's right."

"Name seems kinda familiar."

"Two columns of us in the little O phone book."

"I don't read such thick books."

"It's an easy read."

"Sure with a magnifying glass. Print's way too small." Willett laughed.

"There's action there if you read carefully between the lines and columns."

"Oh yeah, I just bet lots of excitement in them yellow pages. Right, big plot. More entertaining than a Hollywood blockbuster."

"Secret, Mr Willett." I smiled. "Phone book is Hollywood. Where it all started. Pulp and paper."

"Mr Knight, it might be an action book in your trade but the phone book is a real slog. Year in and year out they just go straight to the blue box."

"Maybe you're right there Mr Willett. It's had a long print run but it's probably going out of print."

"Yeah. Figure that, little cellphone gonna knock such a big book out of circulation. I'd say in ten years time the telephone company gonna stop printing that fat thing."

"Mr Willett, a good woman friend of mine once told me, and I might add she is a woman of knowledge—"

"A knowledgeable lady eh, Mr Knight?"

"Yes, she's a very knowledgeable woman."

"That's rich, in my book a knowledgeable woman is way better than a knowledgeable lady. What she say Mr Knight that so tickled your ear?"

"A big book is a bad book."

"I like that, Mr Knight." Willett laughed.

"Yes, there's badness in bigness."

"I say that's talking business now. Gonna remember that. Badness in bigness."

"Thanks for your help, Mr Willett. I hope I can depend on you in the future."

"We'll see. Keep in mind, I'm kept pretty busy round this place keeping it shipshape."

"Liz Strachan is missing, her parents really appreciate any help any person gives in finding their daughter. I can assure you there's something in it for every person who provides information that helps locate Liz Strachan."

Willett said nothing but gave a faint nod of his skull.

"Thanks Mr Willett."

"No problem."

I got up and went into the foyer and rang Connie Yonge's unit. There was no answer. I asked Willett to give me a shout if he saw Connie Yonge return to the apartment building. He said he'd see what he could do but he was a pretty busy guy and that I could count on him but he could only do so much.

I swore at myself. Pay early and pay forever. Like my grandfather used to say, sometimes it's better to have deep pockets and short fingers.

# THREE

I toured the photograph of Liz Strachan around town to the car rental agencies and with some cabbies but came up with nothing. I went back to my Somerset Street apartment and made a cheese sandwich. Good local cheddar from Lanark county on local Rideau rye with a local red Spanish onion. Local. Local. Local. And some dijon mustard. Free French. The first of the fresh apple crop from the Ottawa valley orchards on the side. Very tasty.

There was something about the picture of Liz Strachan's life, the corners of the picture frame didn't true up, but I was not yet near to enough details. I was hoping that Morrison could open her BlackBerry or computer and give me a list of names or contacts. In the afternoon, I could go back to the apartment building and continue with my bellhopping.

I looked at the scrap of paper which I had filched from the living room wastebasket, a long column of numbers running from the top of the sheet to the bottom:

9,50<br>
85<br>
75<br>
98<br>
88<br>
78<br>
65<br>
55<br>
45<br>
59<br>
49<br>
5,9

These might be dollar amounts even if the dollar sign was missing. It seemed plausible, with the odd comma thrown in or misplaced. It could even be French notation, with the comma as a decimal point. The person had started to scribble out the entire number but then abruptly for speed's sake jettisoned the extraneous zeros. The comma in the first number suggested that it was not intended to be read as nine hundred and fifty, but more likely ninety-five hundred dollars. The missing zeros were a consequence of someone in a hurry to do rapid summations or calculations. If the numbers were most likely dollar amounts of some sort and range, the underlining seemed to suggest four periods or groups. On the reverse side of the scrap of paper were names of the months.

Sep, Jan., May;
Oct, Feb, Jun;
Nov, Mar, Jul
Dec, Apr, Aug

The handwriting, although apparently done quickly, evident in the drag of the pen across the paper, in the odd case nearly linking numbers, was still neat and legible throughout.

The phone rang. It was Willett. He told me that Connie Yonge had just returned carrying a piece of luggage. I finished the apple and wrapped the remaining half of the sandwich in wax paper. I went back to the high-rise apartment building near King Edward. I rang up Yonge's unit. Nothing for a long time. I rang again. A brisk confident voice came through the speaker set.

"Yes, who is it?"

"Alec Knight, I am—"

"I don't know anyone by that name." The confident voice abruptly interrupted then terminated the connection.

I buzzed again.

"Please go away."

"Ms Yonge, I apologize if I am disturbing you. I'm Alec Knight, a private investigator. Liz Strachan's parents have hired me. I am with the agency of Lajoie–Chang."

"What do you want?"

"Liz Strachan's parents have asked us to look into your friend Liz's disappearance. Ms Yonge, I was hoping I might be able to speak with you concerning Liz Strachan. Liz Strachan's parents would really appreciate it."

"Wait a moment."

After five minutes, a fair woman about thirty years old, dressed in slacks and a cotton shirt appeared. She was blonde, slim and confident in her manner, no doubt some would have considered her very attractive, but her blonde good looks seemed banal. She opened the glass door.

"Mr Knight?'

"Yes."

"Please show me your investigator's licence."

Her voice unsettled me. I showed her my licence. She read it with detachment and careful scrutiny, in the manner of someone well accustomed to inspecting official documents.

"Do you have a professional card?"

"Yes. Here." I tendered a card.

"Mr Knight, wait in the outer lobby, I'll let you in from upstairs."

"Sure. Thank you."

Connie Yonge went back upstairs on the elevator. I saw Willett poke his head out of the superintendent's office as I stood waiting. Willett approached.

"She come back about a half hour ago."

"Thanks. Maybe I'll have a word with you later." I wanted to shake off the guy, I knew he was trying to tag me again.

"I'll let you in."

"No need. I'll wait Mr Willett."

"Suit yourself." Willett chuckled and left. I was now in some unnamed catalogue of longstanding lobbymen left loitering, to Willett's immense amusement.

She left me standing in the outer lobby for five more minutes then opened the automatic latch. I rode the elevator to the ninth floor and knocked on Yonge's door.

When the door opened Connie Yonge proffered no explanation and I asked for none.

"I hope this doesn't take too much time. I'm quite busy Mr Knight." Hearing her voice again after the lapse I recognized why it put me off. It was high-pitched. It was not put on, quite natural, and the accent was pure Ottawa valley, but it had been polished to an edge which suggested Ms Yonge would put up with no nonsense. To my ear it was an unappealing voice but I had seen mature men near unzip their trousers and let them drop to their ankles when they heard such a feminine high-pitched voice. Cheryl Perron claimed it was an emotional signature in the speech centre signalling reassurance, gratification and ultimately affection, maybe even love. It was honey. It made male hormones flow in the brain, up and down the brain stem and spinal column from the gonads to the neck. Cheryl laughed and went on, it gave certain guys the thrill of their lives, tickled their ear like a woman's tongue, and intimated something about the woman's lips and mouth. I confessed the high-pitched sound grated on my nerves worse than chalk on the blackboard, scratched up and down my spinal cord, gave me an itchy feeling like hives. Cheryl declared, 'My, Mr Knight you are programmed wrong.' 'What's that supposed to mean?' 'It's the lady cooing at you like a little baby when Mummy's nursed you.' 'Gee thanks.' 'Didn't say you'd like the answer.' 'I hear that sort of voice I put it on hold.' 'You don't know what you might be missing.' I studied Connie Yonge's lips. Pink lipstick carefully applied.

"I appreciate whatever time you are able to give. I'll do my best to keep it brief, Ms Yonge."

"Fine. Come in Mr Knight."

We went into a well-appointed living room full of retro art deco furnishings bought new from one of the more fashionable furniture stores, matching tuxedo loveseat and chair covered in pink cotton. A matching table set sculpted to skyscraper shapes. Lava lamps flowing on the side tables. Neither Ikea nor the Bay. She sat in the chair, crossed her legs. I sat on the sofa. Connie Yonge stared at me but said nothing, her eyes and lips confident, smooth, and free of either a frown or a smile. She set my card down on a small side table.

"I appreciate you giving me your time."

"Well." This brevity was matched by a flashing curt smile revealing as fine a set of teeth as my investment adviser–dentist would want for promoting his practice. She turned gracefully a little in the chair adjusting her position, taking on a more sophisticated posture. The smile lapsed and her voice took on a firm inflection. "Well what is this concerning Liz?"

"Liz Strachan's parents hired Lajoie–Chang to investigate what they believe to be an unaccountable disappearance. Liz is expected to start back to law school today. Her parents expected to see Ms Strachan this past long weekend but have not been able to make contact. And they have not heard from Liz recently."

"I do hope this isn't serious, Mr Knight." Her voice took another inflectional turn, it was infused with sympathy and genuinely concerned in tone.

I glanced around the apartment. She noted my scrutiny.

"We hope so. Ms Yonge, do you recall the last time you saw your friend Liz Strachan?"

"It's been a while. Several days ago. Today's Tuesday. The eighth. So well, yes, not since I guess the last Sunday in August, the thirtieth. At least a week ago."

"Frank and Mary Strachan tell me you spent a few days in the last week in August with Liz."

"That's right. We went to the Gatineau. To a cottage."

"Just the two of you?"

"Yes."

"Anyone else around?"

"No. Well a couple of guys dropped in for a little while."

"Who were they?"

"I think they were acquaintances of Liz from the university. I don't personally know them."

"Did you happen to catch their names?"

"Not really. Maybe a guy named Bill and another guy possibly called Ted. Not certain on the names."

"Had you seen or met them before?"

"I'm not sure. Might have in the hall or something. In passing."

"I see. Could you've seen them somewhere else?"

"They were Liz's friends. If I'd seen them before, probably in passing here in the apartment building in the hall or lobby. But on that weekend when they came by I went for a walk. I think they stayed for a beer then left. It wasn't long. It seemed Liz wasn't exactly expecting them." She looked out the balcony window down onto King Edward Avenue. She looked back at me and smiled as if bored. "Faces. And more faces, Mr Knight."

"I understand. Have you ever met a fellow named Ed Stanley?"

"I was not introduced to him. Liz once mentioned an Ed. I don't know him or his last name."

"Could the Ted that came by that weekend be Ed Stanley?"

"Haven't a clue. Might have been. He didn't mention his last name. And I didn't hang around."

"Could you describe these two men who dropped in?"

"Fellow named Bill was thin, about five eight, maybe five nine, dark hair. Looked kind of Med. Glasses. The Ted or Ed fellow, over six. Six two or three. Solid physique. Muscular. Both had short hair. The shorter one darker hair than the muscular man."

"What did they talk about with Liz?"

"Haven't a clue. As I told you they came in and I went out. I wanted a quiet restful weekend away from people. My work has me on a very busy schedule."

"Ms Yonge, how long have you known Liz Strachan?"

"Since she moved in a few years ago. We hit it off. She's great company. Very sharp lady."

"You didn't know her before that?"

"Sort of. Met through a mutual friend. A travel agent some weekend or other. Can't quite remember the occasion. It's vague now."

"Have you ever known Ms Strachan to go off like this without staying in touch with friends or family?"

"Can't say. What with my schedule."

"Right. But as far as you know you haven't seen her disappear before like this?"

"I cannot say. A couple of weeks might pass before our paths would cross."

"Do you know any of her other friends or acquaintances?"

"Not really. We move in separate worlds. She hangs out with a law school crowd. And you must know how it is Mr Knight, once you're out working for a living the university world, whatever nostalgic notions some people carry around, is passé. You did go to university didn't you? I assume you did."

"Yes. Here. Local."

"I see."

"U of O."

"Like Liz."

"And yourself Ms Yonge?"

"Carleton."

"What did you happen to study?"

"Psychology."

I waited for more but nothing followed.

"You mentioned that Liz is in law school. I understand she is to begin her second year this September."

"Right. She'll make a superb lawyer. She's very sharp. It's in her genes."

"Do you know her sister, Brenda?"

"In passing. I met her a few times."

"What about her parents?"

"No."

"Does Liz have someone she goes out with on a steady or regular basis?"

"Not that I know of. There was a fellow Ed she mentioned. Certainly wasn't steady or anything. It seemed Liz wasn't really interested in him."

"How so?"

"You know." Connie Yonge's lips gave an almost impish smile but relinquished the impulse, her eyes became more confident. I was trying to grasp Cheryl Perron's understanding of voice, but the knowledge eluded me. Yonge's lips were a glowing pink. And I tried to remember if she had had on the glowing pink lipstick when she came down to open the lobby door or whether she had put it on after she returned to the apartment but for the life of me I could not remember. And I could not grasp the sequence of expressions in her face. Her features were at once formal but mobile and seemed confident as if she were forcing out gestures but playing with them. Yet she remained radiantly upbeat. I didn't have a clue who she was. Her lips suddenly looked lush even though I couldn't stand pink lipstick. It repulsed me, made me think of pinkish calf's liver slabbed on the meat market counter. Under glass.

"Do you mean this fellow Ed didn't get it? Didn't understand the feeling was not reciprocal?"

"I suppose a man could put it that way." She leaned forward resting her jaw in the palm of her hand, "Some men just don't get it as you put it, Mr Knight. And they probably never will." She leaned back.

"It's a shortcoming we have."

"Ah, to pass through childhood into adolescence into old age without experiencing life. The resting in the cocoon." She paused.

"Do you mean without maturing?"

"Possibly. Mind you I suppose it's not wise to generalize."

"There could be something in your observation. I won't let my position prejudice or compromise me regarding such an intriguing thought. No doubt based on shrewd observations and experience."

"Plenty of material to observe. Some people don't achieve a philosophical disposition towards their own bodies. To say nothing of—well never mind. Life is for pleasure."

"It certainly is. The more pleasure the better. It is what makes North America such a great place. Incidentally, Ms Yonge, who'd you and Liz Strachan rent the cottage in the Gatineau from?"

"A mutual friend was generous enough to lend it to us for the week."

"Might I ask who the friend was?"

"Is this relevant, Mr Knight? I don't like to go about scattering friends' names to strangers."

"Could be relevant. Small details are the little bread crumbs on the pathway to tracing a missing person. I can assure you of the strictest confidence."

"Fine. Joe Parsons. But keep it strictly confidential."

"I will Ms Yonge. Then this was Mr Parsons' cottage?"

"I can't say, as he didn't mention whether it was or wasn't. And I didn't think to ask."

"Would you happen to have Joe Parsons' phone number?"

"I believe I do but I hesitate to give it to a stranger without his permission. It's an unlisted number."

"I understand. Ms Yonge I respect your consideration of your friend's privacy. Possibly if I left my office number you might ask Joe to call me."

"I'll consider it. "

She picked up the Lajoie–Chang card, glanced at it then gave a nice smile.

"By the way, precisely where is the cottage located in the Gatineau?"

"You take 105 out of Hull up to Gracefield, just after Gracefield turn right, it's down a side road towards Point Comfort between Lac Bitobi and Lac Pemichangan. If you go past Bouchette you'll know you've gone too far north. And if you reach Lac O'Hara you know you've gone too far east. I've only been up there once so I hope I've got it right." She scribbled down road directions and the cottage's name, Niibin Masson.

I stood up.

"Ms Yonge I appreciate your time. I'm only in the preliminary stages. Could I contact you again if necessary?"

"If I'm available I'd do what I can. Liz Strachan is a friend. I hope she is okay."

"Mind you I hope it won't be necessary. Hopefully your friend Liz will show up."

"Yes let's hope so, Mr Knight."

Connie Yonge offered her hand. Her lithe, smooth fingers were confident. It was a very firm grip.

I drove back to my apartment, sat down at the dining room table, unwrapped the wax paper and ate the rest of the sandwich. The crows were eating in the back alleyway. I watched them through the double sash windows. The phone rang again. I picked it up.

It was my old man. He hit on me for five hundred dollars until next week. I tried to put him off but he was pressing. Although he denied it I figured he had been to Hull and back. Economists, fund managers, stockbrokers, statisticians, and business columnists carried on with dire warnings, predictions and calculations leading to apocalyptic prophecies regarding debt, the demographic bulge in old age and dwindling national pension funds that drove the investment gang straight into smash-ups like Nortel, Enron and World.com. Such wiseacres clean forgot about the old devouring the flesh of their young. Man, I couldn't afford my old man's retirement. I thought about Connie Yonge's shrewd observations. Her high-pitched voice grated but she knew things. My old man was certainly not searching for philosophical maturity, he was off investigating mathematical incertitudes in the most hostile statistical environment ever conjured up: the casino with its provincial certitudes and inimical odds that always favoured the house. Snowballs in hell sometimes fared better than dice on the felt. I thought I ought to introduce him to Pierre Willett, they'd hit it off at the slots though rumour suggested my old man preferred cards and craps. I agreed to my father's plea for five bills but regretted it the moment I set down the phone. I acquiesced just to get off the phone. There went the gift for Lynda before she sailed away to Japan and probably blissful forgetfulness of this North American male who would never grow up economically because his old man kept tagging him.

I sat back at the table and studied the sheet with numbers. Maybe there was nothing there but the piece of paper nagged at me. I did some quick low calculus and reached the four subtotals and total,

25,500, 26,400, 16,500, 16,700 and 85,100. If money, this was not the small change of a student. It was something else. Or maybe it was just mindless doodling from a game show or really unreal reality TV. The world was full of random scraps of paper with enigmatic doodling that led nowhere, never would lead anywhere.

I went back to Bronson. Morrison was in a high mood. Lajoie and he had just cleaned up the books of a big retail chain—a money shoe box—that was hemorrhaging thousands in inventory loss every month over the last year. I had worked inside as a stock clerk in the storage warehouse while Lajoie and Morrison worked over the tills and account records. We had nailed an assistant manager who had tried to dump the shortfall in inventory onto a shipper-receiver and two stock clerks. The shipper–receiver gave new meaning to the term compulsive liar, but thief he was not, although the heavy handling by the higher-ups probably planted ideas in the guy's head. The stock clerks had habits that mostly consisted of skateboarding and blowing smoke. They were alright kids who just wanted a good time jamming in a basement band that wasn't getting heard except round the neighbourhood, the music amplified through a basement window of a suburban bungalow out Nepean way.

I gave Cheryl Perron the numbered company info and asked her to do a file check. Cheryl told me that she had taken a phone call from a woman inquiring if I were a legitimate employee of Lajoie–Chang. The call had come around the time I had been left loitering in the lobby. Then I sat beside Morrison as he went over the BlackBerry.

"Did I tell you about aandek?"

"Aandek? Is that the password?"

"Maybe. Sort of."

Morrison punched out a-n-d-e-k. "No go."

"Try two As."

"Okay." He tried it again. "No go."

"A linguist told me that's the Ojibwe word for crow."

"So it's not the password." Morrison swivelled in his chair and stared at me. "Alec why are you wasting my time? I'm trying to open up this toy for you and you're trying to teach me a language you don't know and probably will never know. Even less likelihood of you learning to speak Ojibwe than me learning to speak Mandarin. What is this?"

"Did Cheryl or Georges tell you what I found this morning?"

"The password I hope."

"No. A dead crow."

"Alec, do you have any idea where we live? The Ottawa valley is crow valley. This city is crow capital of the crow nation. I need clues not a language lesson."

"I thought you'd show big concern. West Nile virus."

"Right."

"Try Yonge."

"Young? Like y-o-u-n-g?"

"No. Like in Toronto. Yonge Street."

"Okay."

"I called the local health authorities. Guy named Jim, nice guy, friendly sort, came out and bagged the bird. He's sending it to Winnipeg. The bird's carcass. Health Canada Contagious Disease Centre for lab tests."

"No go."

"Try variants."

"I did."

"Try Connie. With consonant and syllable variants."

"Okay."

"So the birds are showing up with West Nile virus. A crow in Windsor and a blue jay outside Toronto. Morrison what do you know about this disease?"

"Nothing. Less than the crow that was felled by it."

"Crow's a tough bird. A smart bird. Admirable bird."

"Wise bird Alec. Next to duck, the wisest of the fowls. The Einstein among birds. Staunch stomach chemistry and numerical neuronal powers."

"What's going to happen, Morrison?"

"That one doesn't work either. What do you mean? Alec, we need alphanumeric clues."

"What's going to happen to this virus and the birds? It's moving pretty quick. Try combinations of letters in her name with nine-oh-nine and nine-one-oh."

"Okay. The birds are dying. That's what I hear. Mosquito is the vector for the disease. The virus has mutated. Avian viruses as a class are powerful and dangerous. Very virulent. Sort of but not quite like malaria and yellow fever. Early on in the research game."

"How early on Morrison?"

"In terms of virology and bacteriological research the paleolithic age. Deep time threshold around 1900 just before they built the Panama Canal. But unrecognized. Mistaken."

"That's deep dark history, Morrison. Scary age."

"Listen, in terms of virology, pre-HIV pre-1970 is like a Stone Age. Anyway there was a famous Japanese bacteriologist died while researching yellow fever. He thought viruses were related to bacteria. Called them bacteriophages."

"Bacteria whats? I'm not going near them."

"Eaters of bacteria. But viruses are something else. More powerful creatures. Species without end. Species unto themselves but as close to crystals as a life form can get. Animate inanimates. Any other hints or clues?"

"Try something with Constant or Constance."

"Sure."

"Morrison, is this bird virus going to be an epidemic? Like HIV/AIDS?"

"Who knows? Maybe like malaria or yellow fever. Could be worse than encephalitis. But hard to say."

"Think about it Morrison."

"About what? The password? Alec, this could take time. Why not just leave me with a list. I'll run them through."

"Think about crows. How many crows do you think there are in Canada. In all of North America?"

Morrison stared at me.

"Does it go? Try a variant. With a K or X."

"Sure."

"I'd say there's at least one crow for every Canuck."

"At least one. Hey." Morrison gave a wicked smile. "You wiz kid. Alec Knight, cracker hacker of the month. King of Kanata. The password worked. Where'd you dig that one up?"

"Just a hunch over lunch. A yard bird told me. How many crows would you say Morrison?"

"From the Arctic Circle to the forty-ninth parallel?"

"Yeah."

"Probably at least ten maybe twenty million."

"From the forty-ninth parallel to the Gulf of Mexico?"
"At least as many, maybe more."
"Let's close the forty-ninth parallel."
"No way. It's against NAFTA."
"I'm worried about this disease, Morrison. How fast can this virus spread?"
"Avian viruses are a class unto themselves. In Hong Kong they put down the whole domestic fowl population three, four years back to contain an avian virus. Millions of chickens, ducks went down."
"That true Morrison?"
"I wouldn't joke about it. Millions of birds. Birds are close to reptiles."
"But I though they were cold-blooded? You got a list of contacts there."
"Looks like it."
"Good man. And aren't birds warm-blooded?"
"Yes, but their reproductive process, some aspects of their organs and of course their brain stem have things in common with reptiles. And their feathers are sort of modified scales gone soft for flight. Took to the skies because they were too vulnerable. Escape the predators."
"That the name of a B-flick, Morrison?"
"No way. You know the way of the world, Alec."
"I'm learning."
"Well if you can't crawl like a creep, flee like a flea."
Cheryl Perron popped her head through the doorway.
"Alec a woman for you on your line."
"Same as before?"
"No." Cheryl smiled, "Not your high-pitched lady. It's Brenda Strachan. Should I transfer it over here? "
"I'll take it in my office. Morrison, can you crank out a list of contacts from that gizmo."
"Sure."
Brenda Strachan had a solid appealing voice with the vaguest trace of an English accent except that it was beginning to acquire a faintly aloof tone bestowed by working in the bureaucracy. She told me to meet her at her place. She would soon be leaving work and would be home in forty-five minutes. I figured ten minutes to get over to Brenda Strachan's address. I used the spare time to check out Willett.

The guy looked vulnerable, broke and not necessarily reliable. From years ago an old criminal charge and some brief time served for theft. I wondered how he swung the job at Melgund. A superintendent job did not necessarily require bonding but maybe it did. I checked out the company that did security for Melgund, a local outfit, Elguard Security.

I went to Elguard Security's web site, a guy's name rang a distant bell, Geoffrey Gagnon, he was in management and investigations. I called up Elguard Security.

Geoff Gagnon came on the line.

"Geoff this is Alec Knight. We were over at U of O together, remember? A crim course."

"Huh. Sure. What is this about?"

I gave him some background. He seemed bored and indifferent. I asked about Pierre Willett. He went off the line for a few minutes. When he came back on, he was more amenable, I figured he was checking out me and Lajoie–Chang and not Willett.

"Yeah. Not much on the guy. He's a superintendent like you say over at one of Melgund's high-rises. Nothing on the guy. He's been doing his job regular for three years now. Since he retired. Causes no problems."

"How'd he get in there. Who were his references?"

"Sec."

Gagnon put me on hold for a few minutes, then he came back on. "Nephew. Guy's high up in Melgund management circles. Gave the old guy a job. Vouched for him."

We talked briefly about the regular security guard on site but nothing had come up concerning Liz Strachan. Gagnon told me they were leaving it to the police. They had nothing on Liz Strachan.

"Thanks."

"No prob. Hey Knight, keep in touch. I hear Lajoie–Chang does good work."

"I will. Definitely. Thanks a lot."

Brenda Strachan's place was in a big house built around 1900 that had been broken up into four spacious apartments. It was in the area called the golden triangle, east of Elgin Street and in the elbow of the Rideau Canal. The phrase golden triangle had little to do with the way the sun shone on this watery city in icy winter or humid summer, rather it was a real estate maxim. Across the way was Minto Park, a pleasant space, where the Argentine General de San Martin shouldered his way into our existence. I vaguely remembered when the Falklands war—although I had heard a few people call it the Malvinas—was going on, a small crew of warmongers called for taking down the good General's statue, a gift from the Argentine government. But the general, a compatriot of Bolivar, showed a brave demeanor and made his way through the season of slander and stayed in place to liberate the park. The houses in this golden elbow of the Rideau Canal were often as not covered with historical plaques. The streets were named after prime ministers and cabinet ministers, governor generals and important diggers of the canal, levees, ports and railroad lines, after the remittance men sent out by imperial London as colonial bureaucrats to run Upper and Lower Canada—up or down. Even Confederation politicians' names showed up. I sat in the park watching the crows and lake gulls and sometimes more aggressive sea gulls bicker over litter. The crows were native but the gulls were interlopers, the sea gulls came in like the eels and zebra mussels with ocean-going vessels on the St Lawrence Seaway. Both the sea gulls and lake gulls had hitched their way up from Lake Ontario following the trash tossed overboard by tourists in motor boats puttering up the Rideau Canal in intoxicated states of leisure.

The houses were spacious, solid red brick edifices—no astonishing architecture, rather stolid late Victorian and staid Edwardian. No risks taken. An after lunch haze had settled in over the Ottawa valley, traffic smog, in the midst of it I could imagine the third floor attics housing maids and servants for the affluent lumber merchants who pulled their fortunes out of the logjams on the rivers. I wanted to go shoot a game of pool at MacLaren's around the corner on Elgin but instead I checked the time, left the park bench and strolled across the grassy park to the big red Gilmour address. I rang the buzzer for the ground floor apartment. The big glass and oak door was opened by a slim woman. She walked with a heavy limp to her right leg, her posture off keel.

"Mr Knight?"

"Yes." I showed her my licence.

"Brenda Strachan. Please come this way."

She had a fine voice, smooth and more resonant in person than it had been over the phone. It was a warm and attractive voice, very direct and appealing. I followed Brenda Strachan to her apartment on the ground floor. We went into a small dining room that looked out to the backyard.

"Would you care for some coffee?"

"No thanks. Don't trouble yourself."

"Tea?"

"Okay. Sure why not, as long as it is no trouble."

"I wouldn't ask if it were. Green tea." She gave a smile. She put the kettle on and made the tea. I started to get up to help carry in the teapot and cups but she broke in, "It's fine. Thanks anyway, I can manage."

I stayed seated. It took two trips for the cups and pot but she managed with no problem.

"My parents said I should tell you anything I am able to that could help in anyway."

"They said you're a lawyer."

"Yes. But I didn't practice much. I tried it for a year with a big corporate firm here in Ottawa but it wasn't my cup of tea. Anyway I prefer research and writing. That's my real forte."

She was not especially good-looking but had lovely eyes and a frank and animate face. I found myself struggling to get by her disability, watching her hobble around on one good leg and one artificial limb was like watching a bird move with a broken wing.

"Ms Strachan, when was the last time you saw or spoke with your sister Liz?"

"Almost two weeks ago. I saw Liz briefly on the Wednesday she went up to the Gatineau with her friends."

"How was she?"

"How was she? Liz was pretty up. She's that way. It would be rare to see my sister in a blue mood. If she gets that way she keeps it to herself. But I can't always tell Liz's moods."

"How's that?"

"We're close but not that close. My parents think we should live together but I don't want to. We're very different people. Liz has her life which is pretty different from mine."

"She's studying law as well."

"Yes. She's in second year. She'll make a great litigation lawyer."

"How so?"

"She likes people and people really like her."

"You mentioned she went to the Gatineau, a cottage with friends. Do you know who they were?"

"Not certain. But I think she drove up with a woman named Connie Yonge. She lives across the hallway in Liz's apartment building."

"Did anybody else go with them?"

"Maybe. But I'm not certain."

"Does your sister have someone she hangs out with?"

"Do you mean lover, Mr Knight? Three minutes. Green tea. This is Gyokuro. It deserves careful timing." Brenda smiled and poured the tea.

"Okay. Whatever."

"I don't know. She saw a fellow named Ed Stanley for a little while but she hasn't mentioned him for some time."

"Since when?"

"Since the late winter or maybe even December. Fact is, Mr Knight, my sister has many admirers. She's never wanted for men getting stuck on her. Liz has always been able to pretty much pick and choose. But I'm not certain who Liz might be involved with, if anyone at all."

"Any names come to mind that were mentioned?"

"There is a fellow named Joe. I met him in passing. I think his name was Joe Parsons. And another university student, I think in computers, by the name of Bill. He was a musician as well. But I can't say, as I don't know them at all. It was simply accidental that I happened to meet them in the first place by being over at Liz's apartment. In any event she wouldn't mention anyone she was seriously involved with. Liz doesn't confide in me."

"What do you know about Liz's neighbour Connie Yonge?"

"Connie? Not much. Liz seems close to Connie Yonge but I don't know Connie. She seems pretty busy."

"What does Connie Yonge do for a living?"

"I believe she works for an airline. Flight attendant. That's what Liz told me."

"They went up to the cottage in the Gatineau together. But you didn't see your sister after that."

"No."

"That didn't seem unusual."

"Not really. Sometimes two or three weeks might pass and we wouldn't see each other. Liz might just call over to see if I needed a hand with anything. Then I tend to get wrapped up in my work. It's pretty demanding, some long hours and, well you know Liz is still in school."

"Your parents said you two are close."

"My parents wish that but it isn't the case. They want Liz to be my minder but neither of us want that. It's inhibiting."

"After your sister came back from the Gatineau on the weekend, did you hear from her or talk to her on the phone?"

"She left a message on my answering service around four in the afternoon on the Monday. The thirty-first. I called her back around seven that evening but didn't get an answer."

"Did you save her message?"

"I don't know. I might have erased it. Let me check." Brenda went over to the phone and checked. "It's still there."

I listened to the message.

'Hi Brenda. Liz. Could you please give me a call when you get a chance. Uh,' a pause, 'It's kinda important. 'Preciate it if you get back to me. Bye.'

I replayed it and resaved it.

"Thanks. You don't mind saving that do you."

"No."

"Can it be copied?"

"I suppose. I don't use that feature much. But this phone can do it." She mucked about and made a copy.

"Thanks. You don't know what it was concerning?"

"Haven't the faintest. But then the landlord Melgund Management phoned about the rent on the third. And I thought it must have been about the rent. I figured Liz must have gone out of town and forgot to pay her rent. I phoned my folks and they said they would cover it but then they were upset because we hadn't been in contact with each other like good sisters. I was a little sharp with my parents on account of that."

"Your parents made the rent for Liz?"

"That's right."

"Is that the first time Liz couldn't make the rent?"

"Oh I think they'd done it before. They'd always help out. It's not a hardship."

"So you didn't think it was unusual."

"Not really. I did think it was unusual that my parents hadn't spoken to Liz in near two weeks."

"Why?"

"Well even if we don't call, they will. And sometimes pop in. Without notice. On the spur of the moment, using some pretext that they had to come up from Kingston to do some legal work in Ottawa, but the truth is they hardly ever have reason to come here. It's mostly just an excuse."

Brenda drank the tea. I stared across the table at the woman. She had very lovely eyes, a certain mirth. But there didn't seem to be a trace of her sister Liz in her features. She looked more like her father's side of the family. The lawyer massaged her shoulder, moved her thigh, adjusting the prosthetic limb.

"Is this your sister's handwriting?" I showed Brenda Strachan the sheet of paper I had filched from the wastebasket in Liz's apartment. I revealed only the surface with the month names scrawled on it.

"Yes. Looks like Liz's. Yes. I'm certain it is."

"Does it mean anything to you?"

"Can't say as it does. Why? Should it?"

"Did your sister say or do anything out of the usual before she went to the Gatineau?"

Brenda looked out the window.

"Not that I can think of Mr Knight. Then maybe. Although this might be stretching it. On the Wednesday morning that I saw her, Liz gave me a computer disk."

"What did she say when she gave it to you?"

"She asked me to keep it in a safe spot. But she said it like a joke. Making light of it. That was Liz's manner."

"So she meant it just as a joke?"

"With Liz it's hard to tell what's serious and what isn't. Liz sometimes has a very sarcastic ironic manner of talking. But it seemed she wanted me to keep it safe so I told her I'd put it in my safety deposit box."

"What did she say to that?"

"She said, 'yeah do that, 'cause there's enough on that to send me back to Kingston for life.' Then she laughed. I said okay what's on it. 'My research papers from law school, I'm gonna flog them to the new class of law students.' She laughed. And I laughed."

"Where's the disk?"

"Here. I didn't get around to putting it in the safety deposit box. I suppose that means I thought she was joking."

"Could you give me a copy?"

"I suppose. Although I wouldn't feel comfortable about it. But under the circumstances I guess I should. Just a sec."

We went into the living room. Brenda Strachan booted up her laptop. She went into her bedroom and came back with a CD.

"Please let me see it." It was labelled transfer disk.

Brenda inserted the disk but couldn't bring up the files or transfer it to the hard drive for copying.

"Sorry, it's encrypted. I can't access the files."

"Could I have that original for a few days? I'll return it."

"Sure if you think it will help."

"It might. Hard to say at this point. Maybe it will and maybe it won't."

I left the apartment, strolled past the silent dignified General, who was not divulging any secrets, and drove back over to Bronson.

# FOUR

I went around town for a couple more hours checking with more cabby connections. Then to the train station near the stadium, which made me feel lonesome for baseball. What's a baseball, just a sphere to toss in the air and let fall into a hand with happy simplicity. I tracked back across town to check at the airport. Then as a last resort to the bus station on Catherine Street, but I doubted that Liz Strachan would leave town riding in a stink wagon for Hogtown or Hochelaga. Judging by the sprawl of furniture in her apartment and the parents' Lincoln SUV, a bus, however fleet, was far from Liz Strachan's style. These little investigations all came up as mighty zeros. Lajoie advised that a PI worth his salt, even if he doesn't necessarily satisfy the client, has the brains to collect information. Current knowledge even if seemingly useless is potentiality, the future itself. And as Lajoie remarked, future knowledge, future solutions. Right. But I wasn't even picking up factoids. I got back to the office and talked with Louise Montpetit, evening assistant.

"How's Morrison doing with the laptop?"

"I think the thing is biting back. The password on the BlackBerry doesn't work on the iBook. Figures. He left a note for Nick to run a cipher program on it. He said to tell you he would give it another crack in the morning if the cipher program didn't open it up. He left this printout for you and asked me to compile a cross list of phone numbers and street addresses. Cheryl did some of it." Louise gave me the printout.

"This is Liz Strachan's electronic address book?"

"Right. Looks like mostly students, friends and family."

I scanned it.

"Okay, something here, these guys Bill and Ed. That's probably Bill di Cesare and Ed Stanley. And Connie Yonge shows up."

"Cheryl pulled this up on the numbered company you asked about." She handed me another printout.

"Norman Innis Burley, Clarence Wilson and Peter Slowikowsky. Slowikowsky?" These names matched with initials NIB, CW and PS on the other printout.

"Of Plante, Slowikowsky."

"The criminal lawyers?"

"I think so."

"Who are these guys Norman Burley and Clarence Wilson?"

"Lawyers."

"Run a background check on them."

"Anything special I'm looking for here?"

"I'm not certain, but up until April that numbered company was paying Liz Strachan's rent. One of the cheques came late. I couldn't decipher the signature off the photocopy the superintendent showed me. Probably one of these three legal lads hanging out in the pad."

"Maybe it's a legal affair." Louise sang in tune and smiled.

"Sure."

"No, I mean maybe the Strachans know the lawyer Slowikowsky."

"Possibly. But I don't think so. Burley? That's familiar."

"Should be."

"Why Louise?"

"He's a bag boy for that Western party. The Civic Unity Party. He's their point man in Ottawa."

"Why do you know that and I don't know it, Louise?"

"Got it from a good source. My neighbour. She hangs out with that crowd. She's in good moral standing with that party. Party member. She mentioned this guy Burley a couple of times. According to her, Norman Burley walks on water. He's an alchemist, turns loonies and toonies into hundred and thousand dollar bills. To quote my teenage son, she worships the ground the dude walks on. Claims he is going to make the Civic Unity Party big big in Ontario and knock the Liberals off the North American continent into the Atlantic Ocean. She says Burley is brilliant."

"Okay. Tell me who's Clarence Wilson?"

"Haven't the faintest."

"Run a search on these characters. JP, probably Joe Parsons. Watch for that, this name Joe Parsons. Liz Strachan apparently had regular Thursday, Friday and Saturday nights with a string of older gentlemen in fine suits and fancy cars."

"I'll see what laundry comes up on Burley, Slowikowsky and Wilson."

I scanned the list further.

"Great. Thanks, Louise. Can you see that Nick or Morrison gets this disk. I got it from Liz Strachan's sister, Brenda Strachan. She could not access the files or make a copy. It is encrypted. Ask Nick or Morrison to give it a crack. Also do background checks on Connie Yonge, Stanley and di Cesare."

"Right."

I went into my office, studied the list and then started working the telephone. Most of people on the list that I reached were students, friends and acquaintances who had not seen Liz Strachan through most of the summer. None had any contact with her in the last several weeks. Many were out of town numbers. I decided to go for a snack.

I glanced at Lajoie's closed door, a seam of light glowed at its foot. I said to Louise, "I'm going down to Saikely's, I'll be back in forty-five minutes. Want anything?" She shook her head.

I walked down Bronson Avenue to Saikely's Lunchroom. More construction. Bronson, that half-commercial, once half-industrial, now partial-residential street with new and old apartment blocks, rammed under the 417, the Queensway. The expressway trashed its congested way east to west through the city on an old railroad embankment. Beyond the 417 underpass and across the Rideau Canal overpass in the vicinity of Carleton University Bronson Avenue brashly widened becoming the scenic Airport Parkway and smashed its way out to the airport. It was as anonymous and rude a street as could be found. Its parallel abbreviated twin on the east side of the canal was King Edward Avenue, once a grand, tree-lined boulevard good for an evening stroll, my mother told me. It had been humiliated by harsh urban redevelopment, an arterial road whose main purpose, like Bronson, was to shuttle hectic north and southbound car traffic across the city between the two river banks. The flow was relentless and getting worse. No doubt in some dream plan of traffic engineering one or both sides of Bronson would soon be levelled to make way for further widening so that it could be an eight lane arterial road. Since my childhood they had talked ominously about widening the street. I could imagine them ploughing the remaining stretch of houses running from the 417 through the Glebe to Carleton University and making the street into nothing more than a freeway from Lebreton flats out to the airport so all the traffic wanks could cheer smooth traffic flow.

In Saikely's I ordered a piece of pie and glass of milk. May Saikely set the food down.

"You good."

"Depends."

"You don't go to the casino in Hell."

I said nothing but shook my head as I bit into the pie.

"See, I said you are good."

"Depends."

"But you don't go over there and play funny."

"No. But someone important to me does."

"Who?" May asked.

"Doesn't matter. Anyway the provincial premiers reassure us that casinos are healthy for the economy. Better and more valuable than a health care system. I mean who needs universal public health care if you got universal public gambling." I laughed.

"They're too stupid. They don't understand it's a disease. But some people quit. Recover from it." She smiled and put her hands on her wide hips. Underneath her middle-aged weariness and long hours in the restaurant I discerned a good-looking, calm woman. She went down the counter to serve a new customer. I noticed a young guy behind the counter at the stove, even in his kitchen whites he looked suave. Vaguely familiar. He was good-looking, lean and dark, beautiful glossy pitch black hair pulled back and knotted at the neck, and two silver earrings. He looked a lot like May. He was working the grill and doing prep work, he did the work with a certain ease, speed and concision.

May came by.

"How's the pie Alec?"

"You know it's good. Albert's a terrific cook."

"I baked the pie not Albert." May Saikely declared. "Some people quit. See."

I glanced up at May Saikely. She deftly motioned with her hand towards the young man.

"My son. He said he has had it with the noise and cheats. Fell out of love with the casino and in love with a human being. Wants to help us." She smiled further, "Do you believe?"

"I got to say that's wonderful. Love cures all. All the hates and sorrows of the world."

She winked at me, then went and served the supper special hot off the grill to the other customer.

I looked back down at the printout and glossed the checked names. Apart from the names Louise was doing background checks on, few still stood out. The JP. Had to be Joe Parsons. But I now had his number and business address on Bank Street. This was going to be a long evening. I thought I better get on top of this one. Tomorrow for sure was going to be a long day.

The door opened, a little heat wave rolled in across the worn linoleum tiles to the counter stools, and someone came in and sat beside me.

"Evenin' Knight."

I recognized the voice. I glanced at the hulking figure on the next stool. The guy was not smiling, he looked grumpier than a trucker with a stalled rig on the 401 cloverleaf. But I proffered a smile all the same.

"Good evening Detective Warnock."

"Knight, don't be too polite polite and smiley. Come 'ere." Warnock stood up and motioned towards the furthest booth. He scooped up my glass and pie plate.

"With service like that I never refuse."

"Shudup Knight. You keep Lajoie happy and Chang chuckling, dontchya?" But there was no malice in the shut up, there was even an upside down note of affection that only deliberate rudeness betrays.

"I do my best to spread felicity all round. It's the way I was raised. My mom told me it's easier to make people happy than to make them sad."

When we reached the booth, Warnock set down the plate and glass. "Sit down." Warnock glared at me. I said nothing, waited and ate my humble pie.

"Cut up the platitudes into a string of angels and hang 'em over the entrance of this leb greasy spoon. There's a lot of bloody unhappiness in the world. It's a shitty world Knight."

"But a beautiful earth. Wondrous green planet. Green is sacred." I glanced into Warnock's face, took the measure of its contours. The solid detective looked profoundly sad. Just now be quiet and say nothing, I told myself.

"What do you know?"

I shrugged my shoulders.

"You see the papers?"

"Sort of. In passing."

May Saikely arrived at the table, Warnock looked up at her, "Just coffee."

He said nothing until she brought it and departed.

"I was talking to Lajoie this evening. Just now. I got, I mean me and my wife that is, we got a big problem. Personal. See this." Warnock reached across the aisle and snagged the rumpled newspaper off the end of the long counter, shuffled through it until he found the city section, grimy with food stains.

"That." He pointed a thick finger at the article about the missing teenager, Laura Cooke, last seen on the Rideau Street mall.

"That's my daughter, our daughter. She carries her mother's last name, Cooke. Nothing's coming up. Nothing. You know these street kids. We need info. But a lot of them won't talk to our people or if the brats do they claim to know nothing. You hear anything— anything—bring it back. My wife is not getting through this very well."

"No problem Detective Warnock."

"Listen. I love my daughter but we, my wife and me, we were having a lot of difficulties. It was a difficult situation on the home front. My girl she was into everything. Crystal meth, crack, hash, acid, you name it she'd try it. This isn't the first time Laura took off. She did it when she was twelve. Lucky the good guys found her on Yonge Street and brought her back from T.O. before anything happened. Then last year when she was fifteen Laura hitchhiked out to Vanfuckover. She was found in a crack house. I'm not gonna blame anyone else's kid but she was running with a rough gang. Really tough. They kicked the veins and arteries out of another kid outside a Nepean shopping mall, all on account of the other girl's ugliness. Only on account of being under sixteen, Laura got consideration from the judge. These little thugs hit on old pensioners, steal from them coming from ATMs and swarm old people in bus shelters. You dig and find anything Knight, it'll help. I'm asking round with you people. Our people are doing what they can. But I can't go in the street and ask round. You know I can't."

"I'll do my very best, Detective Warnock."

"Another thing. This is no exchange so don't take this the wrong way. I know Lajoie–Chang's on this missing person case with Elizabeth Strachan but inside says—not me, I know nothing—she's said to be a high class call girl. Not missing but just on a luxury holiday. Everything points that way. A week with a wallet. The pattern of her behaviour points to it. She's gone off before. Spain, Bahamas, Italy, California, Florida. Some of our people don't exactly want to go through every resort from Montebello to Banff, Monte Carlo to San Francisco if she is just going to swing back into town this Sunday after an end-of-summer frolic. The folks don't want to accept that. Don't even believe it."

"What do you say?"

"I don't know Knight, it's not my case, it's not my affair. I'm just telling you because rumour says there are some very big people who passed through her boudoir. VIPs on her call list. But I'm not expressing any opinion. I think our people are doing their work on this file but the Strachans are very demanding. No, that's not fair. Parents. I should say insisting people. Don't get me wrong, I'm not dismissing them. I wouldn't. I wouldn't."

"Fine."

"On me." Warnock stood up. He hadn't touched the coffee.

When I got back to the office Louise gave me info sheets. I went into the office, sat down and scrutinized them. Ed Stanley, commerce student, twenty-three years of age, shared apartment near U of O, car four years old ... five thousand owing on credit cards ... worked summer job last two years and part-time at Split Second Transport and Warehouse out in an industrial park, two traffic violations, no crim record ... Bill di Cesare, twenty-three years of age, computer science major, U of O, thirty thousand in student loans but money in the bank ... credit cards clean with five thousand dollar line of credit ... part-time computer support person for Split Second Transport ... Constance Yonge, thirty, flight attendant since graduation in psychology from Carleton University, two credit cards maxed out, VISA and MasterCard at eight and ten thousand ... 1998 Mustang on credit... Student loans for twenty thousand still owing, ten thousand in RRSPs. Fifty thousand in a savings account at the International Canadian–Caribbean Investors Bank. Five thousand dollar line of credit in a local bank. Ten thousand dollars in mutual funds ... single, previously married for two years to a pilot, divorced three years ago, no children ... Liz Strachan, four savings accounts at the International Canadian–Caribbean Investors Bank, fifty thousand dollars in a savings account, fifty thousand in mutual fund. No student loans owing. Four credit cards maxed out ... two speeding tickets. Trust fund. A bundle of money in trust, hundreds of thousands but untouchable until thirty years of age without Mum and Dad signing.

My brain went soft. What's the ICCI Bank?

I dialed up this guy Ed Stanley. The phone rang three times, I waited for the fourth ring and obligatory answering machine to kick in, but a male voice came over the line.

"Yo."

"Could I speak with Ed Stanley."

"Right on line. Who is this? You woke me up."

I gave him the line about Liz Strachan's disappearance. I asked to meet him at his place, but he gave a line about no privacy his roommates being so rowdy, and said he'd be glad to meet me at a local near the university on Laurier. He was working the night shift at the warehouse but had time to meet before. I phoned over to di Cesare who was more than willing to talk to me whenever.

Stanley was a big muscular kid. Six three and pushing two hundred and twenty-five pounds, a solid core of muscle, not clumsy but he had yet to grow into physical gracefulness. If he continued to pack on the meat he might never do it but all the same he looked plenty fast and agile on his feet, like he could do a hundred-yard dash down the football field without being winded. In a crude sort of way he was even good-looking. When we entered the bar, some of the young women and men gave him passing glances and smiles of recognition mingled with admiration as if he were a hunk. Maybe a few thought he was hot. He took this recognized popularity all in smooth style, as if it was his due. He told me he had come to school in Ottawa from a small city in southwestern Ontario. His father owned a car dealership. He let me know that it had been in the Stanley family since the time of Sam McLaughlin. Even that his great-grandfather had been an army pal of the good colonel.

I asked him what he wanted to drink and he ordered a high octane brew. I had a soda water with lime. He eschewed the glass. The green beer bottle appeared diminished and disappeared into his mitt like the smallest coke bottle from the 1950s. His hands looked like they could lift an Oldsmobile by the front bumper. The football in his palm would be a wee tiny pebble. But there was no clumsiness in his manner, he even had at moments a certain smooth ease with his body.

"I heard you play on the team."

"Yeah. Fullback." He didn't have to add first string.

"You must be good."

"I'm up there. Rushing a thousand yards. Ten touchdowns last year. I carry my weight. Working at a warehouse keeps me in shape. I hope to do better. If they give me the ball and let me thunderbolt I aim to eat up two thousand yards of turf. I'm ready to run. Built to plough through the line. Guy from Wolverines," he gave me a searching look wondering if I caught the name drop, then he added, "Michigan State, they were up to look me over. Cornhuskers too. You know, Nebraska. Said they wish they had caught sight of me earlier in high school. Build the stamina for four downs as a running back. But I'm staying here."

"That's great. U of O is my alma mater. I hope this season is a winner."

"Better be." He gave a big choppy grin. He still had the virtue of all his teeth. Stanley clearly didn't allow himself to be the victim of pile-ons, chinstraps torn off, and certainly no fists in the face at the bottom of the pile.

"When was the last time you saw Liz Strachan?"

"Saturday, couple of weekends ago. Up in the Gatineau at a cottage. That was the last weekend in August. Me and a buddy drove up there to see her."

"Did you stay?"

"Naw. We had a beer then blew off."

"Who's we?"

"Me and a buddy from university, Bill di Cesare."

"Were you intending to stay?"

"Kinda hoping but Liz seemed to want some time alone before classes start again. That's cool. I respect that."

"So you see Ms Strachan regularly."

"Sort of. We dated up until the end of term. Since April less 'cause through the summer I'm working nights, and she's pretty busy during the day. Not much time to get together."

"Makes sense."

"If you met her you'd understand. She's a beautiful person."

"I haven't had the good fortune."

"Well when you do you'll understand what I mean."

"Her family tells me she is very personable. Very attractive. Very intelligent."

"She's hot."

"Yes."

"Very. Most guys would sacrifice part of their anatomy to get it on with her. She's totally like a superior human being."

I smiled.

"It's true man. I mean it."

"So you dropped in, then what?"

"Well we had a beer." He finished his present one. He motioned for the server. An older guy came over and brought another. There seemed to be some mutual recognition between the two men but it looked like mostly customer relations on the part of the server. "Then we went for a dip in Meech Lake and drove back down to Ottawa."

"What did you and Liz talk about?"

"Nothing much. Just shooting the breeze really. Nice weather. School starting. Good to get out of the city, that sort of thing."

"Was there anyone else at the cottage?"

"Connie Yonge. Neighbour. A woman from across the hall. Some kinda flight attendant. Good-looking bitch. But if you ask me a bit stuck on herself. A real ..." He glanced away.

I waited. Stanley took a long swig.

"Ah it's nothing. It's just that she's kinda stuck up if you know what I mean."

"Was Connie Yonge around when you were at the cottage?"

"Yeah."

"What was she doing?"

"Smirking at her pretty profile in the magic mirror. Actually I don't know. I sure didn't go up there to see her."

"Was Ms Yonge there while you were talking to Liz Strachan?"

"Yeah, she stuck around, wouldn't really let us have a word alone. Bill tried to engage her."

"How long have you known Connie Yonge?"

"Known? I don't know her. I see her the odd time when I happen to see Liz. Rare. I only see Yonge on account of the fact that Liz happened to move into the same building and I guess they sometimes hang out together."

"Does Connie Yonge know you and Bill di Cesare?"

"Sure. Like she knows us to see us. But we don't, you know, socialize with that bitch. No way. Bill tried to take her out but she laughed him off. It was kind of cruel. Hurt Bill. She's a hurtful lady."

"Do you know any other friends of Liz Strachan?"

"Sure." Stanley rattled off a list of names, most of them students on the BlackBerry list.

"Anyone else come to mind?"

"Not really. Just some people. But I don't really know them."

"Do you recall their names?"

"A guy name Benny Rae and another guy Jackie Snoblin. They hang out with a guy called Joe Parsons. He's a buddy of Connie Yonge. But I don't know if they're really friends of Liz's so much as Connie Yonge's crowd. I never had anything to do with them. Just saw them in passing." He gave descriptions of the three men.

"How'd Liz come to know Parsons?"

"I figure through Connie Yonge. Yeah Connie intro'd Liz to the guy."

"What line of work is Parsons involved in?"

"I don't know. He passes himself off as a consultant. But hey you know Ottawa, the city of consultants. Anybody with a suit and tie from Zellers and an MBA is doing consultant work for the feds. I guess that's Parsons' bread and butter. But who can say. He's probably in the phone book. Check it out. Look him up."

I gave a laugh. Ed Stanley was pleased, he laughed as well. He finished the beer and called for another. I knew I had to get out of the joint before he knocked down a two-four. And not good to interview a source that was drinking. Lajoie deplored it, very bad protocol.

"So you're not certain what Connie Yonge's friends Rae, Snoblin and Parsons do?"

"Not exactly. Parsons dresses swell. Nice suits and all. Rae and Snoblin sometimes. But they're more into leather. There's something about that crew. Rae and Snoblin, I never talked to them. Just heard their names and saw them across the hall hanging out in Connie Yonge's apartment. That's all."

"And Liz and Connie Yonge never said precisely what sort of work they do?"

"No. Just that they were consultants. Connie did say they are good acquaintances. Good acquaintances." Stanley mincingly mimicked Connie Yonge's high-pitched voice but he couldn't reach the same level. He was no operatic castrato. He wasn't even in the range of a sixties rock 'n' roll falsetto. Stanley chuckled. He took up the new drink from the server. He repeated the weak imitation, hoping for another laugh. "I guess I shouldn't make fun of her. She's alright. But what a line, I mean, good acquaintances. I'm such a good acquaintance of Liz's too. But not quite good enough sometimes."

"What do you mean?"

"Nothing really."

I sipped on the soda water. Stanley drank a hard gulp, then set the bottle back down on the table and contemplated it for a long moment. He was into the depths of the dew on the shoulders of the bottle. But all the same the booze didn't seem to phase him.

"Wright? That's what you said your name was. Albert Wright. Right?"

"Knight. Alec Knight."

"Sorry about that. Better to be close than completely wrong. Just joking. Well I was kinda close. They rhyme at least. Not good with names like my old man, he preaches the gospel of customer relations. Never. Never. Never. Never—I hear that word so many times—never ever forget a customer's name. Never. Biggest insult you can do to a person on the car lot when making the sales pitch, turns 'em off. Stalls the sale right there. I think sometimes my old man reads the Toronto telephone book practising new names. Rigging up his memory cells." Stanley gave a big laugh. I went along.

"When you tell me Liz is missing like this, to tell you the truth it makes me concerned about her. It's not like her. This doesn't quite seem normal. It isn't, is it?"

"Maybe, then maybe not. Depends on Liz Strachan's routine. Sort of need enough information about a person before her regular pattern can be determined. With some people, some patterns show immediately, others take a little more time to reveal themselves. A little premature to say anything definite. But sooner or later a routine shows itself."

"How're her folks taking Liz's disappearance?"

"Well, her parents are naturally concerned. That's why Lajoie–Chang is involved. As you can see."

"I can understand. They're good people. I met them a couple of times. Lawyers. Brains. Liz is a pretty brainy type. She's not just a face."

"So I've heard. Did you see or hear from Liz after she came back from the Gatineau that week?"

"No. I phoned Liz maybe three times but she never called back. I went over and rang the apartment buzzer. But got no answer." He took a good gulp, "Listen between you and me, Bright, if Liz comes to any harm, I'll brain any jerk who hurt Liz."

"Better not to think along that sort of line, Mr Stanley, we're hoping she is alright. Maybe just went out of town for a week or so. Do you know Liz's sister, Brenda Strachan?"

"The gimp? I mean the cripple. Sure. She's a lawyer too. Smart or so I heard, but not exactly a socialite, no Britney Spears, if you know what I mean."

"What was your impression of their relationship? Close or what?"

"Are you joking man? Liz liked her family but they didn't seem close as sisters. At least as far as I could figure it out."

"How's that?"

"I'm just guessing but I think it goes back to the car accident."

"Car accident?"

"When Brenda Strachan lost her leg. I heard Liz was about five and Brenda was about ten. The old lady, Mary Strachan, was driving. Some jerk ran a red light and banged them up. Brenda was in the front passenger seat. She got pinned between the car door and the frame. By the time the emergency people extracted her, her leg was wrecked. They had to amputate to save her life. Brenda Strachan lost her leg. Liz was in the back seat and walked away from the accident without a scratch."

"Did Liz tell you this?"

"Naw. Liz never talked much 'bout her fam."

"Where did you hear the story?"

"From a buddy of mine in commerce. Penville is his home town. He knew Liz and Brenda. The guy driving the other car was a lush. Rotten part is that Kingston being rinky-dinky, this character happened to know the Strachans. I guess he was some kind of big buck real estate broker. Brokers and bottles go together like cars and collisions. Buddy says the Strachans sued the socks off the poor bugger and anybody in sight. The judge went right down the line, nailed 'em all, whackety whack whack whack, the bar, the bar owner, the bartender, even the waiter that served the booze to the character."

"But Liz Strachan herself didn't talk about the accident?"

"Naw. No way. She never mentioned it. One time I brought it up and she lost it. Couldn't believe her reaction. So I left it alone. Liz is a sweet woman but she's got a heck of a temper. But you got to get to know Liz before you see that side of her. Take it from me. You know something?"

"What?"

"In some ways it's a privilege to see Liz Strachan's temper."

I checked my watch and motioned for the bill. "On me."

"Well that's great. 'Preciate it. Great talking to you."

"My pleasure, Mr Stanley."

"If I can be of any help just call me, Alec like night or day. See I got it right this time, Mr Knight."

"Okay. I'll keep that in mind, Mr Stanley. I might need your help again."

"Yo any time."

As I came up the driveway of the bungalow in Nepean, I could hear a guitar being played. Notes drifted out on the warm night air through the side screen door. I saw down the driveway a nicely groomed vegetable garden with tomatoes, beans, garlic, zucchinis.

I rapped on the screen door. The guitar playing stopped and a young guy, thin, medium height, answered the door. He wore wire-rimmed glasses, and his hair was combed back, he had the manner of a guy trying to project a style of his own.

"Bill di Cesare?"

"Right. You Mr Knight?"

"Yes."

"Mind if I ask to see your licence?"

"No problem."

He gave it a good read, then unlatched the screen door and led me into the small back apartment. It was scrupulously neat. Organizational man's studious existence. Computers neatly set up. The acoustic guitar rested on the stand, looked like a fine instrument. An electric guitar plugged into an amp rested on another stand. A bank of CDs. A work bench for electrical and electronic equipment and tools. A desk of minimalist design, glass and steel. He had economized the space to perfection. Like di Cesare's personal grooming the room sparkled with meticulousness.

"Looks like a great garden out back."

"My parents."

"Good gardeners."

"Sure."

We sat on two chairs at a small table from the nineteen-fifties. In fact the place, apart from the musical instruments and computers, was done out in retro fifties, lamps, side tables and chairs.

"Sounded like good music. Although I didn't recognize the piece."

"Most wouldn't, it's obscure."

"How so?"

"Very early early Spanish guitar. Moorish influences. Not a great composition throughout but it's got some fascinating transitions. And even some minimalist components to it inside the layered arabesque flourishes. Quite modern at moments. A technical challenge. I was trying to improvise on it, give it a jazz feel."

"You play well."

"I wish better. I'm no Leona Boyd or João. I played pretty steadily from the time I was ten to twenty. Should have started earlier. I'm not keen to teach kids guitar. Haven't the sensibility for that as much as I'm into music. Playing more and more jazz. Minimalism's my thing." He gestured towards the electric guitar. "Real minimalism, either Japanese music or jazz."

"That's tough stuff. Head music, I suppose."

"That's right. That's where it's at. As far as I'm concerned. Who needs all that gush. Showy compositions. Strictly amateur." He took off his glasses and rubbed the bridge of his nose and put them back on. "Anyway you didn't come out here to rap on music. What's up? You mentioned Liz Strachan."

"You're at the same university as Liz Strachan."

"Yes. Nearly finished. This is my last year."

"What are you studying?"

"Computer science. It pays. After music it's a breeze. Anyway what's this about Liz Strachan?"

"Liz Strachan is missing. Her parents, Frank and Mary Strachan, lawyers from Kingston, have hired our agency to locate Ms Strachan. Apparently you were one of the last people to have seen her in the Gatineau."

"If you mean I saw Liz in the Gatineau on a Saturday in August, yes. Ed and I drove up there. Ed wanted to see her. It wasn't my idea. It was Ed's. He dragged me along, I wasn't exactly keen to go."

"Why Mr di Cesare ?"

"Ed's a friend of mine. But they sometimes don't seem to exactly get along. Liz didn't really seem keen to see Ed. Well maybe I shouldn't say that or put it that way."

"Why's that?"

"I don't know. He's a football star. First string fullback, sort of used to having things his way with women. I had the impression that Liz Strachan was losing her interest in the guy. Although he'd never say or admit it. They went out for a while off and on but Ed took it more seriously than Liz did."

"How's that?"

"She sometimes went out with other guys."

"How'd Ed take that?"

"Not too cool like a lot of guys."

"How'd you describe his reaction?"

Di Cesare said nothing as if collecting his thoughts. "Not sure how to describe it. It was just an uncomfortable scene. Seemed to frustrate Ed."

"Do you know any of the other people that Liz Strachan went out with or dated?"

"Not really."

"Did you ever ask out Liz Strachan?"

"No. She seemed attracted to older men. Well I heard that. I don't know if it's true. Just a rumour that went round. She was supposed to have a thing for guys with a wallet. I mean she comes from money after all."

"Does she?'

"Sure. You probably wouldn't be here under her parents' calling card unless she did." He smiled.

"Maybe not, maybe so."

"Hollywood's Hollywood but hiring a private investigator costs some money. Mr Knight, her parents aren't exactly selling fries from a chipwagon on Bank Street. Liz Strachan's one of the best dressed women on campus. She has a rep for being sophisticated. And she is. She's a really bright woman. Got culture. She plays the piano with finesse but doesn't care a fig about it. It kind of hurt to see that. All that natural ability with music and such indifference. Complete disengagement. She can really dance. And not just bouncing up and down at some nightspot. She can tango. She waltzes. You name it she can turn her foot to it. She's very cool."

"Did you go out with Liz Strachan?"

"I told you Mr Knight, no."

"What about Ed, doesn't he have a comfortable background?"

Bill di Cesare gave a thin smile.

"I suppose. His father owns a car dealership in some small city in southwestern Ontario. It's all the world to him."

"You ever visit Ed Stanley's hometown?"

"I went one weekend. His parents are small city business people. It's a curling and rye crowd in the winter. And beer on a motor boat or seadoo in the summer at some Great Lakes resort. And church. And more church. His parents are members of the Civic Unity Party. Believe me, Ottawa seems sophisticated, sleek and cosmopolitan next to that scene. Don't get me wrong, Ed's a good guy. Very loyal friend. Very loyal."

"With you?"

"With anybody. You can count on him. There's nothing phoney about the guy. What you see is what he is. It's sort of appealing." Di Cesare paused, "And actually the guy is quite bright in school. Ed Stanley is completely without pretensions."

"A kind of social minimalism?"

Bill di Cesare paused, glanced over at the guitar and then smiled.

"I suppose you could put it that way, Mr Knight. Although I never thought of Ed that way. But I guess there are human beings that fall into the category of social minimalism. I'm gonna give that one some thought."

"No doubt, Mr di Cesare, it is best to think of each person as a human being. An individual rather than just part of a group. How's Ed manage at school?"

"Okay. Actually he passes without a struggle. He's one heck of a football player. Fullback. He'd walk over most guys from what I've seen and heard. I don't know much about the game. But he could just as easily have done track and field. I heard he sprints the hundred yard dash in under ten seconds. Just think about all that speed, muscle and weight coming through the line. To his credit, Ed doesn't struggle with the grade thing like some jocks. He takes it in stride. Mind you, commerce is not exactly a demanding program if you know what I mean. It's on the breezy side of the brain. Like psychology and sociology. Lots of multiple choice exams. Not talking subjects that tax the higher brain functions. Not like calculus, physics, chemistry."

"How'd you meet Ed Stanley?"

"At a warehouse outfit. Split Second Transport and Warehouse. Ed was working on the docks in shipping and receiving and I had a co–op placement there to work on their computer inventory system."

"When precisely did you and Ed Stanley drive to the Gatineau?"

"Last Saturday in August. The twenty-ninth."

"When you were up in the Gatineau that weekend what happened?"

"Nothing much. We just dropped in on them."

"Who's them?"

"Liz and a friend of hers, a woman named Connie Yonge."

"Who's Connie Yonge?"

"I don't exactly know the woman. But Connie appears to be a close friend of Liz's. I think she lives across the hallway in the same building. I heard she's a flight attendant and sometimes Liz and her would holiday together in the Caribbean."

"With other people? Did Ed or you ever go with Liz and Connie on their trips?"

"Certainly not me. And at least as far as I know Ed didn't go, but he might have. But I don't really know. You'd be better off asking Ed. But to tell you the truth I didn't pay much attention."

"Did other men travel with them?"

"Could have but I have no idea."

"Mr di Cesare, how long have you known Ms Yonge?"

"I told you I hardly know her at all."

"Did you go out with Connie Yonge?"

"No."

"Mr di Cesare, did you ask Ms Yonge out?"

Di Cesare smirked, "I told you Mr Knight I hardly know the woman. I wouldn't ask her out. Anyway Connie Yonge probably wouldn't go out with me if I did ask her. But she's not really my sort of person."

"What did Ed and Liz talk about on that Saturday in the Gatineau?"

"Can I say something?"

"Sure."

"Ed's my buddy. I don't want to say anything that would cause him a problem."

"I understand. Loyalty is a great quality in a friendship. I'm not really thinking so much about Ed Stanley here so much as simply trying to establish the sequence of events. Place where Liz Strachan is or where or who she might have gone with on the Sunday after she came back from the Gatineau cottage. Every little bit of information might be handy even if it might seem to you or someone else as useless. Irrelevant. Details are helpful. Sort of like notes in a piece of music, Mr di Cesare. You can't have the score without the notes on the page. As far as we know, according to her family, the people who know her in Ottawa, it was around that last weekend in August or just after it that Liz appears to have been last seen. Mr di Cesare, do you recall what Liz and Ed Stanley talked about that Saturday afternoon?"

"Ed and Liz argued. Well maybe not that strong a word. I suppose more like a little quarrel. Ed wanted to be with Liz. And she wasn't keen on it. In fact she was kind of abrupt. I mean if a woman spoke to me like Liz spoke to Ed I don't think I'd phone her again, let alone pop into her cottage."

"What did they argue about?"

"I told you, Mr Knight, I didn't mean argue. More like bicker. Nothing really. You know a lovers' quarrel. Back and forth but all the passion was on Ed's side. And Liz was distant in her manner. Aloof. She's very sophisticated. At a certain point she disengages. That's Liz Strachan, very cool. That's her manner. Polished."

"Do you recall what Liz Strachan said?"

"Not everything. Just the first bits. Things like, who invited you up here? Who asked you up here? It was a crummy conversation if you can even call it that. Actually it wasn't an argument. I don't want to leave that impression with you Mr Knight. It was actually really banal. Like something off a soap. Actually I don't like talking about my friends behind their backs."

"I understand but I do need your help to locate Liz Strachan. How long did they talk?"

"Not very. Five, maybe max ten, fifteen minutes. I only heard the beginning. I went out on the porch. I didn't even finish the beer."

"Why'd you go on the porch?"

"Why not? Do you like to be in the presence of such things? It's not cool. Not cool at all."

"Was Connie Yonge present?"

"Sure."

"What was her reaction to the situation?"

"Opaque. Connie Yonge just sat there like a lizard. I couldn't tell, she said nothing, but I felt she despised us. Certain vibes. I got that vibration."

"How would you describe the mood?"

"I don't know. Tense. No. Wrong word. Not my style. I don't like arguments. It's not where thinking happens. It's not where my brain's at. Only people who aren't cool argue. Bicker, that's the word. Just a personal observation of mine. Opinion I suppose." He smiled.

"Then what happened?"

"Ed came out on the porch and we took off. Drove over to the lake for a swim and then came back into town, had some beers and I came home."

"Did Ed say anything to you?"

"About what?"

"About the conversation he had with Liz Strachan."

"No. He seemed sort of indifferent to it all. He seemed to shrug it off."

"Can you think of or remember any other men that Liz Strachan or Connie Yonge knew?"

"No. I told you I don't really know their circle. I knew in passing or heard of some people from the university that Liz Strachan hung out with." He gave the same names as Ed Stanley and some of the student names that had come off the BlackBerry. "But I don't know Connie Yonge's crowd."

"Do any of the people that Liz Strachan and Connie Yonge hang out with do drugs?"

"Drugs?" Bill laughed, "Come on. This may be Ottawa but you know. Party music, it's chemical chairs looking for a periodic table. You know that and I know that."

"Did Liz or Connie Yonge do drugs?"

"Sure. They had the loot. They did them."

"What?"

"This isn't going to the cops."

"No."

"They did lines."

"Much?"

"I didn't have the impression they were coke bunnies. Not often. Recreational. Weekends I suppose. I heard. That sort of thing."

"With who?"

"I wouldn't know."

"With Ed Stanley?"

"Not as far as I know. Ed might do the odd snort but I don't know. Look I stay away from that. It's way beyond my pocket. A twenty dollar bottle of Italian wine, that's my high style."

"Have you seen or heard from Liz Strachan since that weekend?"

"No."

"Anybody mention her to you. Or anyone else you know see her?"

"No. Just Ed. He mentioned her."

"What'd he say."

"Once about being in the dumps because he wasn't seeing much of Liz."

"Did Ed go out with anyone else?"

Bill di Cesare's mouth turned up.

"Sure. He screwed around if he got the chance. He plays football. He figures it is one of the privileges of the game. Opportunity showed up he'd grab it. But we're not into morals I hope. Save it for the boys in the Civic Unity Party. It's a drag gossiping about people's bedsheets."

I smiled. "Did Ed Stanley date or sleep with Connie Yonge?"

Bill di Cesare seemed momentarily startled by this then regained his composure.

"I don't know." He gazed down at the floor.

"Did Liz ever mention a Peter Slowikowsky?"

"No."

"What about a man named Norman I Burley?"

He shook his head.

"How about a Clarence Wilson?"

The student shook his head indicating no.

"Does the name Joe Parsons mean anything to you, Mr di Cesare?"

Bill di Cesare gave a long thought. He took off his glasses, rubbed the bridge of his nose, set his glasses back on and stayed in thought. He shook his head. "I don't recognize those names. Never heard of any of them. Why?"

"No special reason. They just popped up because someone mentioned them."

"Who?"

"I keep that sort of thing confidential just as I keep what you've told me confidential."

"Sure. That's cool, Mr Knight."

I stood up and thanked him and headed back into Ottawa.

When I got into my place I checked my answering service. There was a message from Lynda.

"Alec I was hoping you were in. It'd be wonderful to see you tonight if it is at all possible. Please call me."

There was a message from my father. And one from Louise Montpetit to call into the office. I called up Louise.

"Alec, I've got that information for you if you want it tonight."

"I'll pass. I need sleep. I'll check it in the morning."

"The Strachans called, they want to know if you have any leads."

"I'll call them."

I dialed up Lynda first and said it would be great to see her. See someone who didn't hide.

I phoned over to the Strachan's hotel. Mary Strachan answered.

"Your husband called Lajoie–Chang's office and left a message asking that I call."

"Yes Mr Knight. I understand you spoke to our daughter Brenda. She said she gave you a computer disk. I don't want to be too pressing, but we're anxious to have some good word. That is whether you're making any progress."

"Maybe I should come over and speak in person, saves repeating things."

"Yes. Maybe that would be best. We'd appreciate that."

I phoned Lynda and told her I would be a little late.

I drove to the Lord Elgin Hotel across from Confederation Park. It was near the British High Commission and old National Gallery, both 1950s modern international style. The Lord Elgin Hotel was undergoing an expansion but one that was modest and harmonious trying to keep the building in tune with itself. Smaller north and south wings sheathed in cut stone were being added to the core building. Graciously, this 1940s modest hotel had not been subjected to a shiny steel and glaring glass postmodern humiliation. I suppose better not to get hung up on the old for old's sake but there is only so much old architecture escaping the wrecker's ball. Like a city planning buddy once said, they've demolished so much from before 1940 in the sacred name of development that the sixties buildings are beginning to look downright historical. I took the elevator to the sixth floor. A nice modestly spacious room in keeping with their Lincoln SUV. Space is the thing of mind and matter. No space and you're classified as a poor sucker.

"Drink Mr Knight?"

"No. Thanks. I'll pass."

"We're hoping you might have some hopeful information."

"I should say it is yet premature to draw any conclusions. I've checked all the departure points, bus, rail and airport. So far nothing on that front. I have begun a preliminary canvass of the apartment building. At this point, I've spoke to a number of people who knew your daughter. Some of them saw your daughter the week when Liz went to the cottage in the Gatineau. There are some discrepancies but most of it links up, placing your daughter Liz's disappearance sometime between noon on the Sunday when she returned and late afternoon or the early evening on the Monday. But it might possibly be later, even as late as early the next morning, on the Tuesday. But this seems less likely."

"What sorts of discrepancies?"

"Details. Might just be slips in memory on the part of people. I'll have a better idea by tomorrow. I have a half dozen other substantial leads which have to be checked out and then I'll know better the sequence of events and if anyone may have seen your daughter after that Monday. And whether she left town on the weekend and if she did so who with and where to."

"Can you give us an indication if you have any solid leads as to her whereabouts?"

"Not at this juncture."

Mary Strachan got a peevish look. Frank Strachan drank a Scotch and looked like he was exhausted by his alderman.

"Mr Knight we need a good word. Something to be hopeful about. We spoke with the police today and still they have nothing. To tell you the truth our spirits are flagging. Even when Liz would leave the country she kept in regular contact. This is not her way."

"Mr Strachan, we're doing everything possible. Lajoie–Chang Associates has given this investigation a top priority. And placed all its resources at its disposal."

"We made that clear to Georges Lajoie. Money is not a boulder in the road here if you get my metaphor."

"I understand. And Georges Lajoie has made it very clear to me that I am to give this case number one priority. And I have. We have good people working on it trying to secure and compile a thorough list of all your daughter's contacts. Anyone who may have had even the slightest contact with Liz."

"Mr Knight, you sure you wouldn't care for a drink?"

"No, Mr Strachan. I will tell you that our computer person has been able to open up your daughter's BlackBerry. We now have a provisional list of your daughter's contacts. I'm in the process of checking the most important links in her life. I know from experience in cases of this sort that it is hard to relax when someone so intimate to your lives has disappeared. I can assure you we're doing everything we can. We're working as quickly as possible so that if there are any leads we get to them before it is too late, before they fade out."

"We expect as much."

"And you deserve as much." I stood up. "Certainly your daughter Liz does. Incidentally I was wondering who paid your daughter's rent on a regular basis?"

Mary Strachan looked at Frank Strachan.

"Please sit down for a minute, Mr Knight."

"Sure."

"We thought she did but we're not so certain."

"Do you have any connection to a numbered company?"

"Which ones? Over the years we've had dealings with several. But mostly in conjunction with real estate transactions."

I showed them the number of the company.

"No. I don't recognize that company number. Is it supposed to mean something to us, Mr Knight?"

"Well it would appear that for several months from the time Liz moved into her new apartment on King Edward to April of this year that a numbered company issued cheques in payment for her rent."

"This is strange. Liz has more than enough money to cover her rent. In fact all her education expenses without any hardship," Mary Strachan broke in.

"From what sources?"

"Well we paid into a Registered Education Savings Plan. And, well, Frank, should I tell Mr Knight? About the situation."

"Ms Strachan, I think it is best if you were forthcoming about the situation. I thought Georges Lajoie indicated to you that that is essential. Regrettably, clients who withhold relevant information from investigative agencies sometimes get mediocre service because the shared information is inadequate. This may or may not be a serious situation. Maybe Liz went to the Caribbean for a week of holidays on the spur of the moment since she appears to have gone there regularly. And she just neglected to let anyone know about the trip, wanting some privacy. But that's mere speculation. I need all the information family and friends can supply. Any random piece of information can twist around and quickly turn into a substantial lead. If you get my drift."

"No. No. Mr Knight, you entirely misunderstand me. It's just delicate. It has to do with not only Liz but Brenda. Some years ago we were in a very serious car accident. The girls and I. I was driving. A drunk driver ran a stop light and hit our car. Liz was in the back seat. She was knocked against the rear side window. Fortunately Liz had on a seat belt. She was knocked unconscious but recovered. Brenda unfortunately was pinned in the car and, well ..." Mary Strachan began to hesitate, I thought she might weep but she pulled back from her own words. "It's obvious what happened. Anyway there was a settlement from the car accident and trust funds were established for the girls. Liz has sufficient money to go through university. And if she did not we would certainly cover her education."

"Fine. Do the names Peter Slowikowsky, Norman Innis Burley and Clarence Wilson mean anything to either of you?"

"No. Wait." Frank Strachan poured another shot. "Slowikowsky. Peter Slowikowsky. He's a criminal lawyer, isn't he?"

"Yes. Here in town with the firm Plante, Slowikowsky. He's got a substantial reputation as a criminal lawyer. Done some high profile cases."

"Yes, but we've had no dealings with these gentlemen. That's not our area of law. We do real estate. Commercial law."

"Well they're directors of the numbered company."

"Who paid our daughter's rent from after April?"

"Liz did up until this month when you did."

"What does this all mean, Mr Knight?"

"It could be a piece of flimsy information. But according to some informants that I've spoken to your daughter had a reputation for going out with older gentlemen. It might have been one or more of these men."

Mary Strachan shook her head and winced.

"I don't understand."

I got up.

"Listen, maybe you should give yourselves a quiet day back home in Kingston. Try to get back to some of your usual routine. Give us another twenty-four hours and I'll call you at home in Kingston, tomorrow evening or the following morning. When I possibly will have something more substantial to report."

"No. No. Not possible Mr Knight. We're sticking around. If the police saw us go back to Kingston they'd let their investigation drag. And we'd have nothing from them."

"Fine. Just as you wish. You can call me tomorrow after lunch. I have some important things to do tonight."

"Thanks for coming Mr Knight."

I went home. Lynda was sitting on the landing.

"Japan in a few days."

"Thanks." I turned the key in the lock.

"Don't be that way."

"Okay. You're beautiful. A great dancer. Go get a great education in Japan." I threw in a smile.

"I will."

We rolled into bed and did the best thing the universe ever invented regardless what cynics report. I hit the fields of bliss rolling in blue flax flowers until I came across a burnt-out grass field where fire had taken its toll, scattered across the field were the carcasses of crows and blue jays as far as my eye could see.

A spasm in my leg muscle jerked me awake. I woke up so startled that it shook Lynda awake. I felt mortal.

"What is it Alec?" Lynda's voice seemed to be speaking in a strange hazy tongue.

"Nothing. I had a blissful dream. I had a bad dream. I dreamt about dead crows and dead blue jays in a burnt-out field."

# FIVE

The morning came up bright and clear, almost a tap on the shoulder. I went over the printouts on Joe Parsons, Peter Slowikowsky, Clarence Wilson and Norman I Burley. Nick Glastonbury hadn't been able to crack open Liz Strachan's computer or break open the encrypted files on the floppy disk. Morrison sent them out to a wiz kid. A hacker hound, a fifteen-year-old kid in the gifted program at Lisgar Collegiate, the computer companies were already competing to snag the boy like he was the hottest cortex since Stephen Hawking. His father and mother were religious, conservative and strict in all observances. But they lived on the same street in Kanata as the Changs. Under every orthodoxy there is an unorthodoxy struggling to become the new orthodoxy, or so Lajoie had it.

The file on Joe Parsons was long and halfway to interesting. He had a record for cross-border fraud along with a guy called Mike Eaves who was serving time for assault in Millhaven Prison in Kingston. Parsons and Eaves, along with some other financial hustlers, had run a bogus billing scam on yellow pages advertising through the States. They had sent out order forms to US companies to be listed in a reputable international fax directory, claiming the directory would be circulated on 200,000 CD-ROMs. They trotted out the walking fingers logo which had fortuitously never been trade-marked. They charged $895.95 on the fax directory scheme invoice. The suckers were to forward payment to a Canadian mail-receiving agency in Montreal. They'd gulled nearly a thousand US businesses, it meant near to a million bucks before they got nabbed by the RCMP fraud squad.

I whistled. Cunning and conniving lad, commit a crime without crossing the border to hustle the hustlers.

I showed it to Morrison. He laughed.

"Hey Morrison call it all in the interests of the free trade agreement. Do you think the Americans will pursue this and take it to the NAFTA trade panel?"

"No. This one will go all the way to the World Trade Organization."

"This guy is halfway to smooth. "

"What's he up to now?"

"He's running an escort agency called LTD. He's clean since he got out of the slammer, although one of his buddies went up again on an assault charge."

I wandered back to my office, went back over the list of names that came out of Liz Strachan's BlackBerry. There was a Benny Rae and Jackie Snoblin.

"Cheryl, can you check out these two characters. Current address."

"Few Snoblins but some Raes."

I went back in my office and dialed up Joe Parsons, esquire, at his present establishment. Parsons answered himself and was chilly on the phone but said to come over if I chose to squander my time while he emphasized that he knew nothing about Liz Strachan's whereabouts. And next to nothing about the lady herself. He said the cops had already been round. He said he could squeeze me in for fifteen minutes around eleven A.M.

Parsons ran his business out of a little office on the third floor of an old brick building on Bank Street above a shoe store flogging remainders and out of style footwear that even I wouldn't wear.

I walked the two flights of stairs to his office. The hallways were dusty and littered with paper and grimy bits. The linoleum tiles were soiled and cracked. Stains from mysterious materials had been ground down into the tiles. These obscure markings, if looked at a little too fixedly while under the wrong influences, might cause entire malevolent galaxies to erupt like neuroblasts in the observer's brain. I wasn't going there. I kept to the mundane and pedestrian, I just walked on the tiles.

Parsons looked sheepish like he had snorted too much coke. He had on a fine sheer silk shirt that I couldn't afford. He wore Italian loafers with paper thin soles that were only fit for walking to and from a Lamborghini or Ferrari. And he looked like he kept himself trim despite being a snowbird. He put on the appearance and manner of being busy but Wednesday being Wednesday anywhere in the world I couldn't imagine much on his agenda until Thursday, if at all.

"I'm pretty busy so let's make this quick. Alright."

Pigeons were eavesdropping from the window ledge.

"Mr Parsons, I was wondering who introduced you to Liz Strachan?"

"A mutual friend."

"Might I ask?"

"Sure. But I'm strictly answering any questions from here on in as a courtesy. Connie Yonge."

"How's that?"

"I always can use good-looking sophisticated women in this business. I pay a bonus to some of my employees if they recommend a new escort who works out."

"Does Liz Strachan work for you regularly?"

"That's confidential information. As an employer I have an obligation to protect the women's privacy. But she is a good employee. Very reliable. I wouldn't hesitate to give her a reference."

He rolled his head back like he had a kink.

"Could you give me the names of the men who dated with Liz Strachan over the past two weeks?"

"Are you off your nut, mac. That's confidential client info. I told the cops what I could without breaching any contractual agreements with the customers or the female employees. You're just a private citizen. I'd violate my contracts with my clients."

"Sure. Mr Parsons when did you last see Liz Strachan?"

"Maybe three weeks ago. I told the cops. I fully co-operated with them. Okay."

"Who'd Liz Strachan accompany that evening?"

He shook his head but said nothing.

"Okay."

"Okay what? I run a good business. A straight business. I pay my GST and PST. I pay my CPP and EI. Employees come and go in this business. I don't keep tabs on them. Some work for a couple of months, take off. Sometimes I don't hear from them for months. They come back around and want to work again, that's cool by me. That's the way this business is. I don't get in their faces and they don't get in mine. I'm not their father, grandfather or uncle. Okay. Got it?"

"I understand, Mr Parsons. But Liz Strachan, an employee of yours, has been missing for a week and nobody she knows has a clue where she is. Not her friends. Not her fellow tenants. Not her family. You as her employer might have some leads."

He scratched his eyebrow.

"Listen. All I know is that she's a good-looking woman who wanted to work to pay for her education. Help get herself through university. Period. I don't get into my employees' personal lives. It's bad for business."

"That's admirable. More employers should take such an approach."

"Fuck off mac. I don't need this crap. There's the door and remarkably it is followed by a hallway which leads to the stairs which, if you put one foot in front of another foot, you being able-bodied, will take you to the street."

"Mike Eaves took down a guy for you. What was that about?"

"Look. What Mikey Eaves did or didn't do on this side of the law or your side of the law is his business not mine. I had nothing to do with him."

"Mr Parsons, who owns that cottage up near Gracefield? The one you put Connie Yonge onto for the week."

"I don't have any idea. I got a referral for it from a lawyer buddy."

"Peter Slowikowsky? Or Alf Plante?"

Parsons smiled.

"You're in the dark."

"It was Slowikowsky."

"You know dick. You're up here fishing for minnows when there are carp in the Rideau Canal bigger than Harvey Wallbanger's prick."

"Mr Parsons you got me wrong. I admire you. That yellow pages ad campaign was good. Very good. "

"Get out. You can walk your dick through the yellow pages. You're wasting my time. Get out."

I got up.

"Thanks Mr Parsons."

I went down the stairs and sat on a cement street bench outside the building on Bank Street. A pigeon anointed me with a dropping. I laughed.

I went over to Liz Strachan's apartment building. Willett didn't want me around, he seemed thoroughly annoyed, even a touch argumentative, but proved supportive when I gave him a twenty. I worked the units for a couple of hours showcasing Liz Strachan's photo and asking the other tenants if they had seen her.

On the third floor, I met Mrs Eleanor Lowe, a bureaucrat who had lived in the building for twenty years, ever since it had been constructed by Melgund Development. A woman in her mid-sixties, she told me that she had seen Liz Strachan in the underground parking garage of the apartment building at around five on the Monday when she was returning from grocery shopping. It was a fleeting moment in the routine of the day according to Mrs Lowe but she was certain it was Liz Strachan because the man and woman were standing beside Liz's Mazda Miata. And there was only one such car in the entire apartment building and people knew that Liz Strachan owned it. Lowe described a middle-aged man maybe fifty-five dressed in a blue suit. She did not know what they were talking about but she thought Liz Strachan was upset. She didn't recall having seen the gentleman before.

Willett gave me access to the underground garage. When he disappeared into his unit I went and got my camera from the car. I walked the perimeter of the garage in a narrowing circle from the outer edge of the wall using Liz Strachan's parked Mazda as the centre point of an imaginary circle, inspecting each inch of the ground. I found an old running shoe, a dirt-encrusted glove, a soiled scarf in Scottish plaid, scraps of old papers, but none of them near Liz's sports car. Still I took photographs of them. As I neared the car I noted a series of faint marks on the garage floor suggesting that something might have been dragged or pulled across the soiled cement floor for two feet, but the marks were smudged and growing very faint. I snapped a photo. And there appeared to be nothing on the side of the car or on the ground near the car. I got down on my hands and knees and looked long and hard under the car. I saw nothing from the passenger side, then I went to the driver's side. I still saw nothing. Then I went to the front and there was nothing. Finally I looked from the rear fender. At first there was nothing but then I saw a few things in the shadows. I went back to the passenger door and peered under the chassis again. Obscurely, there were two business cards on the ground, one facing up the other facing down just under the car frame and wheel. Under the front wheel there were a few coins and what looked like something small and maybe metal. Any cursory glance would have overlooked these things in the shadows and gloom. I took photos. I sketched a location drawing. I got out three clean paper envelopes, sketched the location of the items on the back of each envelope. Then I lay down on the concrete and with a key I reached and nudged out from under the car the cards, coins and what was in fact an ear clip and photographed them before nudging them into envelopes. I stood up and re-photographed the smudge and the location of the car. I stood in the middle of the parking garage gazing around. Suddenly one of the stairwell doors slammed behind me. It startled me, but as a reflex I stuffed the envelopes in my inside vest pocket before turning around, and there was Willett. He gave me a fishy look and glanced at the camera.

"Hey you been down here a mighty long time. I was beginning to wonder, worry about what happened to you."

"Actually, I just got here a few minutes ago. I had to go back to the office for my camera."

"How's that?"

"Oh I just wanted to take a snap of Liz Strachan's car. Show a photo of it to some people. Hey Pierre, how about a shot." I held the camera up to my eye. I smiled.

"Naw. I'm not photowhatchamacallit ... genic. Cameras are for people who can't remember nothing. I got a memory." Willett backed away towards a pillar. I took four quick photos of the solitary Mazda from the front, rear and sides.

I drove back to the office. I put on latex gloves and opened the envelopes. One card read Peter Slowikowsky, Criminal Law, Plante, Slowikowsky, the other Lester Henderson, Manager, Split Second Transport and Warehouse. The business cards appeared to have what looked like a partial tread mark of a shoe clipped along the edge, no more than a half inch. The coins were coins, Mulroney's favourite item of commerce. Tailors thought the world of the lad who had brought them much weighty business. I took a magnifying glass and inspected the ear clip. A central large pearl encircled by about thirty small round diamonds and a dozen marquise ones were inset in a leaf motif. On the back of the ear clip there was a number and jeweller's signature.

I asked Cheryl what she thought. She only needed one look. And not with the magnifying glass.

"N'est pas cheap."

"Boucheron."

Cheryl whistled, "What do you say to that, you didn't buy them for your latest and greatest lady I hope."

"Funny. Is that silver?"

"No. No. No. You silly garçon. Don't you know jewellery? You'll never make a burglar. Looks like platinum. Nobody in their right mind would set those gems in silver. Especially that pearl. Whose is it?"

"I found it underneath the wheel of Liz Strachan's Miata in the underground garage."

"Only one?"

"Only one."

Cheryl licked her lips.

"I want you to get everything you can get on this guy Parsons, Connie Yonge and two other guys. Peter Slowikowsky."

"The lawyer?"

"Yeah."

"We had him before on a printout, he defended Mike Eaves, Joe Parsons' buddy."

"And a guy named Lester Henderson who is the managing director of Split Second Transport and Warehouse."

"We had that before, didn't we?" Cheryl riffled through her printout files.

"Yes."

"Those two university students. Di Cesare and Stanley work for the warehouse. Looked like summer or part-time jobs for students."

"Yes."

"Coincidence?"

"You know this racket doesn't know the meaning of that word. See if you can set up a meeting with Peter Slowikowsky. And get me a series of photos of Peter Slowikowsky and these guys Clarence Wilson, Alfred Plante and Norman Burley. And this guy Lester Henderson. Eleanor Lowe, who lives in Liz Strachan's apartment building saw Liz Strachan in the underground garage around five in the afternoon on the Monday talking with a middle-aged guy. I'm going to check out another small item and then verify if this ear clip was Liz Strachan's. I'm going over to see the Strachans at the Lord Elgin after I check this other thing."

I ran a scanner over the business card with the small partial smudged imprint from a shoe's sole. I enlarged the image on the computer and printed it. On the way over to the Lord Elgin, I dropped into a shoe store where a high school buddy, Tommy MacAlister, worked as a sales clerk. Despite the name, he came from a Franco-Ontarian family. Originally farming Quakers, pacifists fleeing to Upper Canada during the war of 1812, they had settled in Casselman in the Ottawa valley, intermarried among French and Irish farmers, lost their Quaker name and their English, gained French and become by osmosis pacifist Catholics. His uncle was a Catholic priest, a social activist committed to liberation theology.

That was history Tommy said. As for Tommy, he had done too much booze and hash, partied on the Quebec ski slopes, flunked out of high school, then one summer cycled across the country on his dirt bike. Ski bummed all over Alberta and British Columbia then dragged himself back to the Ottawa valley where his old man, a top-level bureaucrat in Industry, had got Tommy a job working as a shoe salesman at the most respectable shoe store in town, Robertson-Gouley. The commission was good and suddenly all the old school chums he had known were getting married, having kids and dragging them to Robertson-Gouley to get the tots measured for shoes just like their parents and grandparents had done. Tommy was lazy and languid, so fluently bilingual that nobody could tell what his mother tongue was, and almost illiterate. He had an allergic reaction to pen and paper. The automatic tellers, credit cards, computers and Interac saved his life on a daily basis.

"Hey. What's this? You getting married Knight, that what bring you this way? I saw you with that beautiful lady twice this summer."

"Naw. Just hanging out."

"How's things in your racket?"

"So so. And you?"

"Commissions are great. Shoes are another thing. But there's no obligation to sniff the merchandise. What's up?"

"I got a question."
"I don't do questions. They lead to answers. And I'm not good with answers. Skiing is still my thing. Shoot."
"You don't mind."
"Naw go ahead. It's slow. If a cuss wanders in, I'll put you on the shelf. What's up?"
"If I showed you part of what appears to be a shoe print do you think you could identify the model of shoe? Brand."
"Maybe. Give me a try."
I took out the scanned image. Tommy inspected it.
He smiled.
"Don't mind me, I'm trying to think. This is my thinking pose." He nodded his head.
"Okay. Definitely a runner. Not a regular street shoe. Running shoe. But we don't sell them here. I say double check it at a sports shop, that's their stuff."
"Can you?"
"Sure. Give me a couple of hours. Well maybe a week."
"How about better a day at most? I kinda need something pretty quick."
"Okay, I'll ask a bud who works for a sporting goods shop, sells plenty of runners. He'll know in a sec."
"Keep the printout. But trash it after your friend looks at it."
"Sure."

I went over to the Strachans' hotel and showed the couple the pearl ear clip. Mary Strachan recognized it immediately as Liz's.
"What's this mean?"
"I'm not—"
"Mr Knight please do not say you are not certain."
"I'm not."
"Where was it found? Or possibly I should rephrase that, where did you come by it?"
"Full syllables are not always found on the ground. It could mean a number of things. She lost it and just hasn't noticed its loss. It could indicate something more. A fall. An accident. Or possibly a struggle with an assailant, but I wouldn't be quick to jump to a conclusion.

First I had to confirm that it was Liz's ear clip. And that much you have done. Now I need to think about it."

"Sure," Frank remarked cynically. "This is turning into turmoil for us. And it is my observation that the police left this too late. This should have been noticed at the outset. And they might have taken it into account. And taken our concerns more seriously."

"Liz would never lose such a piece of jewellery. It's impossible."

"How's that? These things happen."

"Really, Mr Knight? Do you have even the faintest idea of the value of that set of ear clips?"

"Please tell me, Ms Strachan."

"They're Boucheron. Nearly four thousand dollars. From Dupuis."

"The jewellery auction house?"

"Yes. Liz would notice the loss of such a clip. This is distressing. Where's the other one?"

"I can't say. I found but the one."

"Where's this take you Mr Knight?"

"Possibly much closer. This morning I spoke with a tenant in your daughter's building who saw Liz speaking with a man. I believe her to be reliable. She's disinterested. She knows the building and tenants. Has lived in the building twenty years. She saw Liz speaking with a man, a middle-aged fellow, around five o'clock in the afternoon on the Monday. The tenant was coming back from grocery shopping so the time is pretty definite."

"Did she know the man, I mean recognize him?"

"Not by name. I have some leads on who the man might have been but I need photos to show to this informant. She was candid that she might not recognize the man's face from a photograph but we'll see."

"Let's hope so."

"I need some frankness here from the two of you regarding your daughter's social life. Sexual life. Which appears complex."

"Why? What's this to do with Liz's disappearance? We're not sniffing around for nonsense and gossip. We're talking about our daughter's disappearance. This is not supposed to be some trawling the Seaway for eels, mussels and clams."

"Your daughter and Connie Yonge—you mentioned her, Connie Yonge, and your daughter Brenda mentioned her as well—are acquaintances with a man who runs an escort agency."

"I don't understand." Mary Strachan averted her gaze.

"You will. Connie Yonge, the tenant from across the hallway, introduced your daughter Liz to a businessman who runs an escort agency."

"What's the man's name?"

"In due time. I have to go easy here."

"We hired Lajoie–Chang. We're entitled to know the details. All the details. We're paying for this." Frank Strachan looked livid.

"You will but I have to interview some other individuals involved and regrettably neither Connie Yonge nor this fellow who runs the escort agency were especially forthcoming."

"Shake him down."

"That's for the movies Mr Strachan. Discretion is required when trying to get information from a source. Most people like to talk for pleasure but don't like to talk about touchy issues. Caution sets in. They get either fearful or talk too much, which usually means they know next to nothing. You ever pick an apple?"

"Green ones. When I was a kid. We used to raid a neighbour's orchard. Pissed him off." Strachan half laughed. "What of it?"

"I once worked a summer picking fruit when I was a kid. You don't yank the fruit and you don't pull it. You turn it gently and carefully so the stem of the apple lets go, releases itself into the fingers and palm of the hand. Gives itself up. Fruit picking takes skill. A source is a little like that. If you catch my meaning. I've already got resistance from this guy, he's not forthcoming. He's not talking straight. I expected as much. He's got things to hide. He's got a record."

"For what?"

"He ran a yellow pages invoice scam out of Montreal into the States. He and another guy got eighteen months for fraud. This guy took the lashes and did the time for some big money guys. He claims to be clean since then but probably is not. He does coke. His buddy is back in jail serving time. He looks like he took somebody out for this guy. It was a sort of payback. But this guy was beyond being touched for the assault charge."

"Liz wouldn't have anything to do with people like that, Mr Knight. This is absurd. She's in law school. She'd never jeopardize her future. Never associate with common thugs and fraud artists."

"Ms Strachan, we each have a way of jeopardizing our future."

"I don't understand that."

"Just by breathing. I'll be candid with you for a moment. And I hope you've told me everything about your daughter that you know that is material—however remote or seemingly useless that it might appear to you—to help discover where Liz might be. Let Lajoie-Chang be the judge of whether the information is or is not relevant and trust us not to reveal anything beyond what it is necessary." I paused, hoping that both Strachans would look me in the face but Mary Strachan still tilted her head, her eyes half averted. "Mr and Ms Strachan, Lajoie-Chang does not just live by its clients—we need them to do business, as lawyers you surely know this—but it thrives by its confidentiality agreements. Liz's life is complex. Complicated beyond the usual range of affairs of a university student."

"It goes without saying. Life is complicated Mr Knight," Ms Strachan remarked.

"Yes but this is beyond the usual. Money tends to lead to complexity rather than simplicity. Call it the multiplication factor in the dollar sign. What's apparent is that you are or at least seem to be unaware of a certain side of your daughter's life."

"We've tried to be candid with you. We've done our best."

"Did Liz do cocaine?"

"Yes. I'm pretty certain."

"Mary," Frank Strachan interrupted, "this comes from too much bloody money all at once. I told you Mary."

"Frank."

"No listen. I believe you have to pay your way. Brenda paid her way. She hardly touched the trust money. She didn't want any of it. None of it, because of what it represented. Liz doesn't care where the money comes from."

"Frank this is ridiculous. Liz is Liz and Brenda is Brenda. They are different people. Different lives. Different desires and needs."

"Mr Knight, I always asserted that students should pay their own way through university. Get away from all this nonsense. It just leads to notions of being privileged. I worked. Sure I complained to see the rich kids have it easy getting through law school but I still worked. I believe my law degree is worth more because of it. If Liz had to work, she'd—"

"Frank don't."

"Don't what?"

"Don't run Liz down. Don't compare people. It's crude. It's not fair. It's cruel."

"You had it made, Mary."

"Stop it. I'm sorry Mr Knight. I'm lost by what you tell me. I feel a certain vertigo. Unease. In another universe. Where the laws of gravity have all been changed on us. Liz's disappearance makes no sense to me. It's completely and utterly unaccountable."

"Look. Go through your minds. Work on your memories for any mention of an older man. Or any individual Liz might have mentioned however remote. Even in passing. The key thing here is the safe return of your daughter."

My cellphone rang.

"Excuse me." I went out to the hotel corridor.

It was Cheryl telling me that Peter Slowikowsky would see me at one. I went back in the hotel room.

"I'm sorry, I have to go."

"The ear clip. Mr Knight may we please have it."

"I need to document it. Photograph it. I'll have it placed in a Lajoie–Chang safety deposit box. It might be just a random lost and found item but it also might be material and lead to something more substantial. Leave it with me until I finish my investigation and trust I will return it."

"As you wish."

I asked them to give me the keys to Liz's Mazda in case I needed to check it again.

The law offices of Plante, Slowikowsky were located near Albert and Elgin streets in a ten-year-old building. The firm had a reputation from crappy to classy depending on which side of the criminal fence the person tumbled. They did only criminal law. Slowikowsky handled the punch artists, toughs, thieves, burglars, pushers, junkies, and rumble boys while his partner Alfred Plante, a dignified fifty-five year old, not only a lawyer but also a chartered accountant, handled white collar crime, swollen guys in shrunken suits who worked adding machines too fast, washed strange money through business establishments, finagled gov auditors, and shuffled numbers deceitfully up and down the ledger. Alfred Plante was sometimes referred to obscurely as "all fraud compliant" but this was strictly in admiration not insult of his ambidextrous knowledge. Judges grew flexible, even deferential, in the presence of Mr Alfred Plante, a man reputed to be more versed in the law on fraud than any judge sitting on the bench. Pete Slowikowsky was younger than forty-five but well schooled and known to fistmeisters, needlenaggers and steering wheel artists with an assault charge, disposition to drugs, or a wasted driving record.

The firm was busy and it was reputed to turn away many drunk driving cases unless it was a guy or gal with a referral through one of the big corporate law firms or sorrily dependent on the car for their livelihood. I imagined this was more rumour than strict fact as most criminal lawyers would take a canine as a client. Although it was known that access to Alf Plante required money. He avoided clients who got physical or were on legal aid, pleading a limited knowledge of hard knock society. Plante did handle the odd high profile homicide file. Slowikowsky took legal aid cases but generally the higher profile sort. Being a publicity ego, he'd never seen a newspaper headline about his cases or a shot on the TV news of himself coming out of the courthouse that he didn't admire. Reporters dug Slowikowsky. The camera loved him more. Plante, Slowikowsky had been the first law firm to advertise big in the yellow pages.

I'd had neither the fortune nor misfortune to have met either, although Lajoie–Chang had done some work for them. I could tell Morrison didn't exactly shine to the Plante, Slowikowsky accounts. As for Georges Lajoie, he generally did not let his personal sentiments and opinions of the legal flock be known. The agency lived by referrals from lawyers, and Lajoie tried to be careful about commenting on a lawyer's character or personality.

The Plante, Slowikowsky law offices were fine but used. These legal lads were not out to impress with the furniture. Slowikowsky kept me waiting just to reveal whose fee was higher, that this was a meeting bestowed by him as a courtesy but one he could avoid.

He was a big-boned meaty guy well over six feet, going soft in the waist, but he still looked like he jogged, combatting sag and sloth. A decade earlier Slowikowsky would have been lean and considered handsome, today he was edging towards the banality of middle age before shifting towards a dignified appearance in old age. But he still had a long way to go before wearing his experiences with style. I'd heard a rumour that he was going through a bitter divorce with his second wife, a litigation lawyer with a corporate law firm.

Slowikowsky showed me into his office.

"How's Georges Lajoie these days."

"Alright. He said to say hello to your partner Alfred Plante."

"You guys haven't done any work for us in a while. But there might be something on the horizon. You're staying busy, I hear."

"It's steady."

"I heard a rumour about how you swung a patent case."

"What patent case?"

"That's what I like about Lajoie–Chang." Slowikowsky laughed. "You guys are busy."

"I could use a new pair of shoes." I lifted up my foot.

Slowikowsky smiled.

"What's up?"

"I understand your firm defended Joe Parsons and his buddy Mike Eaves on a fraud case."

"That's right. It was white so Alfred handled it mostly. I covered the court end."

"What do you know about these guys?"

"I'm sorry, I'm not going to say anything at this point. I'm going to plead confidentiality. Mike Eaves is a client."

"Right. What about Parsons?"

"What about him?"

"What do you hear about him and his escort service?"

"It's legit. He pays his taxes. He's trying but I don't know how much he's making out of the racket. It's pretty competitive."

"I better get up front."

"Maybe you better Mr Knight."

"There're a couple of women who work for LTD Escort. Liz Strachan and Connie Yonge. You ever hear of them?"

"Why?"

"Liz Strachan's a very nice looking woman. Some might even say beautiful, a law student at U of O. She's disappeared. Her parents, Frank and Mary Strachan, real estate lawyers from Kingston, have hired Lajoie–Chang to investigate."

Slowikowsky lit a cigarette. He gestured the pack towards me.

"That bylaw is going to do me in." He laughed.

"You could demo city hall on it or challenge it on constitutional grounds. Violating the charter of rights and freedom."

"Nah." He laughed and waved his big hand, "I leave that to the pub and bar owners. Smoking's not a right, just a habit. Unless what makes a guy addicted makes him free."

"We found one of your business cards in Liz Strachan's car."

Slowikowsky gave me a thin smile and faint shake of the head.

"I gave a bunch to Joe Parsons to give to his employees. Just in case they had any problems with the law."

"That showed foresight. Parsons wasn't exactly forthright. I was hoping you would be."

"If I had anything to give you, I would."

"Maybe you do."

"How so?"

"The building superintendent saw you pick up Liz Strachan a couple of times at the apartment building. And a tenant saw you talking with Liz Strachan in the underground garage the Monday afternoon just before Liz Strachan disappeared."

"They must be mistaken." Slowikowsky opened up his appointment book and leafed through it.

"What time on the Monday?"

"Around five."

"Couldn't have. I was here with a client. I was in court all afternoon from one until four and then back here in the office. Must have been a mistake on the tenant's part, confusing me with someone else."

"I guess it must have been. But the superintendent swore it was you. That you came and picked up Liz Strachan three times back during the winter up until April."

Slowikowsky looked out the window.

"Okay. Look. I dated her. But I don't want it to go beyond this office."

"Fine."

"I'm in a super divorce just now. And my second wife is trying to deny me shared custody of my kids. She's gonna hose me even though she's pulling down five times what I make in this shit hole of a practice with grifters, swindlers and cokeheads. The difference is I spend my loot while she works for those corporate thieves who know every trick in the book, how to hide her dough so she comes in pleading poverty due to low pay as a salaried employee."

"I understand."

"No you don't, you never met my wife."

"I've heard she's a very fine lawyer."

"Corporate lady, Mr Knight. She's associated with Vicegrip, Armlock and Chokehold."

"Okay you have my sympathy. Tell me what you know about Liz Strachan."

"Like you say, Liz Strachan is a good-looking woman. Bright. Great company. And," Slowikowsky expressed a deep grin, "worth it. So young and yet so gifted. Knows how to blow up the ego. And placate the libido. The experience would meet with mein Herr Doktor Freud's approbation. No sublimation required after direct handling. I went out with her maybe three four times. But haven't seen her since April."

"Why, if it was so fabulous?"

"Why?" Slowikowsky rolled his eyes. "Why do you think? Parsons knew a good thing when he saw the results. Jacked up the rates. She quickly went to the executive list. She's a very exclusive date. You don't want to see the list. It takes real money to get on it."

"But I do."

"Ask Joe."

"You weren't with her after April."

"Nope. And that's not crap."

I scratched my ear. Slowikowsky gave me a stare. I couldn't stare him down. He knew all the tricks. He had seen every eye trick from every tough in town. I had bluffed him as far as his libido's pride would carry me, but now he was tough. He was all silence like a sharp lawyer until I gave something else to move him.

"There's something more."

"No, Mr Knight. There's nothing more."

"Yes there is."

"Okay be quick. I got a paying client waiting."

I took out a scrap of paper with nothing but the Ontario numbered company typed on it.

"Mr Slowikowsky. You're good with numbers."

"I respect Alf but I do despise the accounting profession. I keep it simple, I know when my account is running an overdraft."

I spread the paper across the desk.

"This number mean anything to you Mr Slowikowsky?"

The lawyer leaned forward and peered at it as if he was glancing at an indelicate and dismissible object. He leaned back in his big leather chair.

"Nope." He shook his head.

"It's not a winning lottery number. Still this number has got to mean something to you."

"Get to the point."

"You're on the board of directors."

"I'm on more than a few boards. I don't keep precise track of the numbers."

"With some lawyers. Clarence Wilson. Norman I Burley."

"So what."

"Cheques were issued by this numbered company to pay Liz Strachan's rent for several months from the time she moved into her current address until April of this year."

"That had nothing to do with me."

"Then who?"

"Clarence Wilson. I told him to stop."

"Was he getting it on with Liz Strachan?"

"Could have been. I don't know. But it doesn't matter. You'll never know."

"Why?"

Slowikowsky gave not a smile but a baffled look.

"Don't you know what happened to Clare Wilson?"

"I know he's on the board of directors with Norman Burley and yourself of this numbered company."

"Was. Was."

"He quit it? Resigned when?"

"Quit it quite completely Mr Knight. Not just the board but life itself. Clare's dead."

"When?"

"In April of this year. Wilson was killed in a hit-and-run accident. He was out cycling in the Gatineau. Didn't you hear? Wilson was a senior partner with a corporate law firm."

"Norman Burley is there as well?"
"Yeah."
"Was he dating Liz Strachan as well?"
"I couldn't say."
"Was he involved in paying Liz Strachan's rent?"
"No way. Norm wouldn't. He would have been royally pissed off."
"You must know Norman Burley pretty well."
"Not well at all. Alf introduced me to Norm Burley. It's strictly a business arrangement. A money deal for investment. Nothing more. I don't know the guy at all. If you asked me anything about the guy I couldn't tell you a thing. You'd get more off the Internet than from me."
"Come on. You don't hang out together?"
"Are you joking. With Norm Burley? He's over there." Slowikowsky waved with his right hand. "With Lord Noir and Lady Noire. He's a bag boy for the Civic Unity Party. If Alf hadn't worked the investment I wouldn't be on the letterhead with that shitface. It was a pure formality."
"But paying Liz Strachan's rent is what? An informality?"
"I had nothing to do with that. That was Clarence Wilson. Entirely Clare's deal. Anyway, big deal. A guy goes the rent for the lady. Means nothing. Come on, politicians on Parliament Hill get blow jobs while chatting on the telephone. We're not into the pyjama game."
"You didn't—"
"Listen Mr Knight. I told you I screwed around with her but I'm not an idiot. When she was priced out of my league I quit the scene. I don't know why Wilson was covering her rent. Maybe she had something on the guy. I liked Wilson. Clare was a good guy. His wife Madeleine Masson is a beautiful woman. She took his death like a roll of logs coming down the Gatineau. But I don't have a clue why Clarence Wilson shelled out for Liz Strachan's rent."
"And you didn't happen to ask him in passing because the dough was coming out of your numbered company account before he died?"
"I asked but he wouldn't say. I asked him to stop. And make restitution to the company account. Before Norm Burley and Alf Plante might get wind of it. They're sticklers. And Clare did."
"What about Burley?"

"Burley only found out after Clare died. He was furious but he didn't know. I can't give you any more time. I've got a client. Look, call me again."

I stood up.

"Sure."

"I like that woman Liz Strachan. I hope she's okay."

"Right. One last thing, what do you know about a guy named Lester Henderson?'

"Mr Knight. You're all over the ceiling and off the wall. You're treading on confidentiality. Henderson runs a bonded warehouse and trucking company. It's all in the yellow pages. That's about it. I've got to see the client." He got up and went to the door.

"I might call tomorrow."

"Sure. Sure. If I'm not available leave a message with my assistant. I'll try to get back as soon as possible. I hope you find Liz Strachan. And I mean that."

"Right. I'll pass that on to Frank and Mary Strachan."

# SIX

Morrison showed me the computer files in Liz Strachan's computer.

"The kid did it. It was a breeze. He's still working on the disk. Tonight or tomorrow. His father insisted he do his homework, his mother insisted he go to his swimming lesson."

"So what's in her computer. Much of interest?"

"Mostly law school material. Essays. Reports. Downloads from the Internet for research. Personal e-mails from friends, family. But I suppose it depends what you want."

"Names. And money. Bank accounts."

"Well. There is a file that is curious and curiouser."

"How so."

Morrison showed the file named BAZAOZBZ.

"What's BAZAOZBZ?"

"Hard to say. I thought you might have a clue."

"No. What's the content?"

"Not much. Letters. Rows and columns of alphabetic characters." Morrison scrolled to the file and opened it.

| | |
|---|---|
| OASJQIGZA | MGMAZFGZA |
| KOOJQJGZA | NVAAZEGZA |
| MGNJQIGZA | OAMAZDGZA |
| NVDJQIJZA | KOJAZEKZA |
| OAJAZHJZA | MGJAZDKZA |
| KOFAZGJZA | MVAAKEKZA |

and so it went for several more lines.

"What do you think Morrison?"

"Encrypted. And then when matched with the encryption cipher somewhere—maybe on a floppy—the data matches. One unlocks the other. But basically this." Morrison paused as if he was going to eat a chocolate bar. He loved chocolate bars. "Liz Strachan was not encoding for amusement, there's probably something here. But your guess is going to be better than mine. We'll see if the computer-meister cracks the encrypted file."

"Well thanks, Morrison."

I studied the encrypted letters. The longer I looked the more I thought people's names. They had to be. My mind lost focus on the meaningless sequences of letters, free association took over: photos of Les Henderson, Alf Plante, Norman Burley, Pete Slowikowsky, Joe Parsons and Clarence Wilson would help. I especially wanted Willett and the tenant Eleanor Lowe to have a good look at the boss boys' faces. I went back in my office and telephoned Pierre Willett and asked him to call me if he happened to see a younger guy in his early thirties, well dressed, or any middle-aged man talking to or visiting Connie Yonge.

"Mr Knight, I'm not a sentry you know. I don't like snooping around on the tenants."

"Mr Willett, could be something in this if someone showed up."

"Like what?

"You understand it has to be crucial, Mr Willett, in helping to find Liz Strachan. Okay."

"Alright. You're alright. I get your snowdrift."

Fink money had a tendency to become inflationary. I had to put a heel on this guy's big toe, otherwise he would keep peeking in the wallet. Then again, Willett's knowledge might be to no purpose and I had to answer to Lajoie and the Strachans. Georges was okay most of the time. He knew snitches and sources were part of the racket, where cashola seemed to have become the measure of information. But it could be delusional, some people coughed up information innocently, others because they were blabbermouths, some out of vindictiveness, revenge or pettiness, others to show off just what they knew, the ego excuses and wallet justifications —from beggary to invaluable even priceless knowledge—were endless. Daily rate + expenses, a nice formulation until the big 'but' and 'if' on the other side of the equation. But if I didn't deliver something of substance to the clients, they eventually went over the invoice and statement with a fine complaint comb. I didn't need that. I figured the Strachans for wanting something. Wanting was a big incentive for spending money.

I did a search on Copernic for Clarence Wilson. A number of articles came up on his death. I glossed them. One read:

# STILL NO LEADS
## IN GATINEAU HIT-AND-RUN CASE

Gatineau area police detectives probing the hit-and-run death of prominent Ottawa lawyer Clarence Wilson have yet to determine the make and model of the vehicle involved in the accident.

Sergeant René La petite said yesterday that Gatineau police were still collecting forensic evidence and assessing it to determine the vehicle involved.

Wilson, 50, of Ottawa was working out on his racing bicycle early Thursday morning just north of Chelsea near his summer residence.

The father of two cycled each morning for a half hour before departing for his Ottawa law office. He was hit from behind by a speeding car sometime between 6:00 and 7:00 A.M. and left to die at the scene.

The police so far have found no witnesses to the accident, although a neighbouring resident informed police she had heard an unusual noise around 6:30 that morning.

Wilson had left home around 6:00 A.M. to cycle along his favourite stretch of rural Chelsea. He was wearing a bike helmet and other safety gear.

Detective Constable Richard Tremblay said the victim was cycling north when he was struck from behind by a northbound vehicle. Autopsy reports reveal that the victim did not die immediately but was left alive but unconscious. Around 9:30 A.M. two hikers discovered his body in the grassy ditch along the side of the road.

The corporate lawyer and senior partner with the law firm of Baldwin Martel Wightman had a long and distinguished career in corporate law, specializing in mergers and acquisitions.

He leaves behind his wife, Madeleine Masson, and two children, André 15 and Mathieu 12.

"It is a tragedy beyond comprehension," said the victim's brother Marshall Wilson in a telephone interview.

Police urge any witnesses who saw the collision or a damaged vehicle fleeing the area to contact the police.

I scrolled down and read another article: "Police disappointed with the failure of witnesses to come forward in corporate lawyer's death."

I printed the articles, thinking this one is disappearing. Two maybe three hours in a ditch and still alive, the worst couple of hours of the guy's life, what a drag. No witnesses. Just an unusual noise. The Gatineau boys were deep in the dark on this one. Probably not much at the scene and next to nothing in the coroner's autopsy beyond death due to brain trauma.

I did searches on Mike Eaves, Joe Parsons and his buddies Benny Rae and Jackie Snoblin. I was scanning for criminal charges and time served. Rae and Snoblin had both done time for assault, Snoblin for armed robbery of a motel, Rae for trafficking marijuana, then the whole claque had been charged two years ago with pushing cocaine. But Pete Slowikowsky had defended them and blow-dried the Crown attorney.

I went back over the articles on Clarence Wilson, then took out Liz Strachan's photograph and stared at it.

I dialed up Madeleine Masson. A young boy answered the phone. I heard him call for his mother in French. She came on the line but when I told her who I was she seemed reluctant. She relented and agreed to see me for some reason after I told her I was with Lajoie–Chang Associates.

There were these bits and pieces accumulating in the file but they did not seem to be coalescing into a significant pattern. They seemed to be dispersing like Manitoba maple keys. The details were not helping to bring Liz Strachan's image into focus. Memory was the slave of time, I could see it in her face. Her face looked simultaneously more alluring and appealing yet more distant and obscure. An unpleasant sensation rippled in my viscera, I consciously resisted it, as I had when I had been startled twice in the garage, first at discovering the items under Liz Strachan's car, then by Willett's sudden appearance in the underground garage.

I took out the sheet of paper that I had fetched out of the waste-basket in Liz Strachan's apartment. Studied it. Then I went back over to Morrison's office. The door was closed. I knocked gently on it. After a long moment, Morrison called out.

"Come on in."

Morrison was hunched over his desk intent on an inventory audit. Sometimes white collar crime looked so smooth and appealing.

"What is it?"

He pushed back his fine dark hair which just carried an auburn glow that was entirely natural. There was not a single strand of grey in his hair.

"Morrison. Sorry to interrupt you. I want you to look at these again."

Morrison snatched the single sheet and scrutinized it. He leaned back in his chair. He went down into the numbers. He did a calculation. He turned the sheet over and read the abbreviations. Morrison had a fertile capacity for silence. He had a skill for lending it to other people so they could think more lucidly and clearly. Not so articulate, at times even brusque and curt, some who hardly knew the guy might have construed it for rudeness but it signalled his intentness. Watching Morrison was helping my brain work. He kick-started it again.

"I'd say ... with reservation ... dollar amounts. That seems most plausible. Although there is a comma out of place here for a placeholder. That might go against such an interpretation."

"Good. Go on. That was my hunch."

"And corresponding to the months."

"Yes. We're in the same groove. Now, Morrison, the clincher. Give it to me."

"Transfers. Under the wire. Variations."

"Meaning?"

"A crude attempt to preserve a record in memory without having to write it down. But whoever did it, did write it down. Checking something maybe? Fabricated inconsistencies to conceal a pattern becoming a pattern. Just spec. Because one of the hidden laws of numbers, even though numbers are infinite, is that all numbers within a finite series, given a large enough sample, will eventually form a pattern or order. Which is a law of capital and money, my friend. Because even, as Georges would say, the circulation of money is infinite but capital itself, despite all the delusions of scam artists, hustlers, racketeers, con-men, fraudsters, money itself is—"

"Finite?"

"Yes. Even though there is infinity within infinity, even infinities within infinity. People are finite. So, the finite within the infinite. Although the circulation of money is infinite, money itself is finite relative to numbers. Numbers are infinite but at any given moment in time they are recurring in finite patterns. And when someone schemes, skims and scams, does a fraud, they leave behind a numerical pattern. A trace. A forensic numerical fingerprint on the account books, the ledger. So to speak. Like so." He motioned towards the account books he had been going through. "It's a law of honest books and crooked books. Honest books are more honestly consistent even when revealing inconsistencies, human mistakes and careless errors. While crooked books are, unconsciously, more honestly inconsistent even while fabricating the appearance of consistencies that try to conceal the fraud. The honesty in a fraud artist is in his persistent consistencies which reveal his dishonesty. Even crooks can be inexplicitly honest."

"So this looks like money," I gestured towards the sheet. "From where to where?"

Morrison shrugged his shoulders. "Alec, is this associated with the Strachan file?"

"It's from Liz Strachan's apartment. It's her handwriting according to her sister."

"This could be just honest reckoning. Ask her parents. Or she could be hiding something."

"What?"

"Not what Alec. Who. Maybe even Liz Strachan is hidden in that encryption."

"BAZAOZBZ?"

He handed back the sheet. Morrison neither agreed nor disagreed, he just shifted his head a little as if in query rather than answer.

"You'll know. Ciphers are both opaque and transparent. They stare you right in the face with all sorts of hints and clues but seem blank. Who does Liz Strachan know? Where does she bank?"

"Bank on the bank?"

"The bank may have all the numbers, not just all the money."

"Thanks, Morrison."

He went back to his book work.

I went to the safe and got the items I had collected from the underground garage and the Strachan file. I went down the hall to Georges's office. I knocked on the half-open door. Georges was taking a break, reading a book and sipping a coffee. He looked up at me. He gestured to enter.

I glanced at the cover of the book. It was a title beyond my time, pleasure and patience. I only recognized it because of Georges. He caught the line of my gaze.

"Stendhal. One of my saviours along with Balzac, Raymond Roussel, and Flaubert. The Pleiade edition. Although we must say that it can never be complete. Alas there will never be a true and complete Stendhal."

"Why? You told me every French writer worth his salt goes there."

"Why? Too many pseudonyms. The great chamaeleon of fiction. Dozens of fictitious names. A man of infinite intricate identities."

"You're losing me, Georges."

"Go ahead. Speak what's on your mind." Lajoie closed the book and set it aside.

"Georges, my mind's out of gear on this Strachan case."

"Be a cold intelligence."

"I'm trying but my stomach's queasy. It's sinking."

"Don't let a hard case heat up your brain. Don't. Stay lucid. Who knows where this young woman is? It is our job to find her. Don't presume anything absolute. Definitive. Don't convey such a numb sentiment to the young woman's parents. In a missing person case it is crucial to remain stable. Optimistic. Even if the authorities are indifferent, cynical, appear to be losing their interest because they think the missing person has shaky morals. The Strachans can't take it."

"Come on, it's not a book, this is life. Look." I spread the items out on the beautiful desk, handling the business cards with a set of tweezers. "I found these under Liz Strachan's car. Her Mazda."

"Good ear clip. Fine pearl. Not cultured. Yes. Yes. The real one. Here we can use the real word, awe, with all its meaning. Awesome craftsmanship. Boucheron. Loose change." Georges scrutinized the business cards. Inspected the tread mark. He leafed through the file, reading my brief reports. Then closed it.

"I heard a rumour. A rumour regarding Henderson and Burley."

"What?"

"Not in connection with this file. Or clients."

"In connection with what?"

"It's unconfirmed. I heard it as mere gossip from a former detective who got it from a Crown who got it from a lawyer who got it from another lawyer who happens to have done some work with a junior who worked with a junior who is reputed—I emphasize reputed—to have got it from a legal assistant at Burley's firm. Which is by way of saying it is nothing. But nothing is something. And something comes of nothing. Otherwise we wouldn't hear the hum of the universe. Or our own human speech. And we must not discount the words of a legal assistant, they are in fact of a very high order, they know things about lawyers but must say nothing. Keep mum."

"Georges please. It's all too circuitous."

"I heard a Balzacian rumour."

"You know I hardly read fiction. Except the toxicological greetings on food packaging."

"A little literacy is better than none. This: that Lester Henderson and Norman Burley paid the legal fees in a cocaine case involving some of these men."

"What's it mean?"

"It means money stacked higher than morality. And morality is not a word that should generally be in one's vocabulary. Mortality is of a higher order. Ethics is a rare and wondrous creature. More rare and fabulous, even fantastical, than a unicorn or gryphon."

"For Christ's sakes. This has got to be a slanderous joke. This guy Norm Burley's in tight with the Civic Unity Party."

"Did you know something even more troubling about the guy?"

"What?"

"Nasty rumour. It's been around for years."

"I thought you despised rumours."

"I do. I most certainly do. Until they become associated with facts. Then I embrace them."

"Tell me."

"You wouldn't know. It was in Alberta many years ago. For a couple of years this man Burley was working as a junior assistant for the Crown. He is said to have raped a teenager involved in a case."

"What happened?"

"Nothing."

"Nothing?"

"That's what happens when you have reputedly high morals. The girl was underage. She accused him but nothing came of it. She had no credibility. Her word carried no weight with the authorities. She was a street kid. She was involved in prostitution and pushing drugs. Well, a little result did occur, it was a little embarrassing for a brief time. Burley stood tall. Let the storm pass and a year later left for private practice. In this way his departure did not appear to be associated with the controversy."

"Norman I Burley and Clarence Wilson. What's your take on that? What could be the possible link?"

"Maybe something. Maybe nothing. Just standard legal work involving numbered corporations. Working in the same law firm. Lawyers trading in financial deals, the usual. Some blindness. Averting of one's gaze. You know the legal advice to clients: I don't want to know. Don't tell me anything I don't need to know."

"Georges look, Wilson was shelling out for Liz Strachan's rent up until April of this year. Issuing numbered company cheques. And he's in tight with Burley."

"Some men are made out of ruthlessness. Their actions are not accidental but transitory. If they had any compassion, they'd quickly mortgage it to a banker and use the cash for an investment on the stock market. Or, if not legit, flush it through the system faster than a janitor flushes a toilet."

"This party is into law and order."

"They talk a civil dialect to the public. Sometimes it even pays off on election day. Good PR. Blame the troubles of society on the government. Tell the public it's the law. So we need fewer tax laws but more criminal laws. Deregulation to make money, but tougher laws to punish criminals. Alec, even in our end of the business we come to believe such rhetoric. A nation can have the finest laws, the toughest laws on the book, but if the citizens are apathetic no amount of law will save a nation. Make it secure."

"Georges," I gathered up the file and items, "that's uncivil speech talking about that party that way."

"Moderation in all things," Lajoie paused, "including virtue. An excess of morality leads to harsh justice. The purpose of the law is not to catch and correct each and every sin but create a just society of reasonable and happy people. Who know when to do the right thing without being told to do the right thing."

"So you say. They'll catch you and set your pants on fire."

"Ah so young, innocent and naive. Metaphysics my friend." Lajoie smiled, then more emphatic, "Incidentally Alec. Be careful when you speak with the Strachans."

"I will. But first I'm going for a hike up in the Gatineau to talk to Clarence Wilson's widow."

"That's smart. Talk to Connie Yonge again. She's in tight with Joe Parsons, his cocaine crew. This tenant Eleanor Lowe is a good lead. And please be cautious with this fellow Willett."

Madeleine Masson's house was in Chelsea, a town north of Hull on the edge of the Gatineau Park. It was located off the main street in a quiet space. An old stone house from before 1900, impeccably maintained.

I knocked on the solid oak door.

A lovely woman with raven hair and crystalline blue eyes appeared. She was of medium height and slim. I knew she was about forty but she could have passed easily for ten years younger but for a certain quality of sadness etched in her features. No doubt Georges Lajoie upon encountering Ms Masson would have found some more engaging, elegant and insightful phrase to describe her. Simply to my eye the woman was a widow. Madeleine Masson appeared to be still in love and grieving the death of her husband, Clarence Wilson. It was hard for me to grasp such sorrow. I'd been in and out of love but it was more or less mutually voluntary, sometimes mutually destructive.

Madeleine Masson was dressed in fine linen emerald green slacks and a short-sleeved golden silk blouse.

"Alec Knight. Ms Masson?"

"I'm Ms Masson. Come this way. We can sit out back on the patio or in the sunroom if you prefer."

"Either is okay, whichever you prefer, Ms Masson."

"This way." She led me across a beautifully polished oak floor into a sunroom of maple with a series of double-hung windows. The sunroom overlooked flower beds terraced up a hillside that became forest.

"You have a lovely house."

"Thank you. It's my family home. My great-great-grandfather built it. He was in lumber. Mr Knight, may I offer you tea?"

"Sure."

"I have herbal tea. What sort would you prefer?"

"Mint would be great."

"Good."

She went to make the tea. I sat leafing through magazines and newspapers scattered on the table, the New Yorker, Le Nouvel Observateur, Le Monde, Le Devoir, the Globe and Mail. I heard French, a boy in the kitchen. The boy went by the doorway. He was a startlingly good-looking kid with a shock of black hair like his mother and a confident posture.

Madeleine Masson said in English, just before she came back in the room with the tea, "Mathieu, when I'm finished speaking with this gentleman I'll drive you and your friend."

She came in the sunroom, set the tea down, "There," and poured it. "Now Mr Knight, you mentioned on the telephone the disappearance of a young woman."

"Yes. The woman who disappeared is a Liz Strachan. Lajoie–Chang Associates has been retained to investigate the young woman's whereabouts."

"Excuse me. Would the Lajoie associated with this—what? private investigative agency?—happen to be a Georges Lajoie from Montréal?"

"Yes."

"My father, who was a lawyer, knew a Georges Lajoie who was a police detective on the Montréal city police force."

"That could have been either Georges himself or his father. They both served on the Montreal police force."

"How old is Mr Lajoie of the agency?"

"Fifty-five."

"I imagine then that it must have been the father not the son. The elder Lajoie. My father spoke very highly of the senior Lajoie. He was said to be a remarkable police detective. In any event, a mere coincidence. I'm sorry to have interrupted you. Please continue."

"No problem, Ms Masson. Well in the course of the investigation your husband's name, Clarence Wilson, came up. He appears to have known Liz Strachan."

"Excuse me, Mr Knight. Maybe we could simplify things. Would you happen to have a photo of the young woman?"

"Sure." I drew out the photograph of Liz Strachan and passed it across the coffee table to Madeleine Masson. The woman studied the photo for a long time, I thought she would not return it. But then she abruptly handed it back.

"She's certainly a beautiful young woman."

"Yes. As I was saying, in the course of the investigation your husband's name came up."

"We don't know any Strachan family, Mr Knight."

"It was Liz Strachan your husband knew, not her parents. I was wondering if you might have any knowledge as to how your husband Clarence Wilson knew Liz Strachan?"

"I haven't the faintest idea."

"It appears to have been in connection with one of your husband's businesses. He was on the board of directors of a company with a number of other lawyers."

"Which one? My husband was on the board of directors of several companies, Mr Knight."

"This one was a numbered Ontario company." I gave her the number.

"I can't say I recognize it. I'd have to check with my solicitor and accountant. Who were the other directors on the board?"

"Peter Slowikowsky, a lawyer with Plante, Slowikowsky. Alfred Plante. And Norman I Burley, a corporate lawyer with Baldwin Martel Wightman, your husband's firm."

"Have you spoken with Messieurs Slowikowsky, Plante or Burley?"

"Not yet."

"Maybe you should. They could probably better answer your questions. My husband is clearly unable. He is dead."

I stared down at the maple floor. My presence was going up the side of her head and I could lose it. I was trespassing, I could hear it in her polite but cold responses.

"I'm sorry, I didn't come out here to upset you, Ms Masson."

"Mr Knight, I am not upset. It is just that I cannot be of any help. I do not know any Liz Strachan. I don't know anyone in the Strachan family. Where did you say these people are from?"

"I didn't. But Liz Strachan's family is from Kingston. Her parents are lawyers."

"Mr Knight, I hardly know anyone in Kingston. I wish you the best of luck in your investigation but, frankly, this meeting appears pointless. I have no knowledge of the persons involved."

"But your husband, Clarence Wilson, knew Liz Strachan."

"What does Ms Strachan do?"

"She's a law student at the University of Ottawa."

"Then perhaps it is in connection with that. It might be more useful to question individuals at his law firm, Baldwin Martel Wightman. After all, there is Mr Burley himself. Have you approached him?"

"Not yet."

We sat for a long minute and drank tea. Then she said, "Mr Knight, is there anything further?"

"I realize this is a bit awkward but you were probably not aware that this numbered company that your husband was associated with issued cheques to pay Liz Strachan's rent."

"I suggest you speak with Messieurs Slowikowsky or Burley. Or even Mr Plante. The living can tell you far more about this arrangement than the dead."

"I have it from a good source that it was Clarence Wilson insisted on paying Ms Strachan's rent. Was he possibly subject to blackmail?"

"For possibly what? My husband was scrupulous. He was held in the highest regard by people inside and outside the law. He held himself to remarkable ethical standards. Unfortunately not the same can be said for all the people he did business with or came in contact with through his law practice. Some of whom prefer to make public declarations of political ethics, great morality plays, but in their personal lives behave in, let us say, a highly questionable manner."

"I guess we live in a morally complicated world."

Her spine stiffened, Madeleine Masson gave me a sharp glance followed by a quick but brittle smile as if to suggest that I were a dupe or fool.

"Not at all Mr Knight. That sort of line is for TV. Hollywood. Politicians. Rather trite, without intending to insult. We live in an amoral world. Some people lack ethics. Others lack spirituality. Where motorists run down innocent good people and no one will come forward for fear of being implicated. I do suggest you speak to the other gentlemen on the board regarding the cheques issued by the numbered company."

"Might I ask how your husband got along with Mr Slowikowsky and Mr Burley?"

"I believe on good terms but strictly in a professional capacity. We didn't socialize with either of them. My husband and I knew Alf

Plante and his wife. They are friends. My husband and Alfred went to law school together. That's how Clarence came to know Mr Slowikowsky. My husband on occasion gave referrals for clients who needed a criminal lawyer to Plante, Slowikowsky. Baldwin Martel Wightman only takes corporate clients. Handles strictly corporate files. Anything involving a client with a criminal charge was referred to Alfred Plante."

"I understand that. And Mr Burley?"

Madeleine Masson gazed long through the leaded glass at the lawn and flowers and into the greenness of the trees of the forest. She appeared to find a hope. Her head turned back.

"I told you Mr Knight, we, my husband and I, didn't socialize with Mr Burley."

"But your husband and Mr Burley were in the same law firm for years."

She gave a thin smile, not at all generous. Excessively shrewd.

"Mr Knight, surely you understand that lawyers who congregate together in a large law firm often have next to nothing in common but the making of a living through the practice of law. Some do it well, while others do it poorly. You can't be too naive on this point."

"Sure, but I thought if they were on the same board of directors together of the same corporation they might have something more in common."

"No more than a legal mechanism and necessity. I suggest you speak with either Mr Slowikowsky or Mr Burley."

"Was your husband a member of the Civic Unity Party with Norm Burley?"

She burst into brief laughter.

"Mr Knight, how absurd. My husband wouldn't have anything to do in politics with the best and the brightest from Alberta. At a big firm like Baldwin Martel Wightman it is the practice to donate to all parties which have the possibility of winning a substantial number of seats. Governed by pragmatism. Why don't you speak to Monsieur Burley."

"I suppose I might."

"Is there anything further then." Madeleine Masson stood up.

"I guess not."

We went out to the vestibule with the slate floor.

"I regret that I could not be of any help. I sincerely wish you and the family which you are investigating on behalf of the very best of luck. I hope you are able to find their missing daughter." She offered her hand. We shook. She had lovely smooth skin.

"Oh one last item, was Norman Burley—"

"Excuse me, Mr Knight, I think I've made it clear I do not wish to discuss Mr Burley. I'm afraid the discussion has reached an end concerning him."

"Right. Uh, excuse me, Ms Masson. Thank you for your time. I really appreciate it."

"My pleasure, Mr Knight." She now smiled.

I stepped out onto the porch. She closed the door behind me.

# SEVEN

In early September, the scenery in the Gatineau was sweet, the air a little cooler and refreshing. But the sentiment I carried back down into Hull and across the bridge over the Chaudière Rapids near the paper mill and into la petite O, was bleak.

I hadn't had such a harsh and sinking gut feeling in a missing person case in a while. The smorgasbord of cases at Lajoie–Chang usually tilted one's stomach with too many choices and unpleasant aromas commingling. No doubt the bread and butter for the agency were cheque and cash frauds, internal corporate theft, inventory shortages in warehouses, computer scams in high tech, intellectual property theft. These one could eat without indigestion. But the downside in the meal were the assortment of side plates that included tossed salads of insurance or the nauseous headcheese of personal gripe cases, someone with too much dough trying to get some dirt on someone else. Missing person cases usually left peelings, rinds and seeds on the napkin but no one sitting at the table. Even if found, a kid on the street in Vancouver, Montreal or Toronto, more in need of mediation than investigation, might remain forever reluctant to go home. If the case involved a missing adult a blunt refusal of the sort 'I'd never live with that headbanger' often led to temporary indigestion from divorce cases. But this case was, in its own amorphous way, grounding down into nowhere and grinding up my guts.

Before going over to the apartment building to show Eleanor Lowe the photos, I stopped for an espresso in a little café on Preston Street, sometimes known as Corso Italiano. Although I didn't need the caffeine, I liked the jolt. I had a petty grudge against tea, a concoction I was too often offered in the name of hospitality, a beverage insipid and innocuous, yet cruel to the bladder. It needs a ceremony because it's so toxic. I suspect it contributes to malnutrition and stunted growth. I relieved my bladder. Ah, the toilet, as one wag remarked, the PI's most coveted private desire.

Eleanor Lowe, a heavy woman thick in the waist, had come from a small town in eastern Ontario near Cornwall when she was fresh out of high school. She dressed carefully, even self-consciously, with a certain pride, in Ottawa's own couture. Her fashion style was strictly public service dowdy. She had joined the bureaucracy as a CR2, in the jargon of the bureaucracy nearly the lowliest of paper shovelers, and had through a diligent forty-two years reached what many hardworking clerks considered the pinnacle of success, the position of PM1. I knew these arcane acronyms mean next to nothing to most Canadians outside the little O but to most Ottawans the term PM1 indicates a symbolic threshold. It clarifies a multitude of obscurities that have to do with power and administration too recondite and arcane to be detailed to the public, only experience can possibly lay bare the real meaning.

As for Mrs Lowe's hubby, Elmer, who was ten years older, he had worked as a mechanic for Public Works for forty-five years and promptly did what more than a few public servants have done upon early retirement. Elmer Lowe, with a smoke hanging from his jaw, keeled over one day at a bingo parlour on Wellington Street West just beyond the railroad overpass. Mrs Lowe collected the residue of Elmer's superannuation hardly touched. His Canada Pension had never been dipped into. This intimate knowledge had been bestowed upon me in our first conversation and turned out to be well worth the two hours and two cups of Orange Pekoe tea followed by a long and prodigious trip to the pissoir. Patience and the pissoir go together. And as my T.O. friend Johnny Olive maintains, in the inquisitor's game, our racket of sundry oblique questions and multitudinous little lies, the lad or lass without a well controlled and capacious bladder is a sorrowful swollen creature. There is, according to one of Olive's more obscure and amusing mathematical formulae, a direct and proportionate ratio between the holding duration and volume of an 'invective's' bladder and the degree of his inquisitive patience and ultimate success.

Mrs Lowe was keen to talk. I knew such avidity all too well. Courtesy was de rigueur. But also auditory vigilance. We went into the living room of her tidy one-bedroom apartment and sat on the colonial couch which still smelt of Elmer's cigarette smoke. The stench of little d lingers in the most banal places. Mrs Lowe was a non-smoker and indignant regarding smoking, this she had let me know in no uncertain terms, it seemed to be part of the post mortem. Being a PI that didn't smoke gave me a certain benevolent status. But perversely, it only made me want to, I longed to smoke.

"Would you like a coffee, Mr Knight?"

"No thanks Mrs Lowe. I just finished one. Although I very much appreciate the offer."

"Just as you wish."

That was a mistake. No possible revenge quite like a widow's except a slighted bureaucrat's.

"On second thought, maybe I will have one. It is going to be a long day. And I could use a refreshment." My capitulation to the cup and saucer. And an indulgence in hypocrisy. Hypocrisy is highly underrated. It can make people happy. It goes so nicely with hospitality. And it can make some people socially gracious.

"I'll just be a moment." She came back with a tray of homemade muffins and cookies. I took a cookie. I took a bite.

"Very nice."

Mrs Lowe made no comment but the glint in her eye indicated pleasure. I had no doubt she'd received many a compliment for her baking.

"Mrs Lowe, how long did you say you've lived here in this apartment building? Was it twenty years?"

"Yes. Elmer and I moved in after our daughter moved out of the house and went to school in Toronto. We had a two-bedroom on the eighth floor but after Elmer's death, I moved down here. What's the point of too much space? My daughter Phyllis moved to Vancouver. She'd like me to move out west to Vancouver or Victoria when I retire next year. But goodness, all my friends mostly live in eastern Ontario. I'd be at a loss. What's life without other people?"

"I understand."

"Are you from Ottawa, Mr Knight? You never said so when we first spoke."

"More or less."

"And your parents too?"

"Yes."

"Do your folks work for the government?"

"My mum works for the government."

"Which department?"

"Health. Mrs Lowe, do you recall I mentioned those photos of some men that I would bring along and let you have a look at?"

"Yes. I certainly do. I'm very keen to see them. Do anything I can to help Mr and Mrs Strachan find their lovely daughter. Having a daughter of my own I can only imagine how they feel."

"Well I have them here. Unfortunately they are not of the best quality. They are digital printouts from a computer. But for the time being these are the best I could do." I placed the photos of Henderson, Burley, Wilson, Slowikowsky and Plante on the coffee table.

She adjusted her glasses.

"Oh dear. My eyes aren't what they used to be. Forty years in the government reading tax returns, as you can well imagine, is not a blessing for my sight. And much of that before computer printers. You would not believe the horrendous quality of some tax returns. Slapdash. Gave new meaning to the word illegible. It is a wonder the government puts up with it. The taxpayers complain but if they saw the atrocities committed on paper that I've seen over the past forty years they might appreciate how tolerant Ottawa is concerning some things. Appalling. And it costs. It costs the very people who complain about taxes. Due to their own sloppiness, carelessness. Goodness." She stared at the men's faces.

"Do the best you can, Mrs Lowe. First select any of the men who you recall seeing in the building. And if possible, I mean if you recognize the face of the man who was talking to Liz Strachan in the garage on that Monday afternoon at around five. If you don't recognize any of the faces just say so and don't worry. Don't feel obliged to identify anyone. And please take your time. No rush."

"Certainly." The woman went through the pile and studied each face for a long time without saying anything.

Finally she gently set two of the photos aside.

"These two gentlemen, I've seen them in the foyer of the building on a number of occasions."

They were images of Norman I Burley and Clarence Wilson.

"How often would you say?"

"Well let me think. This gentleman on several occasions." She pointed at Burley's face. "You know you notice a face when the person does not live in the building when you live alone. You cannot be too cautious with strangers passing through the building. It pays to be alert. I saw this gentleman several times."

"Where?"

"In the lobby or on the elevator."

"Over how long a period of time?"

"I'd say since sometime last year in the fall or late summer. Mind you, I'm not certain on that point."

"And this other man?"

"This fellow I noticed around last September, possibly earlier." She pointed at Clarence Wilson. He came around at the first, middle or end of each month. Like clockwork. It was always at those times. Two or three times a month."

"Always?"

"Yes. Or so it seemed."

"What time?"

"I noticed because it was around five. When I came back from my afternoon walk or from work. I think there were a few months when I didn't notice him. But to be honest I haven't seen him since the end of April or beginning of May."

"Fine. And the other men?"

"Oh it's vague. I'm not certain on them at all. So I dare not say." She looked at me and smiled, "I could say yes or no but only because I think you want me to say yes."

"No. Not at all Mrs Lowe. Not at all. I don't want you to say yes or no one way or the other. I don't want to influence your memory in any way. That's why your word, your memory, your observations are so important. They are neutral. Impartial."

"Yes, Mr Knight. The government is a proper place for teaching one impartiality. I take pride in my impartiality. I would never be a good supervisor or do a good job unless I behaved impartially. I take great pride in my impartiality. It's a matter of principle. I wouldn't want my emotions to interfere with my performance or how I felt about any of my clerks. It would show up in my performance review."

"Good. I want you to identify any of these men but only if you are one hundred percent certain you saw them in the building or the garage. If. If there is even one one-hundredth of a grain of doubt in your mind, Mrs Lowe, as to whether it is a recognizable face then I want you to say you don't recognize the man."

"In that case then only these two specific gentlemen."

"Fine."

I took up the other photos and put them away.

"Now, of these two gentlemen, did you see either one of them in the underground garage talking with Liz Strachan on the day in question? The Monday."

"I believe I saw this man." She pointed at Norman Burley's face.

"Are you certain Mrs Lowe?"

"Good lord, Mr Knight. The world plays tricks on memory. I'm good with numbers. If you showed me ten SINs from ten years ago and a list of names scrambled up, I might be pretty good at matching them." She laughed in pride, "I only slightly exaggerate. I used to go to bed dreaming of numbers. Streams of numbers like the St Lawrence flowing past Cornwall. Goodness, I thought it would never come to an end. But it will I imagine when I retire. I saw this man. Certain. Yes. I saw him. But I am not certain I saw the man and young woman together because after all it was only for a few seconds, as long as it takes to walk from my car to the garage elevator. But I recognize both people because I've seen this strange man in the building before. He's not a tenant here. I know that. I recognize every tenant. I make it my business."

"Fine. Tell me Mrs Lowe. You recognize Liz Strachan?"

"Yes. You know I do."

"What floor does she live on?"

"The ninth. Why?"

"Do you know any other tenants on that floor?"

"Why yes. There's the Baker couple. There's a single man named William Asad who keeps very much to himself, and the Chinese couple, Lee, they moved in two years ago. He's retired. I believe he was a professor in Hong Kong, Mr Lee. Very. Very—what's the word?—refined sort. They came over from Hong Kong. Their daughter's here, she's a doctor. They didn't like it when that Communist regime took over the city from the British. They told me so. And there's two young men. I believe they're gay. Certain in fact. I've nothing against them. They're very quiet. I work with such people in the government, you can get along with such people if you each stick to your work and meet halfway. I'm all for compromise. I can't quite recall their names. Anyway they mind their own business. And there's Mr and Mrs Jolicoeur. Actually she's Yvonne Pascal. They say they're married but I don't think they are. And Ms Yonge. I can't recall her first name. It escapes me. I believe she's a stewardess for an airline."

"A flight attendant."

"Yes. That's it."

"Do you recall seeing any of those individuals on that floor with Liz Strachan?"

"The Yonge woman."

"Mrs Lowe, I believe Ms Yonge's first name is Constance or Connie."

"That's her name. Now that you mention it. Yes I saw Liz Strachan and Ms Yonge together on several occasions. Often." She sat back erect.

"Under what circumstances?"

"With these older men. For the life of me I can't understand what two such lovely women would be doing going out with older men."

"Did you actually see them dating?"

"Not really. I saw the men in the lobby. Or the young women getting in a car with them."

"What else do you know about Connie Yonge?"

"Little else."

"Have you spoken with her?"

"Oh no. She's rather aloof. She puts on airs. If you saw her picking up mail and you said hello to her she'd be quite chilly."

"Is she that way with the other tenants in the building?"

"Seems to be. But Pierre Willett, the superintendent, would have a better idea. She is not a sociable sort of person at all. Not at all. For the life of me I can't figure out how that sort of person can be a stewardess. But between you and me Mr Knight, I've always found those airline people when I did fly not especially appealing. But I suppose it goes with the job. Meeting strangers all day long must surely be taxing."

"I suppose. Is Liz Strachan that way?"

"No. Not at all. Liz Strachan is lively. She isn't one to stand and chatter in the foyer but she always smiles. And such a beautiful, really an exquisite rare smile. Quite charming. And she says how are you and it seems she means it when she asks, she has real warmth. It is only a small thing but it says a lot about a human being, these small pleasant gestures make the day. The world is a horrible place without them. Just an opinion I happen to hold. I know you might be amused by that opinion."

"Not at all, Mrs Lowe. My mother is a very polite person."

"Actually, Mr Knight I don't believe you're just saying that, I can believe your mother is very polite. I can tell by the way you speak with me. You don't just speak to me. I deplore it when people speak to me. With."

"So you never spoke with Connie Yonge."

"No. I was not in her social register." Mrs Lowe smiled. I smiled in accord.

"Did you hear any rumours about her?"

"Yes, but mostly malicious gossip. I wouldn't dare repeat it. The sort of gossip that men want to make about a good-looking single woman. I did hear a rumour that Ms Yonge was divorced. That she had been divorced from an airline pilot. But that's hardly malicious."

"Who gossiped?"

"If I say you won't repeat it to that person?"

"No. You have my word."

"Pierre Willett."

"What did he say?"

"What did he not say, you mean. His mind is in the gutter. Ms Yonge is divorced. He said that. And that's probably true but the other stuff is trash. Junk. I do not repeat it. Pierre asked me to go out after my husband died but the man's entirely desperate. Too desperate. After being married to a man of Elmer's calibre, it would be quite impossible to consider someone like Pierre Willett."

"Mrs Lowe. Thanks for your time." I stood up. "You've been a big help. If necessary, could I call on you again?"

"By all means, Mr Knight. I'd do anything to help the Strachans find their lovely daughter."

I went out to my car and dialled Yonge's number on the cellphone. Her high-pitched girlish voice came on the line.

"Hello."

"Ms Yonge."

"May I ask who is calling."

"Alec Knight. I spoke with you yesterday regarding your good friend Liz Strachan. I was wondering if I could come over and speak with you for a few minutes."

Her voice went down a register.

"Only if it's absolutely necessary."

"We still haven't been able to find your friend Liz. There is a good possibility that you could clarify a few things that would be very helpful and establish where Liz went or who she might be with."

"If you must. When?"

"I could be there in half an hour. I'm across town."

"Alright, Mr Knight. But I haven't much time. Make it quick."

"Certainly."

I sat in the car mulling over the situation, then I drove around the corner and parked out of sight of the apartment building. I got out and went down the street and sat down on a distant bench from which I could view the apartment building. I opened up a newspaper. Shortly I saw a blue Olds pull up and park across the street in front of the building. Joe Parsons got out of the passenger seat. Another man with short blond hair sat in the driver's seat, another was sprawled in the back seat, both were loafing and laughing over something. I scribbled down the licence plate number and phoned it in to Louise Montpetit. Parsons went into the lobby and rang the buzzer. He disappeared into the elevator. After about five minutes Parsons came out. I had an impulse to track him but it was too bright out and time was tight. I watched him walk back to the blue Olds and waited for him to drive off with his buddies but the car did no more than drive around the next corner and park at the curb. They waited. I got up and went to my car around the other corner. Then I drove back around the block on time and parked near the apartment block.

I got out without looking back. I went into the lobby.

Connie Yonge was shining. She was startling. Her hair finely coiffed. She had on a rich silk dress. It was a dashing yellow with geometric black lines swirling around her form. Her nails were finely polished and had a rich glow, her lips were rich, a red gloss, almost shimmering like glass.

"Mr Knight, I hope this won't take too much time."

"No. May I come in."

"Why not?"

We sat in the living room. She sat across from me in a matching tuxedo chair. She crossed her legs and smiled.

"Well."

"I happened to be talking with Ed Stanley and Bill di Cesare. If you don't recognize the names, they are the two university friends of Liz's that dropped in on you two at the cottage. They confirmed most of what you said. But they mentioned that they thought you were in the room when Ed spoke with Liz on the Wednesday."

"Surely those boys must be mistaken. I went outside on the porch. They are so boring. Especially that Ted. He behaves like a boy. "

"Do you mean Ed when you say Ted?"

"Whatever. Ed, Ted, it's all the same. I told you I hardly would recognize the fellow. He doesn't know when to flake off. He hasn't an ounce of maturity. But what can be expected. I heard he grew up in some small place. Is that true?"

"I wouldn't know. We didn't get into any sort of personal discussion. Bill di Cesare says he went out on the porch because Liz and Ed Stanley began to argue but that you remained in the cottage."

Connie Yonge smiled, a truly delicious smile, and gave a small laugh. A careful laugh. It was beautifully modulated. Very appealing.

"He's so ridiculous. Those boys, they were probably drunk."

"Were they?"

"I don't know, but if you know Ed the rumour is that he drinks far too much. Liz can't stand him. He, well he argued with her sometimes. But I don't know if they did that day."

"I see. I understand Liz Strachan had problems sometimes making the rent. Ms Yonge, did you ever happen to help out Liz Strachan with her rent?"

She smiled and laughed again, now there was something charming in her manner.

"I would've if Liz ever asked. I would have done anything for Liz but it was hardly necessary. That's a ridiculous rumour. Even an exorbitant rumour. I don't know where you heard it. Who said such a thing?"

"It hardly matters."

"Well it is absurd. Liz comes from money. You've met her parents. You know it, Alec, otherwise you would not be sitting in this room asking me these sorts of questions. I know you mean well and are doing your job but from this side of the room they are banal, very banal rumours. Please don't listen to this sort of gossip concerning Liz. She has her act together." Connie Yonge uncrossed and recrossed her legs, glanced at her gold wristwatch. I noted it. It looked real. And as Lajoie said, watch people's jewellery, especially if they like to show it off.

"I don't mean to bore you, Ms Yonge."

"Connie please. You sound like a job interviewer. And I haven't had one of them in years. I'm not that cold and formal with reasonable men."

"Do you know if Liz knew a man named Clarence Wilson?"

"I don't recall the name."

"What about Lester Henderson?"

She shook her head negatively.

"Or a lawyer named Peter Slowikowsky."

"I've heard that name before but maybe only because I think it's a local name and Liz was studying law. She might have mentioned him. What sort of law does he do? "

"Criminal."

"Where?"

"Here in Ottawa."

"I've never heard of him. I never met any such person by that name."

"Mr Slowikowsky knows Liz Strachan."

"Could be, but as I said, Liz and I are very close friends but we live in entirely different social worlds. Not even parallel universes of any sort. She is outgrowing such people. Only a matter of time."

"I believe both you and Liz know a gentleman named Joe Parsons."

"Yes I know Mr Parsons."

"He runs an escort agency, LTD. Have you ever done any work for that agency?"

"I believe you're prying now. And frankly I can't see what that would have to do with Liz Strachan. Liz's disappearance."

"No?"

"No. No is a very good word, Alec. Liz is a mature woman. She does what she wants. I'm sure she'll return, when she chooses to. She probably took a trip. A little holiday for the week. Ottawa can be a real drag in the summer with all the tourists crowding about confused and looking for their Member of Parliament. Mistaking a light show for life. Silly shenanigans on Parliament Hill to amuse the nationalist tourist sentiments."

"How can you be so certain that Liz Strachan will return if you don't know where Liz is?"

"I have confidence in Liz's common sense. What's more I can't countenance the notion of something negative. I don't listen to what comes off negative wavelengths. That's not my channel." She smiled and looked at her gold watch. It glinted and winked at me, it was real gold. No bauble from Wal-Mart or Zellers. "In any event I'll have to ask you to leave, Alec. It's been a pleasure but I'm busy this evening. And running late."

"Sure."

She stood up and waited for me to walk towards the door ahead of her.

"You're a pleasant person, Alec. I do wish we had met under more congenial circumstances." At the apartment door, she offered her hand. The firm grip was there. I noticed that her voice stayed down a register throughout the conversation. It was more stable and appealing. It unsettled me. She looked much better tonight than she had previously. In fact, my optical memory was floating in chaos, I had thought she had been a sort of banal blonde with the potential for good looks but nothing appealing or striking, whereas at this moment she could have been devastating if she had relaxed. But she was not relaxed. Her appearance was sharp but entirely made-up and the earlier image of her from yesterday would not quit my brain no matter how attractive she appeared at this instant.

"Ms Yonge, thanks for your time but I should indicate that, despite what you say about Bill di Cesare and Ed Stanley's reliability, these discrepancies are unsettling. How can they be accounted for?"

"Jealousies do troubling things to men's memories." She smiled.

"If you have anything you wish to clarify possibly you could phone me." I gave her my card, she read it and then smiled, she stared into my face. She had on a light perfume. She knew how to wear things.

"You know, Alec, insinuation is not good for a man's character."

"I know but it is better than rudeness."

"You are polite. Too polite." She rested her hand on my sleeve fleetingly. "I suppose it's Ottawa. Ottawa's too much politeness. You're from here aren't you?"

"Sort of."

"This town holds back the best people. Smart people. It's the capital but it's the most provincial of capitals. Real creative people's imaginations are thwarted. Dynamic people deserve a better place."

"It's what we've made it."

"Do you go to the casino in Hull or Montréal? Preferably Montréal."

"If the occasion arises. Taking a risk is sometimes necessary to find out about life." I smiled. She smiled.

"It's an amusing relief to see so many losers in one place, so many losers who think they're winners of the universe. They're trying to break down the tedium of cautious lives. Are you cautious, Alec?"

"Cautious? I never thought about it."

"I deplore cautious men, they're so timid and tedious. Should I keep this card? I wonder." She smiled.

"Be bold, Connie, keep it."

"But it seems so ... so ... what? Superfluous."

"I'm a superfluous man. In a superfluous town."

"Wonderful. Wonderful. You have delicious wit."

"Call me. It might be a wise act."

"Considerate too."

"One last query."

She opened the door.

"Really. Overstaying is a rudeness."

"Did you happen to know a lawyer named Norman Burley?"

Connie Yonge smiled. "Alec, it's as if you were rhyming off the phone book to me. And as everyone knows the phone book is so very boring. Good evening."

"I do hope you contact me before something troubling comes to light concerning your good friend Liz Strachan."

"If something troubling comes to light Alec, I do hope you contact me." She closed the door.

I went back down to the garage and walked around Liz Strachan's car. I opened the car door and went through the vehicle interior thoroughly but found nothing. In the trunk there was the Hudson Bay blanket, school texts, a water jug, a cardboard box full of junk. In the box were music CDs. I shuffled through them. There were half a dozen with no labels on them. Five were brand new and unopened. The sixth was also new but had been opened and looked like it had been used once. I took it and slipped it in my pocket. I closed the trunk. I stood by the side of the car and inspected the smear on the garage cement floor. It was beginning to disappear under the back and forth of tire tracks.

I went up and knocked on Pierre Willett's door. He poked his head out in his furtive manner. He smelt of rye and stale smoke. His eyes were red.

"You. What the hell is it now?"

"Can I have a word with you, Mr Willett."

"Alright. Come in."

He let me slip in and closed the door. I could smell the thick odour of bacon and a disorienting combination of other putrid, even lurid smells that were at once powerful, familiar and yet strange and peculiar. They hung below the ceiling in a vapour. I had no desire to stay. Intimacies with some people's personal space can trigger moments of vertigo. And Willett didn't look exactly like he wanted me to hang around unless I was dropping loose change. He sniffed, maybe on account of the smoke. But I thought he was sniffing me to determine if I had bills.

"Can you tell me what you know about Ms Yonge. The tenant across from Liz Strachan in 910?"

"Didn't you ask about her before?"

"Yes. But I need more information. I was wondering how long she has lived in the building?"

"Three years. I think. Yeah near four."

"What do you know about Connie Yonge?"

"Not much. To tell you the truth the woman's a snob. She puts on airs like a lot of people today. Puffed up. Thinks she's better than a lot of the other tenants."

"I've heard that. Have you heard anything about her?"

"I told you she acts like she's got connections and money. She plays. None of my business but there's more going on up there between units 909 and 910 than appears. But because they pay their rent, don't make a racket and the cops don't come buzzing 'round, I stay out of it. I got a policy of staying out of the tenants' affairs. Melgund Management people like it that way. Unless of course it violates the lease or breaks the law."

"Well tell me what you think is going on up there, on the basis of your considerable experience and knowledge as a superintendent. You've been here how many years?"

"Enough. And I've seen a few things."

"I'm sure you have, Pierre."

"Ray. It's Ray. Nobody calls me Pierre unless they don't know me. They turning tricks. It's high class stuff. We're not talking blow jobs in the market and quickies, pick-ups. We're talking more dress-up. Fancy stuff."

"You said you saw a number of older guys with Liz Strachan and Connie Yonge."

"Yeah. That's right."

"If I were to show you a series of photographs could you look at them and tell me if you recognized any of the men?"

"I suppose. But I'm half cut. I've been putting back a few."

"Just do the best you can."

I showed him the photos from the coalition of the willing. He recognized Clarence Wilson, Norman Burley and Lester Henderson.

"These other two. Sort of vague."

"That's very helpful."

I slipped him a ten.

"You're alright. Come by anytime."

I went out to the car. The cellphone rang. It was Louise Montpetit. "Alec, that licence plate number you gave me, it's a stolen plate. Possibly on a stolen car."

"Figures. Give it to the police, Louise."

"The Strachans phoned, they want you to call them. Their daughter Brenda called as well. And you've gotten two calls from a university student. Stanley, Ed Stanley. He says he needs to talk with you."

"I'll give the Strachans a call. What did Stanley say?"

"Just that he needs to talk to you. Wants to know what's up with his girlfriend, Liz. He was a bit pressing."

"I'll call him when I get a chance."

I phoned up Brenda Strachan and asked if I could see her again. She said to come over. I phoned up the Strachans at the Lord Elgin Hotel. They had left a message that they were out for dinner. Fine by me, I wasn't exactly keen to talk with them at this juncture, but I left a message that I had called.

I parked on Lewis Street beside Minto Park. As I was saluting the Argentine General, someone called out in a laughing voice, "Hey Lantern."

I glanced in the direction of the voice. Three young guys were sitting on a bench. I recognized one of the fellows. A kid about nineteen years old, known on the street as Inky Baby. He had on a big leering grin, slightly bad teeth but a good smile all the same. If the kid could manage to get some dental work there was still time to salvage the teeth. He appeared a little worn down, but still nice looking. Complex tattoos showed up his arms. He was dressed in a sleeveless shirt, more a rag than a garment, and elaborately patched jeans, patch upon patch of multitudinous colours, materials and stitches that seemed to create a new topsy-turvy cartographic perspective of the continents and seas. He wore a stovepipe hat at least a foot tall, a stiff blue satin brim stitched to a black stem made from the leg of a pair of jeans. I didn't recognize Inky Baby's two buddies. One wore shorts, sandals, a cap and a T-shirt with the face of a man with a big refined moustache, black print on a red background with the slogans, Viva Zapata and Plan de Ayala. The other guy was wearing a white shirt that read across the front, The Right to Squat is a Human Right. I knew Inky Baby from the street. Baby was his true surname, no joke there. I had no clue where Inky came from, even less notion of what Inky's first name might be. Our paths had first crossed during a landlord case. Inky worked in a street soup kitchen that the mayor and companies hated to see on the streets of Ottawa. He knew all sorts of people, had travelled across the continent from city to city since he was fourteen, his appearance and manner belied the store of information he carried around. He was a sourceless source. And often one that would not tell anything if the mood, even so much as the location of the sun, inclined him not to say anything. Inky could be both garrulous and petulantly shut-mouthed. He had been kicked around and had kicked around so much that he was not afraid of authority.

"'Lo." I returned a smile.

"Lantern, you got any smokes?" Inky Baby called out.

"Sure, Inky." I got out my street pack. I saw me-toos in the eyes of the two guys. "Here take it, there's only a half dozen left."

"Thanks, Lantern." Inky accepted the pack with a smile, took a cigarette out, broke off the filter and shared the pack with his buddies. They nodded their heads in appreciation. "This is a guy called, uh ..."

"Knight." I smiled.

"Yo, right, Knight. He's a Lantern."

The other two guys gave me a dubious look. I nodded towards them.

"This is Diderot. And this here's Helium."

Diderot was tall and very thin and dressed in the red and black T-shirt and cap. I took him for about twenty-six or seven. Helium had a shaved head and tattoos circling his neck. An elaborate indigo latticework necklace, something more than a choker. They both nodded towards me but said nothing. Now the three were smoking.

"How you been?"

"Ah you know. They won't leave us alone. It's the same old same. You know the way of the world. Property trumps human beings. They're trying to throw my buddies here from the squat out on the street. Maybe you heard. The city harasses the street kitchen. And we're only trying to feed some hungry people."

"I read something in the paper."

"Collecting for the squat. What you say? People there need food."

Diderot doffed his soiled sailor's cap, waved it and proffered an ambiguous smile.

"Sure." I dug in my pocket, found two toonies, a looney and a half dozen smaller coins and tossed them in the cap. "I don't need a charitable receipt for income tax purposes."

"You're alright." Inky laughed.

The three smoked on.

"Inky, there's Valerie." Diderot and Helium stood up. "Thanks for the coin. Back in a sec." Then Diderot and Helium were off across the park towards a woman who looked in her thirties, dressed in jeans and T-shirt with auburn hair to her shoulders.

"Inky, you living at the squat?"

"Naw. Not just yet. Maybe later. We're supporting each other. Like political allies." Inky laughed. "Wouldn't you know it, the homeless and the hungry got a lot in common."

"I suppose it makes sense."

"Would you know, Lantern? You ever been there?"

I said nothing to this.

"Forget it. It's just that the situation is crappy. Some people don't believe it. But we got a lot of people who support us." Inky glanced at me, "You know something?"

"What?"

"Those people know more about the law than the judge and Crown. They don't need a lawyer." Inky grinned. "Hey don't look so dubious. It's true. Valerie is really smart."

"Sure. If you say so." I leaned forward resting my elbows on my knees. "Listen Inky."

"Lantern, I don't care for that tone."

I glanced over at him.

He spit out a choppy bit of tobacco that had got caught on his tongue.

"Just kidding. K. What's niggling your nightbrain?"

"You ever hear about a girl named Laura Cooke, sixteen?"

Inky bent his leg, rested his chin on his knee and just puffed away on the smoke. Very meditative. Then he said, "You too. That's that shithead dick Warnock's daughter. There's some weird shit out there."

I said nothing. I waited while Inky smoked.

"You know something?"

"What?"

"You tell Warnock that there's only certain kinds of I-stuff you can buy. Info is not Instanta pack from the freezer to the microwave. You know." His voice changed inflection and Inky began to recite a recipe in commercialese, "Read instructions carefully before preparing. Put one pack in microwave ware. Pour in one cup of water. And mike harris for one minute. Presto. That isn't food or I-stuff. Most people aren't for sale, eh?"

"You could be right. Laura Cooke's mum's pretty broken up. Very sad lady in sad lady land."

"They all are out there in the 'burbs. And bidonville babes. That's the SUV crowd." His voice changed inflection, and he began to sing, "Just driving along in my SUV ... with no particular mall to go ... my kids strapped in the back ... crying desperation row." Inky lowered his leg, hunched forward and lit another smoke off the old one, he gazed at his companions on a bench across the park.

"That girl could be hurt."

"I got news for you Lantern. She is hurt. Damaged way beyond her old man's knowledge and old lady's imagination. But all they want to do is spend time outlawing everything. So they de-legalize us guys."

I stood up.

"Here, not for you, give this to your buddies in the squat." I gave Inky a ten. "And by the way, don't presume where I've been or whatever. Like you say I don't care for that tone. Got to go." I started off across the grass.

"Hey Knight. Take this." Inky called out. I looked back. "Come here. Take this cell number."

I went back and typed the cellphone number into my own.

"Give me a call late tonight or tomorrow at that number. K."

"Thanks." Then I crossed the road and went up the steps.

Brenda Strachan let me in. We sat in the living room. She had a corner of the couch padded up.

"I'm glad you called, Ms Strachan. There are a number of things that have come up over the last twenty-four hours that you might be able to help with."

"Is there anything solid that would help tell where Liz might be?"

"Let me say I've spoken to a number of individuals, sources so to speak, who have provided some leads but I still need some clarifications. If I might speak for a moment in generalities. In dealing with investigations involving a missing person, sometimes family members are not necessarily aware of what information might be of assistance to a private investigator. Things that seem pretty obvious to the family sometimes get overlooked."

"I suppose it is a case of objectivity. Objectifying information. Or our concern. Maybe even anxiety."

"Yes. A family is possibly afraid of being embarrassed by certain aspects of family members' actions or life. Such reluctance is entirely understandable. After all, I am a stranger."

"I don't feel you're a stranger, Mr Knight. I trust you. I feel I trust you. I can trust you. I told my parents that we should trust you."

"I appreciate that. That's very important. Very necessary."

"I must confess. Confess is such a terrible. Worried word. But I can't just now find another word." She bit her lip and shifted about. "Would you like a coffee or a drink."

"Coffee's fine."

She made the coffee and this time let me help her bring it into the living room.

"Mr Knight, I wasn't as forthcoming regarding my sister Liz as I should have been."

"Why?"

"Petty things. People think I'm jealous of Liz because she's so beautiful. People imply. Or say it behind our backs. And she is. But I'm not jealous of Liz. I love my sister. I thought I would leave it to my parents to be frank with you regarding our family. To set aside their notions of pride and to divulge what you deemed necessary. But they weren't forthright. That much is apparent."

"How so?"

"I had an argument with my parents yesterday evening. Late in the evening after you spoke with them. Concerning candour. It was meaningless but it happened. One of those petty family squabbles that Russian authors are so good at depicting and American writers are so good at evading, reducing it to sentimentalism or angry melodramatic yelling. Sentimentalism rules, Mr Knight. And if not that, bitterness."

I smiled.

"I mean it." She smiled, an agreeable smile, she did have a beautiful smile. "As soon as one starts talking about one's family in North America it all runs to Hollywood sentimentalism. Self-deception. But even the bitterness is rotten to the core because then TV rules and it is all for show. We're not a congenial family. We have a surface loyalty and all that but we don't get along."

"Could that have any influence on your sister's disappearance?"

"Possibly. But I don't know. Maybe. I'll be frank even if my parents disapprove. There is no point in binding your hands by withholding information that might potentially be useful. I'll allow you to be the best judge of what is not relevant and what is. I'm adopted. Liz was born five years later. My mother had an affair."

"Do you know the man?"

"No. My father knew of this affair but I don't think he knows who it was with. He's really quite generous. He loves my mother and Liz regardless of the affair. He has always considered us his daughters in the fullest sense."

"Who was the man?"

"I don't know his name. I have heard various rumours. One that he was a lawyer. But that is not at all certain. I also heard it was a businessman. A local fellow who moved west."

"I see. When was your mother in law school?"

"Back in the early seventies."

She sipped the coffee.

"Liz found out about it in her teens. She was very cruel to my parents. As if she despised them. It was very hurtful. In high school she was wild. To be honest I don't know how she got through it and passed. But she's always been very bright. My parents told you about the car accident?"

"Yes."

"Well Liz thinks I always got more attention because of it. That happens. I suppose I did. I was in and out of hospital so many times and in therapy. I took a lot of my parents' time. It's a fact of the situation. She was younger and felt neglected. The situation was difficult. She craved attention, I suppose. Maybe that's not fair. But she got into a lot of meaningless trouble that had little or nothing to do with having fun but mostly caused problems for my parents. She argued a lot with my parents."

"How were your parents about it?"

"Mostly okay. You know that lovely Canadian word." She flashed a smile.

"Tell me."

"Decent. Beautifully tolerant, decent and patient. But my mother was disapproving, even harsh with Liz and herself. Liz screwed around a lot with both boys and girls through her teens. One time another mother found Liz in bed with a teenage girl. The girl's mother, a very religious woman, blamed it all on Liz and our family. Liz was older than the other girl. She threatened to file a complaint against my sister with the police. It was touch and go."

"What happened?"

"Oh on one level not much. These high-minded moralists are bigger windbags than a bagpipe. But even a bagpipe has the virtue of occasionally being deflated. The other girl's mother did not do anything official. But then my parents did the clamp down thing. Sent Liz away to a very strict private school. Liz got through high school and came up here."

"You mentioned that you know Connie Yonge."

"Yes."

"Do you know more than you told me?"

"Probably. I mean yes. I'm not doing well for a lawyer, am I?" She gave a faint smile. "I'm afraid of being a snitch or gossip on my sister. I'm caught betwixt and between, being perceived as a jealous snitch on my beautiful sister and being profoundly anxious as to her whereabouts. This is serious, this case, isn't it?"

"I don't know. It could be. Yes. It could be. But then it might not. I don't like to speculate. I prefer to leave that to others."

"You found one of my sister's Boucheron ear clips?"

"Yes."

"What's that mean?"

"First tell me what you know about Connie Yonge and your sister Liz."

"I believe they're lovers. Actually I'm pretty certain."

"Do your parents know?"

"Actually, I don't know. Maybe but they probably wouldn't acknowledge it. They might suspect it but my sister has learned to be more discreet living on her own. She doesn't throw it in their faces. My father is not troubled by Liz, he seems to have come to accept it, but my mother really disapproves. She's not especially tolerant. If it were strangers or acquaintances, say a couple of gays, educated people, people with money, she'd be sociable and polite, even superficially tolerant, but because it involves her own daughter, well it sets her off."

"And you?"

"I view any loving relationship as a good thing. In this world it's hard enough to find someone loving. When people see me they feel troubled by my appearance. They can't accept it. It unsettles them. Or they are indifferent, which masks their attitude. This being I'm in is everyone's fearful damaged future but the thing is, I am living it out now before people's eyes. And they don't want to see. I know I might seem aggressive to defend myself, people don't like it. But I won't settle for the complacency society dictates that I should accept. I refuse it. I don't see myself as disabled. I see the society as disabled. The accident. Time tore up and left my body behind but it threw my brain into the future." She rubbed the edge of the chair's arm, then stared at me.

"I'll take what you say as so." I glanced away from Brenda Strachan's gaze. "You're right, it is unsettling. There is a lack of honesty about bodies."

"Thank you Mr Knight. Now tell me what the found pearl ear clip really means."

"I don't know what it really means. It could be just an ear clip that fell off and your sister didn't happen to notice it. Or it could have other implications."

"Might it suggest a struggle, an assault of some sort?"

"It could, I suppose."

"Rape?"

"Maybe, but I think not. The police would have found some evidence in their investigation and their approach would be very different at this juncture. The fact that they are treating the situation as a missing person file suggests that they found nothing of that sort."

"My parents are anxious on account of the police. Have you spoken to them?"

"Not concerning that."

"They feel or believe the police are taking the tack that Liz left town on a trip. It is all about the company Liz keeps. The authorities are not impressed to say the least."

"That sort of thing can influence them. But the local police have a good record. I'm confident that if they found anything that suggested a crime they would go after it. A missing person case does have some elements of ambiguity. Strictly speaking it is not a crime in itself. Context determines if it is. And when a missing person case involves a person living on their own, a responsible adult, and the person has committed no crime and that person might appear to have gone on a trip or holiday then they obviously have to be a little more circumspect. Especially if the person acted of her own volition. Strictly speaking it may not even be considered a missing person case. It is more an unlocated person. They are careful not to appear to be intruding on a person's privacy. The ambiguity makes the search a little more intricate. Difficult."

"Is that the case in your opinion?"

"No. But the police have your parents calling up and stating that your sister is missing or has disappeared. They get this often from parents. Keep in mind your sister is not a minor, she is an independent person. Just because a parent wants to know the whereabouts of a child does not mean they're entitled to know. It doesn't mean they can call up a police force in some city and ask them to go searching. They give some credibility to your parents but obviously as they find out anomalous details, a different routine, that the family either didn't know or may have deliberately withheld, well then it is understandable that it will shade or influence their approach. If they found a crime scene then of course all of this would change. But they have not."

"Is that definite?"

"Look. The senior partner, Georges Lajoie, is a former detective on the Montreal police force. He has substantial experience. We're giving it our best. Lajoie is very capable."

"I see."

"I have to go but I have a few last questions that maybe you might be able to shed some light on. Did your sister ever happen to mention any of these individuals? Norman Burley, Lester Henderson, Peter Slowikowsky, Alfred Plante or Clarence Wilson."

She gave a long thought. "No. Except that first name Burley sounds familiar."

"How so?"

"I work in a legal branch of the government and his name came up."

"In connection with what?"

"I can't quite recall at this instant but it had to do with a bank. Maybe just a coincidence. Probably."

"He's with the corporate law firm of Baldwin Martel Wightman."

"That's it. I should've recognized it. How foolish on my part. I must have been confused. Context and association is nearly everything. I needed my memory jolted."

"What was it concerning a bank?"

"It was a research document, submission paper, during an inquiry into international banking regulations and proposed changes in legislation. Canadian banks doing banking in the Caribbean. And the regulatory process. Protecting privacy of depositors. Burley made a presentation at a committee hearing or conference defending strict privacy rights of bank depositors. That the new regulations concerning money transfers being contemplated might infringe or encroach on the Charter of Rights and Freedoms, demand mandatory rather than merely discretionary and voluntary disclosures by the bank officials to the police authorities concerning suspicious bank deposits and transfers by depositors. It covers an important issue but it is just the sort of thing the public only pays attention to when it actually comes up. The Burley paper is in the public domain. You can read it if you want very exciting stuff."

"Sure. I'll take it out of the parliamentary library the next time I drop into the Rotunda." I got up. "Thanks for your time. I don't want you or your parents to get too down. Your sister might have taken a brief holiday to the Laurentians. Montebello. The Eastern Townships. Vermont. Nothing more."

"Let's hope so. In a way no news is good news. Right?"

"Call me anytime if anything further comes to mind."

"I will. One last thing Mr Knight."

"Yes?"

"In mentioning Connie Yonge." Brenda Strachan stopped. "Well it's nothing."

"Are you certain?"

"Yes."

# EIGHT

Back at the office I went through the file and pulled out Lester Henderson's and Norman Burley's addresses and phone numbers. I asked Louise Montpetit to dial up Burley's house doing a telemarketing racket. While I waited to hear from Louise, I checked the CD from Liz Strachan's trunk. It was no blank CD. It was a series of photographs of men and women embracing, potentially semi-compromising pictures. Young women with older men. But none of Liz Strachan or Connie Yonge.

Louise came back and said Burley was in. She then checked out Henderson's house. He was also in. I tossed a coin in the air, it came up Henderson.

I drove over to the transport company owner's house. The guy lived in a big house in the west end beyond Parkdale Avenue near too busy but scenic Island Park Drive. A hospital zone bracketed by The Royal Ottawa Hospital to the west and the Civic Hospital to the east, the neighbourhood looked and felt bucolic. The air was soft and gentle. The streets quiet. I told my bladder to prepare itself for a long wait. I slouched down and waited, feigning to read the mop and pail, a newspaper that did not cease to provide amusement by manufacturing real events into trivial banalities, paranoid slogans and tedious opinions daily. Over its lifetime, the rag reputedly had gone from loudmouth imperial British tory sloganeering to singing sycophantic Yankee doodle dandy ragtime. Its editors had ranted through the nineteenth century in a state of imperialist high dudgeon, needing rest they had slept through the twentieth in a state of smug senility, and now early and short into the twenty-first, exhausted by diatribes, they had fallen into a conservative coma. No doubt they would wake up in the twenty-second century on the starship Free Enterprise gliding into the universe of unlimited free trade. I was gliding near to sleep under the landslide of numbers in the stock market columns concerning the coin I lacked for investment when I saw Henderson in the faint dusk light come out, get into a white Buick and drive to Carling Avenue. The car had an oval dealership sticker from SMP, Stanley Motor Products.

He drove east on Carling then through the Glebe onto Bank Street. A sedate day, most of the shops in brick buildings of two and three storeys with wooden signs, faux antique, were closed. Here rents were a whack on the wallet, property taxes gave businesses in the net-net leases high blood pressure, while the meter minutemen were vigilant in applying the five second rule to an expired parking meter, working their little meter ticket machines like a prospector's precious metal detection device. The big Buick rolled on, crossing the canal on the Bank Street bridge, through Old Ottawa South down the hill towards the Rideau River, where the ducks and geese congregated in the reeds of the speckled green isles, the rare red and white copie could be spotted and black swans in couples glided by like out-of-place summer dreams. No doubt the black swans were dreaming of upstart crows and the coming of autumn. The big car crossed the river at the Billings Bridge and continued up the hill into Alta Vista. It pulled into a strip mall near Walkley.

Henderson was a small wiry man who was going bald. He was dressed in cotton slacks and a polo shirt with a designer logo on it. Everybody wants to be as recognizable as a beer bottle sign in neon. This is identity theft of a new order. A refrain of trademarks and brand names are stealing our identities while we are asleep inside our wallets. Henderson went into a doughnut shop, bought a dozen doughnuts and an extra large coffee. He glanced around, the place was half empty. Henderson took his coffee over and sat at a window table. I went in and ordered a coffee and muffin and sat at the next table. I pulled out what looked like a walkman but was an amplification headset and put it on, pretending to listen to Charlie Parker, opened up the mop and pail and pretended to slop a mop through its slush.

Shortly, I noticed through the shop window a man coming across the parking lot. The man entered, there was a moment of recognition between the man and Henderson. He was tall, solid in the limbs, straight-backed, straining to appear upright, it seemed his right shoulder was a little higher than his left. His face was hard-featured which made him look inclined to be argumentative, although in a more conciliatory and complimentary vein he might be described as combative. With Henderson, he expressed initially a companionable manner but seemed governed predominantly by ambition, a guy who likes money. His clothing suggested an endless fondness for garb that signalled money and appearance over human beings. I immediately and unmistakably recognized the puffed up lad as none other than Norman Innis Burley. He sat down across from Lester Henderson. Burley was the sort of personality you immediately would have preferred to forget but having once seen him, he was unforgettable. He would no doubt one day make a successful politician.

Burley and Henderson shook hands. Beside Burley, Henderson seemed the salt of the earth.

"Les, good to see you again."

"Norm. How was the Caribbean?"

"Hot. Too hot. The islands are great from November through to March, great place for a game of golf. But between you and me, not my sort of climate to spend the first week of September in. If it weren't a necessity I'd never visit the place at this time of year."

"Coffee, Norm."

"No. No. Just had one."

"Have a doughnut, Norm." Henderson pushed the box towards Burley, the lawyer glanced at the box but did not take one. Henderson's voice lowered and I adjusted the amplification and moved the device a little closer to the edge of the table. "Norm, something's come up."

"What? Couldn't it have waited?"

"I don't know. There's a guy snooping 'round Joe's people."

"Who?"

"Some hired flunky with a private outfit."

"Well. I think it's just a question of staying clear of them. Probably just one of Joe's people with a personal issue."

"Listen. You must have heard about this stuff with one of Joe's ladies, that sharp-looking one, thinks she's pretty smart, Liz Strachan."

"I haven't heard anything, Les, I've just been in the Caribbean for the last week, since last Tuesday on business. Just got back late yesterday."

"It goes round that she's gone missing. Her family called in the cops then hired some piss-eyed snoop to check it out."

"My good fellow, you're overreacting. Just let it go. What's it to us? Nothing. Nothing." Burley started to get up. "Is that all. Is that why you called me out?"

"Norm, wait."

Burley sat back down.

"Les. Why don't you just relax. Take a bloody holiday or something. Go play a game of golf."

"It's a luxury."

"Les. Take a reasonable approach."

"The snoop braced Pete."

"So? That's Slowikowsky's pecker caught in his zipper. What do you care about that. Some two-bit hack. Trust me, Slowikowsky can take care of himself. And if he isn't up to it, it's his problem."

"Norm. Think this through."

"I am and in my opinion Les, you overreact, calling me out like this. You've done it too many times. If I may say so, a foolish alarmism."

"I'm worried about that guy Parsons, Norm."

"Listen, Les. Say nothing to Pete and his pimp. They'll have to take care of themselves. None of those side rackets of theirs touches us. None of it. Everything is properly in order. I've kept everything on the up and up, here and with the people on the island. As long as you and your people follow instructions to the letter."

"I'm concerned that's all. 'Cause this Strachan girl's family calling in the police and a PI, they can stir—"

"Forget her, okay. She's nothing. She's just a little holiday hustler. A year of law school and she's full of fancy ideas."

"I don't know. You ever talk to her?" Burley said nothing. Henderson went on, "She's pretty sharp. Her and that Connie Yonge seem to have their own ideas."

"What do you mean, you don't know? She's a little tramp, she's probably run off on a two dollar vacation with one of Parsons' fancy pants."

"Maybe."

"Look, if you're so damned worried hire an investigator and get her number."

"Christ, another cost."

"The cost of doing business. And you know it, especially if guys like Parsons are involved. Even on the margins."

"Norm, I'm trying to get out of a hole, not dig myself in further. You people came to me. Don't forget you people needed me."

"Lester, we carry you."

"I had a good business before I got into all this."

"Shut up Les. You know why you're here. You liked it when you were getting the dough. Parsons is your person. You brought that con in."

"Norm, be reasonable."

"Look. I haven't time for this, Les. Some little trash goes missing and you get your balls tied in a knot. She's probably been laid more times than she's eaten croissants. Listen, my good man."

"What?"

"I can tell."

"What do you mean you can tell."

"You got something big on your brain, Les, otherwise you wouldn't be talking this way. What's this really all about? It sure isn't about sleazebags like Pete Slowikowsky balling his brains out with one of Parsons' hired women. I had you tracked, Les, so don't lie."

"Okay. I was getting some stuff with some of Parsons' ladies."

"I was informed of that by my source. You guys are too much. You are a bloody idiot to mess around with a hinny. We didn't hire Parsons for that. Don't mix business with pleasure. I told you guys the rules of the game. Number one, stay away from the mules. That's Parsons' racket. His front. I tell you that again and again. No mules in your stalls. But you guys don't get it."

"It's human. Okay. Not everybody has your impeccable self-restraint."

"Shut up, Les. I got to go. Listen. Don't talk to Parsons. Don't go near that apartment block. That's an order. Keep off this topic with Pete Slowikowsky if he brings it up. Pete was balling them. That idiot Wilson was doing it. And ripping us off. What's with you guys? I know it all. I tracked you guys after I saw what Wilson was into. They got something on you now. You are a certified idiot. That's the way Parsons' women work. They're potential blackmail bait. Tuck in your sweetbreads, zip up your trousers and keep your stupid mouth shut. Those women are trouble. Parsons is a risk. I told you to watch your back with that character. Worse, bedding those girls is even bigger trouble. You are so incompetent. I'll get some people to take care of this."

Burley left abruptly. I went out and followed him back to where he lived in Rockcliffe.

I sat and waited a long time but nothing happened. Time went into my head. It came out as a long list. Of men. I thought of all these guys that Liz Strachan knew. I thought of di Cesare and Stanley again. I thought of Slowikowsky and Parsons. A police cruiser came by. I rolled down my window, the policeman asked what I was doing and asked for my driver's licence. He checked it back in his cruiser then returned it. I said, thank you officer. He said, a neighbour called in your licence number. I said thank you again. He drove off. I followed his good example, drove to the next main street and parked when the cellphone rang. It was Louise Montpetit. She told me the Strachans had called again as well as Stanley. I called Ed Stanley's place. He sounded half loaded. Voluble and drunk, he was, as ever, eager to talk about Liz Strachan so I decided to drive over. Chronic talk about the lady was Stanley's displaced way of engaging in intimacy with the woman. For Liz Strachan, even glancing at her watch probably would have been giving him too much time. The theory of sublimation was sort of like the theory of life on other planets—fine to speculate on, even amusing, but you really didn't want to live there. Call me lacking in curiosity but interplanetary travel just doesn't seem to be what it is all cracked up to be if I have to leave behind the people I care for. My mind drifted elsewhere, I didn't give a hang about Ed Stanley's hangups over Liz Strachan. I was more hung-up quite suddenly over Lynda's imminent departure.

Stanley shared an apartment near the university with two other guys who played on the university hockey team. The joint was all too familiar. Piles of unread textbooks on commerce, psychology, economics and sociology stuffed in the corners and covered with dust. A sweet collection of hockey sticks for both street ball hockey and ice hockey racked up. The requisite collection of running shoes ranging from one hundred buck cheapies to four hundred dollar specials and hand gloves of various sorts from hockey to roller blading. The acrid smell of sweat mingling with the odour of beer, the beer bottles and two-four cases piled up along the walls as testament and edifice to academic commitment and accomplishment. The torn and worn sofas and soft chairs bought at used furniture shops, Goodwill, Sally Ann and Neighbourhood Services, suggesting hope or hopelessness depending upon which end of the bottle you stared through at the soiled furniture. At the end of the school year it would all be consigned to the dump and the students would have no memory of a year blurred by a six-month long hangover.

Stanley's roommates were two solid fellows. One near to handsome, except for a coerced look that lurked in his features. His physique, one of power, size and ease, suggested that he was probably a tough and fine hockey player. But facial features suggested his old man might have bullied him down to the hockey rink and through the regime of hockey training, seeing the luminous way of Wayne Gretzky Parkway in his son's spartan sports future. Mingled with the look was apathy. But I could discern that he would be the first to jump up and defend the national sport against all heretical agnostics and antagonists, without believing much in the rhetoric. A piled up character due to a lack of true enthusiasm for the game.

The other fellow had that tough intelligent look, quiet, reflective and inarticulate, unhappy in school but no doubt brilliant on the ice. Some guys only found their intellects when they had the skates strapped on and the stick placed in their gloved hands. For certain, graceful and cunning on the ice. Also dangerous and capable of split second subtle gestures but strictly in the game. A real live accident waiting to happen when the sports career exhausted itself in five or ten years and he was doing sales on commission for a sporting goods outfit or stuck working the assembly line at an auto plant, jobs wrangled through buddy connections. The all sports networks fabricated these guys and their parents' ambition a dime a dozen across the entire continent. To produce one top notch athlete the industry devoured ten thousand young brains.

"Yo, Alec Knight here. Meet two of the greatest hockey players in Ottawa. Phil Smythe and Tommy Hobbes. You'll see them at the Senators game at the Corel Centre. In their favourite viewing spot. The penalty box."

"Ed is still playing for the Ottawa Rough Riders." The two hockey players laughed and watched the TV and drank their beer.

"Why don't you jerks blow off. I got to talk to this guy about something kinda important."

"Whack off, Stanley."

"No. Come on, goof, I mean it."

"Stanley. I never know you to talk about anything important except your dick."

"Get out, you third strings. I mean it. I got to talk alone with this guy."

Smythe and Hobbes looked at each other, exchanged smiles. They dragged themselves up out of the furniture. "Hey hey no blow jobs in the shower you boys. Keep it strictly talkie talkie."

The two hockey players left.

"Beer, Knight?"

"Thanks but no thanks, Ed. I've got to drive."

"I got nothing else."

"That's cool."

We slouched in the sagging furniture. Ed drank.

"Have you got any good news about Liz?"

"I have some leads thanks to people like yourself."

"Can I tell you something, Knight." He was more than half cut.

"Sure. Go ahead."

"I love that lady."

"I'm sure you do Ed."

"No. You don't understand. I mean it. We're hoping to get married after she finishes law school. Well we kinda talked about it."

"Do Mr and Mrs Strachan know?"

"Not yet. It's not a topic of conversation at the dinner table or anything. We didn't want to let anyone know. Keep it kinda private." He rolled his big head on his neck. "I love her and I can't bear the thought of anything happening to her. It tears my guts out. You know something. She makes me something better than I am. You ever get that way with a woman?"

I said nothing.

"Sec."

Stanley got up and went into the kitchen and then came back with two cold beers. He offered me one.

"Have a brew. I don't like drinking alone. It's antisocial."

"I understand. Entirely understandable." I took the beer but didn't drink, I held it in my hand as if to sip at any time. "Remember you mentioned that last week of August that you dropped into the cottage where Liz Strachan and her friend Connie Yonge were staying?"

"Yeah. But Connie isn't really a friend. If you know what I mean."

"There might be something there in what you say. Well I spoke with Connie Yonge and she claims she was there in the living room of the cottage and that you and Liz Strachan—I don't know precisely how to put it."

"What did she say?"

"Ms Yonge said Liz Strachan and you had an argument."

"That, that Yonge, she's a parasite. 'Cause she's got nothing herself. A leech. She knows Liz's family comes from money so she latches on. I know her kind."

"Ed, was Ms Yonge in the cottage at the time?"

"Yeah." He punched the armrest of the torn chair, a burst of dust went into the air and some of the cotton stuffing pushed further outward from the tear. "Yonge makes people weird. She makes Liz kinda weird whenever she is around. Alone Liz and I get along grand. We had such a great relationship before Liz started hanging out with that—ah, forget it."

I said nothing. I glanced at Stanley, he stared back. I raised the beer bottle to my lips feigning a drink. He stared at me then looked away and took a powerful swig. Stanley half grinned "Rotten thought, I can't stand to think about it but that Yonge she's got the hots for Liz. Yonge's a blipping lezzie. I got that on good authority from people around campus. It's true, Knight."

"How can you be certain?"

"Liz told me. Liz really regrets moving into that building."

"I see."

"Tell me something. I understand you work at Split Second Transport and Warehouse."

"That's right. Why?"

"Who's the manager or owner over there?"

"A guy called Les Henderson. Why? What's this got to do with Liz?"

"Does Liz know him? Has she ever met him?"

"I dunno. I can't see it. I mean there'd be no reason for her to meet Les Henderson. She's never been to the warehouse."

"Have you ever met Les Henderson, personally?"

"Sure. My old man knows him really well. They grew up together. He's a hometown boy. He's originally from my hometown. That's how I swung the job."

"What's Mr Henderson like, Ed?"

"Les? He's a good guy. Bright guy. According to my dad, his old man had next to nothing but a lousy quarter section. The worst quarter in the entire township. Run down. All rock and rubble, sand, even the wood lot was nothing but ash and ironwood. Pretty crummy patch of soil. Farmed out. Soil exhausted. Les's a hustler. When he was sixteen Henderson started hauling this and that in an ancient Dodge half-ton, then he bought a fifteen-year-old dump truck when he was 'bout twenty, hauled garbage for the city, then got himself a ten-year-old rig, and he turned that one dumpy transport rig that only had two pistons driving into a national transportation outfit. My old man says Les is one of the most brilliant businessmen in Canada. And he knows the guy. The guy's loaded but you wouldn't know it by the way he lives, he's not living in Rockcliffe or some fancy place in Kanata. Henderson's not into that showboat stuff."

"Ever talk to him?"

"No. Not much. Not much reason to. I work in the shipping–receiving end. On the loading docks. Where's this going? I can't follow the drift of this. I'm half cut, Knight." He gave a fat fatuous good-guy grin.

"It's nothing to do with Mr Henderson. It's an employer of Liz's."

"Who?"

"I can't divulge the person."

"Okay." He sat for a moment slouched in thought. "What's this got to do with Liz?"

"I'm not certain yet but—"

"You're not thinking of Bill di Cesare just 'cause he works at Henderson's outfit?"

"Why do you ask?"

"Ah, for nothing. Bill's okay but he's a nerd. A computer crackhead. He's desperate, he can't get laid. I like the guy. He's useful. Like a lot of nerds. But you don't want to really hang out with his kind. He's kinda a drag."

"How's Bill di Cesare useful?"

Stanley chuckled.

"Come on. Give a guess. He does papers in stats for the guys. He knocks off the stats homework like a chimp chomps back bananas. He's a wiz kid at calculus. Makes a good buck, that's how Liz and I got to know the jerk."

"What did he do for Liz Strachan?"

"Nothing." Stanley grinned, "Okay, he did her stats in the psych course. She aced it."

"I understand Liz Strachan is pretty sharp in school. I can't imagine she'd need that sort of help."

"She is. She is. But she's a busy lady. Liz asked me to scout around for somebody."

"Are you certain Bill di Cesare did her homework?"

"Yeah. I intro'd them."

"I see. Did Bill di Cesare go out with Liz Strachan?"

"What? No way. Who tol' you that?"

"Nobody said he did, it's just that someone suggested that Bill di Cesare might have gone out with or, well, might have asked Liz Strachan out."

"That's crap." Stanley laughed, "Liz would never go out with a tube of toothpaste like di Cesare."

"Well did you intro Bill di Cesare to Ms Yonge?"

"Sure."

"Did he go out with or sleep with Ms Yonge?"

"Sleep with Yonge? No way. He asked her out. I told you. But she brushed him off."

I got up. "Thanks for the beer, Ed." I set the beer down on the table.

"You hardly touched it."

"I got to drive. Lot of driving this evening."

"Sure."

I went to the door.

"Hey Knight let me know as soon as you hear anything about Liz. I've been having fierce nightmares. I dreamt I was in bed with Connie Yonge. Can you believe it?" He laughed, "Now that's a nightmare. Okay. She got up with a knife and started pumping me in the chest with the blade. There was blood everywhere. Everywhere. Now that part of the freakin' dream is no joke. Even if being in bed with that, that that is a joke. She's more Bill's type. He so badly wants to lay her. Go figure it out." Stanley shrugged his shoulder and chuckled.

"A dream like that would shake up anybody."

"It was a helluva bad dream. Shook me down to my socks. Like being locked inside a locker with a bobcat and never getting out. Locked inside forever. Right rippin' 'n' rockin' trip. I was trying to get outside that bloody dream and I couldn't do it. At least not until I woke up from it. Thank god I woke up. Then I was outside. You know it's all on account of me being really worried about Liz. What the heck, it was only a dream. And like my mom used to say when watching the horror video, it's only a movie. Tomorrow's school. And I'd say, now that's the real nightmare. Well actually even that was alright. I was pretty good at it." Stanley laughed.

I parked on a side street and walked to the hotel. I rang up the Strachans from the desk phone. They told me to come straight up. They were impatient and anxious.

I sat in the soft chair by the lounge window. Frank Strachan was working a martini. Mary was drinking a glass of white wine.

"Drink, Mr Knight?"

"No thanks. I've still got a long night ahead of me."

My cellphone rang. It was Lynda. I went out into the hallway.

"I want to see you, Alec. I'm lonesome to see you."

"I'll come by. I'm almost finished with seeing a client. I'll be by in a half an hour or so."

I went back into the hotel suite.

"Mr Knight." Frank Strachan stared at me. "Have you made any headway?"

"I'm still getting much information from many sources."

"I know we seem impatient but between you and me and my wife, we're beginning to think horrible thoughts the longer the time passes between Liz last being seen and today."

"From experience I realize these situations are frustrating, even sometimes distressing and difficult. I reiterate that Lajoie–Chang Associates has put all its resources at this case's disposal."

"Mr Knight, I realize Georges Lajoie has an excellent reputation. A good friend of ours, a fellow I went to law school with who is a prominent criminal lawyer in Toronto recommended Georges Lajoie. But when all is said and done an excellent reputation is not enough in itself. It does not alone solve the situation. We need some concrete results." He sat down near me in the matching window chair and rested his big thick hand on my knee. "This situation is causing us tremendous anguish. Today we spoke with the police and they indicated to us that they believe our daughter has left the city with an older gentleman. Although they would not state precisely who they believed that person to be. The detective in charge, although he was sympathetic, said that there are aspects of our daughter's behaviour and the people she associated with that suggest that she has not gone missing but has probably left the city of her own free will and will return. They have spoken with what they describe as various interested parties and unfortunately some of these people are quite unsavoury."

"Frank."

Frank Strachan looked at his wife.

"Mary."

"I think Mr Knight is working hard."

"I've been on this case near non-stop since the morning when I first spoke with you."

Strachan leaned back and took a huge breath. He started to weep. It was not a heavy crying but a slow sad series of small tears that smeared his face.

"Let me tell you Mr Knight I'm thinking some horrible thoughts after the conversation with the police detective."

"The Ottawa Police Service is top notch Mr Strachan. There are some very sharp officers in the criminal investigative services."

"I can tell the detective does not believe that Liz is a missing person. He didn't say so but he as much as said it."

"But did the police detective actually say that she wasn't missing? That this wasn't a missing person's case, Mr Strachan?"

"Well, implied it. Oh he says it is a crime against persons in the category of, er, potentially a major crime. But all the while in his other words, the way he speaks to us, he seems to be shifting it over to the category of whereabouts unknown or some other jargon. I don't know how they shuffle and downgrade the cases, it's not my area of law. I've got rotten thoughts."

"Don't Mr Strachan. From experience, let me convey to you that you and the other members of your family need to think hopeful thoughts."

"Fine thoughts, Mr Knight? Fruitless thoughts."

"Not at all. Stay hopeful. I've seen people who went missing appear or be found quite suddenly when a few key details came to light that had been overlooked. Ms Strachan, you mentioned that your daughter Liz had suffered some sort of head trauma when in the car accident."

"That's correct. Momentary. Liz was knocked unconscious during the car accident. She actually has no recall of the event. But she was thoroughly checked by a neurologist and was fine after the accident. Apart from the temporary loss of memory no other loss."

"Has she ever experienced a memory lapse or been unconscious since then?"

"Not to my knowledge."

"Recurrent amnesia is a possibility. It is known to occur years later after a head trauma."

Frank Strachan stared at me. He took out a handkerchief and wiped his face.

"Excuse me Mr Knight."

"It's understandable. You might want to have Liz's medical records checked. Could you do that?"

"I suppose we could try. We'll speak to her doctor but I'm not certain they'll disclose anything." Mary Strachan sipped her drink.

"Mr Knight," Frank Strachan touched my knee. "We spoke to the police about the bulletins they had put out but they have come up with nothing. They ask us to be patient until they have heard from other police services across the country."

"Mr Strachan, your daughter could still be in the Ottawa vicinity."

"But the police department does not think that is so. In fact the detective is persuaded, based on her luggage and her past patterns of travel, that Liz has left the city. Why do you hold that opinion? It is actually contrary to what the police believe."

"Partly based on the people who know her and partly based on my survey of the train and bus stations and the airport. Admittedly Liz could have driven out of town with someone. If something comes to light in that direction then I'll pursue it immediately."

"Waiting is futile. It breeds anxiety."

"Patience is a necessity in such a situation. There is another matter which I regret I have to broach which might unsettle you but I can't see how it can be avoided. And it might in fact make understandable the more cautious position the police are beginning to take towards Liz's disappearance."

Mary Strachan looked at her husband then me.

"By all means Mr Knight. Please go ahead."

"You neglected to be forthright with regard to your daughter's past. And that has obscured things and certain associations she might have with certain individuals."

"Such as?"

"She's no doubt bisexual and has had several affairs. Did you tell the Ottawa police about Liz's past experiences?"

"Certainly not."

"In itself it is not overwhelming. Sexual experience is various. In investigative work we see all sorts."

"Excuse me, Mr Knight, but Liz is not all sorts. My daughter is not a lesbian, bisexual, or anything of that sort."

"Ms Strachan, please give me a moment. Nothing really shocks. You needn't have withheld such information. It would have remained confidential. And it would have helped in the search for your daughter. Best to let the police know. Although they probably have it."

"Our daughter's reputation is important. A few indiscretions in adolescence doesn't make a person, whatever. Our daughter is not a lesbian. This is so distasteful. Really disgusting."

"Your daughter hasn't got a reputation that she worries about, Ms Strachan."

"That's terrible. That's an appalling thing to say."

"Not really. She hasn't one reputation, it appears that she has a half dozen or dozen reputations. Depending on who she is sexually involved with at any given moment."

"Mr Knight, you're going too far. You do not know our daughter."

"That's probably part of the reason why the police may have backed off just a little from the case as a missing person case. Liz probably has at least a couple of relationships that make her vulnerable. Reckless even. What's more, you didn't disclose to me that she had a turbulent adolescence and you didn't get along. By the way, the police find out these things and it tends to influence their assessment of the character of the persons involved."

"That was years ago. Character has nothing to do with this."

"Nothing is ever years ago. Everything is contemporary Ms Strachan. Our pasts in the form of time leave us behind, but we don't leave our pasts behind. Liz has got herself involved with many people who could cause her trouble, difficulties."

"What sort of people? Who are they?"

"I suppose they are the unsavoury people you alluded to that the police detective insinuated Liz was connected with. You need not conceal this from yourselves or be embarrassed. Most parents who come to us as clients don't know a side of their children's lives. Sometimes they don't even know their children at all. And Liz, although she is your daughter she is no longer a child. In any event, no need to go into details concerning these particular individuals at this juncture, it can wait, but there is also another vital fact I need. Mr Strachan would you mind if I had a word alone with your wife?"

"I don't see why I can't hear everything you have to say."

"Frank, do as Mr Knight requests. It'll be fine. Go have a drink in the bar."

Frank Strachan got up, he looked weary and there was trudge in his step as he left.

"Okay Mr Knight what is this about? I'm beginning to get a little short with your manner. It's gone too far. And Lajoie–Chang is not showing much for all the money that is being spent."

"One question. Who did you have an affair with twenty-five years ago?"

"This is too much. We hired you, Mr Knight, to find our daughter not investigate our private lives. Frankly I've had it with you people.

Highly recommended or not. I can see nothing for all the money we've spent. Now it turns out you aren't doing the job but simply rooting around looking for malicious gossip. I've heard about your sort. Your type."

"Fine. You don't need me." I stood up, "I'll write up my final report and submit Lajoie–Chang's account statement if that is what you prefer."

"I know when I'm speaking to an upstart. You're an utter mediocrity."

"Better an utter mediocrity than to utter mediocrities." I smiled.

"I'm going to speak to Georges Lajoie. This is contemptible."

"It'll do you no good. It'll be a waste of time. Mr Lajoie will back me on this case. He told you at the outset that you were to give me full cooperation which means full disclosure. Lajoie–Chang does not deal with clients who refuse. Missing persons cases can rarely be solved without going through messy family relations, family history. It's the 401 of a missing person case."

"You're too much. Over the top."

"Fine. I'm sorry about this. I'm really concerned for your daughter." I stood up. "A small word of advice. Please don't speak to the police this way. We're private investigators, we have to take such nonsense. But they aren't. They don't like to waste their time, they are working on behalf of the public, their duty is to protect the public interest, not any one private individual's personal opinion, desire, or reputation for that matter. I wish you the best of luck in your search for your daughter. And I mean that. You may not believe this but I am genuinely concerned."

"Wait Mr Knight." Mary Strachan stood up and stared directly into my eyes. She had nice eyes but her face was a little puffy from the wine. Initially, she had seemed composed but now she appeared vulnerable while sustaining an erect and dignified posture. "Why do you need to know this? Something that possibly happened years ago, is it truly germane?"

"In my opinion it could be. It might well shed light on a number of anomalous facts that are only opaque."

"This can't have anything to do with Liz's disappearance. But I will tell you this much. Many years ago I had an affair with a married man. The man was nobody in Ottawa. He lived in Kingston. He was an engineer in the oil industry. He was ten years older than me. He's dead now. He died five years ago in Calgary. My husband knows I had an affair but not who it was with. I don't want him to know. It's in our past."

"I see. Could Liz have had contact with her biological father? Or be off in search of him?"

Mary Strachan kept staring into my face but said nothing, her eyes blinked a few times then she said, "No. It's not possible. I cannot see it. Liz has no knowledge of that affair. Frank and I have kept it between ourselves. I don't want to hurt my husband. Frank accepts Liz. He's never reproached me. He's been ever so loyal. Will that suffice?"

"I suppose at this juncture. If you say the man has died. And you are certain Liz has no knowledge of the affair."

"I spoke a little hastily. Please stay on the case. Brenda says she has real confidence in you. Brenda trusts you, Mr Knight, that means something. I consider Brenda a good judge of character."

"Fine. Say good-bye to your husband."

I sat in the parked car and looked at the cellphone. Call Inky Baby. I blocked number display and digited the number. The phone rang on the other end. A woman's voice answered.

"Hello."

"I'd like to speak with Inky."

"Who's this?"

"Tell Inky it's," I glanced through the windshield, "it's Lantern."

"Inky's not here. You want to leave a message." The woman's voice was a little raspy with the sound of smoke. But it was a voice with a rich immediacy to it. The sort of voice I had not heard in years. It was direct and knowing in its tone, even in its brevity it had confidence.

"That's alright just tell him that Lantern called."

"No number?"

"Please just tell him I'll try later."

"Just as you like."

"Thanks."

The woman's voice disappeared. I despised cellphones. They made me feel worse than credit card or loan forms. I tossed the phone on the car seat, who needs this crap? Then I drove over to Lynda's place on Wilbrod Street near Strathcona Park overlooking the river. As I was parking the Honda I felt a sudden jolt, a car had rear-ended me. I got out. A tall fellow in leather got out of an Olds. I recognized the car immediately.

"Hey mac, whadefuckyadoin'?"

"Sorry about that. But I could have swore you nudged me."

"No fucking way."

"Let's take a look, maybe it's nothing much."

"Dontchya know how to park, asshole."

"Hey be cool. Come on let's take a look."

I noticed his buddy get out of the passenger seat. I glanced at the car bumpers. Although there was a slight new mar on the Honda it was not enough to get into an argument.

"Hey look buddy, it's next to nothing. Just touched bumpers. Let's call it even." I smiled.

"No way. Look at that. You put a dent in my car."

I peered where he pointed.

"That looks like an old ding. Even in the dark it looks like it's got a little rust on it. Couldn't be recent. Come on let's call it equal. No hard feelings." I started to turn away.

"No way." The guy grabbed my arm and yanked me around. I could feel the strength of a weightlifter in his grasp. As I spun around he drove a fist into my gut. It was like a bucket of nails. I bent over, he slugged me again. I tried to move aside but I was too winded. His buddy grabbed me from behind and pinned my arms. He gave me two more solid punches in the solar plexus. This guy knew how to smack, he wasn't looking to leave a subdued impression. I kicked up and hit him in the crotch but it didn't do enough damage to stop him. He raised his fist again to whack me in the face, I turned my head just fast enough to get it more on the side below the cheek rather than take a direct blow on the schnoz, otherwise I could have kissed it a long goodbye. He gave me a kick in the stomach and his friend let me drop down on the asphalt.

"Watch where you're driving asshole. Get the message."

They got in the Olds and took off.

I was crying. I dragged myself up and limped to Lynda's place and pressed the buzzer. She came down in a kimono.

"Alec. Alec."

She got me to her apartment and I flopped out on the chesterfield.

"What happened?"

"I got mugged."

"I better get you to emergency." She rushed into her bedroom and came out dressed so fast like she was working in the garment trade.

"I don't want to go. I'm just winded. I'll be okay."

"We better call the police."

"Wait."

"I don't understand."

"Wait. I got to think it through. I think it's the case I'm on."

"What kind of case is this? This isn't normal. It's too much, Alec. You look terrible. We've got to get you to a hospital. Got to call the police."

I stretched out on the chesterfield. The pain eased off and I began to feel better.

"Nothing. I'm going to be alright."

"You look terrible. What kind of case is this?"

"It's a missing person case. I want a glass of water."

"Where did they hit you? Are you sure you should drink?"

"In the head a couple of times. A couple of times in the stomach. I need some water."

She brought me a glass of water. I drank it slowly in very little sips. And finally sat up.

"The side of your face is swollen and red, Alec. Below the eye. It looks terrible."

"Lucky not my finest feature." I rubbed my nose and laughed, "That slugger could have knocked it clean off my face and clear across the river into Hull. I can see it in the morning papers. The nose. A lonesome nose was discovered early this morning wandering the streets of Hull. After doing hiphop all night in the beer halls. Owner wishing to lay claim to errant nose—"

"Stop it Alec. This is serious. I'm going to take you to emergency. What kind of missing person case could get you like this?"

"Do you really want to know?"

"Yes."

"Don't say anything to anyone?"

"You know I wouldn't, anyway you know very well I am leaving for Japan."

"Don't bring that up or I will not talk."

"Can't you see I care? Don't be that way."

"Listen." I paused and looked at Lynda, I wanted to embrace her and stop talking.

"Well." Lynda folded her arms across her breasts. Her kimono was worn, I'd hardly noticed before. She rubbed her upper arm in a slow but worried way. "Go on. I'm listening. Don't play silent picture show, I see it in your eyes. I know you."

"A young woman, she disappeared from an underground car garage. But I really can't talk about it. In fact I mustn't. Lajoie and Chang would snatch my shoelaces and buttons."

"Did you find out anything?"

"I'm still working the case. I can't talk about it."

"What happened to the woman?"

"Don't know yet. The police were investigating but they seem to have backed off. Especially once they began to dig into her life and shovel through her history. It looks like she might have disappeared from the underground garage in her apartment building last Monday afternoon. Nobody's seen her since. The police are now of the mind that she left town with someone. Of her own free will. They may even believe that she is in another city. I don't know."

Lynda sat down and for a long time stared at me. I said nothing. I stared back at her. Then she said. "You look like a scarecrow."

"Scared crow." I laughed.

"No. A scarecrow, one that speaks a speechless dialect. At least the blood, the colour is coming back into your face."

"I'll be alright."

"I'm worried."

"Don't be."

"What about the disappeared woman?"

I said nothing.

"Well."

"Honestly Lynda, I don't know. I'm worried. Between you and me it looks bleak. Too many permutations and combinations in this case with difficult people who she knew. Some real nasties. But to boot, even the woman's mother lies."

"Why?"

"'Cause her daughter's bi or lesbian and the mother doesn't like it or can't accept it."

"That's terrible. Then how can you find her if even people close to her are lying?"

I shrugged my shoulders.

"I found something of hers in the underground car garage that troubles me. The police missed it. We're going to have to turn it over to them."

"What?"

"A piece of jewellery. You should see it. A platinum, diamond and pearl ear clip."

"Pearl ear clip? Where was it?"

"I found it the second time I went back and looked around her car. You had to really look to find it. I was lucky. A fluke. It was behind the wheel and sort of underneath. I went back a third time and found CDs in the trunk. A pile of them. They looked like a half dozen blank CDs that you would buy at an office supply. No labels. No nothing. I thought it was a bunch of blank CDs but one had been used for photographs. That might be, well, forget it."

"No. Tell me, Alec."

"I can't mention what was on the CD but I mean, wouldn't you notice if you lost a platinum pearl ear clip?"

"I suppose I would if I could ever afford to have one." Lynda smiled.

"We're not talking Wal-Mart or Zeller's Lynda. The ear clip is worth thousands. The pearl's this big." I gestured with my fingers. "And Georges Lajoie says it's the real thing. And believe me Lajoie knows his gems. So it's got to be so."

"Tell me more."

"No. I'm wasted." I glanced at my watch.

"Let's go to bed." Lynda rubbed my shoulder.

"Sec. I got to make a phone call."

She gave me a rare look, one of exasperation.

"I'll be with you in a sec, okay. It's for work."

When Lynda went to the bedroom, I telephoned Inky Baby's number. The woman with the wonderful voice answered.

"Hello."

"Evening. Could I please speak to Inky."

"Ummh. Sec." I heard her call out, 'Did Inky arrive?' Someone said 'No, he's not in yet.' 'It's his caller.' 'Not here.' Her terrific voice returned to the telephone, "He's not here. Any message?"

"Tell him I'll call tomorrow morning."

"Give me your name."

"Lantern."

"No. That won't do." Her voice was passionate and commanding. I had not run up against such confidence, almost felt as if I could not defy her.

"He knows who I am."

"Right. But I don't and I don't like people calling my number who I don't know."

"I apologize, I don't mean to disturb you Ms, Inky gave me this number."

"Listen. This is my phone number. I didn't call you. You called me. Understand?"

"Yes."

"Give me your name and number."

I paused.

Then she said, "Okay. You got one last chance. I'll give Inky your message. But do not call this number again after tomorrow unless you are prepared to leave your name and number. Do you understand?"

"Fine. Thanks for your time."

"You're not welcome."

I clicked off and drifted off to the bedroom.

I was so far away that the planet Earth had vanished from existence, reduced to a single incinerated molecule in some distant galaxy. It was a reassuring sensation. I was going to stay with this dream.

Then Lynda nudged me awake, I looked up at her. She was sitting up. She looked so appealing, but unsettled.

"What is it? I was having a swell dream. A far away safe dream."

"Alec I'm worried. I'm worried about that woman. I had a bad dream."

"Everybody is having bad dreams. The guy who claims to love her is having bad dreams. I got to sleep. Really."

"Listen Alec I had a dream about that disappeared woman you're looking for."

"Lynda, you couldn't have. It's an empirical impossibility. You don't even know her. You never laid eyes on her."

"In the dream, she came speaking French."

"She speaks English."

"She was running across the garage to escape. Running towards a closed door."

"Sure."

"Don't mock. Did I ever tell you what happened to me in the subway when I was living in Toronto?"

"Go ahead."

"I was coming back on the subway. It was pretty late. I was going up the subway stairs and some creep grabbed my ankle from behind. I was lucky. I had a camera. I really nailed him with it. I was so lucky. I had it there close to me and turned around spontaneously, instinctively and let him have it. There was blood all down his face."

"Served him right. He got exactly what he deserved. Did the creep back off?"

"Yes. He ran up the subway stairs and into the street. The night. But in my dream the missing woman you're searching for was being chased by the subway prowler, he still had the blood streaming down his face. Waiting in the underground garage."

"That's a bad dream, Lynda. I shouldn't have said anything to you about the case. Lie down. Try to go back to sleep."

Lynda slipped down under the sheet. She gave me a hug.

"Alec?"

"Yes."

"Promise me something."

"Sure. Go ahead, take advantage of me when I'm not mens sana in corpore sano. Go ahead. You know I'm crazy about you and going to miss you. You leave for Japan and I'm going to the casino in hell, mens insana in corpore insano, no matter what the Saikelys say."

"Alec, promise me you'll go back to that car garage again and look."

"Here I am confessing, and you want me to work a mental overtime shift for Lajoie and Chang. What a drag."

"Go back there. No woman loses an ear clip like that and leaves it behind."

"Sure. Sure I'll go back. I'll do whatever you say. You and Georges Lajoie command my attention. This is mission imperative. This is your sublimated consciousness speaking."

"Stop it. Promise?"

"I promise. I'll even get Georges to go with me."

"There's a door there. Go to it."

"Alright. Everybody else is telling me what to do. Why not you. Minutes ago I was happy in another galaxy. Now I'm an alien back here on planet Earth. What dialect do I speak? You said it before. But I forget."

"A speehless dialect."

"Do I?"

"We all do."

"Is that the linguist speaking or Doc Freud?"

"No. And no. It's a worried woman."

# NINE

The next morning I phoned over to Split Second Transport and Warehouse to talk to Lester Henderson.

"I'm afraid Mr Henderson is very busy. May I take a message."

"Could you tell him it is an urgent matter regarding an intimate friend of his."

"One moment, please."

His assistant went off the line or left me on the line, depending on which end of the line one was dangling from.

"I'm sorry, but Mr Henderson is too busy."

"Actually this is urgent. It really is important."

Exasperation was her middle name by this point and although she did not know it I entirely empathized with her, she didn't need this at this hour of the morning in a busy warehouse.

Lester Henderson came on the line.

"What's this about Mr Knight?"

I spun him a line about Connie Yonge's friend Liz Strachan and asked if I could have fifteen minutes of his time. Henderson muttered an abrupt sure and hung up without saying good-bye.

The warehouse was in Nepean west of the Rideau River near Colonnade Road. A series of bleak prefab commercial and industrial buildings sprinkled with the odd eatery and beer joint to reinforce the waist line of the SUV set. But the moniker for this asphalt zone was the valley of mattresses. More king size mattresses were warehoused in this neighbourhood than in the entire city of Montreal. Something to accompany the monster liquid TV screens and swank bedroom sets in the three-car-garage houses for the nouveau mortgaged set. I drove through the Merivale Acres Business Park like I had entered the outer circle of a Wal-Mart parking lot where the multitude of determined SUV drivers morphed into earnest shoppers engaged in a major struggle with the satanic forces of the credit card.

The Split Second warehouse was a cinder block and aluminium building that ran the depth of a lot surrounded by an imposing and formidable chain link fence. Such precautionary measures announced that valued warehouse inventory even in transit has its price. The place also looked like it had been thrown up according to its name.

Henderson kept me waiting in a small outer office. This I thought only appropriate. Concerning time, Chang and Lajoie had taught me that the longer the mandatory wait the greater the prospect of a lead having substance. I was happily leafing my way through car, tractor and trailer, and truck mags. I was busy on my diploma in truck maintenance when Henderson finally came through. I recognized him though he gave me no such look of recognition.

"You Knight?"

"Yes. Mr Henderson?"

"Mac, I wouldn't be asking if I wasn't."

I offered a hand but he ignored it, he was already heading for his office door.

"Come this way. I haven't got much time."

His office was jammed with paper, customs and brokerage documents, invoices, statements, bills of lading and more. It looked mostly well organized except for the mare's nest on his desk.

"Okay what's this all about Mr Knight?'

"I've been hired to locate Liz Strachan."

"Let's see your licence."

This was more a command than a request. I showed my provincial ID.

"Okay. Sit down."

Henderson lit what looked like a nice cigar. "I give you fifteen minutes. Pretty busy. Got to move a lot of freight."

"I appreciate the time. It is my understanding that you know Liz Strachan."

"Not really. In a passing sort of way."

"That's all? That's not what I was led to believe."

"Nothing more. I can't say as I'd be certain to recognize her."

"Mr Henderson, I understand you had a more intimate relationship with her."

"No. Just someone to have a drink with."

"You know Connie Yonge?"

"Yeah. Yeah I know the lady."

"Intimately?"

"What's this intimately mean? Out with it. Get to it I'm a man of direct words, Mr Knight." Henderson smiled. "The only women I'm intimate with are my mother, my wife and my two daughters. Okay. I didn't get where I am by pussy-footing around with words. I handle a lot of freight but not intimately. You're not talking to some soft-headed slobbering bureaucrat. Some guy who doesn't know plain English. Tying his tongue into knots trying to avoid, to friggin' hide what he's got to say. Worried about stepping over the line, that he actually might say something that makes common sense. Means something. No way, mac. I don't talk that way. Get it?"

Henderson moved his cigar around in his fingers then tapped it against the ashtray.

"You do know Liz Strachan and Connie Yonge?"

"What's this all about? This isn't a shakedown?"

I shook my head.

"It better not be. 'Cause if it is, the loading dock's out there. And there are some boys who know how to use their hands for more than lifting."

"Nothing of that sort. This is concerning a missing person case. You can check with the police regarding the disappearance of Ms Strachan. I might even be doing you a favour by visiting you."

"How so? Sounds like guff."

"The police might come round soon."

Henderson said nothing and puffed on the smoke. The time outside with the mags told me to wait. I said nothing.

"Look around you, mac. This is a bonded warehouse. I cooperate with the police. And so what if I was getting something on the side, some socializing with a chick, what's that got to do with you?"

"Mr Henderson, do you know where Ms Yonge and Ms Strachan live?"

"I know where I live. Mac, I don't know where you live or for that matter anybody else. People move."

"They live in the same building. You were identified as being in the building approximately around the time Ms Strachan disappeared. Last Monday, the last Monday in August in the afternoon. And specifically in the underground garage with Ms Strachan."

"Must be a mistake. Mistaken identification. I was here in this warehouse. Okay. Got it?"

"On another occasion you were also with these women."

"Listen mac, I don't know this Ms Strachan."

"Sure you do, Mr Henderson you said as much. Some friends of yours know you spent time with her."

"I had maybe two drinks with the lady. She dropped by Yonge's apartment when I was there one day. She came in had a martini with us, left and she went about her business whatever it was and we went about ours."

"When was this?"

"Months ago. In the spring maybe March or April. Who knows. It's not exactly the kinda thing that I keep in my friggin' social calendar."

"And you haven't seen Liz Strachan since then?

"Nope." Henderson looked at his watch. I stared at his cigar then at his thin face. He puffed on the cigar, smoke came out. He wasn't savouring the cigar. It was unkind of me to ruin the pleasure of what looked like a pretty good cigar.

"Mr Henderson, do you know a Mr Joe Parsons?"

"I can't say as I immediately recognize the name."

"He's an acquaintance of Ms Yonge. And I believe Ms Strachan."

"Maybe so but not of mine. I'm not intimate with him." Henderson smiled.

"Ms Yonge works for Mr Parsons' escort agency. LTD."

Henderson shrugged his shoulders.

"That means something to you."

"Nope. I told you I'm not into your intimacies. We're running out of time here Knight. See this, I got a pile of freight to move." He gestured with the cigar in his fingers towards the mare's nest of paper in front of him. "My assistant out there is tearing open just as much, she's a real doberman pinscher when it comes to the envelopes and invoices. I got real business to attend to. I'm not interested in verbal hanky panky."

"I had the impression that you hired Ms Yonge's and Ms Strachan's services through Mr Parsons' agency."

"I told you I don't know Ms Strachan. What's more why would I go and hire a jerk-off when I got a pecker of my own." He laughed.

"That's what I was led to believe. So I was wondering—"

"Being led to believe something by a fool or a liar or a loudmouth is more idiotic than dreaming up the story yourself Knight. You're skirting round the skirt." He grinned. "Take it from me, far better to get inside. Anyway why pay twice? I don't need that sort of graft outfit. That's for jerks. Expose 'emselves to extortion. Forget it. If I wanted that kinda trouble, I'd stroll Dalhousie looking for a floozie."

"But Ms Yonge said she made her arrangements with you through LTD Escort."

"You're dreaming in pixels." He shoved at the pile of papers on the desk, "Look Knight, you got nothing here. You trying some little extortion racket?"

"Never. This is a legitimate inquiry, Mr Henderson, in the interests of some very genuinely concerned parents. You know the young lady—"

"Listen I got a lawyer. I don't know nothing about Parsons and LPD or TLD or whatever agency. This is still a free country and I can screw around if I like with whoever I want without the chatter. Or the friggin' Charter for that matter."

"You certainly can."

Henderson puffed on the cigar.

"Big shits do it. Little shits do. Learn your verbs. We're a fucking nation. You're too young to remember, Trudeau give us that, we can party. A fucking nation makes a happy nation." Henderson gave a salacious grin. "Getting a little on the side ain't no crime."

"I suppose."

"No suppose. Believe me, you'll get there one day. You married, Knight?"

"Yes."

"Kids?"

"One and one on the way."

Henderson grinned.

"Happy?"

"Very."

"The young lady happy?"

"Still wants me. Hasn't booted me down the porch steps and taken up with the postman."

"Well wait twenty years. Then you'll be a barking dog."

"I'll still love her."

"But will she still love you? Knight, you don't get it. You being in the business that you're in Mr Knight, divorce is your bread and butter but you got to know divorce isn't what it used to be for a guy with assets."

"Certainly isn't."

"Then you understand."

"I understand."

"Maybe I spoke a little hastily with you. A little rough but a man has to protect his interests. And I protect my interests, Mr Knight, if you understand my meaning. Protection comes first."

"I understand you entirely Mr Henderson."

"Good. I'm glad we've reached an understanding. Like any two reasonable men. Reasonable men remember what's important. Unreasonable men remember the unimportant things." He stood up. I got up.

"Thank you for your time Mr Henderson."

"My pleasure. Believe me even if you don't believe me. Mr Knight, I can tell you're a smart kinda guy."

"Thank you, I'm still learning but I do appreciate compliments."

He offered his hand. We shook hands.

I was to meet with Lajoie. Before I left I had given the Strachan file to Cheryl Perron and asked her to give it and the CD to Georges. I had anticipated Henderson would stiff me in the interview. It was a hard luck gamble. But certain interviews have to happen even if the talk on both sides is nothing but lies, implied threats and gestural pantomime. Buster Keaton is still alright to watch, talkies only supersede so much in the silent pics. It's still amusing to watch certain monsters chase a character around a table or a davenport flop on chaste lovers or a Murphy bed fall down on the head of a baddie. A confrontation with Henderson had been risky but I thought I might shake something loose from a guy in debt running scared and not wanting his marriage to go down the tube. At least I figured that he had screwed around with Liz Strachan and Connie Yonge, one or both, and probably come to them through Joe Parsons.

The weather had grown warmer again, I was sweating in my suit jacket. This was the last ragged end of summer in the Ottawa valley. Just right for cruising the Gatineau on a mountain bike hoping not to get clipped by a limo speeding towards Meech Lake and Kingsmere.

I loosened my tie and hauled myself into the office.

"Alec, you look like you were just zapped in a microwave." Cheryl smiled.

"I near was. I just came out of a hot warehouse talking to a dude who's screwing 'round on his wife and he wants me to be the blanket. Not a comfortable ménage à trois. To quote a prominent chief of police, there's a lot of things that can happen with a blanket."

Cheryl laughed.

"I gave Georges the file and CD. He says he can see you this morning."

"Thanks. You, you I can trust."

"By the way, Alec, you got two phone calls. One from a guy who left a simple initial 'I' but no phone number, he said you'd know what it would mean. And another from a woman. Sec. Here it is, a Ms Madeleine Masson."

I took the slips and went back to my office. I phoned Inky Baby.

The passionate woman answered, when she heard my voice she said simply, "He's here." Inky Baby came on the phone.

"Hello Lantern. There's something out there. But like, the people I spoke to are afraid. Do ya understand?"

"Yes. Is there anything I could do? Anything that might help."

"No. I don't think so. I can't give ya any names. These people they're like afraid of some people. They're afraid of the cops. Worse, they're afraid of 'em giving things out that will go to snitches in the street who will take it further down the line. These are not my friends. Do you understand?"

"Yes."

"These guys aren't with us. Like us. These guys, like, are jus' scrambling. Scrapin'." He paused. "They have like no organization. They don't trust people much, like anyone, including people like me because who I'm with. It's really complicated stuff. They're very suspicious of people like us. Not you, but I mean like the people I hang out with. Something is out there. They're kinda afraid of guys like your party. Some of them said they heard—" Inky Baby said nothing for a moment.

"Inky?"

"I'm still here. Sec."

I heard creaking of wood like footsteps going across a wooden floor in a distant room, a door closed, the sounds echoed over the cellphone, and I waited, it seemed a long time, muffled creaking of wood again, the slipping of socks on wood, then Inky Baby's voice came back.

"Listen. I need a few more days." His voice sounded a little twisted and out of shape, even anxious, a quality that I had not heard in Inky. "But you tell your party. That the ... the ... the person is maybe travelling."

"Where?"

"I got to get off this phone. My friend said I cannot, she said I cannot give out this number to anybody without her say–so or unless she has their number. She's a really good person but she's kinda pissed off with me for me giving ya her number. Don't give it to anybody, k?"

"I wouldn't. Don't worry."

"You give me your number and I'll give it to her, that okay?"

"Fine. Give her my cell number." I gave it to Inky Baby. "But don't call this office number."

"Whatever. Don't use call blocking when you call her cell. K?"

"Fine. Where's the person travelling?"

"You got to wait. Give me some time."

"Fine. You need anything Inky?"

"No. No. I'm doing this as a favour for someone. Someone I really care about. I don't want nothing from nobody. K."

"Thanks Inky."

When I got off I dialed Warnock. The police detective was not available, I left a message. I phoned Burley's office but he was not available. I left a message with his legal assistant. I then looked at the note from Madeleine Masson. I called her number.

"Ms Masson, this is Alec Knight. I understand you phoned this morning and requested that I call you."

"Yes, Mr Knight. I appreciate you taking the time to return my call so promptly."

"No problem. My pleasure."

"Well," she paused, "Mr Knight, I am not calling concerning the disappearance of the young woman you inquired after. But I do wish to speak with you regarding another matter."

"Yes."

"It concerns my husband's death." She paused.

"Yes."

"I must admit that when you initially called I felt uncomfortable speaking with a private investigator. But after you left and over the evening I gave it some thought. I should say that I entertained the notion of engaging the services of Lajoie–Chang Associates. I must admit to a hesitancy and I do not wish to go into details on the phone but it is difficult living in this—what shall I call it—empirical limbo. The fact of the death of my husband so to speak, but no facts of the death itself. The crime itself."

The other line flashed up.

"I think the best thing to do would be for you to come in and speak with Georges Lajoie, the senior partner. He can give you some notion of what we may be able to do."

"I'd very much like that. It would be a pleasure to meet Mr Lajoie."

"Fine, I'll transfer you over to Cheryl Perron and have her set up an appointment. Just give her some idea when it would be best."

"This afternoon or tomorrow afternoon would be fine. I'll be in town."

"Just let Ms Perron know that."

"One other thing, Mr Knight."

"Yes."

"Would you be working the case? Having met you, I would prefer someone I feel comfortable with. Someone I have at least spoken with."

"That is a decision that rests with Mr Lajoie and Mr Chang. But I'll let them know of your request. And you might just mention it to them."

"Thank you, Mr Knight."

I transferred Madeleine Masson as quickly as possible over to Cheryl. Then I listened to the message, it was from Pierre Willett. I phoned Willett.

"I seen one of those guys come in the apartment building. He's gone into Connie Yonge's place."

"Fine. I'll be straight over. If I don't make it in time could you try to record his licence plate number and the car model."

"Sure thing. Like I said I'm sharp with numbers."

I clicked off, told Cheryl to tell Lajoie that something urgent came up and I'd catch him later, then I ran out like I was on steroids doing the hundred metre dash.

I arrived at the apartment building like a wasted lover having multiple affairs running between bedrooms. Willett was hanging round the white cement bench outside the apartment building, watching pigeons and murdering a cigarette. He looked red-eyed and hung over.

"You come too late Knight. You missed your main man."

I sat on the bench with Willett.

"But you got a good look at the fellow?"

"Sorta."

"Well Ray, what did you see?"

"To be honest I'm not right certain which of her lover boys it was. I tell you, from the time I was shoved into the principal's office to get the strap, men in suits sort of looked pretty pushy and pretty much all the same to me."

"Isn't that the truth." I laughed. And Willett laughed as well.

"Mind you I figure a suit's got its place, weddings and funerals. There it's an equalizer. But suits 're not exactly my crowd. Don't take offence." He gazed at me up and down and grinned, "Not exactly the most friendly kinda people in this world. But you're kinda different, I figure. You're alright Knight. I know you only wearing that get-up 'cause you got to on account of the job."

"I suppose. You read it right Ray, myself I'm not exactly keen on this." I flapped the suit jacket as if to dismiss it.

"I can tell you go for real trousers. And C & W."

"You bet Ray."

Now I knew we were talking more than suits and men but the necessary accessories, jewellery, wallets and money, and looking at

Willett I could see he had a point. He'd probably never seen enough bucks in the wallet to call it a billfold. I was near there myself. I'd leave Lajoie–Chang in a minute if someone came rattling a tin can with more coin in it. I eased my hand into my pocket. Willett observed the gesture.

"But as it was, I was kinda lucky to have a pen handy. I know them guys the city medical officers condemn smoking but a smoke pack can be a handy thing to have around. Kinda like a notepad. I scribbled down the fellow's licence like you suggested. Right here on the cigarette pack. But I did it outside so the bylaw officer don't catch me." Willett grinned.

"Ray you're a good man. No phoney in a suit. And to boot a law abiding citizen."

"You bet I am. Only laws I ever violated was speeding, smoking dope on Sunday, drinking on my front lawn when the LCBO said it was illegal, screwing around with my neighbour's wife when he was at church and being too drunk to go to my former boss's funeral. Although I come to my senses and made the after funeral feast." He puffed and grinned with his quicksilver thin lips. I smiled. "By the way you want some inside dope?"

"Can always use it. Might come in handy."

"Smoking on Sundays is better than Mondays. That's a kinda law, Knight."

"How so, Ray?"

"The Willett smoke bylaw says a guy got to smoke on Sundays and Tuesdays."

"How's that Ray?"

"Them the most boring days of the week."

"You're a shrewd fellow Ray."

Willett revealed the number. And I furnished a greater numerical revelation. He slipped the bill into his trouser pocket.

"Ray, what model of car?"

"Blue BMW. Pretty fresh off the line. The paint job looked so new I could almost smell the paint. You put your hand on it you'd have smudged it."

"Thanks." I got up as if to leave, then turned back. "Oh by the way, you mentioned Connie Yonge's car."

"Did I?"

"I thought you did. Before I think. You said it was—"

"She drives a yellow Mustang."

"That's right. Thanks Ray."

"No problem. Anytime."

I went back to my car which I had parked around the corner from the garage entrance. I called in the licence plate to Cheryl.

I sat in the car. I put on my Lynx baseball cap and sunglasses, slouched low and waited. I was entering nothing-nothing land. This could be a long wait, I wished I had pissed before leaving the office. The heat was coming on. It was going to get up there. The cellphone rang, it was Cheryl.

"BMW."

"Right."

"Ownership under the name of Peter Slowikowsky."

"Maybe we've hit something."

"Want his traffic record?"

"Sure, to pass the time. Maybe I'm in for a long wait."

Cheryl gave it to me, nothing aggravating but he did get caught speeding down the 417.

Avoiding boredom. I was lolling back down into nothing-nothing land, balancing myself between patience and observation. An almost automatic subliminal alertness that did not tax my brain but kept things under watch. This was a good state to be in.

A long while went by. When I floated to the surface I felt dehydrated. Then the garage door rolled open and a yellow Mustang spun out. It headed towards the 417. I followed. It sped east on the 417. I kept some distance tailing Connie Yonge. She cruised through the suburb wasteland of Gloucester and Orléans onto provincial highway 17 heading east towards Montreal along the Ottawa River.

She drove on through the farmlands of Prescott and Russell County until she reached Alfred. A stretched-out small town with its share of placidness, fear and gossip. Too sedate to be as quiet and obscure as it presented itself.

The Mustang turned off into the gravel parking lot of a motel. I kept on a half block to a gas station. I filled up the tank of my car, took a quick voyage to the pissoir. When I came back out, I tried to chat up the garage man while I was paying but he was too busy to really want to talk. I grabbed a cheese sandwich and ginger ale and sat at the picnic table on a little patch of grass by the gas station and waited, yawning my way through a newspaper, the National Ghost with its spooks, horrors, fears and hysteria. Her yellow Mustang sat parked in the motel lot. The garage man gave me a nervous look. A half hour later an OPP car glided into the garage lot.

Just as the OPP patrolman scrutinized my driver's licence and provincial investigator's permit, Connie Yonge came out of the motel, got in her car and drove off west down 17, back towards Ottawa. The patrolman seemed displeased, as if I was going to bring more scandal down on the locals. He took the documents back to the police cruiser and sat with them like it was a ham and cheese sandwich. I feigned indifference and kept reading the Ghost quoting virtuous former prime ministers on the accomplishments of the free trade agreement, politicians on the achievements of the casinos, the justice minister on legislation.

The policeman brought the licence and permit back. He was friendly now, I had to be friendly back to ease his boredom cruising the highways and sideroads of eastern Ontario where there were more rocks than crops. He got back in his patrol car gave a wave and a smile to the garage man as if to indicate all was swell and pulled out. I waited until the police car disappeared then drove over to the motel parking lot.

I was just about to get out of the car when I sighted Norman Burley come out of the motel office and head across the gravel lot to a silver Cadillac. He looked pissed off, his big head ploughing the air, his face had a grim look around the mouth. His straight grey-blond hair looked a little out of line as if messed shaking his head in vehement speech or by a siesta in the sack. This contrasted with his fine conservative suit. With the grimace, the part askew and the beginning of angry jowls, Burley did look like a reformed alcoholic but one who wasn't enjoying the dignified state of sobriety. For a moment he looked like he had maybe even hit the bottle and knocked back a few swigs. But I put a brake on those thoughts, after all why think badly of someone you hardly know. Burley got in the Caddy and drove off. I was tempted to follow but let it pass. The guy was in some kind of grumpy mood.

I went in the motel. A middle-aged woman was behind the counter doing the ledger books while watching with side glances a soap. Her hair had a vehement red rinse that turned the roots orange. She was friendly and gave a smile.

I smiled and intro'd myself, it turned her mood.

"We've had enough trouble in this town for a century. Okay."

"Yeah, it's tough, the big city media types beating up on the small places in the counties when they got nothing better and are bored stiff. I can really sympathize with you, I'm originally from southwestern Ontario before moving up here to eastern Ontario."

"Whereabouts?"

"Exeter. It's in Huron County."

"Never heard of the place."

"Near Grand Bend. That's a resort town on Lake Huron. Plenty motels in the area. I got friends running a motel and they let me know it is no easy task."

"Yeah. I heard of that place, 'pose to be pretty wild in the summer."

"Yeah. It's fun. But the big city media people give us the same kind of aggravation you folks see around Alfred."

"They certainly do and for no other reason as I can see than to get people to watch the TV news and sell newspapers that aren't worth next to nothing. If I believed half of what I see and hear in the media, I wouldn't even be on this planet. Frankly I despise the TV reporters. Despise them people. Phonies. They got no respect for people suffering misfortune."

"I assure you, I am no reporter."

"Well let me tell you, lucky for you because I would never ever rent to another reporter in my life. They come. They go. But I stay. And have to look my neighbours in the eye." The motel woman looked me in the eye, she gave me the gospel gaze.

In the banality of the world I'm just a private eye for hire with no sophisticated optics but no one's going to tell me how private an organ the eyeball is. By observation I know the eye, however mysterious, is anything but private. The wanderer. Promiscuity is its long middle name. At moments of visual confrontation with utter strangers, I appreciate the tact my mother taught me, to look people in the eye as a show of respect. The eye can feign a lot of things but it can't fake respect, worse between strangers it often risks revealing mutual contempt or suspicion. Now my Latin and shop teacher, Mr Wolsey, was a more mundane moral instructor who lectured on the fine arts of vision, demanding direct eyeball contact from students out of respect for authority. Now that was quite another moral fable. And then came Lajoie, that connoisseur of the optical psychic arts, who advised me to be quick and direct in my sight and scrutiny. No PI could afford to be shifty-eyed and delaying. Best to immediately find some quality to respect in the person being interviewed. Looks, wealth, surroundings, even clothing. Although superficial, they might do, especially if the person took pride in them. But usually work was the best thing, the nonpareil thing, but the common thing, because it runs deep and requires no fakery on my part. Most people never quite receive the respect they deserve for the work they do. Work, like love, gives self-esteem. Even when it hurts. And it's pretty tough to be rude to someone who signals respect through the retina. Now it goes without saying the PI can't love everybody, that's risky business unless he wants to lose his licence to gullibility, stupidity or licentiousness, but he can convey respect to the common person. Of course there are glitches in this theory of an honest gaze, the hustlers and grifters who wouldn't sweat a straight job are problems. A low-stress lot if ever there was one. These sleazoids brag their cheating takes effort, skill, and brains, that's Hollywood hype, they actually hate work. And worse, these egomaniacs despise the common people like my mother and father and Mr and Mrs Lowe who stitch the world together. The logo, brand name and trademark of the petty con artist, swindler and fraudster is his utter contempt for work. So I learnt, in the field geometry of the gaze, velocity of vision is crucial to creating the sight lines.

The motel woman's stare was steady. I returned it with pure innocence. Until she relented and said, "Okay. I guess you look alright. Jus' what is it?"

"I'm on a good deed."

"How's that?"

"I'm looking for a missing person. A young woman. A student. I was hired by her parents to find her."

"Well now that's an entire different thing. The Jackson family's daughter Julie disappeared two years back. The farm out back behind the garage there. Sweet girl. Just disappeared. They thought some guy did some harm to her. But the police found nothing for more than two years. Then they found the poor girl out west in

Vancouver. Addicted to drugs and a prostitute. Poor thing. Family couldn't do anything for her. Wouldn't wish that on any parent. No, I wouldn't."

"Happen to see this young woman?" I showed the picture of Liz Strachan. The motel clerk gazed at it for quite a time as if she were under a spell.

"Lovely young woman. Face seems faintly familiar but to tell you the honest truth you best speak with my husband, John. He does most of the work at the front desk. It might catch his memory."

"Might he be around?"

"Yeah. Doing plumbing. He's down in room 12."

"I'll go down and see him if you don't mind."

"Suit yourself, go right ahead."

I went down to the motel room and knocked on the open door.

"Yeah. Come in," a man shouted. "I'm working on the plumbing in the bath."

I went in.

"'Lo."

"Howdy mister. I done told my wife not to rent this particular room until I was finished. You'll have go back to the front desk and get another room mister." This without looking up at me.

"No problem. I'm not here about renting this room. Your wife sent me down. You're John?"

"I still am. Some guests sneak away with stuff but they haven't as yet snitched my name." The guy in overalls with a fat gut was crouched over the toilet drain, he had removed the toilet and looked to be doing a repair. He finally looked up, "What is it then? If you're an asswipe salesman peddling paper bejesus we got enough to hold us until the next century."

"I'm a private investigator from Ottawa looking for a missing person."

"Well this isn't Hollywood mister. You're on the wrong movie set."

"Maybe not. There's a possibility the person I'm looking for might have stayed at this motel."

"The only person gone missing in this town is the young Jackson girl and everyone knows where she is. You come by just at the right time. Back out a bit willya. I'm going to re-seat this blasted toilet with a new wax seal. You got a good eye, just lend it to me and tell me if I've got the alignment right on the floor screws and over the drain hole."

"Sure thing."

John inverted the toilet and set the wax seal on the ceramic bottom. He hauled up the toilet. I helped guide him to set it over the screws and floor hole. He gave a great grunt. Then a sigh of relief and one word, "There." He smiled. "Thanks mister. Big help. It can be a bugger to do it by yourself sometimes. Now what's this about a missing gal?"

I showed him the picture of Liz Strachan.

"One looking like that I wouldn't miss in a million years." He wiped his hands then bent over and tightened the nuts and washers over the protruding floor screws. He reconnected the water line to the toilet tank and switched on the tap. The cistern filled up. He test-flushed the toilet.

"There, works like brand new. Two things I hate. Condoms and tampons. Wreck a toilet drain." He washed his hands in the sink.

"Then you've seen this woman?"

"Sure. Never forget a beauty like that."

"When?"

"Couple of times she come out this way with another good-looking lady. A blonde gal. In fact I think I just saw the blonde go across the parking lot about ten fifteen minutes ago. But I was too busy with repairs. Anyway I think I saw her. Ask the wife."

"Did you rent to this woman?"

"I don't think so. Maybe the wife did. I was in here doing a mighty task."

"So this woman came with the other woman twice?"

"Yes."

"Did they stay overnight?"

"Yeah. And the first time they left in the morning together. Second time the blonde left. And a big fellow come out and paid the bill and met this one." He gestured towards the photograph of Liz Strachan.

We walked back to the motel office.

"We can rent the room again. You maybe want to go down and give it a quick wipe. The floor's a bit mussy."

"Sure. I see you found my husband."

"Thanks."

She went out pushing a cleaning equipment cart. John went behind the counter.

"When was that?"

"To be honest I can't remember exactly. Let me see." He leafed through the card registration index. "Hard to say. Got to put a face to a name. Sometimes easier to put a name to a face."

"Maybe I can help." I palmed a five on the counter.

He scrolled through.

"I'm not sure I recognize the guy."

"What'd he look like?"

"Wore glasses and drove a rented car, I think."

"Tall? Short? Thin? Fat?"

"Tall type. Over six, I'd say. Solid frame. Looked like a middle-aged football player."

"Glasses?"

"Yeah. I think he wore glasses. I'll go ask my wife. Be right back. Why don't you read a good book." He laughed and flopped the telephone book on the counter and breezed out.

I grabbed the registration rolex and flipped through. No Liz Strachan. No Connie Yonge. No Henderson. No Slowikowsky. No Burley. I gave it another whirl to the current guests where I saw Mike Eaves registered most recently today. I scrolled through and found the name three more times. I copied down the information on the cards. The desk man came back in.

"Say, if I showed you some photos of a few men maybe you'd recognize some of the guys who register."

"Pass them by."

I showed pictures of Slowikowsky, Plante, Burley, Henderson and Clarence Wilson.

"These two." Henderson and Burley. "Mind you I'm not absolutely certain. Probably, but who can say. I see an awful lot of faces from this side of the counter. Guy around fifty-five with a miracle looking young thing, twenty, twenty-five years old—well, not exactly talking father and daughter. If you know what I mean. At my age you'll recall the gal and forget the fellow. Every time. I say why bother remember him."

"Makes sense. Do you remember anything they said here in the lobby?"

"No. But I remember them arguing. Well actually not me but my wife."

"How so?"

"Alice, my wife, was cleaning the room next door in the morning. And the gentleman, I mean guy, was going ballistic."

"Over what?"

"Over money, what else? I mean what else do men and women fight over. You best speak to my wife if you want the details."

"Sure, thanks. That was a good read." I left the five hanging out of the yellow pages.

I went back to the motel room. Alice was cleaning the bathroom.

"Excuse me. But your husband said you happened to hear an argument between an older man and a young woman."

"Which couple? I hear them lotsa times. This is not honeymoon suites. As much as I prefer it quiet and most are but some aren't."

"An older gentleman and this woman." I showed the pic of Liz Strachan again.

"Yeah. That's right. I forgot about that."

"Do you recognize this gentleman?" I showed Norman Burley's photo.

"Maybe."

"Wasn't he just here?"

"Come to think of it. He asked about a room then decided not to take it. He left."

"Was he the man who argued with this young woman?"

"Might've been him. Maybe it wasn't. Can't be certain."

"But you remember an argument over money."

"What world do you live in? Everybody argues over money."

"Your husband said you overheard them arguing one morning while cleaning a room next door."

"Now I recall. That's right. I have a terrible memory. Terrible. Terrible argument. I thought he was going to beat the woman. To be honest I was getting ready to call the OPP if I heard that guy smack her. There's a lot we put up with but I don't allow that. Beating up women. Not in our motel."

"What did he say?"

"He just kept going on saying ugly things. Something to do with a bank account and whether the woman grabbed money out of the account."

"What else?"

She gave me a stare.

"Ugly things like, a lot of swearing, he's got a dirty mouth, he said, 'you' ..." she paused, "called her a ..." she paused again, "stuff I don't like to repeat. He said to her, 'you ripped me off. You didn't make those deposits.' I left. I didn't stick around. It was an ugly argument, enough to give a person a splitting headache. I got to finish this bathroom. Looking at the guy you never would have thought it. He had a foul mouth. He never said much otherwise. Although he was always polite as peas at the check-in desk. I got to clean."

"Right. Thanks for your time." As I left I put a five on the table beside the TV.

# TEN

Back at Lajoie–Chang I rapped on Georges's door.

"Alec." Lajoie looked impeccable and breezy.

I slouched in a chair, glanced at Lajoie's familiar in the photo.

"You look rough, my friend."

"I took a couple."

"Who?"

"I figure cronies of Parsons. Either on their own entrepreneurial enterprise or stimulated by Burleyan bravado. They were driving the same car as before when I spotted them outside an apartment building except I could have swore there was no licence plate on the front of the car and the rear plate looked like a Quebec plate. But too dim to be certain. I mean not only the light but myself after the punch-out."

"We won't let this pass. Be certain."

"I will."

"Are you okay my friend?"

"I'll manage. The one guy carried a punch. Georges, this case is going off the wall. I made a mistake. I confronted Henderson. I wasn't expecting much but I thought he might provide a little piece of info as to where Liz Strachan has taken off."

Georges sat down across from me. He looked meditative. He said nothing.

"I figured either Burley or this guy Henderson have got to know something about where Liz Strachan is. But I blew the interview with Henderson. Or maybe I should say he covered me in a cloud of smoke. That means he'll squeak to Burley. Although those two are not getting along. Or so it sounded in the doughnut shop. Henderson's got money problems. Burley's hosing everybody. What do you say Georges? Don't look at me that way like I got caught five-fingering a boolabag of jujubes. I'm not five."

"You got caught. It could be rougher from here on in. After this." He waved the CD.

"There's potential in that."

"Maybe. Potentially extortion. But potentially innocuous. Depending on who these women are. Who are they? Do you recognize any of the young women in these photos?"

"No. Liz Strachan and Connie Yonge are not among them."

"Who took the photographs?"

"Hard to say. Maybe Connie Yonge or Liz Strachan. Possibly Joe Parsons. Maybe one of Parsons' buddies. Possibly this represents some sort of profit for Parsons and his crew of lowlifes. But I don't think it directly involves these young women. They were being used."

"Possibly. So Strachan and Yonge aren't in any of the photos. Why?"

"I don't know. I can't quite figure it."

"How did Liz Strachan end up with this CD?"

"Probably through Connie Yonge or Joe Parsons."

Lajoie looked meditative for a long moment then breezed through my series of reports in the file folder. He took the CD and inserted it in the drive. Lajoie rotated the monitor so we could share the view, the photos began to appear on the screen. He glanced up and said emphatically, brushing the sheets, "Not Parsons. This is part of his life blood. He wouldn't relinquish them if he had them. He'd use them to squeeze people. I see Peter Slowikowsky in here. No?" Lajoie worked the images onto the screen revealing older men embracing charming lovely younger women.

"Yes. Who else, Georges?"

"Who's this?" He showed a series of photographs with the same middle-aged man.

"That's Lester Henderson."

"But I don't see Burley," Lajoie interjected, click-streaming through many photographs.

"Right. Burley's not among them."

"But guess who is?"

"Who?"

"Here." Lajoie stopped at an image that showed a solid middle-aged man with a cigarette in his hand and his arm around the waist of a slim woman. "This is Marshall Wilson. Lawyer. You probably wouldn't recognize him. You've never met him, have you?"

"No. Clarence Wilson's brother?"

"Yes."

"Who else is in there? Is Clarence Wilson there?"

"No. The other three men I don't recognize."

"What about Alf Plante?"

"No. Alf is mister monogamy. He'd never cheat on his wife. She is a devout Catholic. So too Alf. They mean it. Made the pilgrimage to Rome. Saw the Pope."

"Never? That violates the laws of lust. Never say never. Always avoid always, so you remind me. Remain open to possibilities."

"Alfred Plante and his wife love the Church. They are very chaste people. Very high-minded sort. He reads Lonergan."

"What?"

"Who. Bernard Lonergan. Jesuit priest. Some people consider him Canada's greatest philosopher. Alf takes pride in the fact that he was born in the same town as Lonergan. Buckingham. Almost sacred ground."

"Are you joking?"

"Alec," Lajoie gave one of his condescending thin smiles. "Let's focus on this."

"Okay. See anyone else?"

"Not that I recognize." Lajoie rotated back the monitor.

I sat back. "Ah Georges you know so many interesting people. That's what I like about you. What next?"

"Give me the afternoon. I'm still thinking on this. We're dealing with a discontented fellow who passes for a marvellous gentleman. I can't figure if he stands behind the mirror or in front of the mirror."

"You mean Norman Innis Burley?"

"Yes. In all of this, he's the master quick change artist in front of any mirror or shop window entertaining tailors and clients, while behind the mirror counting coin for any passing banker. A starburst of megalomania. Seems he even wants the sun to flatter him."

"Well he was in the Caribbean. But was complaining. The guy's a complainer."

"He'll buy a Versailles mirror the size of a shop window to show off in. An illusionist."

"You got it Georges. All ego. Big phoney. The man's all image. Smoke and mirrors."

"Be polite Alec, we're not talking crows and turkey vultures."
"If he raped that young girl out west, I want to nail the bugger."
"That's going too far. Assimilating another person's vengeance is unwise. Save it for the law. Let's be careful here. Retribution is a negative sentiment. I need only remind you, you are working a very basic missing person case, Alec. Which admittedly has possibly turned upside down."
"I only show these emotions with you Georges. I don't know why I do it."
"It is a necessity of investigative work. Every investigator or police detective needs a confesseur—to make certain he does not seep to a source or a suspect when questioning them. That's why they go in pairs. Doppelgänger."
"Come again?"
"Twins. Confidants in the best sense of the word."
"Yeah, but you're right, it's a waste to get excited. I shouldn't do it."
"We're no longer dealing with a tyranny of trifles. Possibly something more complex. From this point, you must be careful with anything that might be construed by police as material evidence. We will have to turn these items over to the police. They might already have a copy of this CD. But first let me give this a good thought. Unfortunately I'm too busy today, Morrison has finally accumulated something substantial in a client's accounting computer system. Looks like the accountant was working a salami shave in a throughput manipulation in the account files. Morrison had the shaved pennies flow into separate covert files. The total amount matched the amounts that the guy was hiding and transferring to his own secret files and then out to his own account. Pinch the pennies, pile up the pounds. Morrison nabbed the crook. I have a meeting with the client and their lawyers to discuss whether to seek restitution from the joker or pursue criminal charges."
"Just try giving the Queen a quick shave and Morrison will catch 'em every time."
"The lady is not for shaving. Early in the morning we'll go back out to the garage where you found this material. If we find nothing then we must of necessity turn these items over to the police. Immédiatement." Georges gestured towards the envelope, CD and Strachan file on the desk. His nicely starched shirt cuff revealed a

fine jade stone. "We need to know what Liz Strachan was hiding in her computer files and we don't know. Hopefully Morrison's hacker boy will crack the encryption."

"Georges, sometimes I got a ... I don't know what. Liz Strachan wouldn't drive out of town with someone else. She'd fly. She's got the loot. She might take the train. There's a certain pattern in her movements that has been broken."

"Don't be so certain, Alec. If the police think she has left town of her own free will they have good reason to believe so. The Parsons factor is a potent component. Also, don't necessarily assume she has the cash. Her parents, even if they have substantial incomes, tie up her cash flow. One thing seems possible, Liz Strachan is living beyond her means. Remember, money and avarice breed bankruptcy even for those who have the dough."

"She's broke?"

"Possibly. But don't forget she drove into the Gatineau with her friend Ms Yonge. So let us not dupe ourselves. The men Liz Strachan and Ms Yonge are involved with are talkers not doers, though they no doubt think themselves men who can get things done. All men striving after big money perceive themselves as men of action. Only men who have obtained such comfort as to shed either label are able to relax with self-assured indifference towards actions and words, relax in the comfort of their accumulation. Henderson and Burley would hire someone. Talkers are not good doers. Maybe once upon a time they were. Be assured they want someone who uses his own hands and not his tongue. A tough guy who goes straight about the rough business and gets things done. And incidentally, my friend, your cheek there is clear enough evidence of their calibre."

"My cheek is my cheek."

"It is. It is. But don't be cheeky with bruisers."

"I'm going to see Norm Burley tomorrow."

"You might as well, for Lester Henderson no doubt will have contacted Mr Burley instantly. But go carefully, and before noon tomorrow we'll check out the apartment garage."

"Georges, have you ever met the man?"

"Yes. In passing. Some years ago. We did some work for Baldwin Martel Wightman."

"What's the guy's weak spot?"

"Two things. His former affection for the bottle."

"A lush?"

"A former one. His wife is the daughter of a Croatian refugee, a chemist. The old man came over after the Croatian fascist regime collapsed. Fled communist Yugoslavia. Hung out with the hard right-wing crowd from Central Europe. The Ustasha. Rumour went round that Burley's father-in-law collaborated with the Nazis when they occupied Croatia. But nothing came of that. The old man's a runaway success, founded Clear Chem Dyes in Montreal. His daughter read Burley the riot act on the bottle. Either stop nibbling on the bottle or out she'd go. The Civic Unity Party says they won't let him run as a candidate unless he gets his drink under control. A year ago Burley quit cold but with great resentment. Apparently the guy has ambitions to be leader of the party."

"And what's Burley's other Achilles tendon?

"Not tendon. Cartilage. His wife's nose." Georges smiled.

"His wife's nose?"

"The nose. A conspicuous asset for her face, but not her dignity. She supposedly had a nose job to scale it down. It is not a topic of dinner table conversation at polite parties. Burley is, to say the least, as conspicuously sensitive about the subject as her nose was formerly conspicuous on the lady's visage. They say the lady is good-looking. But to tell you the truth my contact with Burley was no more than a legal handshake at a meeting. He can listen but he does it like a con artist calculating an angle. The man is reputed to be ruthless. Not so much bright as willing to do the dirty jobs for corporate execs who want a guy who can put a legal cover on a dirty merger and buy-out. He used to specialize in a tough area of law. And was strictly a purist."

"Labour relations?"

"You got it. Corporate side only. That's Baldwin Martel Wightman. They'd never touch a union side case."

"Burley's their man at BMW?"

"You got it. Apparently a veritable pit bull in labour negotiations. A nasty bit of work. That was yesterday. He paid his dues to the corporations. Now he's collecting appointments to boards of directors. I heard he's gone over to the financial side of corporate law. Dirty business but with a bourgeois table napkin over the shirt front. He likes being praised. A compliment is his weak spot. And if it comes from an American with money he stands on his hind legs and wags his tail."

"You forgot something, Georges."

"What? Illuminate me."

"He's got a nasty mouth when he gets impatient."

Georges smiled.

I stood up to leave.

"Alec, one further thing."

"Yes Georges."

"Detective Warnock called. He wondered if you got anything."

"I got a source. Maybe good, maybe lousy. But he's come through in the past. He knows the street. I use him rarely."

Georges gave me a stare.

"Georges, he's not buyable. The police can't get anything from this sort."

"But can you, Alec?"

"Depends."

"On what? Don't be coy."

"Georges, I can't tell you." I glanced over at the photograph on the bookshelf. "Georges that guy behind you, is that a photograph of one of your cronies, whatchamacallit, Stenzac, Flaudahl, Boussel or Ralbert, you know whatshisname?"

Georges' voice was rich with laughter. But he said nothing, not even yes or no. He was doing the ignoring thing, the prerogative of the boss. Changing subjects did not work with Lajoie.

"Give me your source, Alec."

"I can't, Georges."

"That won't do."

"Georges please. I can't. These people will not speak to me. Half the time I'm not there for them. I'm lucky if they even will look at people like us. Believe me. I can't let such a source go to Warnock. They can't be bought. You can give them coin, loose change, that sort of thing, but you can't buy them. They know the street better than the police Georges."

Georges' gaze was no longer conciliatory, it was stern, and strictly former police detective. It unnerved me. I'd never want to be braced by Lajoie. I relinquished.

"Fine. This is it." I related the telephone conversation with Inky Baby leaving out bits that might clue Georges.

"A verbatimist. Rara avis in this racket. A very fine attribute of yours, Alec. Such an ear, don't misuse it." Lajoie paused, "Such an ear signifies a sense of honesty."

A verbatimist. This was one of Lajoie's schnozological neologisms. In spite of the crossed circumstances of our meeting, it could only be taken as a high compliment

"Keep in mind, we owe the police information. We owe Warnock information. In our racket it's our lifeline. Now listen." Lajoie's gaze was softened, even kind, but steady. "Not a trace. The police have got nothing. Not snared a thing from their snitches. They've shaken down all the little druggies, the street kids. And the usual gonads with headaches in trenchcoats. Zero. Do you hear me. They're now travelling through the toilets into the sewer. They still have nothing. Accept that this young girl, Laura Cooke, was last seen on Rideau Street Mall around seven, seven thirty on the Friday. Zero after that."

"I understand. I know Warnock and his wife are wrecked."

"Alec," Georges paused, he rested his hand on the desk. "There is a certain disposition, opinion, among some police officers that when a person joins the force they join for life, until retirement. Detective Warnock is a lifer. He disdains any police who leave for personal gain, profit. He's strictly old school. To serve the community. The oath with him is the highest honour. He does not respect private operators. Retire, then maybe it's okay to go off and do something else. Otherwise, you lose your standing in that community."

"Georges, that's a hackneyed word."

"Nevertheless, I must disabuse you of certain false assumptions. Morrison and I have no special standing with the police as former officers. We are simply, in the routine way of the law, outside sources sometimes useful, sometimes a nuisance. Do you understand? But we still have to play by their rules. Understand. We cannot be interfering." Georges paused.

"I understand."

"A piece of advice. Don't be cunning with a complicated source. And don't trade them information. If they have a dictum, no money, follow it. Don't give them coin. Go your way. But Alec. Do be careful. When you start dealing with sources beyond the reach of police, then you are in very dicey territory."

In my office I called up Pete Slowikowsky. He was not happy to hear my voice or eager to see me again, but said as a goodwill gesture he would squeeze me in for ten minutes. Burley's assistant had also called back asking what it was I had called about. I phoned Burley's office at Baldwin Martel Wightman.

"This is Alec Knight from Lajoie–Chang Associates."

"One moment please. May I put you on hold." This was no question or request. But I said yes anyway.

I waited five minutes. Finally a man's voice came on the line.

"Norman Burley."

"Mr Burley this is Alec Knight with Lajoie–Chang Associates. I was wondering if I could have ten minutes of your time concerning a case that Lajoie–Chang Associates is investigating. It is possible that you may have some information that may be of assistance."

"I'm exceedingly busy. Tell me what it is about."

"Lajoie–Chang has been hired to investigate the disappearance of a Ms Liz Strachan. Her parents are our clients."

"Strachan? I'm afraid that name means nothing to me."

"I'm surprised, Mr Burley. Your name showed up on Ms Strachan's BlackBerry."

"I have no knowledge of the person you have mentioned."

"Mr Burley, ten minutes of your time with me might expedite the situation."

"I don't have any further time to discuss this matter."

"Please give me a moment, Mr Burley. Lester Henderson suggested that I contact you."

There was a pause.

"Very well Mr Knight. I'll give you ten minutes of my time and no more. Tomorrow morning eight sharp."

"Thank you Mr Burley. It's very much appreciated."

"Good day to you sir."

When I got to Slowikowsky's office he looked wrecked. The best thing about the guy on this afternoon was his suit. It had a certain style, a notch above Harry Rosen. But just about any set of rags looked better than the trash hanging off my shoulders trying to pass as a suit. I notched up my brain, come on be professional ask Lajoie–Chang for a clothing allowance. Yes, my superego murmured. Fat chance with Morrison doing the expense accounts. And Lajoie inspecting my record of accomplishments. Two twins forever inspecting the bottom line of the agency. Lajoie played congenial to Morrison's caution. They were rolling in the dough and I was dragging myself through the streets in rags. No respect. Worse, today I hadn't exactly made fast friends with Lajoie refusing to divulge Inky Baby as a source.

Slowikowsky appraised me. I could feel it in the lawyer's indifferent handshake.

"Look Knight, I hope this is quick. I have a heavy case load. I'm only doing this as a favour to Alf. I hope you understand that. Alf thinks very highly of Georges Lajoie."

"They discuss Lonergan."

Slowikowsky looked at me as if I was daft. "Let's make it quick."

"I'll do my best."

He didn't offer a seat but sat down behind the desk. Slowikowsky hunched forward on his elbows smoking a cigarette.

"You didn't come clean with me."

"You shitbag, don't come in here and try that con. That's going too far buddy." He rolled back in his big leather chair.

"You know Connie Yonge."

"So."

"You didn't tell me you knew Connie Yonge."

"You didn't ask, mac."

"It was there."

"You've got to ask." Slowikowsky half smiled. "And you know it."

"This isn't court. I'm trying to save you aggravation."

"No it's not court. But you've got no more rights in this office than the chair your arse is parked on Knight. And by the way that's my chair." He laughed.

"You know I'm on a missing person case. Lajoie–Chang has had good relations with your firm. It's worth your time to cooperate, Mr Slowikowsky. As you ask me to cooperate with you concerning your relations with Liz Strachan. Or maybe I should leave. And let the police carry it."

"Maybe you should."

I started to get up.

"Sit down, Knight. What do you want?"

"What is or was your relationship with Connie Yonge?"

"You know." He shifted his hips raised his shoulders, then smiled.

"Both women?"

"Come on grow up. This isn't the tot lot. You're no chambermaid changing rumpled linen in the Gold suites of the Chateau Laurier. A guy's got to get his socks off to get his rocks off. Two's better than one and three's better than two unless you're a handicraft artist. You dress like a rag picker but you don't look like a solitaire hand artist. You know this town can get awfully boring. Do you want some, Knight? Is that what this is about? Eh? You want to go to the happy humping grounds? Come on. You come up here to bargain for a piece of ass. Huh?" He exhaled disdainfully and half smiled.

"This is not good Mr Slowikowsky."

"Cut the Mister crap, leave it for the foreign affairs troopers at Lester B. Call me Pete or Slowikowsky. What's not good? Humping is the hum of life. Keeps a man alive. Listen to your molecules."

"The disappearance of Liz Strachan. Were you with Liz Strachan on the Sunday or Monday before she disappeared?"

"No. I told you that. And that answer is not going to change. Ever. She's probably cruising in the Caribbean on a holiday. Connie Yonge said as much. She goes there all the time."

"With your buddy, Norm Burley?"

"What's that supposed to mean?"

"You figure it out."

"I figure you're looking around to get laid or something. I don't have time for this shit. I thought you had something of substance and wanted something of substance."

"Her disappearance grows more obscure."

"You're blowing things up. Way out of proportion. I got some stuff that tells me that the police are taking a laid-back posture. They figure she's on vacation, will show up any day now that Labour Day has passed. Probably be back in town this weekend. This is no missing person case with a ten-year-old grabbed off the street."

"Who's your source?"

"A guy in the can."

I said nothing but gave Slowikowsky a good look.

"Bad source. Listen, between you and me, this is not a good situation. If the police dig even a little deeper your name is going to show up. Now they're going soft on the missing person case 'cause they made a link between Parsons' LTD escort agency and Connie Yonge and Liz Strachan. They're thinking just a couple of fancy trollops making a buck on the side. That's momentary. Sure the police are spinning through the idea that Strachan went on a holiday. But she didn't."

"What the fuck do you know? I heard she's out of town on a holiday."

"Sec. Be careful if you say that Mr Slowikowsky. Do you mean that as fact?"

He said nothing.

"Fine. Sooner or later the police will come back and dig a little deeper. The woman's parents aren't going home to Kingston. Sooner or later they will have to tell the parents something of substance or drop the case. That won't look good. If they drop it the Strachans will be none too pleased. They're not the sort of people who will go away. I give the police maybe twelve to twenty-four hours before somebody goes back very thoroughly over that missing person file and sees it is not right. A good detective gets on it and then Pete ..."

Slowikowsky turned his head and gazed out the window. He said nothing. He looked back at me.

"Knight, you're like a cat pawing over a bird. What do you want? Do you want to get laid? That it? Is it? Is that what this is all about? I'll talk to Parsons."

"What's the link between Norman Burley, Liz Strachan and your friend Lester Henderson?"

"I don't know. Haven't the faintest. I told you I don't hang out with Burley's crowd. That would be one heck of a liability in my practice. And you know it. Burley's people and the Civic Unity Party are for reinstating capital punishment. They want a national referendum. Want longer sentencing. Come on. Think about it. What a liability. In this practice if I were in with that crowd I'd guillotine myself. And there's nobody to carry the skull. It was Alf, and I'm not bullshitting you. Alf and I had some investments with those fellows. Burley and Henderson. It looked like a quick turnover, high rate of return. I needed the cash real bad. I had a pile of legal aid cases that

I had not got any coin on, the Law Society's legal aid fund was near depleted and a long queue for coin. I was stretched out on my lines of credit. I needed cash bad. Alf turned me on to this investment fund with Burley. That's all. Strictly financial. But human. And you can see that."

"You're on the board of directors of some of Henderson's and Burley's companies."

"Look. A guy has got to invest his money somewhere. Somehow."

"What do you know about the International Canadian–Caribbean Investors Bank?"

"Next to nothing. Except its location in the Caribbean. And I wouldn't know that if you hadn't mentioned it. I mean, that's not my personal bank. I bank down the street."

"It's Norman Burley's bank."

Slowikowsky said nothing. He butted out his cigarette. He folded his hands together like he was going to do the kid's rhyme with his fingers: here is the church and here is the steeple, open the doors and here are the people.

"You finished Knight?"

"Not quite. I want to meet with a client of yours."

The lawyer said nothing.

"Mike Eaves."

He seemed to mull it over, lit another smoke then said, "You're treading on toes. That's almost next to impossible. I got to protect my clients. Anyway it would really take time."

"As soon as possible."

"You want to get me in shit up to my eyeballs with the Law Society. That's next to impossible. Anyway it needs time."

"Time's evaporating, Pete."

"Screw you. You want to fuck me over with my clients."

"You're holding back something from me. So you get nothing."

"You haven't anything to give. You're like a loser on reality TV. You finished?"

"Thanks. When the police reshuffle that Strachan file you could be finished. I was going to tell you about something going to the police. But not now. No. You didn't give me anything that I couldn't get off the computer. And you know computers. They're good for numbers but useless for knowledge." I got up and went towards the door. "Pete, I hope Liz Strachan is alright."

"So do I. I told you I think she is one cool chick."

"Pete, you're a smart lawyer but not a bright client."

"Get lost asshole."

"Don't go see Connie Yonge again. Stay away from her."

"That a threat?"

"No. It's cheap advice. Two three days the cops are going to be all over that apartment block. They might even find your pinky print or used condom."

"Since you're into the advice column, well here's some. Buy a new suit. A Jehovah's Witness wouldn't be caught in that felt outfit. And forget about Mike Eaves. Asshole, that'd flush my articles down the toilet."

I went over to Saikely's and ordered a fried egg sandwich with lettuce and tomato and a glass of ginger ale.

It was slow and May Saikely wasn't around. Albert was working solo on the grill and serving. He set the fried egg sandwich down before me.

"There," he said.

"Thanks," I said.

"You're welcome, Alec."

"So are you Albert."

"You're polite Alec. Always. I like that."

"Got to be. Goes with the work. Anyway it's a habit of my mother's."

Albert smiled.

"Hey Albert I got no luck these days. Give me some of your luck."

"Alec, believe me I thought I was out of luck. But maybe it's coming back. My boy wants to work here, learn to cook. He quit the business program and says he wants to be an artist. He has a new girlfriend. She has a lot of jewellery in her face but she is a nice influence. My boy's giving up on the Casino d'Hull."

"That's great. This town is going to enfer and back. It's what a regular paycheque will do to people."

"The government people get regular paycheques and waste it at the casino."

"That's why it's there. Casino operators want to be in a town where there's a steady flow of cash. Big money comes out of lots of little piles of money slipping through lots of little hands."

"I got a cousin in Windsor works the assembly line says casinos parasite on the worker's paycheque. Otherwise those scumbags couldn't survive."

"That's right."

"The casino in Windsor's taking over the auto business in that town. Competing with the assembly line. My cousin says a lot of guys want to work at the casino instead of in the car factories. Imagine that. Guy can't keep his mind on the job for thinking all day about getting over to the casino and tossing the dice, flipping the cards. Casino is the big assembly line in Windsor. Bad. Bad for business all round. Casino hurts business on this side of the river." Albert wiped the counter then took up the scraper to clean the grease build-up on half of the grill. "I swear casino operators are in tight with the loan sharks. And those jerks in Queen's Park want to give those casino creeps another half a billion dollars. Five hundred million dollars for the Windsor casino. Do you believe it?"

"It's—"

"Alec, it's criminal. They make good wages down there in the auto plants. The union has a good contract but it's not enough. My life, you should see the houses down there along the lakeshore."

"I never got beyond video games on the computer."

"Me, no time. I got no time for those games. See where I stand, Alec?" He gestured to the long narrow aisle behind the lunch counter. "This is my place. Back and forth. Back and forth. From five in the morning to ten at night. What's a casino to a guy like me? Huh?"

"You got good luck Albert. You and May got your own business. Good business. You work hard. You made it. You're not greedy. You make your own luck."

Albert said nothing, continued to scrape the grill but glanced over his shoulder and grinned at me.

"I mean it Albert. I respect a guy like you. People like May and you. You got no idea, the cheats, leeches, chisellers and louts I come across in my racket."

"Don't you worry. Security sells."

"I'm out of it Albert. Even the pigeons crap on me. Pigeon pooped on my head yesterday." I laughed. Saikely laughed.

"Alec that's not bad luck. That's a sign of good luck."

"How's that?"

"Old country people say a pigeon dropping is good luck. A blessing from heaven. Angels are watching over your soul."

"How's that Albert?"

"Birds are heavenly creatures, that's why they fly. Messengers from the heavens. Like angels."

"Speaking of birds. Great fried egg, Albert. Great. Not greasy. Normally I wouldn't touch it."

"That's the bird. Versatile food. I don't fry it in animal fat. Other places mix it up with lard, no good. Phew." He scraped the grill, drawing back the residue and scraping it down the grease gutter of the big Garland stove. As he worked with the stone grinding the metal, half the grill began to come up clean and shiny. "Got to keep the grill in good shape, Alec. This is where the food happens."

I laughed. I was about to pay and leave when big Detective Warnock rolled in.

"Two coffees, buddy. Back booth," Warnock ordered Albert Saikely, motioning to the back of the long restaurant.

Albert glanced at me, I said yes with my eyes.

"Sure," Albert remarked.

I followed Warnock to the booth. We sat and waited until Saikely brought the coffees.

"Food any good in this joint?"

"I wouldn't be here."

"Okay give me something solid," Warnock said to Saikely. "What do you recommend, Knight?"

"Depends."

"I'm a meat and leftovers kinda guy. Cold pasta. Good cut of pork or beef."

"Albert, give Mr Warnock your house steak special."

"Mac, grill it quick and hot, burnt on the outside, rare on the inside."

"Right." Albert moved back to the grill.

Warnock looked depressed. I'd never been there. I had no kids. I didn't have a clue what it carried, the toll it might take.

"I talked to Lajoie." Warnock paused, but I said nothing, I wanted to know what Lajoie had told Warnock. Warnock wanted to know if I had something that I had not told Lajoie. I stayed quiet. Warnock broke the silence. "Lajoie said I should speak direct to you. Our people went all-out. Nothing from the snitch tribe. Nothing from the bribe tribe. Nothing's come up and that's creepy. Really creepy. All the worms and weeny wankers, combed out the lice. The little diddlers and big diddlers. Still nothing. Laura's lousy headbanging smart-ass crew says they know nothing. None of them saw her since after school. For once the little headbangers didn't lie. A miracle. Laura went downtown on her own. That we know. Bus driver told us she took the 98. We got one kid who saw Laura on Rideau between seven and seven thirty. That's it. But this kid is just that. Some kid from Lisgar High School. A stranger. A total innocent. Living in the Glebe. Saw her alone at the bus stop. And that's it. Nothing out of Vanfuckover. Nothing in Hogtown. Hochelaga. So okay. I mean not okay. You called."

"Detective Warnock, I need a little more time."

"I was afraid you'd mumble something like that."

"I got a little, a hangnail lead."

"Okay. Let's hear it."

I gave the conversation that I had had with Inky Baby, dropping out the Lantern tag and Inky's own name and any little clue that might be a hint to Warnock.

"That word for word, Knight?"

"Pretty near."

"Hey, hey. I wish I could do that. I could do both sides of the yakyak. Like a fucking ventriloquist. Lajoie said you had a pretty accurate ear. Freaky Knight. What's Lajoie call it? Call you? Whatchamacallit?"

I said nothing.

"Source said. Quote. The person is maybe travelling. Unquote. That's it?"

"Yeah."

"Laura's the person, right?"

"Right."

Albert brought the grilled steak.

"Thank you." Detective Warnock stared at the meal and waited for Saikely to go away. Then the detective picked up the Lea and Perrin's Worcestershire sauce and drenched the steak. "Would it be too much to ask if I could talk to your person?"

"It would."

Warnock cut into the steak, took a bite and chewed on it.

"Thanks for the coffee, Detective Warnock." I stood up. "I'll call you tonight or tomorrow. I got to get back to work."

"Shudup Knight 'n' sit down. You didn't finish your coffee. You are so fucking rude." He motioned with the stainless steel fork. "Good steak. The leb can cook."

I sat down.

"I want your source."

"This is not good."

Warnock took another bite. He buttered a bit of the roll and stuffed it in his mouth. He chewed. I just waited.

"I'll tell you what's not good." Warnock's face was grim. "My daughter is missing. My wife is wrecked. I'll tell you something personal. This is very personal. She's almost having a nervous breakdown. Do you know how much I love my wife? Do you have any idea? She is the most beautiful woman in the world. She does not deserve this. She's not garbage like you and me. The trash we associate with. The muck from the gutter splashed all over our trouser cuffs. Stink. Stench. My wife's a human being. I told Lajoie I need information. We give you people a break. Now you sound like you got something. And I want that source. Otherwise I wouldn't speak to you so politely."

I still said nothing, stared at Warnock's big thick hand holding the cutlery. He cut into the steak again, set the fork tines into a french fry and then pressed them into a bit of meat, stuffed the food in his mouth and chomped.

"Well."

"Detective Warnock, I'm going to repeat the conversation for you again." I recited it again.

"That's a pretty fucking bright trick. I got guys on the force who been there ten twenty years can't pull that stunt. But it's pretty fucking goofy too. But it's just repeat. I heard it already."

"Well then it can't be bent. You'd lose the source and information."

"I probably know the character."
"Maybe you do. Maybe you don't. I can't say. You're letting your headspace get in between your judgement of the situation."
"You're a fucking idiot. I'm talking about my wife. Gimme the source. I didn't buy a steak dinner for nothing in this leb shit hole."
"I can't."
Warnock leaned back from the plate and stared at me.
"You know something Knight? You're an asshole. But Lajoie's right too, you're a smart fucking asshole. You didn't tell Lajoie, didja? So I guess you won't tell me. Nobody else knows this character?"
I shook my head negative.
"Good. So it's clean?"
"Cleaner than a grain of polished rice."
"Call me as soon as you can. I appreciate any help you can give me. I won't ask about the source. Let me get your meal."
"Thanks."
"Don't take what I said personally."
"I never do, Detective Warnock."
"Don't repeat it, eh?"
"I wouldn't dream of it."
"Hey, Knight. Come here."
"I got to work."
"I got something civil to say. You're hurt. I can see it. Give me the guy's name. We'll get the bastard charged. You're alright. I talk crummy but you're alright."
"I appreciate that."
"You don't need to take that crap. I'm on the level."
"Soon. I don't know them. But when I get it, I'll give it to you."
"You do that. I mean it. Don't take it into your own hands. No need. Give it to me. And we'll fix their arses. They won't sit in a pew until Christmas Eve Mass."

When I got back to the Bronson Street office, Louise Montpetit told me, see Morrison. Chang was grinning.
"I only got a minute here. The kid cracked the computer. He also deciphered that ciphered file. He says it was pretty basic stuff. BAZAOZBZ. The first Z column in the first row is a month marker.

Basic alphabetic shift of one alphabetic character: A becomes B, C becomes D et cetera until Z becomes A. Each column runs on a variation. You read both down and across. Alphanumeric combination." Morrison handed me the sheets. "Here, it probably means more to you than me."

"What is it? Names?"

"No. Looks more like dates and money."

I glanced at the sheet. "Looks a little the same but with numbers." I laughed. "Could it be another cipher?"

"Not a chance. He swears it goes no deeper."

"And you, Morrison?"

"No. The ciphermeister's right. It's basic stuff."

"Thanks Morrison."

I went in my office and sat down and read it. It ran like this:

NBS999500
JPO998500
LHN997500
MWD999800
NBJ008800
JPF007800
LHM006500
MWA005500
NBM004500
JPJ005900
LHJ004900
MWA005900

And so on for a few pages. Morrison and the hackerhound were right. It now seemed obvious. I opened the file folder and took out the scrap of paper I had filched from the wastebasket in Liz Strachan's apartment and compared it. I wrote it out in full.

After Lajoie and Chang were finished dealing with the client Lajoie called it an evening and I stayed late with Morrison Chang to go over the info he and Nick Glastonbury had compiled on the International Canadian–Caribbean Investors Bank. Morrison declared with his emphatic empiricism, as if he were setting up pieces of stone in a wall, "This is a dirty bank Alec."

"How so?"

"Look. The ICCI Bank has received plenty of attention from the US grand juries in Miami. Imagine that. Just figure out what that means. Miami of all places."

"A nice town. Plenty of sunshine."

"Well it had a branch there up until 1979. And believe me Alec, the ICCI was not there doing mortgages and backing up auto loans, but working US citizens to set up accounts in one of its Caribbean branches."

"Which means what Morrison?"

"Major dough was being taken from drug trafficking and deposited in the names of shell companies. In 1978, a Miami grand jury subpoenaed the records of branches of the ICCI Bank located on the Caribbean islands. The case involved a drug cartel. The Florida branch stood tall to defend depositors' confidentiality and the courts fined the bank."

"Where are my people? Where's my man?" I smiled.

"Which man?"

"Norman Burley."

"The lawyer? Are you joking, Alec?"

"No way Morrison. I got that as incidental knowledge from a source."

"No such thing as incidental knowledge. All knowledge is crucial knowledge. Integral knowledge."

"I never understood that word Morrison."

"What word? Knowledge?"

"No. Integral."

"Every thing is integral. From integers to interrogation. Anyway, the next year in another drug case a fine was levied against these bank brats."

"How much?"

"Two hundred and fifty bucks a day."

"Because they didn't want to put the documents on the table?"

"Constitutes contempt of court because the bank would not show its records."

"So they paid up. A one-day fine, and showed the judge padded records. I assume."

"Assume nothing. The bank pulled out of Florida or let us say it made an honourable and dignified but cowardly retreat from peninsular justice to the protective isles."

"Where'd the head office go Morrison?"

"It settled on an idyllic isle. To keep good company with five hundred banks, ten thousand corporations, and four hundred insurance companies."

"With stats like that the place has got to have more people than China."

"It has 10,000 mopeds. And a population of 20,000 permanent residents catered to by 20,000 domestic servants, many migrant workers."

"Why's it got so many mopeds, Morrison?"

"'Cause it has very strict environmental laws. None of which have to do with financial environmentalism. Even stricter car licence and ownership laws, and yet stricter car parking laws than Singapore."

"Kind of noisy, them mopeds."

"Listen, the US department of justice—"

"Is there such an entity?"

"Listen Alec, quit interrupting. These guys in the justice department brought down on the heads of the board of directors a criminal indictment involving tax fraud and cheque kiting."

"I thought that kiting cheques died years ago."

"It did. Internal. This was between branches of the ICCI Bank. But the joint was implicated in giving bribes to the new political bosses."

"CIA? FBI?"

"Maybe. But who can say. That didn't exactly come out in the print-out from the justice department."

"Who was involved?"

"The Prime Minister of the island, a guy called Lloyd Winston Balfour, who took bribes from casino operators."

"This is rich. I'm gonna tell Albert Saikely about this place."

"Listen up Alec. You wanted all this garbage I don't know for what. You had Nick Glastonbury digging through the electronic trash."

"Go ahead Morrison. I'm just amused."

"Be amused. This is not the Master of Ballantrae. Don't waste research time. The client's money."

"I'm not."

"There better be reason to this madness."
"There is."
"Okay. Anyway a convicted cocaine smuggler claimed to have withdrawn $250,000 from Prime Minister L W Balfour's account in the International Canadian–Carribean Investors Bank and to have passed it on to Richard Balasco who was a former CIA spy."
"So they are there."
"Come on. You think guys like Noriega work solo? El Presidente General Noriega's in jail not for stealing but for what he knows about who."
"Whom. Lajoie."
"Alec. Next you're going to tell me how to pronounce Sun Yat-sen and Mao Zedong." Morrison gave me a stare to end all stares. "This might be near Miami but this is not Disney World. Balasco was a former CIA spy but now wanted by the CIA and the USA justice department."
"Why does everyone want to be on the justice department's celebrity list? Can we get on their list, Morrison? What's it take?"
"Alec. Listen. I want to go home. My wife's parents are coming over for dinner. According to the witness, Balasco gave the dough to the Prime Minister L W Balfour. A British solicitor, a guy named George Arnold Eden, was convicted in relation to laundering money from a British drug smuggling ring. Most of the cash had been deposited in the International Canadian–Caribbean Investors Bank then transferred back to London England then rerouted to various New York City banks. This guy George Eden got eighteen months and was out in nine months."
"Good schoolboy."
"Not likely."
"Where's he live?"
"Guess."
"That glittering isle in the Caribbean. What have you got on this guy George Eden? Who's he know here in Canada? Miami?"
"No one in Miami. But he knows a very interesting person you mentioned. Sec." Morrison shuffled through another stack of papers. "The Burley guy."
"Very nice. But this is so old nothing can come of it."
"Okay. It's your trash, Alec. Nick and I are only laundering it."

"Go ahead."

"Two years ago. The Organisation for Economic Co-operation and Development's Task Force put the island nation on its blacklist of fifteen countries for not cooperating in trying to halt money laundering. The Group of Seven in its 1997 report had placed the island with banks in the worst category of the failure to produce anti-money laundering legislation. In the International Narcotics Control Strategy Report of 1998 released by the US department of state this island was rated as a primary source of money laundering."

"So small, yet so influential." I gave a sigh. I wanted to go swimming but I didn't have five hundred dollars in my bank account after my old man had cleaned me out the other day. "That is still yesterday. A long time ago Morrison. I need something closer to now."

"Yes it is. Task force after task force. But it's going nowhere. None of this is serious."

"Why?"

"Because legit banks take the money after it has passed through the system and no one wants to be the first to say no. We're talking lump sums. None of them wants to be a chump's son. What they all want, construct, is structural distance from the taint."

"Which means?"

"They want the dirty dough flowing through their banks but they don't want to be implicated with the corrupt source. Original sin. The big governments are busy constructing legal systems which showcase the big ten banks worldwide and the G7 countries as cleaner than surgeon's robes entering the OR and clamping down on money-laundering. But at the same time they have dams and sluice channels that divert the continuous flow of capital back into the G7 countries. They compete for this capital, it comes cheap. Every central banker knows a country without capital is sicker than a dog with rabies. That scares them more than a system full of dirty money."

"It'll infect the system."

"Capital is capital. Capital only knows capital. It doesn't even recognize her Majesty's face even when it is plastered on every dollar bill. It is indifferent to source. Illegal money and legal money do not distinguish themselves from one another once they merge to become capital. Like water pouring into the Ottawa River, polluted or unpolluted both become the Ottawa River water. Anyway, Alec, you can't have a water system without storm sewers, sewage sewers and a sewage treatment plant, otherwise the effluent just flows into the lakes and rivers and water table. Ever hear about Walkerton? The role of banks is to clean up the money."

"It stinks. Where's Burley in all of this?"

"Buried my man. Buried so deep. Anyway there's something else."

"What?"

"Trying to sort through the dirty money, it's like trying to move a slag heap of nickel trailings. Sure, dogged bureaucrats, lawyers, accountants, regulatory people slog away trying to do respectable honest work at their gov job, try to stop the flow. But no nation is genuinely interested in clamping down. In the USA the money markets and banks and credit card companies are in such bad shape. The whole country is haemorrhaging debt. Federal, state, corporate, public, private, personal. You name it. It's debt. The USA is so desperate for capital from anywhere and everywhere. Interest is a pack of wild dogs devouring the lean sheep. While the euro is tearing through the US dollar like a wolf through a flock of fat sheep. Soon, the petrodollar will be matched by a petroeuro, no doubt followed by a petroyuan. Watch it, mark my word, oil's going to hit two hundred bucks a barrel. You get off the gold standard something has to be the standard. Stability."

"I can't follow Morrison. You're into higher finance."

"Correlates."

"Another word I do not understand."

"International money marts. Currency trading. Something has to bring stability to the international trading of currencies. The US buck can't do it alone. So. Petro. Petrodollars. But when oil and gas are depleted—and they most assuredly will be. Categorical. And imperative. And an empirical fact despite all the SUVs—then there's water, soil, and air. Followed then by drugs, coffee, heroin, cocaine, and hashish followed in correlation with oil prices. Until they supersede them. You wouldn't remember tea, salt, sugar, coffee and opium. Made the sun rise on the British Empire. It's axiomatic, you've got to know Scottish distillery history of the eighteenth century. And their banks."

"I'll pass."

"Then you miss a great moment in economics and understanding Adam Smith."

"I'll pass on the Scottish banking system. Go on. Morrison, I dig your rap on money. It's funnier than some hip hop."

"Capital does hopscotch. More value in dirty money than clean money. No tax. No tax. Tax evasion is where it's at. Drugs are great for generating large sums of liquid capital very quickly while disappearing and not leaving a trace of evidence behind. Heroin, coffee, hash and coke make the moon glow on the new empire. Ready cash. Pays for armaments. Pays for agents. Proceeds of crime legislation. So," Morrison paused, he smiled at my lack of comprehension, "the Canadian bankers are complaining about restraints and extra costs of the new anti-money-laundering laws. They're pissed off over the new plateau of bringing in fifteen thousand across the border."

"And chatting with CanCuss?"

"You can swear all you like."

"Burley's a nasty bit of work. You should hear the guy talk to people he considers friends, associates and business partners. He's even ruder to women."

"No surprise. Dirty money, dirty mouth."

"Will they get the guy?"

"Alec, are you joking? This guy is so politically insulated by US neo-con politicians that nobody up here would dare touch him."

"Did that come out?"

"Listen Alec. He's hired as a consultant for this and that on cross-border deals and trade. He's an adviser on banking regulations. He advises on free trade agreements. He does presentations on the World Trade Organization. He submits papers to committees. Who do you think you're talking about?"

"I don't know. Maybe Bambam Baloney."

"Laugh again. Stay away from this guy. Burley's bad news in spades. He's got golfing cousins in Florida that you'll never want to meet. A golf club is more than a sport's implement. They make those guys in the Civic Unity Party look like a fringe group in a peace demo. I'm not joking. And if that's not enough, listen, we do business with Baldwin Martel Wightman. Okay. They're clients."

"I understand all that Morrison. But I got to talk to this guy. Georges said I could make a social visit."

Morrison smiled.

"What is it, Morrison?"

"I suppose it's integral?"

"It is. You could put it that way. If you wanted to use a nice word."

"Good luck. But you'll get nothing from that guy. Burley's a calculating customer. If he wants something done, he hires out and hires out and hires out. He knows the logic of distance. And you'll never trace it."

"Makes sense. But he's impulsive. And look at this, Morrison." I waved the sheet. "He's in here. In the alphabet, NB. Nota bene. I actually studied a little Latin. With Wolsey." I smiled.

Morrison stared at the sheet. He took a deep breath.

"Alec, did you know Detective Warnock was here?"

I shrugged my shoulders.

"Don't be an ape. Do you know what Warnock said about you? Okay, I see you know when to shut up. You know what Detective Warnock said about you Alec? He said you're just in this racket to get laid. He elaborated, said you were smart. And coming from Warnock that's not a compliment. He said it as polite as Warnock gets. He said, and I'm quoting because out of respect for my wife I don't use this language, I'm going to pretend to be a verbatimist, Warnock said, quote you're a smart fucking asshole unquote. How am I going to disagree with the man? Think. Think about that when someone of Warnock's stature runs those three words together they're not at a loss for words, they're not searching for something to say. Don't toss sand in Detective Warnock's face. He's pissed off and a very worried man. A missing daughter, sixteen years old. You put Georges and me on the spot by not giving Detective Warnock that source. Now you want to go like the Easter bunny hopping through the grass selling chocolate eggs at Baldwin Martel Wightman. I got news for you, the Easter bunny does not lay eggs." Morrison took a breath.

"Burley knows something about Liz Strachan. He's the last guy to have seen her before she disappeared on the Monday afternoon. It's that simple."

"Okay. But a word of advice."

"What?"

"Keep your mouth shut and let Burley do the talking. Please don't interrupt him."

Morrison dropped the papers on the desk and left.

I went over all the documents, hundreds of pages, that Morrison and Glastonbury had prepared. When I was finished it was late. I double-checked Norman Burley's address. I checked the city garbage schedule. Back to basics. It was garbage day in his lullaby neighbourhood and I figured it was my day to take out the garbage. I got dressed in my old jeans and T-shirt, put on my old ball cap, work boots and a pair of yellow work gloves. Rockcliffe Park looked swell. The houses like gems studded along the arc of the Ottawa River. In the stretch of the river, Kettle Island slumbered like a small whale. Burley's house was near little Lake MacKay. I parked a few houses down from Burley's. The lights were out. I grabbed a couple of big black heavy duty garbage bags and slipped out of the car. The Burleys' garbage pail stood beside the black recycle box like a sentinel. I took a deep breath, rushed it, tore off the lid, flopped the bag over the top of the garbage can, and upended it quickly. I set it back up, slapped the lid on it, tied the garbage bag with a tie and then stuffed the other bag full of the paper from the black box. I tossed the bags in the trunk and took off back to the office.

The night was quiet. Nick Glastonbury, the nighthawk, came out back in the parking lot with a lamp. We put on white face masks and heavy duty yellow rubber work gloves and sorted through Burley's trash.

"Alec you said anything financial. Right?"

"Right, Nick. Anything with a number, address, anything from a bank."

"This guy's a banker?"

"Yeah. And a corporate lawyer."

"You going to make a deposit, Alec?"

"I'm going to redeposit this."

"Proceeds of crime, Alec. Theft of garbage. This is private property."

"Nick, tell me about it. Garbage goes public."

"Okay, theft of public property."

"Tell Mike Harris about it. Tell Mayor Chiarelli. Anyway first it's got to go in the garbage truck."

The moon came out. Like two raccoons we pawed our way through the trash. We collected an assortment of papers, some crumpled, some torn, some whole. Numbers and words, soiled and torn, the world was a place of used up numbers and disintegrating, decomposing words.

We scooped up the residue scattered across the parking lot asphalt and hustled it back into the garbage bags.

"Nick, could you give these papers to Morrison when he arrives in the morning. If you see anything fishy—talking money—fish talking money, mention it to him."

"Maggots talking money, Alec."

"Yeah. Highlight it. And bring it to Morrison's attention. I'll check it out when I come in. I'm bushed."

# ELEVEN

I got into work around seven and talked with Morrison Chang. He said the garbage that Nick Glastonbury and I sorted the night before was a zero effort. Utter waste. Not a single item linked to ICCI Bank, not a trace to link Burley with Liz Strachan, mostly finely shredded credit card slips, the odd shopping list for groceries, and a few personal notes to pick up some things.

I arrived at the law offices on the dot. Burley kept me waiting in Baldwin Martel Wightman's reception area. The receptionist chanted behind a long sleek polished mahogany counter. "Baldwin Martel Wightman how may I direct your call. Baldwin Martel Wightman how may I direct your call. Baldwin Martel Wightman how may I direct ..." I counted and admired the equanimity and cadence of her velvet voice. I lost count after a hundred. It became almost a mantra, meditative and soothing. An hour passed. I jolted up when the cadence of her voice changed. I glanced over then I approached the receptionist.

"I had an appointment to see Mr Norman Burley at eight."

She gave a cheerful but patient look with her green eyes.

"Yes Mr Knight, I have indicated to Mr Burley's assistant that you are waiting. She said Mr Burley will be with you as soon as possible."

"Could you please check again."

"Certainly."

I stood waiting. The receptionist spoke into the phone.

"Mr Knight is waiting to see Mr Burley." Pause. "Yes, I'll tell him."

"Please have a seat Mr Knight, Mr Burley's assistant indicated that he will see you as soon as he's finished with his present client."

I sat and waited.

Ten minutes later a slim tall woman with blonde hair cut very stylishly came out to greet me.

"Mr Knight?" Her voice was in the imperative mood. I was at her mercy.

"Yes."

"Mr Burley will see you. Right this way. Follow me."

Dwelling so deep in boredom I would have followed her anyway.

She led me down a long white corridor where stylish po-mo art barked at me that I lacked the sophistication to understand it. And I whispered back, yeah but I've got patience in spades. And a work of art wants above all else a patient viewer. We passed three spacious boardrooms before she led me into an antechamber. I knew it was so because she said in a nonchalant, anticlimactic way, half suave but so pleased and amused, "Have a seat Mr Knight."

I sat. And she sat behind a desk with a mahogany veneer. There's a limit to squandering law partners' profits, it usually stops at the legal assistant's desk. She overcame her appearance and went fast to work on the computer. I admired her, if she had been driving a car she would have been doing the equivalent of 190 and taken every curve. I could not hear the sound of her mistakes because she made none. We take such things for granted but know nothing of the fingers until we use them. She tore up the typographic road map.

The keystrokes on the computer keyboard metronomically measured time. I was so bored she began to look beautiful. Indeed I convinced myself that she was beautiful. Another half hour gnawed away. Burley's assistant said, "Mr Knight. Mr Burley will see you now."

"Thanks."

She rose and showed me to the door. She knocked lightly on the mahogany door and opened it.

"Mr Burley. Mr Knight."

Burley came about a half pace forward but no more, I went to his desk. He extended his big hand. We shook. His handshake was moderately firm and politic as if not to convey his strength. He was impeccably dressed in a fine blue pinstripe suit with a discreetly textured red tie, a red carnation in his left lapel. His pale blue shirt was silk. His hair, blond with touches of grey, was perfectly parted, his face puffy in the jowls like a retro Diefenbaker, his blue eyes very cool, distant, even indifferent.

"Alec Knight, Mr Burley."

"Please be seated sir. I didn't realize yesterday when you telephoned that you work for an investigative agency which our firm has employed on occasion."

"Mr Burley, I believe you may have met Mr Lajoie or Mr Chang."

"I've had the pleasure of meeting Mr Lajoie." He paused.

"Mr Lajoie has informed me that you have made an impressive contribution to Canadian politics. And in particular to this province through the Civic Unity Party."

"I like to believe that I have. It gives me immense gratification to know that I'm working with the best and brightest minds—the very keenest men committed to the national interest. Minds who are endeavoring to revitalize this nation. And if the electorate shows its wisdom and confidence in the next election, the party may have the honour to serve the interests of the public with good common sense. After all, the foundation of the party is common sense. And the Canadian people are, at least in my experience, a very common sense people."

"I think that you are in tune with my generation."

"I think we are a party ready to redress the past mistakes of other parties. Previous generations fell for the swindle of socialism. Sold this great nation out to the socialistic demagogues. What we desire is to rectify the past by bringing capitalism to all the people. The welfare state, socialism robbed people of all incentive to do business. To reform the tax system. That's the goal of the Civic Unity Party. To uplift each and every citizen. Each and every taxpayer. Relieve Canadians. To get them out from under the burden of a horrendous tax load. Horrendous squandering of the public purse. No giveaways to people who won't work. Who won't do business. No taxing those with a good business to give to those who won't work."

"That's the wavelength of so many of my business friends. People are tired of too many taxes. Exhausted."

"I concur. The welfare system destroys the will. Destroys the moral fibre of a self-reliant person. The state must stop meddling in the lives of people. It must stop seeking to regulate the economic life of its citizens. Regulating the emotional and moral lives of the electorate towards cynicism and pessimism and defeatism. Those are three political diseases that plague this nation, rot the economy and lead its citizens to apathy. The state's intervention leads to moral slackness." Burley paused, his fingers fidgeted as if he itched to smoke. He folded his hands together on his desk. "If I might be philosophical for a brief moment. There is a certain purity to money. The pursuit of money makes us better human beings. Transitory philosophies—mind you I ought to call them what they are, ideologies, worse, truly speaking, demagoguery—such as communism and socialism don't grasp the essentials of the human spirit. This principle of purity in the pursuit of money, property, money instils a moral incentive, unleashes a creative impulsive. It gives a crystal clear focus to men's lives. Their desires, wants and needs. So essential to survive. We might take a leaf from the history book of our wise American cousins and neighbours who have shown so much more moral courage, vigour, and fortitude. Their refusal to fall back on the state and government for all their needs. Instead they have looked to individualism, independence, and self-reliance. Admirable qualities. Admirable qualities we might cultivate. Admirable American values. Instead of this socialist swindle imposed on us."

I nodded. Burley's blue eyes were stern.

"By this, I mean money purifies itself into capital which sustains the necessities of life. And as it does so, if I might speak metaphysically, it purifies our spirits. Pragmatic idealism."

Burley paused.

"Mr Burley, I think it's only a matter of getting that message out to people of my generation."

"Yes but the liberal media stand in our way. The state-owned media. The CBC and other negative forces with their anti-americanism seek to subvert our grand project. Those newscasters of nihilistic negativity. They delude, mislead and confuse Canadians. But it is only a matter of time, reason will prevail and we will win over a new generation of minds. Then the media will stop their liberal whining. But sir you surely didn't come here to discuss this. You have something more imperative."

"As I indicated on the phone, Lajoie–Chang is involved in investigating a missing person. A Ms Liz Strachan."

"But surely you recall, I clearly indicated on the phone yesterday that I do not know any such person."

"Mr Burley, I'm hoping to help you avoid embarrassment."

He said nothing to this.

"The police are investigating the young woman's disappearance as well."

"That's fine. I assume it's a matter for the authorities."

"Ms Strachan's parents have hired Lajoie–Chang. They are solicitors from Kingston, Mary and Frank Strachan."

"Get to the point."

"In the course of our investigation your name showed up in documents in Ms Strachan's possession."

"What sort of documents?"

"Some electronic, others on paper. A business card of yours was discovered in one of her purses."

"This is trivial."

"I'm inclined to differ."

"Listen. Any stranger can receive a solicitor's business card. Or pass it on. This in itself is insignificant. And certainly does not warrant coming knocking at my door."

"Ms Strachan, along with a number of other young ladies, worked for an escort agency."

"I know nothing of such businesses."

"It is known as LTD Escort. And according to one source we have, you used their services."

"This is utter nonsense. You can't come in here insinuating such nonsense."

"Are you certain you don't know Ms Strachan? Have not had intimate relations—"

"I told you sir and repeat, I never heard the woman's name until you mentioned it to me. This is boundless arrogance on your part to come in here like this."

"What about a Ms Connie Yonge? I understand you had—"

"Enough. I'm not going to go through a checklist of names to either amuse you or satisfy your curiosity. It was a mere courtesy to discuss this issue. This is too bold on your part. You've overstepped yourself, raking up worthless gossip on Dalhousie Street and then coming in here with a list of worthless questions. I'll call your agency and have you sacked if you continue."

"Call."

"Sir, if you possess any wisdom you will leave."

Like some in the Civic Unity Party, Burley was being trained by media handlers from the sun belt. TV performed quirky inversions projecting liars as visionaries of the truth. I fantasized Burley as telegenic in Televisistan, a veritable statesman.

"Wisdom is in short supply. We've had a drought this summer across the province. The crows and blue jays are keeling over. The squirrels are becoming bold, surly and ruthless, biting back. Mr Burley, when was the last time you spoke with Ms Strachan?"

Burley said nothing.

I'd made a few jabs, but a rude miscalculation trying to land a left hook. It was apparent that Burley was image but he was no inflated dummy.

"Mr Burley, you were seen in the underground car garage with Liz Strachan on the Monday, the last Monday in August, the thirty-first, in the afternoon around five P.M."

"It couldn't have been me. I have no idea what you are on about. I was out of the country." This very breezy.

I saw him. Here I sat in Televisistan watching Burley stay cool. Under no circumstances would the lawyer back down, he went on to get the message out on the airwaves, ignore tough questions, speak the aura of truth, ignore the substance of the truth. And never backtrack to a difficult fact. Pass over contradictions and stay on message. There were far too many facts in the world for people to understand.

"Where, Mr Burley?" I asked.

"No concern of yours, Mr Knight."

"This young woman is missing and I have an exceedingly reliable witness who identified you as being with Ms Strachan. The time and place are correct."

"A clear and plain and simple case of mistaken identity."

"I think not. I want to know what you discussed with Ms Strachan on that Monday afternoon."

"Enough."

"Because. Because you, as far as can be determined you were possibly the very last person to be with Ms Strachan before her disappearance."

"You sir are a liar."

"In this line of work I have found that lying is a very great virtue and useful tool. Even a virtuous vice to discover a virtue."

Burley relaxed, leaned way back in his chair then leaned forward. His voice's inflection changed. It lost its self-regard and came out harsh and blunt.

"Listen. And listen good. You little lying fleabag. Get out. I won't say it any more politely. You never got a referral from Lester Henderson to talk to me. You came out of a flophouse. You're a tramp jumping up and down on a box spring and going through the floorboards. I don't know Liz Strachan. I never met Liz Strachan. I never heard of Liz Strachan."

"Saying so won't make it so."

"Get out. I've a mind to file a complaint with the Ontario Registrar of Private Investigators."

"I'd love it. It would be a splendid hearing." I got up and went to the mahogany veneer door. "Incidentally what ever happened to that young girl you hustled out West?"

"Get out." Burley half rose from his leather chair, he rested his big palms on the desk. His face was flushed.

One wants to leave on a high note after visiting a solicitor, preferably with a cheque in hand from the lawyer's trust account. When that's not possible I'll settle for a colourful display. Burley was livid, he was living up to his reputation. A man of mirrors, platitudes and postures mingled with impulsiveness and self-importance. He gave new colour to the phrase puffed up. Only thing was he had his hand on far too much money for this to pass quietly. Lajoie was going to blow a gasket with this one, maybe even no more referrals from Baldwin Martel Wightman.

At this very moment as I left the law offices, Burley was probably in his comfy leather chair leaning back and reaching for the telephone and dialling Lajoie–Chang. I'd manufactured myself into a fool. Not cool.

# TWELVE

Lajoie and I were driving over to the apartment building to go over the underground car garage. I was hanging onto silence after the brawl with Burley. I thought avoidance was best. But Georges brought up Burley.

"How did it go with our friend Burley?"

"Well, let's just say we moved from politic words to impolitic fairly quickly."

"This is a political town even if it suffers from hypersomnia."

"Huh? How's that Georges?"

"Hypersomnia. The opposite of insomnia."

"Sleepy town."

"You had impolite words."

"Why ask if you know, Georges?"

"Knowledge is never certain."

"Word travels fast."

"Yes. We got a call from Claude Martel. One of the founding partners at Baldwin Martel Wightman."

"Sorry Georges. I really blew it."

"Proportion." Georges gave a very thin smile. "Burley's got a rude lip. You'll come off looking good in some people's eyes if anyone should happen to hear about it. Anyone who gets a tongue lashing from our friend Burley takes it as a compliment. But," he paused as I turned a corner, "listen."

I gave a quick glance at Georges, he was being considerate. I could discern by the focussed gaze out the car window that he was not pleased.

"You're pissed off Georges. You're being polite. It's hard on referrals."

"Alec," Georges tilted his head towards me, "we live by referrals. Not by confrontations. I think you showed poor judgement in trying to brace Norman Burley. He's a combative man. I tried to caution you. Morrison did as well. Now. If Baldwin Martel Wightman wanted to punish us, Elliot Wightman would have telephoned. Fortunately for us it was Claude Martel who made the telephone call. He has no fondness for Norman Burley. All things considered, it was an amiable chat after the initial formality of a reprimand. Claude Martel had no choice, he had to at least make the call. He can't and won't let such things pass. It is a matter of the firm's dignity. And Claude Martel is a man of formalities and dignities. He has aspirations."

"Don't tell me, another guy who wants to be a judge."

"Yes. And he should be. He's a good judge of character. Claude Martel is a man of real intellect. He is very cool to Burley because Burley lacks respect for people. Martel and Gaston Laing make the referrals, Burley has no say in the matter. We tried to caution you away from this course."

"Then why didn't you say so more explicitly?"

"Explicitness is for amateurs. This is your case. You'll handle it your way. You note I am sitting in the passenger seat and you are the driver."

I said nothing. Time sat on the dashboard, then Georges said, "Burley's capable of rape. He's capable of much else. But we can't fight injustice Alec, we are no more than a private investigation outfit. Nothing more and nothing less, I emphasize."

I pulled up at the apartment building and parked. I took the keys out of the Honda's ignition and glanced over at Georges.

"And I reiterate it. We cannot in the course of our work assimilate a crime. Give me the keys."

I handed the car keys to Georges.

"There. See." He handed them back to me. "You are quite capable of following instructions but it would do no good to instruct you to drive the car here."

We went in and got Ray Willett. Georges surveyed the garage. He checked the stairwells then worked out from Liz Strachan's Miata. All the while I watched silently. He came back to the column where Willett and I stood.

"Did you check each fire exit, Alec?"

"No."

There were four fire exits plus an extra door. Georges looked at Willett. "Mr Willett, did the police check the fire exits?"

"I can't say."

"What's that other door over there?" Georges pointed across the garage to a distant white door.

"That's to the garbage dumpsters."

"Is it locked?"

"Yeah, it locks automatically if it slams behind you. But there's no automatic spring or anything like that. I got a key so I can open up from the outside if I go out and it locks me out."

"So someone can get out that way?"

"Sure I suppose. But it goes nowhere."

"Let's have a look."

Georges and I went out the door while Willett stayed inside and held it open.

"Alec, check the dumpster."

"You don't think she's in there," Willett scoffed.

There were four dumpsters. I climbed the side and threw back the lid of the first. The stench came up. I peered in, nothing but trash. I checked the other three. Georges checked around the sides and backs. There was a high cinder block wall of eight feet behind the dumpsters.

"What's behind the cinder block, Mr Willett?"

"An overflow work supply shed."

"Is it for the apartment building?"

"Yeah."

"How do you reach it?"

"Through the fire exit."

"Who goes back there?"

"Just me and some of the company maintenance guys."

"When was the last time you used the shed?"

"I don't know. Not recently. Month or more. I store most of what I need for the summer inside the garage's storage sheds and the winter gear goes in there for the summer. I haven't much call to go in there through the summer months."

Georges looked down on the ground.

"Fine. Let's go back in Alec."

We went back in the underground garage.

Ray Willett looked bored and irritated. Georges gazed at him, it was Georges's remarkable gaze that shook a person down. Authority commingled with gentleness, it was near irresistible in its insinuation and influence. He could lure a person with it or drive a person away.

"If you don't mind, I got some things to do," Ray Willett said. "I'm going back upstairs, give me a shout if you need me."

"Sure, thanks for your help, Mr Willett. It's much appreciated." Georges was all affable now.

Willett smiled.

"That's fine Ray," I added. "Go ahead and do what you have to do."

Willett left. Georges watched the superintendent leave.

"Come back here, Alec."

"Sure." We moved towards the exit doors.

"That one's into the fink fund."

"Yeah. But mostly small change."

"But not necessarily reliable."

"That's going too far. So-so. I've been bringing him along. He's improving but ..."

"Blabbermouth?"

"Half and half. But he does see what he does see. If given an incentive. That counts for something."

"Does he talk to the police?"

"As little as possible. I think he's afraid of them."

"Why? Did you check him?"

"Yes. He got into a little trouble many years back. Nothing serious. Petty theft from an electronics shop. Accessory. Did six months. Looks like the poor sucker was used by a buddy. He drove the car without maybe realizing what the friend was moving. So he's afraid of the police coming down on him again even though it was years ago."

"So he talks."

"No. I don't think so. More uses the law of avoidance. Saw-nothing heard-nothing said-nothing sort of guy. He doesn't want to lose his job here in the apartment building."

"How'd he get it?"

"As far as I can tell, a nephew of his is high in management circles with Melgund Construction. I think the nephew swung him the job."

"Reverse nepotism. So at least ninety-nine point nine percent of what he tells you is crap."

"I thinks that's going too far Georges. He could tell more but we'd have to pay a lot more and then it might be a problem of making up stories to feed us what he thinks we want to hear."

Georges Lajoie said nothing more. He just stood there and gazed around the garage. For me this was always a wonderful and rare moment, reassuring, Georges radiated energy that was good to collect if you were connected to the guy in a positive way.

"Show me exactly where you found the ear clip and business cards."

We strolled back to the side of Liz Strachan's car. I pointed out the spot on the pavement under the vehicle.

"Did you see anything else Alec?"

I stared at the car.

"There was a smudge or smear."

"Yes."

"And you've got the stuff from the trunk."

"Yes." Georges squatted down and stared at the side of the car. "Here. See here." He pointed his long thick finger at the side panel.

I bent over. I was staring at a very fine purple fibre about two inches long. It suddenly looked huge.

"Don't touch it Alec."

"Hell." I muttered and shook my head.

"What colour of dress was Liz Strachan wearing when the other tenant saw her on that Monday afternoon?"

"Mrs Lowe. I don't know."

"Go ask her. Now. Quick. But don't let Willett know you're talking to Eleanor Lowe. Call her from here on your cell first and take the stairwell, avoid the lobby and elevator. Willett'll be watching."

Eleanor Lowe was in.

I took the stairs to her apartment.

The bureaucrat was drinking tea and watching Jerry Springer.

"Mrs Lowe, I was wondering about that Friday you said you saw Liz Strachan in the underground car garage."

"Yes, Mr Knight."

"Do you recall that day?"

"Yes. As I told you, I certainly do."

"Where was Liz Strachan standing when you saw her?"

"By her car."

"Did she have her back to you?"

"No. If I remember correctly, I walked towards the elevator and Ms Strachan had her back to her car and the gentleman who she was speaking with was facing her. I saw them first as I got out of the driver's seat and then in profile with my peripheral vision. Is that the expression?"

"Yes if you say saw and you mean out of the side of your eye."

"I meant I was not exactly looking directly at them because I didn't expect them. You know I was busy getting out of the car and seeing them was purely accidental. Incidental. I saw the man's back as I approached and he half concealed Ms Strachan and then as I went by I caught them with my side vision, I didn't really look their way. You know I was being discreet. It didn't seem the sort of situation where they wanted an outsider interrupting, maybe even a hello or a good day might have been too much on that occasion. It was a little awkward. They were involved in this conversation. Ms Strachan didn't even glance my way. She didn't so much as acknowledge me. So I thought it best to be discreet and just be on my way. You surely understand what I mean."

"I understand. You were being courteous."

"Exactly, Mr Knight. I appreciate that some people understand what it means to be polite."

"Do you recall what Liz Strachan was wearing?"

"I believe a dress. Mind you, you know how dim it is down there."

"The colour?"

"Oh, very dark colour, I can't say for certain but it might have been blue or black, awfully hard to say, you know the light down there, it's not terribly good. Everything looks either black or white or just grey at times. But definitely a dark shade. She was always dressed terribly well."

"So the dress could have been a dark shade of blue or black or purple?"

"Could have been. But I wouldn't be confident to say that it was anything more than a dark colour."

"Fine. You've been a big help." I turned towards the door.

"No problem, Mr Knight."

"By the way," I looked back. "Maybe you could keep this between us, eh?"

"If you prefer."

"I think it would be better."

I zipped back downstairs to the garage.

Georges was circling the car.

"A mess. A botched mess. If there was a crime here, this is a corrupted scene. Thoroughly. Time does its number but trampling through it does more. What does our lady friend have to say?"

"A dark dress. She wouldn't go beyond that with any certainty. Liz Strachan dresses well."

Georges looked down at the thread again.

"Silk. I'd say purple silk. You?"

I bent over and gave it another look.

"Yes. Purple. Silk? I'm not certain. Maybe very fine cotton."

"No. Silk. Look at the shine and sheen and turn of the thread. Only a few rare cottons, Sea Island cotton and long staple Egyptian cotton, can approach that calibre and this thread has a finer quality than the finest cotton. Let's check that other exit to the storage shed."

Georges picked up a scrap of two-by-four and propped the door open. He stood on the doorstep and stared around, then down at the dusty hard packed soil. "See." A cluster of shoe prints of various types were tramped in the dust, a scramble of them went forward about three feet in the dust then appeared to stop then to turn back. "Some people already checked here but went back. I count," Lajoie said nothing for an entire minute peering at the prints, "I count five different shoe prints. How many say you?"

I stared and stared. "Not sure Georges. At least four."

"Stay close to the fence, go carefully, and watch for anything on the ground."

I followed behind Georges close to the cinder block wall. The storage shed was down the path about ten paces, the narrow laneway was about ten feet wide. About six or seven feet away from the shed an unpleasant smell circulated in the air. The closer we approached the more the air became stale, humid and putrid.

Georges moved slowly, pausing and inspecting the ground as we went. There was a series of faded dusty shoe prints.

The lock on the shed door had been forced.

Georges took out his handkerchief and opened the door. Inside, the stench was a little diminished but the stale air had the odd, fetid, mouldy odour typical of enclosed spaces. There was a random assemblage of maintenance tools and equipment, snow plough, shovels, ice choppers and other winter paraphernalia.

I felt a little dizzy from the putrid mix of smells. I turned my head aside. I swallowed, I had a slimy taste in the back of my throat.

Lajoie approached the back wall, pulled back a heavy orange plastic tarp covering more equipment and machines.

"Outside. The other side of the wall, Alec. Check it."

We backed out of the shed avoiding the scramble of dusty shoe prints and went along the side of the shed towards the back. The stench came up in a wave. My throat was thick. I covered my nose and mouth with my sleeve. I stared downward, on the ground was Liz Strachan's other Boucheron pearl and diamond ear clip, it was in tight against the base of the shed wall nearly out of sight.

"Georges. The other ear clip."

"Leave it, Alec. Be careful, something here." Georges went on towards the back wall of the shed.

We peered into the space between the shed wall and the cinder block wall eight feet high. The stench was near overwhelming. A one-foot length of an extension ladder protruded from a blue plastic tarp covering the rest of the aluminium ladder.

Georges reached over and pulled the tarp back slowly.

A body was draped along the ladder as if scrambling up the ladder rungs to escape to a higher place that could never be reached. Her purple silk dress was torn and rucked. Animals had been clawing and biting at the flesh. A cord was knotted around her throat and her flesh bloated. The stench was overwhelming.

"Christ," I muttered, turned away, gasped then vomited down the side of the shed wall.

I heard Lajoie's voice murmur, "Steady Alec." I heard the blue tarp fall back over the body and ladder. Georges rubbed my back for a fleeting moment. I wiped my face.

"Georges."

"Death is never subtle Alec. Back away very carefully. We fucked the scene. You got your cellphone? Call them."

Georges Lajoie was stolid even stoical. There was no tremor or discomposure in his features. He stared down at the splash of vomit. Then for a moment put his hand on my shoulder and motioned towards the doorway to the underground garage.

"Alec, give me the cell. I'll make the call."

I handed Lajoie the cellphone. Georges Lajoie was matter of fact and stoic on the phone. He stood on the spot not moving, his features at once detached and philosophical. He said nothing and I had no inclination whatsoever to say a thing.

Through the humid air, we could hear the distant sirens of police cars converging on the apartment building.

Finally I spoke.

"I blew it, Georges."

"No. I think not. The unfortunate young woman was probably dead before you came to the case, Alec. Judging by the number of prints in the dust, some look like prints from a constable's boot, possibly the police might have been here very early on and checked the shed and found nothing. Possibly the body was moved and dumped there after the initial police search of the underground garage. But who can say at this point. Alec, you did your best. But this one goes way beyond our moment here. We're off the case now. Fact is, it was always a police case."

# THIRTEEN

The police grilled Lajoie and me over the discovery of Liz Strachan's body. It was her. The detective on the case was Detective Sergeant Hélène Johnpine, ten years on the force, new to the homicide division from the drug squad. I recognized her from U of O's crim program. Stellar student. Johnpine had been completing her master's in criminology when I entered first year. She was admired and envied for both intellect and physical prowess. She went straight out of the crim department onto the Ottawa police force. She was a fine athlete, a canoeist, speed skater, a marathon runner—top twenty finisher in the Ottawa marathon. Johnpine had an abrupt manner. She was understandably displeased with the mess, the corrupted crime scene. But the police detective took it in stride as a consequence of the situation, the passage of time and the location itself, the underground garage a heavily trafficked area.

After Johnpine's questioning, I took the rest of the day off. I wandered around downtown, had a gelato and espresso at Pure Gelato on Elgin Street that gave me a jolt. Then I decided, hang it, even if I was broke and my old man had stripped me of my reserve loot, I'd still buy Lynda a gift. I wanted her to remember me—we'd had some beautiful moments together through the summer—even if we didn't see each other again. My mother said, give a woman something she can't throw away without a touch of remorse even if she loses interest in you, at least she might remember you a little better when she sees or touches the thing. I went shopping, something I rarely did. I was one of those in and out customers grabbing pretty much the first piece of clothing or shoes that appeared and racing away to escape the boredom of it all. I knew from security work in retail that all the world's a big department store and that all the shoppers in it were actors. Some suave, others anxious. For myself in my own life, after watching all the petty thievery and five-fingering, I was one of those bare minimum shoppers going for groceries and a few other necessities at the smallest shops to be found in my neighbourhood. Herb & Spice around the corner on Bank Street and a string of Middle East shops and Chinese grocers on Somerset. I wandered along Sussex Drive window shopping, stumbling into shops and stuttering my way out, until I bought a gift way beyond my wallet, put it on plastic, something I rarely did outside of the job.

Lynda considered the gift for a long moment, touched it with her fingertips but didn't say you shouldn't have. She just said thank you. But it was that voice of hers that carried a resonance.

I spent the weekend with Lynda. Early Sunday morning I drove her to the Ottawa airport and then went back to my place.

Clean the bathroom, some strange animal growled in the base of my brain. I watched a news program on TV for an hour. I couldn't believe there was one war going on and another in the marketing. I figured the world was all screwed up. If I could really get into watching a reality TV program I might delude myself that it was all messed up because Lynda and I had parted ways, but the earth is a beautiful planet and not a reality television program. I consoled myself with two-bit philosophy on a Sunday morning, guessing the world is always upside down and the earth is always right side up. Listened to three messages from my old man, each one more intimate and more pleading. And didn't call back. There was one from my mother. I phoned my mother, who was nice to me and said she hoped to meet Lynda since I seemed to spend so much time with her. I told her forget it. She seemed disappointed when I told her that Lynda had left for Japan. She said, I don't understand. I said neither do I. She invited me over for supper and cards. We played cribbage for a little while. Two of her neighbours dropped in and I was dragooned into playing bridge. I played the dummy to my mother's great pleasure. I kept thinking of Lynda's sotto voce thank you.

On Monday morning I dragged myself into Bronson Avenue, Cheryl Perron gave me a sympathetic look.

I said to her, "Thanks but don't feel sorry for me. Yesterday was my day."

"I forgot." Cheryl gave an even more sympathetic look, "Your friend left. Right?"

"Yeah. I dropped her off at the airport early yesterday morning."

"Where is it she's off to?"

"Japan. She wants to study over there."

"Right. She's the smart one. Into languages."

I said nothing.

"You'll keep in touch. She'll e-mail you."

"We live by the computer and die by the computer."

"And love by it. Think of it as computerized love letters."

"How charming. The computer, an insignificant instrument, makes all of us even more insignificant."

I half laughed and headed towards the office.

"Oh, by the way Connie Yonge mentioned she would not be back until tomorrow."

"Right. Tell Georges I'll be with him after I get my messages and call the Strachans."

I closed the door and turned on the answering machine. One from my old man who wanted two hundred more. It put me to sleep. The next message was from Connie Yonge, her voice edgy and nervous and sad.

"Alec Knight. This is Connie Yonge. I've just been interviewed by the police. I was hoping to meet with you preferably not at my apartment. I'm worried. And need some (inaudible). And I was hoping"—her voice dipped down again and she sounded as if she might be weeping but I was not certain—"I have not told the police that Liz and I were intimate but they know about Parsons. Could you please give me a call tomorrow after one when my flight returns. Or I'll call you again. Thanks. Connie Yonge. My phone number is two three ..."

I played it back again then sat at the desk for a long moment.

I dialed up the Strachans at the Lord Elgin. There was no answer. I left a message with reception. I went back out to Cheryl's desk.

"Cheryl, did you or Louise speak directly with Connie Yonge?"

"Louise did briefly on the Friday. I did this morning."

"What did she say?"

"Not much. Except that she wanted to see you, had to do a flight and would be back on Monday. And that the police had questioned her."

"How'd she sound?"

"Sound? Like one very nervous, even, I'd say, scared lady. But that's just me putting it on her. After all, it can't be too much fun living in an apartment building across the hall from your friend who just got murdered in the underground garage. I sure would be nervous if I were a single woman living in that building. The newspapers seemed to suggest that Liz Strachan might have been raped."

"It's a drag. She didn't say why she wanted to talk to me?"

"No. Just that she wanted, well actually needed to. By the way, Georges still wants to talk to you. He's got something on his desk."

"Thanks." I knocked on Lajoie's door.

"Yes. Come in."

Georges looked a little tired. But he said nothing of Liz Strachan.

"Sit down. This." Lajoie tossed a file on the desk towards me. "Something for you. But you don't have to take it if you don't want it after Friday. Something came out of your work on the Strachan file."

I opened the folder. It was Madeleine Masson.

"I should tell you I knew the Masson family in passing when I was a kid in Montréal. Her father was a Québec judge. My father knew him. The Duplessis crew despised the guy but the Massons are an old family. Masson père had a reputation for being a thoroughly incorruptible personality at a time when the expression had some meaning." Georges paused as if he wanted to read a book rather than talk. "There's money in this one. It could be a long haul. But look, if it looks dry let me know as soon as possible. Madeleine Masson has taken her husband Clarence Wilson's death in a tough way but it's been near five months. And, well from experience, with hit-and-runs that involve a death the fellows are on top of them fairly quickly and as a rule get the vehicle and driver quickly. After a few months the picture doesn't look so good. This is not an insurance case so it is going to be very tough. You'll need more than patience. To be honest Alec, I would be surprised if there is anything new to be found out. It seems that a fundamental is missing from the tragic triangle of time, location and evidence." Lajoie paused and with a flurry of his hands made a transitory triangle with his initial fingers and thumbs. "The time side and location foundation don't find equality in a hypotenuse of evidence. No eyewitness or a precise piece of physical evidence from the crime scene linking it to the specific vehicle which was immediately involved in the hit-and-run accident. Which in turn would allow the vehicle to be linked to a specific driver. I tried to discourage Ms Masson, told her it was better to leave it with the authorities, but she has lost her confidence in them."

"I go out there?"

"Yes. When I spoke with her I told her I'd send someone from the office on the Monday."

"Sure."

"Few other things. Johnpine is riled over that first ear clip."

"I understand. But their people missed it."

"All the more reason. More urgent from their perspective is the footprint on the card and the thread on the car. Detective Warnock is assisting Johnpine on this homicide. He'll probably be around to talk to you. So prepare yourself. Also I want a complete final report prepared to give to the Strachans as soon as possible."

"Right. I do it before I go over to Quebec. Get it to you this morning."

"Fine. Have you spoken with the Strachans?"

"I called, they weren't in. I left a message. By the way, Georges, if Connie Yonge calls in could you speak to her? She's one nervous woman. She might be vulnerable."

"I'll stay with it. What do you see?"

"I don't know. Blackmail. Those flicks. Money laundering. I can't say. She was tightlipped the couple of times I spoke with her but now she wants to talk."

"She's holding back from the police." George brushed his upper lip with the edge of his first finger. "She's wanting to pump you for information. Either for her own protection or to turn it over to some people who are on to her."

"Liz Strachan and Connie were lovers, Georges."

"It will come out. Johnpine and Warnock probably already know. That's the sort of thing that comes out almost immediately in these sorts of cases."

"Sure, but she's pretty edgy."

"She no doubt has reason to be. Whoever killed Liz Strachan is not interested in negotiating a deal."

"Connie Yonge sounded all broke up."

Georges nodded his head and said nothing.

The ride up to the green hills of the Gatineau was a relief. The radio started up with some good music but the news came on. The media were reporting Liz Strachan's death as a homicide and a suspected rape although a complete autopsy had yet to be made and the police were withholding any definite details. I thought of the thin silk purple thread stuck on the side of the Miata. I flicked off the radio. I drove through old Chelsea to Masson's house.

Madeleine Masson opened the door. She looked austere in a grey sleeveless linen dress. Her lithe but finely contoured arms were lovely, the skin almost satin. I had the impulse to rub my fingers along her upper arm. I felt an abrupt and spontaneous longing for Lynda. The residue of desire floated around me. Almost as if she intuited my impulse, Madeleine Masson folded her arms across her chest.

"Mr Knight, thank you for coming up here."

"No problem, Ms Masson, Mr Lajoie asked me to. I hope we can be helpful."

"Please come in. Could I get you some coffee or a tea."

"No thanks. I just had lunch."

We sat on the back verandah in the white Adirondack chairs. She said nothing for a long moment. A crested blue jay landed on the tree across the garden. The sun was above the trees moving westward. The air was soft but a faint breeze came up, it could not sustain itself and collapsed. I caught the fragrance of cedar and pine. The needles on the pine trees were exquisitely traced out on the sky.

"After your visit out here the other day I must admit I was troubled. Not knowing you, I was reluctant to speak candidly regarding my husband and the accident."

"That's understandable."

"It was not just my husband Clare's troubling death and the circumstances. It was the mention of several other aspects in our conversation."

I glanced at her. She had been leaning forward but now sat back in the Adirondack and folded her hands in her lap.

"Are you sure I couldn't offer you a coffee?"

"Only if you're going to have one yourself. Don't make it on my account."

"I'll be a moment." She went in the house.

I watched the birds in the trees. A quarrel of squirrels.

Madeleine Masson came back with a tray of coffee and set it down on a small wooden table.

"I need my coffee more than ever. Although I shouldn't have too much caffeine." She near smiled.

I took the cup and threw in a teaspoon of dark sugar.

"Demerara. Hmm. Good, very good."

"I had a very candid conversation with Georges Lajoie. I suppose I half fool myself that much can be done to solve my husband's death but I can't leave it unresolved. It weighs on my mind. My children, my two boys want an answer."

"This is understandable. Entirely. I suppose we seek meaning even when it is a troubling answer."

"I'm not seeking revenge. I'm not. I'm not. At least I tell myself I'm not. I think it was cruel. So terribly cruel to have hit Clare in that way and crueller to have left him and not even have stopped and made a gesture to assist him in some small way. Even if he had died instantly. And I suppose I'm granting the person who did it the possibility that it was an accident. I also tell myself maybe the person who did it panicked. I can contemplate such a moment. Some young person. Inexperienced. Or some man. Someone who just lost themselves in the confusion of the event. Lost their reason. And didn't know what to do."

"You're being generous."

"It's my inclination. I've had almost everything, Mr Knight. But I don't want to be angry. Maybe if we found out who hit my husband I would try to seek some understanding and forgive the person who committed the crime. Clare was that way. He was such an admirer of Trudeau. He declared that when Trudeau worked for the abolition of capital punishment in Canada that that was the greatest day in the history of our country."

"It makes a difference. Although not everyone would agree with such a sentiment."

"I know Clare wouldn't be seeking vengeance. He deplored such emotions. He believed that justice was best served through a spirit of generosity. My father, who was a judge, believed the same. Not vindictive law." She paused. "I'm going on. Sorry."

"Not at all. No problem, Ms Masson. It's good to know where a client is coming from. It clarifies expectations. Desires."

"My brother-in-law Marshall Wilson is livid. He wants the man, I mean the person who did such a thing put away for life. I certainly want to see him arrested and brought to justice, knowing what happened, but I don't want revenge. Now Georges Lajoie, whose agency comes highly recommended, told me that the chances of resolving a hit-and-run accident grow more and more remote the longer the case is unresolved."

"A cold case is tough. Evidence. Evidence is what is needed. But it gets trampled upon. It evaporates. Disintegrates. Witnesses are lacking. The evidence disappears into new matter. Changes its molecular form so to speak before our eyes. Time does its trick of disintegration. It is an unfortunate aspect of any event, any crime of this sort."

"I know the authorities have done their best but it seems insufficient. My husband's family is upset and impatient. I spoke to my brother Gilles Masson about your visit. He is a doctor. He recalled my father mentioning Georges Lajoie when Mr Lajoie was on the Montréal police. My brother-in-law also gave it some thought. My brother Gilles urged me to contact Lajoie–Chang Associates. And hire the agency. I hesitated. But I wanted to talk with you, so I called your office. But after I heard about the young woman's death—"

"Liz Strachan?"

"Yes, the woman who you were searching for. I was convinced that it was worth a try."

"Why's that if I might ask?"

Madeleine Masson looked across the garden towards the line of conifers then back at me. She gave me a forceful gaze.

"Mr Knight, can I speak with you in the strictest confidence?"

"Of course. It's part of the contract Ms Masson. It's a standard part of the agreement. We're very careful on this point."

"I'm especially concerned regarding my in-laws. After you came out here looking for information regarding Liz Strachan I was unsettled. I misled you, Mr Knight."

I half smiled without intending.

"You knew I did. Didn't you?"

"Let's say it was nothing more than a probable hunch."

"That's being gracious. In fact, I lied outright. But I felt at the time that I was under no obligation to delve into my husband's personal life with a perfect stranger. Then I thought, after you left, that if Ms Strachan were missing and I had some information which seemed meaningless to myself but might prove to be useful in your investigation that I should give it to you but ... nevertheless I hesitated to call you." She rested her hands on the arms of the Adirondack chair. Her fingers were long, she still wore her wedding band. "This is so roundabout. I hope I didn't compromise your search for the young woman. It's horrible, what I read in the newspapers. Would it have made any difference if I told you about my husband and Liz Strachan?"

"Well first, I'm not certain what you will tell me. Second, probably not in terms of saving Liz Strachan's life. By the time her body was discovered it's hard to say whether anything to do with your husband and Liz Strachan was relevant. But that's hard to say for certain until the police finish their investigation."

"Who found her?"

"I can't say. I don't know."

"I had the impression from a rumour I heard that a private person found the body, not the police."

"Where did you come by that Ms Masson?"

"Through my brother-in-law. Marshall Wilson. Actually he even suggested that Lajoie–Chang was involved."

"It is better not to go into details. These sorts of homicides generate a lot of speculation. Worthless speculation. Innuendo."

Madeleine Masson said nothing. She rubbed her hand on the wide armrest for a moment.

"I believe my husband and Liz Strachan had an affair. In fact I think he contemplated leaving me for her."

"I see."

Madeleine Masson began to cry then wiped her face with the back of her hand and stopped.

"Fact is. That as much as I loved Clare, as loyal as I was to him, Clare was promiscuous. He was not loyal. He made little of it. He said he was loyal where and when it counted. In appearance we were loyal but it was not that way for Clare. I almost divorced him after my second son's birth, he had an affair with a woman, a legal assistant at the law firm. But we had become so financially entangled that it was not possible. Clare swore he'd have no further affairs. I half ignored it. It was a lie. The affair with the legal assistant, who also was married, lasted two or three maybe four years. My husband was a fine lawyer. Served his corporate clients well but like so many lawyers, like so many professionals, in his own personal financial affairs he bordered on incompetent. His financial affairs were very complicated and entangled."

"How so? Maybe you could give me some idea. Some details."

"He was involved in some high profit, quick profit but high risk investments with a number of individuals."

"Who?"

"Well." She paused. "At least one person at his law firm, Norman Burley."

"Who else?"

"A Mr Lester Henderson, who is an acquaintance or business associate of Mr Burley. Mr Henderson runs a series of bonded warehouses and a transportation company. My husband came to these investments through his brother Marshall Wilson and through our good friend Alfred Plante. Alf Plante is a criminal lawyer in the law firm of Plante, Slowikowsky. Maybe you have heard of him. He is quite a prominent criminal lawyer."

"Yes I have heard of the firm Plante, Slowikowsky."

"Marshall and Alf said these were good investments. With a good record of fast turnover, quick return at a high rate. Marshall needed funds fairly quickly. Marsh and Clare didn't exactly have it rough but their father, Hugh Wilson, an accountant, was not a prudent man. He was a compulsive gambler and alcoholic."

"Excuse me for a moment. Where did your husband attend law school?"

"Kingston. Queen's University."

"And his brother Marshall Wilson. He's a lawyer as well?"

"Yes."

"Where did he go to law school?"

"University of Western Ontario. After he did his MBA at McGill."

"Okay. Please continue."

"The Wilson brothers' life was anomalous, they were not by any means poor. In a manner of speaking they had many opportunities but grew up in a family that was financially precarious, because their father Hugh was entirely lacking in prudence. The situation was one of constantly being broke but having the illusion of money. A sort of artificial affluence, if you can imagine it, where credit at high interest rates and constant borrowing were daily passions. Their father, Hugh Wilson, kept shuffling things around through a series of revolving debts and trust accounts among his clients and their accounts. Infinitely complex and risky. And somehow, for some people, exciting. My father used to say the best men are shaped by their mistakes, errors and faults and become much better from being a little bad, even self-destructive. I'm inclined to think that of Clare sometimes. He had so many admirable qualities. And people were so naturally drawn to him. That he was so charming maybe because of his faults. You can't really judge someone you love. Anyway, Marsh and Clare didn't gamble like their father but gambled in their investments. They went for high and quick profits on risky investments. They hit a bad patch in the early nineties. Against my better judgement I allowed Clare to use money from my inheritance in one of the trusts to bail himself out. He was very involved with Norman Burley's Caribbean banking ventures. From a financial perspective it was squalid. I think the worst but dare not state it because I can prove nothing."

"Did your husband lose big time being involved with Mr Burley in this Caribbean investment venture?"

"Nearly. But my trust funds salvaged him. He swore after I bailed him out that he was finished with Burley and his high-flying investment crowd. Hedge funds. Money markets. Junk bonds."

"But he wasn't?"

"No. He was a little more cautious and did look to me because I told him I would not jeopardize the children's future. In any event, my brother Gilles Masson is trustee of the family estate and wanted nothing more to do with Marshall Wilson and Norman Burley and the International Canadian–Caribbean Investors Bank. Particularly after the collapse of the fast investment market in the nineteen nineties. Anyway the short and long of it is that Clare put at risk my inheritance."

"Did your brother know?"

"Not initially. He's a doctor and was out of the country a good deal of the time. He does relief work with NGOs. But he discovered some things but not everything. You mentioned that numbered company and it was clear that Clare was back involved with this man Lester Henderson, Norman Burley and other high risk investors." She paused. "I want to show you the coroner's report and a few other documents."

She went in the house and returned with a legal folder, simply labelled Clare's Accident. She handed it to me.

"You might look at this."

I leafed through it glossing the items. There were press clippings. Numerous obituaries. There was the coroner's report. Then a photocopy of a letter addressed to Clarence Wilson at his Ottawa address.

"Read it, Mr Knight."

Printed caps from some standard printer in the centre of the page. It read: STAY AWAY

"Well, if nothing else, concise." I inspected the photocopy of the envelope, the stamp had been franked in this year Toronto ON.

"Yes. Very."

"The police have the original?"

"Yes. But I only recently found it. Two weeks ago. I had told them my husband had been promiscuous. They knew as much. Even more than I knew. Even so, they are still convinced or they seem to be working on the assumption that Clare's death was an accidental hit-and-run. Rather than deliberate."

"Did you tell the police about Norman Burley and Lester Henderson and Peter Slowikowsky?"

"I mentioned that we had financial difficulties but that they had passed. In any event, they were more than convinced after the coroner's report that it was an accidental hit-and-run. It says as much."

"Up to a point. It's not that explicit Ms Masson."

"Only because they have no suspects as to who the driver was or even the vehicle."

"Can you take me out to the site where the accident occurred."

"Yes. If you think it is useful."

"It might be helpful. Although it is some time since the accident. Things can be overlooked. It happens. It's a while but it doesn't hurt to have a look see. May I take this file and make copies?"

"Certainly."

We drove out through Chelsea, I followed Madeleine Masson's silver Camry in my Honda. We went by way of little-used roads that passed through heavy rock outcrops, red and grey, and by dense forest, mostly conifers, some birch and a few maples. Shadows created by high outcrops of rock lined stretches of the road even though it was a clear sunny day. This old logging area had been clearcut probably three times over. I'd heard that the new growth trees, pines and other evergreens, only obtained about one third of the original height of the old growth in the virgin forest before the logging companies moved into this region. Give the trees forty or fifty years and cutting would start again. Only the forest in the wooded parkland was gaining back height, but it would be centuries before the trees would regain the magnificent height of the virgin forest. Throughout this wooded area, beautiful and serene as it appeared in moments of seclusion, the powerful rock jutted out and was bleak and cruel. I suddenly felt old, even weathered, and haunted as the shadows of the trees moved through me.

Masson's Camry pulled over before a long bend in the road. I pulled over to the side of the road behind her car.

She got out and without a word I followed her about ten paces up the gravel shoulder. The woman stopped, stared about. Curving round the bend there was nothing in view but rock and green trees, a rocky ditch on either side of the narrow worn asphalt road bereft of any yellow line with only narrow eroded gravel shoulders. A perfect spot if there ever was one for a hit-and-run accident. Not a house or cottage in sight. Not even a broken down barn or silo. Not even some lonesome wood shack or decayed log cabin so common to the area. No village store trailing down the line. Nothing for a clear mile on either side of the curve and twisting road up ahead.

"About here as far as I can recall Mr Knight."

There was a chill in the air as we stood in the shadow of the trees. A shallow gully below was hard with rock and some verdant patches of surprising soft grass.

"Clare's body was found down there by those rocks." She pointed towards some grey rocks with rusted iron striations. I followed her gesture and went down through the gravel, weeds and rocks to the spot. He had been thrown about fifteen feet from the edge of the road. I glanced about. There was not a sound in the air. I stared over at Madeleine Masson, she had her cool arms folded across her chest.

I came back up out of the hard rock and approached her.

"Bleak but beautiful all the same."

I said nothing for a moment and surveyed the area. I got out my digital camera and took snapshots of the site.

"Watch my back for any cars coming round the curve, I'm going to take a look up the road." I paced along covering the ground about twenty feet up ahead. I saw a small shard of glass that looked like it came from a headlight. I left it. Took a photo of its location. Thirty feet on I found two more pieces in the gravel. Recorded them with the camera. I turned around and went down the shallow gully into the rock and weeds and surveyed the area from below. Coming back across the rock I noticed another small piece of glass a half inch long about five feet from where Madeleine Masson had first indicated her husband's body had been found. I took a photo of the ground. I came back up and stood beside her.

"Well Mr Knight?"

"Nothing really. Did the police find anything that might identify the vehicle? Paint chips. Glass pieces. Broken metal. Plastic fragments. Anything at all from a vehicle."

"I think so. Yes. Several pieces of glass but none that could be linked to Clare's bike."

"Some paint from Clare's bike probably ended up on the vehicle's fender or grill or even body panel of the car, maybe a side panel or hood panel. There was probably a dent in the car panels."

"Police didn't say or wouldn't say. They never got around to even suggesting what make or model of car it might have been. They were very prudent in everything they said."

"Understandably cautious. Careful not to leak any information that someone might hear by rumour and then address."

"You know there was another hit-and-run a week later. Which they tracked down. And they thought it might be linked to this accident."

"How so?"

"It involved a small child. Five or six years old. Back about five miles along this same road. Fortunately the child survived although she was badly hurt. A man about thirty-five years old was charged with hit-and-run. Criminal negligence. At first the police thought he might be linked to Clare's death because he initially reported his vehicle stolen. And the police found the man's car in the river. The man had been drinking at a bar in Maniwaki and left, according to some people, intoxicated but that was never proven because he only reported his car stolen the next day. So there was no possibility of doing a breathalyser on him. But they finally determined that the man himself had dumped his own car in the river after hitting the child to conceal his involvement. The attempt to link Clare's death with this man's car went nowhere. They found evidence on the car that it had hit the little girl but nothing to indicate that it had been in a collision with a bike."

"Interesting." I could feel the cool evening coming on, she looked a little chilled. "Look, why don't you head back to your place. I'll go over the situation. If I have any further questions I'll be in touch."

"Thank you, Mr Knight." She offered her hand. There was something formal but awkward in the gesture, she held it out as if at a reception. We shook hands. I watched her drive off.

I went back down over the stretch, took measurements of the locations of the various shards, photographed them again then picked up the shards of glass with tweezers and put them in the paper envelopes, drew the locations on the back and dated them. Not much here, probably nothing more than fragments from recent cracked glass.

I went back to my car. I drove back and parked in a spot before the curve. I pulled the car as far onto the shoulder as I could without getting into the ditch. I took out my binoculars and got ready for a long wait and see. Up until five thirty it was quiet. I saw five vehicles go by, three of them half-tons. I copied down the licence numbers one by one. Dusk approached. Six went on to seven. Four more vehicles. The forest of the Gatineau was dark and darker with a longitude of shadows instilling loneliness. Just as I was about to wheel around and head home telling myself I would be out early tomorrow morning, a fast-moving car came down the road hitting near to ninety kilometres. I just barely got the licence number but the car looked familiar. An Oldsmobile with a rear Quebec licence plate. I followed it at a distance. It was driven by a guy who knew every inch of the road. He handled every twist and turn in the low hills with ease. He headed north towards St-Pierre-de-Wakefield by another sideroad but I lost him. He was speeding all the way.

I turned the Honda around and headed back into la petite O.

I dropped off the licence plate numbers and asked Louise Montpetit and Nick Glastonbury to run checks on the ownership, and ID the cars and half-tons.

There were messages for me from Ed Stanley, the Strachans and Brenda Strachan.

# FOURTEEN

I called up Freddy Asad, a former client of Lajoie–Chang who had gone through a bitter child custody case with his former wife. It involved trawling for a hardnailed family lawyer to get everything on the former wife's mothering. Did the tyke eat too much junk food, how late did he go to bed, were there any baddies and abusers among the former wife's immediate relatives. Did the kid walk to school in freezing blizzards without his toque and mittens on, did he munch Joe Louis and swill coke for breakfast and lunch. But Freddy's former wife was not only implacable but also an impeccable mother. There may have been a mistaken marriage but there was no mistake in mothering. I came out of it feeling more grimy than a sieve straining old grease from a deep fryer but reason prevailed and Freddy Asad got the boy one weekend out of four and two visits a week. Asad was a manager of an auto parts shop out south Bank Street near Alta Vista. When I arrived, he was finishing with the last customer, a trucker with an emergency, a rig motor that was kicking back. When Freddy was finished he flashed a smile.

"Alec, Alec my friend. Good to see you. What's up? Car troubles?"

"In a manner of speaking but not my Honda."

"Guess what." He was still beaming, "I'm married again."

"Congratulations, Freddy, I wish you the best of luck in your new marriage."

"Not new. Not new, my friend. Old marriage. I'm back with my first wife. She's my second wife. I'm a bigamist with the same woman. We got remarried if you can believe it."

"Only in the movies Freddy. But I'll believe it if you tell me it's so. A big double good luck on this one."

"Alec, Alec, I got you to thank in a way. Only you, my friend."

"For marriage?" I laughed, "You're joking. Come on most people think that people in my racket do nothing but lay waste marriages."

"No. No. Not at all. You always said more than anyone else, be reasonable. That she's a good mother. A wonderful mother. She loves the kid. You didn't do dirt on her. No you told it straight. That she was a good mum to our kid. You kept telling me to be careful 'cuz divorce makes people bitter. And that lawyer, I tell you, that lawyer. Boy oh boy. Something else. Only in it for the divorce fees. Jeez." Asad shook his head.

"They're only doing what's legal and what the client asks. Don't forget they need a client willing to argue. Willing to be unreasonable."

"And boy did he have one in me. My boy's just great. Just great."

"Wonderful to hear it. I can always use a happy story. Listen, Freddy, I could maybe use your help. Your expert knowledge. I got a little difficulty. You may or may not be able to help."

"Anything Alec. Just name it."

"If I showed you pieces of glass, do you think you would be able to identify if they came from a car part? Say for example a headlight or windshield or whatever. And if so which model or make of car the lamp or glass went with."

"Maybe. Maybe not. I'll give it a shot. It's possible unless the pieces are just too small, then I guess you'd need some kind of specialist. But like I say I'd give it a shot. Let me lock up."

I spread out the six shards of glass I had collected on the counter. Asad peered at them for a time without saying anything.

"This piece is too small for me to identify except by the plastic. It looks like it's made from an automotive plastic but probably not a headlamp. More from the side of a car. Like a piece from the inside, like the dash. This piece isn't from a car. It's glass more from a bottle of some kind. It's not an automotive glass or plastic. Now these three pieces. They're automotive. They each came from different vehicles. They're not the same glass." He looked up at me. "Is that so?"

"I don't know. You tell me."

"This last piece, it's kinda small but it is different too. You see, these three have lines. Whatchamacallits. The structure of the lamp moulding is different. Come on back here."

We went down the long aisles lined with auto parts to the headlamp section. Freddy started matching them.

"Now I'd say this one and that one came from a half-ton truck. See?" He held the piece up against the new headlamp. "A match.

That's a 1995 GMC. And this one here, it's a Dodge half-ton. And this other piece is from a car lamp not a truck." He shifted down the aisle. "Looks like a Japanese model. A Toyota. This fourth piece like I said it's too small for me to match except by the material. And this fifth piece? Well I'd say General Motors product." He moved back up the aisle. He matched it against Pontiac, Chevy, Buick and Olds. "Looks closest to an Olds."

"An Olds then?"

"Yeah. I'd say it's from an Olds. See." He motioned for me to come in and take a closer look although the light was on the dim side in the aisle. I tilted my head. The lines in the moulding of the structure, apart from the hairline scratches and worn fading of the material seemed a perfect match. I nodded my head.

"Let's take it back up front where the light is better, bring the new lamp Freddy."

"Sure."

At the front counter he set the lamp down and the piece next to it. "What do you say? Don't it look like a match to your eye?"

I peered more closely. Scrutinized the piece matching with the new headlamp. It seemed very close. But I still had doubts.

"I'd be inclined to say yes. But I trust your judgement more Freddy. You've seen a thousand of these things."

He looked at me. He was clean-shaven but he had a heavy five o'clock shadow, no doubt the sort of guy who if he was going out in the evening had to do a second shave. But he had a friendly if slanted smile.

"Listen Alec. The only way to be really certain is to fit it. Like a jig saw puzzle. You'd need to fit it into the original lamp if you wanted to be hundred percent certain. But for myself I tell you this. I'd swear on my old grandmother's prayer beads that this piece," he gestured with the wedge shaped piece of glass before my eyes, "came from an Oldsmobile headlamp. I don't want to be claiming too much is certain. If some joker had told me I was certain to take a second wife who was a first wife I'd have laughed in his face and said man you're off your rocker. But I've spent twenty years matching up auto parts, fitting car parts to cars. And I'd swear this is from an Olds."

"Great."

"What's it mean?"

"I don't know yet."

"That's something. You sound like you're celebrating. You found something, went looking for a match and you still don't know what it means. Kinda screwy." He grinned.

"That's right."

"You know something Knight, you're a funny kinda guy." Asad half laughed, "I don't know you but I know you. I'd trust you with my wife. I mean my life." He laughed again. "If you say you don't know what this means, I'll trust you. But I bet you do know what it means, right? Way back there in the back of your head, eh."

I photographed the new headlamp and the shard beside it. I took the fragment from Asad's fingertips and slipped it back into its envelope. I wrote the make of the car and possible years on the envelope and the date and time of identification by Asad.

"You've been a big help. You mark this date on your calendar, okay, Freddy. I'll let you know what happens."

I headed back home to Somerset. I looked at the telephone, thought about messages but left it. I made a pan of chili beans with jalapeno peppers and a red sauce. I boiled a pot of rice, very simple technique on the stove top, measure two or three cups of rice in deep pot, wash the rice in cold water, drain and then cover with cold water just three fingers above the rice, put it on the stove, bring to a quick boil then put the lid on and simmer it at a low temperature for precisely twelve minutes. Don't remove the lid. Let it sit for fifteen minutes. It doesn't fail. The brilliance of rice is in its simplicity. I cooked while listening to the radio news. Delegates were walking out of conferences in Africa. A politician resigned, there was back-up on the 417. The temperature was down to 24 degrees. It might rain.

I ate. Rice and beans. Eaten slowly. No higher culture. Then listened to the phone messages. One from my dad about the two hundred, I ignored it. The well was dry. Another from Louise Montpetit telling me the Strachans had called and were anxious to speak with me after having dealt with the police, and then a message directly from Frank Strachan himself returning my call telling me that they were sorry they had missed my call but would be in their hotel all evening and that I could call anytime. I phoned Ed Stanley and Brenda Strachan and told them that I would attempt to meet them later this evening time permitting. Ed Stanley was pressing but I put him off. I stopped by the office to ask Louise Montpetit to photocopy the material that Madeleine Masson had given me and leave the originals and copies on my desk. I did an extra copy of the letter sent from Toronto, and stuffed it in my suit coat pocket. I phoned the Strachans and told them I was on my way over.

They were building a new addition onto the Lord Elgin's south end having completed the north wing. The grey building was covered in the dusk's red glow.

I went up to the Strachan's suite on the sixth floor. They were watching the news. Frank Strachan shook my hand. He looked sad and slow as if he had been knocked to the ground and like any middle-aged guy out of shape he was hurt and winded, struggling and slow to get up, his face was drained of something vital.

Mary Strachan made no effort to rise from her chair, she sat there poised and very reserved, she nodded and offered a flaccid handshake, a mere formality. I had the impression that she had no further desire to see me considering the way things had turned out. I figured this would be the briefest of meetings. She said with more politeness than necessary, "Please sit down Mr Knight." I sat down across from the couple.

"We are returning to Kingston tomorrow and hoped to speak with you before doing so. We've spoken with the police. The coroner is still working on the autopsy. They have not given us much information except the basics of when Liz was found. And even that they have asked us to keep confidential until they complete their investigation. However it is my understanding from talking with Detectives Johnpine and Warnock that you and Mr Lajoie made the discovery."

"Yes. That is correct."

"Can you say what led you to search that area?" Frank Strachan paused, "To be candid Mr Knight, I don't understand this turn of events at all. One day our daughter is on a brief holiday and then this. Maybe it is harsh but it seemed that the police were gearing down their investigation. Or at least insinuating that Liz was not so much missing as difficult to locate, possibly travelling outside the city or some such nonsense, on a vacation."

"It would be best that you spoke to the police on those points Mr Strachan. I can't really say anything on those aspects of their investigation."

"I'm angry."

"That's entirely understandable."

"And that's a platitude, Mr Knight," Mary Strachan broke in. "Just another platitude in a series of platitudes from you and the police. Things might have been a damn sight different if you people had taken this case with the real gravity, urgency that it warranted."

"Ms Strachan, I can't speak for the police but speaking for Lajoie–Chang, I can state that we took this case with seriousness from the outset."

"You gave no indication that you suspected the worst."

"Maybe we can speak on another occasion when you are not in such distress." I stood up.

"Sit down, Mr Knight." Mary Strachan's voice rose and was harsh. "You people owe us an explanation. The police can stand on the necessity of keeping things close to their chest but that doesn't apply to Lajoie–Chang. We paid you people to investigate."

"I can't explain your daughter's death. I don't have sufficient information. It's beyond me at this point. And it is now a criminal investigation. In the hands of the Major Crime Unit of the police service. It would be inappropriate to discuss the case. What's more Mr Lajoie and myself may be called as witnesses. In fact the police—"

"Look." She was very forceful, her voice firm and distant, the lawyer in her was coming to the fore. "Mr Knight you suspected worse when you came up here that evening with my daughter's ear clip. Why didn't you tell the police and be candid with us? Maybe Liz would be alive."

"The police have asked us not to discuss the case with the public or media."

"We're not the public. We're her parents. We hired you people. We paid you. We're entitled to know what you found and what you know about our daughter's death."

"My speculation. And keep in mind, I'm not a coroner. I'm not in any way a medical authority or anything, but in my limited opinion,

I believe, Ms Strachan, that your daughter was dead days before Georges Lajoie and I happened to discover her body."

"How can you be certain? Even the police haven't said as much."

"I told you it's a mere opinion. A belief. I'm not trying to pretend that it's anything more. But you're pressing me. You're putting me on the spot."

"Why do you have such an opinion?"

"The decomposition suggests such a possibility. The police only disclose what they have to especially prior to completing their investigation and to laying charges."

"We have that much from them as a formality and there's nothing we can do but wait. And hope they do a proper investigation and capture the person who did this horrible thing. But from you, that's a soft excuse from you."

I shrugged my shoulders.

"You're disgusting, Mr Knight. Our daughter's dead and all you can do is sit there and shrug your shoulders."

"I think ..." I paused.

"What do you think, Mr Knight? Go ahead, just tell me. I'm waiting."

"I think you are speaking in sorrow. You're in mourning. I accept that. It is not wise to go into details."

"You suspect someone. Or have suspects in mind. Don't you."

"I have my own thoughts. It is inevitable."

"You knew something after you found our daughter's Boucheron ear clip. You came and asked us about those men. Who are they?"

"I have detailed those points in my report. Mr Lajoie now has it. I assure you I have prepared a thorough report. As is the practice at Lajoie–Chang. In light of the unfortunate unfolding of events, both Morrison Chang and Georges Lajoie who are former police officers, will go over my report very carefully before it is given to you to ensure that nothing is omitted."

"You're holding back information on these men. And this woman, this Connie Yonge woman. Holding back, that's your method, isn't it Mr Knight?"

"Actually, some think me too candid."

"Disgusting irony." Mary Strachan turned away, she looked out the window and spoke to the glass. "You know something and won't speak. I hope to God you told everything you know to the police. And if you didn't, I hope they can rattle it out of you." She turned back. "Why did you mislead us so much? It's a double blow."

"I never misled you, Ms Strachan. You would have despised me if I had left you without a trace of hope however unsettled my thoughts were. It is best to keep postulations when doing a private investigation to oneself, and let the facts speak for themselves."

Mary Strachan stared at me with an angry glare.

"Drink, Mr Knight?" Frank Strachan finally asked, as he poured himself a gin and tonic.

"Thank you for the offer, but I don't drink when I'm on a case or working with clients."

"That's admirable." Frank Strachan half smiled. "I admire such forbearance. I don't have it by half. I don't think I could deal with some of my clients if I couldn't have a good stiff one now and again. Real estate agents are something special. And home buyers. Business people looking to make a buck through property speculation can be worse than used car dealers. Every home buyer wants a Michael Cowpland mansion on a McDonald's salary." He started to cry. "I regret to say I'm pissed. I'm pissed and depressed and sad and fucked up and fucked over and fucked. Well generally as fucked as any man and father can be. I'm a lawyer but this is way out of my league. I never came to Ottawa to hear this not even in my most rotten thoughts."

"Stop it." Mary Strachan said sharply.

"No one could cope with this one. It can never go down," I remarked.

"Never mind that," Mary Strachan broke in. "Mr Knight, tell us who you suspect did this horrible thing. You've got names on your mind. Suspects. You couldn't have found Liz without suspecting someone. Someone going through your mind."

"It wouldn't be appropriate . In fact it wouldn't be—"

"Don't bloody well say ethical. I hate that bloody Ottawa word. Ethics. Parliament's passionate password. Preparatory to telling a lie. It's just trite. Frank and I hear it all the time. It's just boilerplate. When a person wants to sound smart and say nothing. This stupid town is full of such nonsense. Ottawa's famous for nobodies standing up for the national ethic."

"Ms Strachan, I didn't bring it up. I avoid the term. But some people live by 'em."

"And some people die by 'em," remarked Frank Strachan, then he sipped his drink.

"Shut up Frank."

"As you can imagine, we've been crying and arguing all day," Frank Strachan continued. "Our daughter Brenda left us. She couldn't take it anymore. Do you know what happened to Brenda, Mr Knight? I mean concerning her leg."

I said nothing.

"A bloody real estate buddy of mine. A supposedly good friend from way back. A lush full flush coming home from a friend's Christmas party."

"Shut up Frank."

"We sued the pants off the bugger. That guy got off lucky. Now this."

"I think I better go."

"Not yet." Mary Strachan approached my chair. "There's a lot on your mind, Mr Knight. Don't hold back. Please tell us what you know."

"It's not a matter of ethics. It's a matter of the facts of the case coming out to reveal how your daughter died."

"Not died. Killed. Murdered. Raped. All the ugly litany. Why did she die this way?"

"No, better first how and then—"

"What do you mean by how, Mr Knight?"

"Just that. How it happened will lead to who. This much is apparent. It wasn't a robbery or a mugging for theft. Or a result of an accidental encounter."

"Then what?"

"A guy with a kink? A weirdo?" Frank asked.

"Well maybe. But I'm not qualified on that."

"Liz was raped then murdered."

"Or murdered then raped? The autopsy and coroner's report are needed."

Mary Strachan stared at me.

"Why do you say that?"

"Let's just call it a hunch."

"You aren't going to speak of the men you investigated."

"No."

"What of this woman Connie Yonge? We hear that she's a lesbian."

"That's a rumour."

"What do you know about her? At one point you insinuated that she was Liz's companion or friend."

"Some said lover."

"I prefer not to use the word lover for such relations. I find it distasteful. Disgusting. Liz was not a lesbian. Why did this woman latch onto Liz? What was her motive? Who are these people that she brought Liz into contact with?"

"I don't know. I never got quite that far into the case. This speculation becomes very—"

"Risky?" Frank queried.

"No. Just not useful now. But I have something I want to show you. If I may."

"Certainly."

I took out the envelope with the photocopy of the cryptic letter Madeleine Masson had given me. I slipped it out of the blank office envelope. "Do either of you know anything about this letter?"

The Strachans read it and looked baffled.

"It means nothing to me. Is this in reference to Liz?" Frank asked.

"I don't know. I don't know who or what the letter refers to. Did you send such a letter Ms Strachan?"

"Never. Absolutely not. Who was it sent to?"

"You stated that things could have been different if I had been more candid. How did you put it, Ms Strachan?"

"Hold back. You held back details."

"Let me put it this way. You showed discretion when you said you had an affair with another man. And that the man was an engineer and had moved west to Alberta and since died."

Mary Strachan blushed.

"Why this? It's true. Are you intent on humiliating me?"

"No. Not at all."

"Let's leave this alone Mr Knight. You've stepped over the line."

"Your daughter's life was as complex, even more complex than your own life, Ms Strachan. You had an affair with Clarence Wilson didn't you? And you sent him this letter when you found out that he was having an affair with Liz."

"That's disgusting. What you say is vile. I did no such thing. I don't even know this person you mention, Watson or Wilson. I've never even heard of such a person."

Frank Strachan moved his glass around the surface of the table.

"Mary, don't mislead Mr Knight. We knew a Clarence Wilson. He was in Mary's law class at Queen's. But Mary never had anything to do with Clarence Wilson. She told you the truth about John Anderson. A chemical engineer. He was a mutual friend of ours. Some thought that he was Liz's biological father. But he wasn't. That's it, nothing more. Liz and Brenda are both my daughters. It's the past. Done. We've made our peace."

"Ms Strachan did you write this letter to protect your daughter?"

"Never. It's disgusting."

"Clarence Wilson had, or appears to have had, I'm not sure how to put it, an affair. Or may have been involved with your daughter Liz."

Mary Strachan began to cry. She went to the window.

"That man was such a bastard. Such a parasite."

Frank Strachan got up and went to his wife.

"Maybe you ought to leave Mr Knight. This is going too far."

"No. No. Frank, it's my fault. It's going to come out." Mary Strachan turned around abruptly. "I did have an affair with Clarence Wilson but Liz isn't his daughter. I swear I didn't know anything about Liz and Clarence Wilson. If I had I wouldn't have written to the man. I would have come and told him to his face to stay away from my daughter Liz. I wouldn't have wasted the postage. He wasn't worth the fifty cents. The cost of a stamp. He was a parasite. A sexual predator. So charming. A real bloody bastard."

Frank Strachan washed a hand across his facial features.

"I don't understand this. This is beyond me."

"Mr Knight. How did you come by that letter?"

"I can't divulge the source but it was mailed to one of the men who appears to have had relations with your daughter. Wilson. It would have helped if you had told me about the affair. No doubt, the police are probably going to confront you over this at some point because they are going to dig all through Liz's personal life. I know you won't much believe this but I'm trying to protect you a little from the unforeseen. A lot of what you will consider ugly details are going to come out in this investigation and I hope you don't take them personally."

"That's too much. That's over the top. How else are we to take them?"

"I don't know."

"For God's sake. Our daughter has died. Has been killed."

"This is one of those very difficult situations where you will have to sort out what you wish to believe and not believe concerning your daughter Liz." I stood up. "It's late and I have a few other people to see this evening. I am available tomorrow if it is essential."

I offered my hand but Mary Strachan just said. "Good night Mr Knight."

"I'll see you back to your car, Mr Knight. I could use a smoke." Frank Strachan went out with me.

We said nothing to one another in the hotel corridor. It was not until we got in the elevator that Frank Strachan spoke.

"Mr Knight. Believe me when I say I didn't and don't think my wife sent that letter."

"I believe you, Mr Strachan. But why do you emphasize that?"

"Because I'm going to tell you a few things that I don't want you to misconstrue."

The elevator stopped. We went through the hotel lobby to the street. Strachan took out a pack of cigarettes and lit one.

"I've tried to quit. I don't know how many times. That's a no smoking floor." He gave a quick thin smile. "Anyway. I was going to tell you something about Clarence Wilson and my daughter Liz."

"Your wife knew Clarence Wilson."

"Yeah. I know the guy too. How'd you come by that?"

"They graduated the same year from law school at Queen's."

"That's right. Where'd you come by that?"

"One and one makes three in this game."

"They had an affair. She was always interested in the guy. Thought him charming but complained about him. Attraction repulsion syndrome. It's kinda complicated. Mary had a very brief affair with this character Wilson. Just a weekend. He seduced her. It was quite quick and all. Lasted a few weeks. Nothing much on his part but momentarily overwhelming for Mary. You had to know Wilson.

He was one of those," he puffed on the smoke, "I suppose not nice to trash people, but, well Wilson was one of those thoroughly self-absorbed egotists that exude a certain charisma but just use up people along the way getting things their own way. Mary and I separated for a year after Liz was a year old. Later, I found out that Mary had had an affair on the rebound from this jerk Wilson but with a mutual friend of ours. A nice guy. John Anderson, the guy was a chemical engineer. People thought he was Liz's biological father because of the time and everything. But it isn't so. We had tests. Liz is my child. It's the past. Done. Mary and I got back together after the trial separation. She's my daughter in every way despite whatever rumours you might hear." He took a deep drag on the smoke and exhaled. "Do you understand?"

"Sure."

We had come to the car. Strachan rested his thick fleshy hand on my arm and said, "Let's go for a drink."

I looked at my watch.

"Okay, a quick one."

We went back into the bar of the Lord Elgin Hotel.

"This is between you and me." He pointed a finger at my chest.

The waiter came over. Strachan ordered a double martini. I went for a soda water.

"Admirable self-restraint Mr Knight. I admire that. I wish I had it. The legal game is a crappy career. Contact with all sorts. Brash bullies, flunkies, bootlickers, coke-heads, lushes and pinheads. Contractors, developers and speculators who got in their heads they'll make millions but are no more than trimmers, corner cutters and angle men. What a lot. I sometimes wonder."

"Congenial sociable crowd with eclectic manners and habits."

"Yeah, you could put it that way."

The drinks came.

"Where were we at?"

"I didn't want to put your wife on the spot."

"I know. While we were separated. Mary saw other men. Maybe even Clarence Wilson was one of them a few more times. I didn't go that far. Although I heard rumours. I never asked her. You don't have to either."

"The cops might."

"How so?"

"If Clarence Wilson had an affair with Liz, and it looks like he might have, the police will check it out."

"I don't think so. Something maybe you don't know."

"What?"

"If you don't know already, Mr Knight—"

"Go ahead."

"This smoothie Wilson is dead. Dead seducers don't murder four or five months after they died."

"You have a point."

"You know the guy had to be a real bastard, if you know what I mean, if he had an affair with Liz after being with my wife."

I said nothing.

"Do you have any idea who Clarence Wilson was married to, Mr Knight?"

"Who?"

"Madeleine Masson. Real old Quebec money. Her great-great-grandfather started a lumber company. The old guy came out from the Saguenay in the 1840s and worked western Quebec. Built up Gatineau Masson Pulp and Lumber. Company logged out half the Gatineau and old E B Eddy the other half. I heard it merged with MacDonald-Glengarry. It's Fleet-Glengarry Consolidated now, one of the biggest multinational paper companies. Clarence Wilson's father-in-law was a big judge up in Quebec. Supreme Court material but he really pissed off the Quebec government after he ruled on some native land claims. So he never got to be a Supreme Court justice. I understand his daughter, Madeleine Masson, is a pretty good-looking woman but it wasn't enough for Wilson. I was a few years ahead of him and Mary at Queen's but Kingston being Kingston, it's a small town through and through. He was always out trying to get laid."

"Lady's man."

"Polite. Shouldn't badmouth the dead. The guy was a top notch corporate lawyer. But he had money problems like his old man, who was a bent out of shape accountant."

"How's that?"

"Rumour mill."

"Go ahead."

"You guys live and die by info, right?" Frank Strachan exhaled.

"Sure. That's right. Every trade has its ambient noise level."

"I like you, Mr Knight." Strachan smiled wanly. "Wilson's old man, can't recall the guy's name, was by all accounts a pretty sharp number, a C.A., very sharp with numbers, too sharp. I also heard the old man was a compulsive gambler. Liked a high stakes poker game. Always on the edge and in and out of financial trouble. He had several brushes with the law and regulatory people in chartered accounting, but always got himself a good lawyer who saved his bacon. So I understand old man Wilson kept himself clean. But he certainly had an influence on the Wilson brothers. Clarence Wilson has an older brother, Marshall Wilson, known to be quite a legal shark, handles a lot of risky financial work for the corporations. As for the Wilson brothers, in their investments they moved with a crowd of guys deep into hot money in Florida and the Carib. Shell companies, quick takeovers, buyouts, mergers. Phoney baloney manoeuvres staying one jump or even a half jump ahead of the authorities. I don't know the details. Local real estate is my limit. It all came to a crummy ending."

"How so?"

"I heard Clarence Wilson died in a hit-and-run accident up in the Gatineau. Maybe you heard. The guy was a skirt chaser but nobody deserves that."

"A heck of a way to die."

"Truly crappy."

"Mr Strachan, is John Anderson dead?"

"No. He's in Alberta. Forget about him. I want you to tell me about this woman Connie Yonge."

"I can't say much. I don't know much."

"I want to know about these people my daughter Liz was supposedly involved with."

"The police will tell you."

"Not likely. They're very close-mouthed. Very circumspect."

"Once they get Liz's murderer it will come out in the trial."

"That's two hypothetical statements. First if they catch the rotter. Second will the dirt on these people come out at the trial? Not likely. Even if the courtroom is hardly my usual space, I know enough to know that not much will come out about what got Liz to where she arrived. What will come out with any criminal defence attorney worth his salt is dragging my daughter's life and reputation through the muck trying to defend the brute."

"You could be right. It is very hard to second guess a homicide case."

"Okay. These things are important but I want something."

"What?"

"I want you to stay on but investigate all these people who knew my daughter. I want to know who they are. What they did to my daughter."

"To what end? That's an expensive research project for the mere sake of knowing."

"Let me be the judge of the value of the information. This is separate from the other thing. I don't want my wife or my daughter Brenda to know about this."

"You certain?"

"As ever."

"Think it over, Mr Strachan. Also I'll have to check with Morrison Chang and Georges Lajoie as to the propriety of such an investigation while a homicide investigation is being carried out that involves some of these same persons. Or parties of interest to the police."

"I just want information on these people. Liz didn't get there on her own."

"Okay. Think it over for a few days. If you still feel the same way, drop by the office and sign another contract with Georges Lajoie. It will have to be treated independent of the missing person file on your daughter which we worked for you. Everything has to go across Lajoie's desk or Morrison Chang's." I finished my drink and stood up. "I got to go."

"Mr Knight, I'll get the drink. Thanks. You're a good sort. I trust you a damn sight more than my own legal tribe."

# FIFTEEN

I went back to Bronson, Ed Stanley and Brenda Strachan had called and wanted me to call back as soon as possible.

"This guy Stanley again." I stared at the pink slip.

"He called three times Alec," said Louise Montpetit. "Third time sounded pretty loaded. Weepy and in a pretty sad state over Liz Strachan's death. Is this guy her boyfriend or what?"

"Supposedly Liz Strachan's lover boy. But more by claim than reality. What's he want?"

"He just kept repeating that he's got to talk to you. Has to talk to somebody who knows what's going on. What happened to Liz Strachan. That sort of line."

"He's dialing the wrong number. I don't have a clue what's going on."

"Some admission from a PI."

"The best kind. Information starts with admission of ignorance."

Louise smiled. "And Brenda Strachan called again."

"It's late, I'll call her tomorrow. I didn't expect to be that long over at the Lord Elgin with the Strachans."

"Actually she was fine with you calling however late. She was calm. Nearly the only reasonable person that I've spoken to about Liz Strachan. Call her Alec. She needs the call."

"Okay."

"Oh yeah, Madeleine Masson called as well." She handed me another message slip.

"That looks like a different number than the one she gave me."

"Her Ottawa residence over near New Edinburgh. She wants you to call if you can."

"Tomorrow."

"She sounded upset."

"About what?"

"Wouldn't say, just said she needed to talk to you if it was possible."

"Too late."

"And Connie Yonge."

"I called her number but there was no answer."

"And you won't get one."

"What do you mean?"

"Ms Yonge says she doesn't need to talk with you."

"Did she say why she changed her mind?"

"Nope. Just said that she'd changed her mind and that everything was alright."

"Is that how she sounded?"

"That she had changed her mind?" Louise half smiled. "Or that she didn't need to talk with you? Or that everything was fine?"

"Multiple choice. Too late in the evening, Louise. Give me a break, my brain is winded."

"One, Connie Yonge sounded like a person who had had someone change her mind for her. Two, that she needs to talk to you but won't."

"And three?"

"That everything in the world is crappy, from barbie dolls to cocaine, from barbequed sausages on Bank Street to sliced sushi on Wellington. Not fine."

"And your astute telephone assessment please."

"Lady in distress. Demoiselle under duress. And you're her shining knight."

"Not tonight. She's Liz Strachan's lover more by reality than by claim, fame or name."

"And finally this." Louise pulled out a printout sheet. "I got the ownership on that licence plate you called in from the Gatineau."

I scanned it.

"This. 1995 Olds. Benoit Rae. In the Gatineau. That's the one. It says July owner, since then."

"That's right."

"Only since then?"

"Yes."

"Find out all previous owners for the last two years to when Benny Rae bought the car."

"When do you want it?"

"As early tomorrow as possible. I'll try to get in early. This one is on the Madeleine Masson file. The hit-and-run."

"Okay. I'll leave it for Nick."

"Sure."

"Oh something else, one last thing from late yesterday. Some guy named Tommy?"

"Tommy MacAlister?"

"Yes. He called and apologized for not getting back to you sooner but his buddy in sports goods had trouble tracking down the shoe based on the partial print but he said to tell you to call him anytime."

"Great. Thanks. Not much of a big deal now. That was for the Strachan file."

I went into my office and called up Brenda Strachan. She wanted me to come over that evening even though it was late.

The night had that late summer hazy quality that lingered over the Ottawa valley. The air was humid. The Argentine general in the park was quiet and stoical, a contrast to the noise from the bars up on Elgin. The university students were rolling back into town for the beginning of the term and getting loaded. Seeing the general made me think of Inky Baby. I put a mental notch on my brain to remind myself to call Inky Baby again.

Brenda Strachan looked pale and fragile when she answered the door. She was using a cane.

"Thanks for coming over. I know it's late and you've had a long day. Ms Montpetit was very considerate on the phone. And I know you've been through the wringer with my parents. So I really appreciate you dropping by."

I felt like saying nothing but spoke anyway against my better sentiments.

"I understand." I was now descending into the platitude side of the menu and didn't like the sound of my own voice.

We went into the apartment. Brenda Strachan settled herself into a chair rather than in her usual position in the corner on the couch.

"I can get you a coffee or tea."

"I'd be awake all night. And I need a good night's sleep. I've got to get up early."

A white Persian cat which I had not seen before stepped out. It stopped in the middle of the room on a small deep blue, black and saffron Kurdistan rug and appraised me. Not at all impressed, it slowly turned its head, paced towards Brenda Strachan, paused and leaped on the couch, not to be petted but near enough to observe the two of us. It was wary, eyes half closed. Even though the cat was within reach, Brenda made no effort to pet the animal.

The cat was aloof from either of us.

"I'm a lawyer. But it does me no good to help me understand what's happened to my sister. I tried to talk with my parents but it alternates between depression and self-accusations, anger and accusations towards the police and, I regret to say, towards you Mr Knight. We even bickered a little, if you can believe it."

She stopped for a moment as if I ought to say something but I said nothing.

"Well I tell them that it is unfair. I'm confident you did the best you could."

"I did what was within my capacity. It has to be shattering for you and your family. It doesn't surprise me that your parents are upset. Maybe it can't be helped."

"That's generous, Mr Knight."

"No. It's reasonable. It came out badly."

"You found my sister. You were asked to do that. You did. Lajoie-Chang Associates did do what it was hired to do." She paused, "Can I call you Alec?"

"Sure."

"Truth is I need someone to confide in. I have friends, coworkers in the department but I can't confide in them, as sympathetic and supportive as they are. And I feel strangely," she looked at the cat then back at me, the cat lifted its eyelids all the way then drew them shut and adjusted itself as if it might sleep, "possibly unaccountably, but intimate with you although I hardly know you. Maybe it is the peculiar and unfortunate circumstances under which I met you. It's not in my nature to confide too easily in people. Truth is after the car accident I don't trust people much. That's a bad quality in a person. And an especially bad quality in a lawyer. But I trust you. You seem without deceit. And beyond manipulation." Brenda Strachan shifted her artificial leg. The Persian opened her eyes and stared at Brenda, it jumped off the couch, stretched itself then slunk off to the bedroom.

"She doesn't trust me." Brenda smiled. It was a splendid smile, her face lost some of its wary quality, and it seemed as if a trace of her sister's features came into her face. "Because I'm quite the opposite. I'm anything but free of deceit and hardly beyond manipulation. In fact, my family is highly manipulative. Each of us in our own way. Imagine that's how we express our individuality."

"I can't comment on the other characteristics but individuality has to come out somehow."

"Don't trust my parents, Mr Knight. I mean Alec. I shouldn't confide in you."

"Why?"

"Because it's manipulative."

"I'm not over for that. Why do you want to see me?"

"I have some information which I want to convey to you and that you will convey to the police to assist their investigation into my sister's death."

"Why don't you tell them yourself?"

"It would potentially be a breach of confidentiality. My oath. And security status."

"How so?"

"I work for a department that is involved in investigating money laundering. New legislation is in the works."

"I've heard. You've even mentioned some of this before. Go on."

"One of the men you've mentioned in connection with my sister, Norman Innis Burley, variously known as Norm or Norman Burley or Norman I Burley is under, shall we say, scrutiny."

"If the term works for you."

"It will at this moment."

"He owns a bank. Or rather is a major shareholder and on the board of directors of the bank."

"Which bank?"

"Little known. It's offshore. The ICCI Bank. The International Canadian–Caribbean Investors Bank. Its name reveals its location. Have you ever heard of it?"

"It is not up there in memory with Chase Manhattan, Bank of Nova Scotia or the Royal."

"No. It wouldn't be. It's on the anonymous side of things." She half smiled. "It's on an inconspicuous island where there are inconspicuous people engaged in conspicuous consumption. Many banks. And thousands of registered corporations. ICCI was charged with handling laundered money through its Miami branch. Maybe you heard about that. Although it happened years ago."

"No."

"The US authorities want to see ICCI shut down, cease operations, but it is beyond its jurisdiction since it fled Miami Florida. ICCI was heavily involved with some US agents who became involved with military figures who were running a drug cartel in the Caribbean. The US agents were using ICCI as a conduit to launder the drug money. The money was reputedly used for purchase of weapons for Cuban exiles and Contras working in Central America. Didi Cabosa was one of them. He had done some work for the CIA and Cuban exiles who were operating anti-communist brigades. They had a general on the payroll. A guy named Jesus Lopez-Schmidt. He ran a junta, knocked off an elected official and seized office. The CIA had it with Lopez-Schmidt because the general decided to cut himself in for the bulk of the drug money and he stopped buying his weapons from US and Israeli manufacturers and turned to Belgian and Japanese weapons manufacturers. They scooped Lopez-Schmidt, put him on trial along with some of their own rogue agents that they could catch. And they went after the ICCI officials and some US savings and loans that were implicated in the money laundering and weapons sales."

"Was Burley charged?"

"No. Burley has some high up Florida politicians both state and federal who give him some support and cover. He's basically their man. It was all made to look local. Local individual. A single local corrupt employee with bad habits. The Miami branch manager took the rap. And they were fined for several days for refusing to provide depositors' records to the US courts."

"This is public. The Canadian police will know all this."

"Yes. But Connie Yonge and my sister made regular trips to Miami and the Caribbean island where the head office of the ICCI is located. Liz and Connie knew Norman Burley."

"What are you suggesting?"

"I'm suggesting nothing."

"Do I hear a mule kicking in a stall?"

"You have very good ears, Mr Knight. Since there are no mules in the general vicinity of Ottawa."

"Only donkeys. I hope I don't turn into Pinocchio, Brenda."

"Some people, Justice people, would like further charges brought against ICCI. Others want to stay clear of this. There is a possibility that the Canadian authorities may close down the Canadian branch office in Toronto. However, there is a political wrinkle."

"How so?"

"Imagine if you were very good friends with certain highly influential individuals in a Canadian political party and some of these individuals had been on the board of the ICCI before being elected to parliament or provincial legislature. And what's more that certain high Republican elected officials at both the state and federal levels had links. And were connected to dozens of US S & Ls and banks in the US where the money was rerouted."

"Highjinks?"

"Yes, with the ICCI. One of them happening to be the brother of a governor in a very powerful US state. The savings and loans people do not want this bank to fail or be closed."

"So we are talking hesitation."

"Hesitation. Procrastination. Anticipation. Obfuscation. Consternation."

"Extrajudicial constipation? Euphemistic legal stagnation?"

"All the stag nations in the world Alec."

"And you want me to be the leak for what?"

"I want you to illuminate the authorities without—"

"You breaking your oath to the government and losing your security clearance."

"It is my sister's life." Brenda paused, "I like my job. It's a good job. I do good work. I have secret security clearance. I don't like to see criminals beyond the reach of prosecution due to political influence. I want to serve the public interest."

"Do you know this town?"

"I know." She paused. "This town, famous only for its banality, compliancy, boredom, is one of the most complex capitals in the world. There are only two other countries in the world that have such legal duration as Canada. And both those nations had civil wars. Alec, I know this town is completely and totally upside down."

"The O in Ottawa stands for obscure. The two t's for totally."

"And anonymity is a good companion."

"Problem, Ms Strachan."

"Brenda."

"Brenda."

"What problem, Alec."

"Norm Burley had nothing to do with your sister's death."

She gave me a severe and riveted gaze. I could see her mother's features in the look.

"How do you know?"

"I don't."

"Then why declare it if you don't know."

"Because if he did he would be too distant from it to prove it."

"The man's a rapist. He's a brute. He raped a young woman years ago in Alberta. My sister Liz was raped and murdered. She was a lesbian."

"Liz was bisexual."

"Okay. But nevertheless even if she went with men, she would never go near a man like Burley. She never slept with any of those men. It was all a front. LTD is a front for Burley's money laundering schemes. A channel. A conduit to the isles. To ICCI. I can prove it."

"How's that?"

"It's in the—" She near cried. "I can't say. I'm deep into it."

"It?"

"Yes knowledge of it. Deep into it."

"We're deep into the world. The world is a deep place. And as soon as we happen to discover where we are, it is a sphere of mere smooth surfaces concealing the folds, convolutions and fissures of complexity from sight."

"Burley raped and murdered my sister Liz."

"Don't declare it, Brenda, please be careful."

"He's a brutal man. Behind that proper facade. All that Civic Unity Party virtue."

"He'd be hard to bag."

She started to cry then stopped.

"I loved my sister. Although we never quite got along, we were close in our own way. After our own fashion. Even intimate at times."

"I'm sure you were."

"Burley did it."

"Burley's ruthless. He'll be next to impossible to take down. Especially if he is as you suggest in close with the savings and loan crowd."

"The law can be corrupt but nobody is beyond prosecution for homicide. He used my sister. Connie Yonge dragged Liz into this ugly mess with these ugly people. It was foolishness. Pure and simple stupid greed. Connie loved Liz but she is a fool for a dollar bill. She can't help it."

"Maybe. Possibly. But we must be very careful in accusing Connie Yonge of far too much. It may not be fair. Foolishness is not a crime."

"Burley's not untouchable if the info went to the police from a reliable source."

"Brenda, be careful of suggesting it was Burley."

"Through a good dependable channel. You could find the way. You have the knowledge, the ability to make it come to them. You'll catalyze them. Show them the rubble, they'll dig through the rubble on their own and find the facts. I have confidence in you Alec. I do."

I stood up.

"It's late. I'm afraid I've got to go."

"Please think about what I've told you."

"I don't want to compromise you, Brenda. Your security status is hard to come by. Why should you lose a good job? A job that you need."

"You wouldn't compromise me."

"I would if I didn't have other sources. Totally independent."

"You can work it out. I'm confident you could."

"Think about this. I was there for a moment thinking about Burley but it is a tough one. He'd use someone else. He'd be careful to put distance between such a brutal act and himself. An untraceable distance."

"That would at least make him an accessory. But you don't need that. Burley's an impulsive man with a terrible temper. His arrogance and his anger make him overstep himself. That's what I heard happened out in Alberta."

"What do you know about Alberta?"

"I made it my business to know about Alberta. I went out there."

"You went out there."

"Yes. I went out there and spoke to the woman."

"Then you know that nothing came of that case."

"A great injustice was done to a vulnerable woman. The investigating officers were clumsy. They sided with Burley."

"Nothing came of that. It was a mess. He was young then. Middle-aged men don't necessarily act consistent with their impulsiveness when they were young reckless bucks. Burley's changed. He is governed more by financial greed and political power and influence. He's a different man than he was thirty years ago. In some senses more dangerous and ruthless and calculating. He has the means to destroy you."

"It's not that." Brenda Strachan smiled. It was an unsettling smile.

"I'm not sure what you mean."

"You're afraid of him."

"Not at all. I'll think about all that you've said. The police will come up with some solid information. Give them a chance. And if Burley's in the equation, they'll go after him. Better that way."

"I'm quite disappointed."

"Don't be."

"These men used my sister Liz. Burley, Henderson, Parsons, Slowikowsky. Even that oh-so-respectable Clarence Wilson."

"Clarence Wilson? What do you know about Clarence Wilson, Brenda?"

"Nothing. Didn't you mention him?"

"Maybe. But I don't recall."

"Liz made a mistake getting involved with Joe Parsons and his crowd of financial leeches and sexual parasites but she never deserved this, however promiscuous she was. She wasn't one of them. Those men exploited her."

"You're right there. They certainly did. But she knew what they were about."

"You don't know half of it, Alec."

"Tell me the half I don't know."

"No. I've said far too much. You won't help so there's no point in saying anything more. I shouldn't have said anything about Clarence Wilson."

"What do you know about Clarence Wilson and Liz?"

"Nothing."

"You spoke with your parents about him this evening didn't you?"

"No. I didn't have to. I happen to know all about that man."

"What do you know?"

"He messed around with Liz. Messed up her head."

"Must have made Connie Yonge upset."

"It did. Connie was wretched over it. Connie suffered over it. She didn't deserve to. She didn't care about the other men. She knew they meant nothing to Liz. Clarence Wilson was different. She could see that manipulator had some hold over Liz. Connie's a very jealous person. She was just wretched."

"Were you upset too?" I put my hand in my suit coat pocket and drew out the copy of the letter Madeleine Masson had given me.

"He's dead but he was a very destructive man. Very very destructive man. Extremely manipulative."

"So you sent this?"

"What?"

I handed her the photocopy. Brenda Strachan unfolded it and read it.

"Where'd you come by this? You shouldn't have it. You've no business having this." She tore it up and threw the pieces of paper on the floor.

"I'm sorry. I didn't mean to hurt you." I sat down. "Brenda."

"Shut up. You side with the men. Do you know what Clarence Wilson did to my mother? Do you? And I trust you. How can you? I trust you so much."

"I know they had an affair."

"Can you imagine what it would have done to my mother if she had found out Clarence Wilson was seeing my sister Liz? Can you just imagine? He told Liz he was going to leave his wife, Madeleine Masson, and told Liz he would marry her. I had to stop him."

"Clarence Wilson would never have left Madeleine Masson."

"He told Liz he was going to divorce his wife and marry Liz. Liz wanted to marry him."

"Liz didn't know Clarence Wilson had had an affair with your mother?"

"No. Liz knew nothing about it."

"How did you find out Brenda?"

"I just did."

"How?"

She said nothing.

"Connie Yonge told you. Right?"

"No. Yes."

"How did Connie find out?"

"Pete Slowikowsky told her. Connie loved Liz. She wanted to protect Liz."

"So what did you do?"

"I told you, okay. I wrote that letter. But it didn't do any good. He's such a nasty man, vile, without any conscience, without remorse, he still went on seeing Liz."

"So then what did you do?"

"Nothing. I couldn't. Anyway ..."

"Anyway what, Brenda?"

"He was killed. You know. You've got to know this much. In a car accident over on the Quebec side of the river. In the Gatineau Hills."

"Sure. And that's all?"

"That was it. What more is there?"

"How was Liz after that?"

"I don't know. She was upset. Pretty devastated. She went back to Connie. But they had trouble getting along."

"Who ran over Clarence Wilson?"

"I don't know. It's still unsolved. I understand it's still under investigation." She gazed at me. The cat came back in the room, stared at both of us.

"You shouldn't have written that note, Brenda. It was foolish."

"I suppose you're going to tell the authorities."

"No. I know you didn't have anything to do with Wilson's death. A pretty obvious empirical impossibility."

"How so?"

"You don't own a car and you don't know how to drive a car."

"So what are you going to do?"

"I'm going to think about it. It could look very bad for your parents. All the more reason to think about it very carefully."

"How did you come by the letter?"

"I can't say, it would be a breach of confidentiality."

The cat came and sat at the foot of Brenda's chair.

I stood up.

"I better go."

"Good night."

"'Night, Brenda."

I went out, took the night air and walked a little along the canal. The night was rich. The sky and stars were covered in a light haze like a muslin cloth. As I went along I came upon a dead bird, a blue jay lying under a tree. I stood and stared at it. I went back to my car and drove to my Somerset Street apartment. I left a message on the municipal Health Department's answering service about sighting the dead blue jay and its location on the canal on Queen Elizabeth Driveway between Somerset and MacLaren streets.

# SIXTEEN

Bagged. I was in a plastic bag. Then I was in a shower stall and a white cat came strolling along the white ceramic floor. It came to the edge of the shower, I pushed it away, but the cat persisted even though its white fur became covered in water. It entered the shower stall. I scuffed it aside with my foot. It meowed and put on a malevolent face. I thought it was going to attack my naked foot. The cat was strolling along the canal, a dead crow in its jaws. I was at the slots in the Casino d'Hull with my old man. He was urging me to plug coins in the slot machine and kept muttering, boy oh boy, you'll win boy, you gonna win. I can tell. You're a winner. I put a coin in and won, the coins gushed out and wouldn't stop. Brenda Strachan was there. She said, look Alec you made me whole. I did? You did. I stared and she had two legs. We embraced and she slipped back her blouse revealing beautiful creamy white breasts. Oh I love you Madeleine. Do you? Then why call me Madeleine. It was a slip. What sort of slip? The coins were still pouring out of the slot machine and rolling like crazy across the casino floor. My father was scrambling around on his hands and knees scooping them up. Madeleine Masson was standing beside me as I kissed Brenda Strachan. She murmured, he was very promiscuous just like you, Alec. But I'm not, Madeleine, I protested, I'm Canadian.

I woke up to the alarm. It was six. To the ancient ruminations of the dream floating through my skull, I washed, shaved and dressed, then had breakfast, rye toast with peanut butter and a bowl of yogurt. I wanted to go back into the dream but the early dawn wouldn't let me.

I drove over to Bronson. The traffic was heavy. I greeted Nick Glastonbury.

"Did you get the ownership history on that Olds?"

"Sorry, buddy, I was busy all night with an emergency Morrison laid on me. I'll get to it first thing I can."

"That's okay. I'm going up to the Gatineau to do surveillance on these guys Benny Rae and Jackie Snoblin. Phone me on the cell when you've got it. I need an agency car."

"Take the Chevy." Glastonbury rummaged through a drawer of keys, ticked off a sheet and had me initial for the keys.

The heavy traffic from the suburbs and towns of Quebec to the government complexes on the Ottawa River near the confluence of the Rideau Canal, Gatineau and Rideau rivers had not yet begun. Les Terrasses de Chaudière across from the old E B Eddy paper mill and Place du Portage and Place du Centre facing the Parliament buildings looked stolid and bleak beside the sinuosity of the Museum of Civilization curving along the Ottawa River shoreline.

I drove into the Gatineau. The hills wore a sombre green shroud. I parked down the road from Benny Rae and Jackie Snoblin's cottage in the shade of some trees. I got out my binoculars and digital camera. I sat in the bushes for a good hour before Snoblin and Rae came out. They looked rumpled and worn. I got some good photos of the lads. They tooled around on their motorcycles for a half hour then stumbled into the Olds and took off down the road. I ran back to the agency car and tailed them. On 307 I jumped ahead of them until they hit downtown Ottawa.

They parked on a side street off Bank and headed towards Joe Parsons' LTD Escort Service. When they entered the office building I gave the car a good going over. The right headlamp appeared to be newer than the left one. With my digital camera I took close-up shots of the car lamps then went down to the office building.

I crawled up the stairs to the third floor where Parsons' office was located. The door was closed. I slipped past it and stood to the side. I listened. One guy was shouting while another voice was so soft it was inaudible.

"We did it, get it?"

Inaudible.

"Where's the dough?"

Inaudible.

"Joe. Come on Joe, this isn't you."

Inaudible.

"Who's the bastard?"

Inaudible.

"Well tell the creep to come across or we'll ream his butt with a crowbar."

Inaudible.

I heard footsteps pounding on the floor and approaching the door. I stepped around the corner out of sight. Then the two guys in denim and motorcycle boots came out into the hall. Rae slammed the office door. The door vibrated and bounced against the doorjamb swinging back and forth, slowing down, creaking lamely for a few more seconds on its hinges until it eased to a standstill staying open a few inches. Meanwhile, the two angry men went on stomping down the stairs.

Through the crevice I heard Joe Parsons talking, his voice barely audible but anxious.

"Look I wanna talk to Lester Henderson. This is kinda important."

A pause.

"I don't give a damn if he's in bed screwing his brains out. Put the jerk on the line willya."

I heard a chair scraping the floor. I slipped back. The office door was pulled shut tight with a slam. I came closer but could hear nothing.

I slipped out of the building. The Olds was gone. I scuffed at the curb.

Back at the Bronson office Nick Glastonbury had left the ownership history on the Olds with Cheryl Perron. I took the printout and went over it in my office. It made me sit up. The car had been owned by Joe Parsons and before that by Liz Strachan. I asked Cheryl to print the digital photos of the Olds.

I phoned up Madeleine Masson. She said I should come out that morning.

I phoned up Freddy Asad and queried him about tracing the purchase of a replacement Olds headlight. He said no problem, that he'd check among various auto parts dealers.

I went down to Saikely's for a coffee and a good think. Then I nudged myself and recalled that I was supposed to call Tommy MacAlister. But I figured since I was no longer working for the

Strachans, I'd put it on the back burner unless Frank Strachan called back. My thoughts turned to current business. Benny Rae, Joe Parsons and Liz Strachan in the chain of car ownerships made a rich equation. I sat drinking coffee in an aura of sudden awareness of the unexpected. I felt overwhelmed.

"You, Mr Knight, look lost." It was Albert Saikely.

"Hey don't worry, my old man took me to the casino last night, Albert."

Albert Saikely looked grief stricken. "I'm really sorry to hear that. Here I thought you was a good guy. An intelligent kinda guy. Had the smarts to stay away from such crap."

"We made a big haul. I won on the slots Albert."

"Mr Knight. Mr Knight. Be careful, you gonna trick yourself. There's only two ways in life to truly make a living in this world. By this," Saikely held up his worn, wrinkled and scarred cook's hand, "or by this." He pointed to his temple. The cook shook his head in consternation and disillusionment.

"Hey, Albert come on, it was a joke."

"No joke Mr Knight. By the hand or by the head. Some say by the heart. Meaning somebody loves you gives you or leaves you some money."

"Albert, I was just dreaming."

"No dream. Nightmare, my friend. The casino's no joke, it's bad news place for the man who works for a living. Hard on your bank account."

"You don't get it. It was a dream, Albert. What I mean is that last night, my old man, my father took me to the casino in my dream. And I just dreamt I was winning at the slots. Coins pouring out all over the floor in a dream."

Saikely laughed. May Saikely came over.

"What's this?"

"May. Listen. He says he dreamt he won at the casino on the slot machines with his father."

May Saikely laughed.

"That's a rich dream. You're lucky. Go back to sleep. In our dreams we're all rich."

I went back to the office. Cheryl told me that Freddy Asad had called up. He left a message that Mississagi Auto Parts out Walkley

Road had sold a new headlamp for a 1995 Olds back in April. I drove out to Walkley. The service parts manager was a thick bald little guy about five two whose girth was giving his height stiff competition. But like many corpulent people he moved over short distances with suprising speed.

"Yeah, Freddy A phoned 'round. You that guy Knight that he mentioned?"

"Yes."

"Let's see your eye spy licence."

I showed my provincial ID.

"Okay. I guess you know how to quack like a duck. What's this all about?"

"Your shop sold a headlamp for a 1995 Olds in April to someone."

"Right."

"Recall who did the sale with the customer?"

"I sold the headlamp. See." He showed me an invoice. "Those are my initials. Whoever makes the sale initials the invoice. I initialed it."

"Recall what the customer looked like?"

"Not really. Apart from the fact he looked like he had balls dangling down between his legs."

"Anything on the customer? Glasses. Moustache. Clothing. Unusual appearance. Age. Height. Anything?"

"Nothing mac. Really that's a long time back as time goes in this business. I mean we see hundreds of people a week. In and out faster than a bar full of drunks. This much though."

"Go ahead."

"He wasn't a regular customer. I'd remember a return customer I mean. We watch for that. Also the Olds wasn't his."

"How's that?"

"I don't know, I think the guy might have mentioned something about it being not his car or having borrowed it."

"Was the guy young?"

"I don't know. I'm struggling here. I got to think." He paused a long time. "Christ I can't say. I guess I'd say yes maybe no. Maybe, what the heck, I don't know. Don't want to swear on it. Under thirty-five. But to tell the truth. To be honest, the older I get the worse I am with the age thing. I see somebody who's twenty-five and they begin to look fifteen. I see someone thirty-five and they look more like twenty. Aging is wearing the friggin' brain cells out. I don't want to swear on this guy's appearance or anything. I couldn't begin to remember who he was or what he looked like, to be honest. There's no sense bullshitting, telling you the guff you wanna to hear but making it all up. That's the friggin' TV, isn't it? Some hot cop show where, you know, some character suddenly remembers something, someone from twenty years ago. That they like saw for three seconds. So traumatized they can't forget and they got like a superduper memory more powerful than a friggin' computer." He shook his head.

"What colour was the Olds?"

"Haven't a clue. The guy came in and purchased the lamp. He just gave us the part and the make and year of the car. I never saw the car itself. He could have parked it on the other side of the Atlantic."

"Can I see the invoice again? Purchase record."

"I suppose. But there's no name or nothing on it."

"How'd he pay?"

"Good old cashola."

I stared at the invoice but there was nothing on it to reveal the purchaser.

"Can I get a copy of this?"

"Mac you certain you aren't with RevCan?" The guy laughed.

"They come this well dressed?"

"Just joking." He chuckled again. "I suppose it don't hurt since it hasn't got any personal info on it." He photocopied it and handed me the sheet.

"What happens with the old lamps?"

"We send them for recycle."

"Where?"

"An outfit in Toronto."

"Do you have the name?"

"Sure. Quik-Kar Parts Recycle." He gave me the address and phone number.

I went back to the office and phoned up Johnny Olive, an independent investigator with Mellos and Olive that Lajoie–Chang used as a contact in Toronto. Olive sounded hung over.

"Maybe you live in the darkness Knight. But I sleep there."

"Time to wake up."

"No. No. Heck of a night."

"Tied one on, eh?"

"Oh yeah. And I need privacy at this precious moment."

"Hit-and-run case, my man."

"Sec." He put me on hold. "You are disrupting a beautiful relationship that is only beginning. Go ahead. I need a glass of water. I'm drinking but listening."

"I got a shard from a 1995 Olds. I need a match with the headlamp that it came from. The headlamp apparently may have gone to recycle in a joint in your neighbourhood. Company called Quik-Kar Parts Recycle. Ever hear of them?"

"Sure, sort of rings a bell. Somewhere on the border between Etobicoke and Mississauga. I think near Dixon Road."

"Sounds right, Johnny. Look I'll quick courier the piece today. Listen, treat this shard like the holy shroud. See if you can rummage through the headlamps and find a match."

"I will. I will. But I'll sleep until the midday messenger sings a song at my door. Night Knight."

# SEVENTEEN

I made the overdue phone call to Madeleine Masson at her Ottawa residence and she asked if I might come over. I got there before noon. She lived in New Edinburgh. A solid old neighbourhood squished between Rideau Hall, the residence of the Governor-General, and the mouth of the Rideau River. The green parks, river falls and island gave the area a bucolic quality. The Masson house, an old stone one, was on a short dignified street. It was made with good solid stone masonry and traditional carpentry to the windows, doors and porch. The casement windows on the first and second levels remained in fine shape and appeared to have the original leaded glass.

Madeleine Masson greeted me at the front door. We went into the front room. A Chinese carpet spread across the old maple floor. The chairs were not fakes. The room with its veneer of solid but subdued plasterwork suggested restraint and tradition go together, but you have to have coin to maintain this sort of house. It wasn't just available from do-it-yourself kits for TV viewers watching remodel your home programmes. Individuals who lived with this style probably had very frightening nightmares called Wal-Mart.

Madeleine Masson looked as good as ever. Last night's dream, which I had forgotten, slapped me across the cheek. I forgot it once again. I noted the old botanical prints of flowers and leaves hand-painted with water colours. There was a survey of the Gatineau. Masson followed my gaze.

"I've closed the summer cottage. My boys have returned to Ashbury. If you wish to contact me it is better to call here."

"That's a fine survey map."

"My great-grandfather was involved in the surveying of Western Quebec. That's his work."

"Impressive. Must be a pleasure to have things from your family going back that far. Shows a feeling and attachment for our country. Most people are lucky to have an old bathrobe of their granny or shaving mug of granddad's." I gave a laugh.

"It is and it isn't. It's important to keep our culture alive. But there can be something delusional in such possessions. We shouldn't dismiss them but we shouldn't overrate personally possessing them. Having them. It took me a long time to realize that people are far more important. I wasn't always of that disposition. I trained as an architect. Aesthetics. Beauty. Beautiful objects had a powerful hold over my mind."

"I can see some of that thoughtfulness in this house."

"I worked on historical restorations before marrying Clare. This house was in my family, actually built by my great-grandfather, but my grandfather sold it when he built a new house in Outremont. This house had fallen into a decrepit state. When I married and moved to Ottawa, I repurchased it. We had many personal photographs of the house from the nineteenth century that helped with the reconstruction. Restoration of heritage architecture was a second choice of mine."

"How so?"

"Oh I wanted to do something radical as an architect." She smiled. "But the first architectural firm I worked for was not exactly into becoming Mies van der Rohe or Cardinal. Architecture's a beautiful but cruel art, it's for the idealist but it swiftly, even cruelly makes one a pragmatist. But then some notable architects who seem so radical in the contemporary moment, their works comes to look stale. The new doesn't necessarily last in architecture. It can age badly. The new just becomes stale. Some radical works even become banal. Worn out. Clichéd. So developers knock it down and we start over. Anyway I had no pleasure in designing cubicles for bureaucrats and middle managers in safe commercial office towers. So I started my own small office doing heritage restoration. Then the kids came. Well I still do some but not as much. In any event I'm far away from why I asked you to call me."

"No problem."

"Mr Knight, I had a very unsettling conversation yesterday evening after I spoke with you." She paused. "I hesitate to mention who it was with."

"Don't if it is a problem. Unless it is essential. I'll let you know if I need to know."

"I think I better. In any event the details would mean next to nothing unless you know who the conversation was with. It was with my brother-in-law, Clare's brother, Marshall Wilson. He's a lawyer as well at Baldwin Martel Wightman. He's upset that I have hired Lajoie–Chang Associates to investigate Clare's death."

"Why's that?"

"I'm a bit perplexed. I don't quite understand. Initially Marshall was upset that the police were unable to solve the hit-and-run. Marshall sometimes is an impatient man. In fact all the Wilsons are. Clare was inclined that way. They get it from their father. They say it is because they are meticulous, capable, supercapable, competent people who have to put up with incompetent people. But it is no more than impatience, wanting things to go their way and instantly wanting people to go along with their decisions and plans."

"And other people don't necessarily."

"The Wilsons can be very persuasive but people don't always comply. A person needs to be flexible. In any event, first Marshall was impatient concerning the police. He declared it was an accident probably by some local driver who panicked, fled the scene of the accident, and it ought to be solved fairly quickly if the police were competent. That impatience didn't exactly win friends with the authorities. It subsided after July. He let it drop. He was argumentative but stopped. I thought it best to let the police do their work. Work through their investigation. However, my brother Gilles Masson was upset with the way the investigation was handled. Not so much thinking the police had failed or anything of that sort but that the investigation was stalemated. In fact he was the person who urged me to hire Lajoie–Chang after the first time you came to the house. I told Gilles about your initial visit. Gilles still lives in Montréal and he knew of Georges Lajoie. He said Monsieur Lajoie had a top notch record on the police force as a detective. Also that Lajoie–Chang did investigative work on hit-and-runs for insurance companies."

"We do."

"In any event Gilles was the one who urged me. Simply on the premise that it wouldn't hurt to have an outside eye take a look at the situation. But somehow Marshall found out, he came up to the cottage in the evening after I saw you. Now he was insistent, even forceful in his manner, that it was a mistake to bring a private investigator into the case."

"What did he say?"

"He said it was meddlesome. He said things about Georges Lajoie."

"What sorts of things?"

"Marshall said Monsieur Lajoie is incompetent. That he was drummed out the Montréal police department years ago like his father had been. That neither had left by choice. Is this so?"

"Georges Lajoie was with the Montreal police department years ago but he was not drummed off for incompetence. He resigned. It was of a personal nature. I really can't discuss it."

"Why?"

"It would be better if you spoke directly to Mr Lajoie."

"Then there could be some substance to what Marshall has said."

"Georges Lajoie's departure has nothing to do with the abilities or competency of Lajoie–Chang. It's not in any way relevant to the case you've asked me to investigate. His father was a notable police detective with the Montreal police as well. I never knew the man. He had nothing to do with Lajoie–Chang, at least to the best of my knowledge. I know next to nothing regarding his departure. This has no bearing on the work I do for you Ms Masson."

"How can there be two such contrasting opinions of the same man? My brother-in-law argues that the authorities in Québec will be furious if Lajoie–Chang is involved."

"I think not. We're in no way interfering with the official investigation of the accident. We would never do that."

"I need reassurances."

"Ms Masson, trust me, Georges Lajoie and Morrison Chang are two solid people. They put the clients first. They would not do anything to compromise an investigation."

"I'm, I'm not close to my brother-in-law. But he is a very competent lawyer. He says that he has spoken to some legal colleagues in confidence who said that if we wanted to hire a private investigator that we could do better than Lajoie–Chang. But he also said that his colleagues in criminal law think it better that any private investigator stay out of the picture until the police have formally charged someone."

"Were you aware that Baldwin Martel Wightman, in particular Claude Martel, has given referrals to Lajoie–Chang?"

"No. Marshall didn't mention that."

"It's so. You can verify it. I wouldn't say so if it weren't. Go ahead, check it out if you want. I can assure you it is so. Call Claude Martel if you like."

Madeleine Masson uncrossed her legs and recrossed them but she made no motion to verify by phone what I had just said. "I want my husband's death solved even if we no longer had a, well, the relationship we once had had. As for yourself," she gave me a direct gaze, "I'll be candid. Although candidness always seems a little, what? Forced."

"Declarations of candour conceal something more complex."

"Precisely. I want to trust you but you unsettle me. I mean this unsettles me."

"How so?"

"I don't know. I can't say. I wish I could."

"You'll figure it out, I suppose. Hopefully after I've solved what you've hired Lajoie–Chang to do."

"At times, Clare's brother Marshall can be difficult. Sometimes he is too vehement. Mr Knight, you have to understand I can't be arguing with him. It would be stressful."

"I understand. Better not to. Refer Marshall Wilson to me. Let us handle him. He could even talk to Morrison Chang or Georges Lajoie." I smiled.

"Are you certain?"

"Sure. Georges Lajoie would like nothing more than to deal with a skeptic. He's a fan of skepticism. Anyway isn't that what you want?"

"Yes."

"What do you think accounts for Marshall Wilson's strenuous opposition to the agency?"

"I suppose what he told me. I take it at face value."

"Why?"

"Because I asked my solicitor if there was any substance to what Marshall said and my solicitor, although not entirely agreeing, did confirm it in a way by saying that Georges Lajoie had left the Montréal police in the midst of a controversy."

"Who's your solicitor?"

"I go to Hélène Sénécal at Constable Strong. However, Ms Sénécal recommended that I speak with Alfred Plante before hiring Lajoie–Chang. Bear in mind I've never had any need for a criminal lawyer. That sort of thing is entirely beyond my regular legal needs. Plante happens to be an old friend of my family."

"I see. Is Marshall Wilson also a friend of Alfred Plante?"

"I don't think so. But who knows, he could be."

"Marshall Wilson is a friend of Norman Burley?"

"Yes. They're in fact very close, not only on account of being in Baldwin Martel Wightman but also because, as I mentioned, they did numerous business transactions together. Why do you ask?"

"With a numbered company involving Norman Burley and Clarence, I didn't notice that Marshall Wilson was on the board of directors."

"No. They're involved in other ventures. Marshall is an old friend of Norm Burley's, they went to law school together and worked out west before moving back here and joining Clare's firm."

"How'd that come about?"

"Clarence joined Baldwin Martel Wightman first, then when Clarence became a partner he urged the firm to invite Marshall in. Marshall wanted to move back to Ontario. Some years later Norman Burley was invited in. Not through Clarence but through Marshall's doing. Then Norm Burley and Marshall Wilson also became involved in the Civic Unity Party."

"Was your husband or other lawyers in the law firm involved with the people in the party?"

"No. The fact of the matter is that that was a point of friction between Clarence and his brother Marshall. They stopped talking politics. Clare was opposed to the Civic Unity Party. But Marshall was committed to it along with Norm Burley. Although I don't think nearly as deeply involved. Mr Burley is a major fundraiser for the party."

"Did they argue politics?"

"Initially they argued in a partisan sort of way, the usual fraternal sort of thing. Because Marshall had always been a supporter of the Conservatives and people like Mulroney. But he got frustrated and disillusioned with the Conservatives after Mulroney left. The arguments were sort of in the family politically. But when the Civic Unity swept the West in the last election, Marshall became quite earnest, even strident. It was unpleasant. Clare didn't like it. Nor did my brother Gilles. Gilles and Clare at one time had been close and are still very loyal to the tradition of Trudeau and liberalism. They even jested that they'd sooner be with Dalton Camp than have anything to do with the Civic Unity Party. That really irked Marshall. He thought Camp destroyed the party."

"I suggest that if Marshall Wilson brings up the issue of you having hired Lajoie–Chang that you drop the subject. I'll speak to him. But I should tell you that I have a potentially promising lead. I wouldn't want it compromised in any way so I'd prefer that you not speak to anyone about Lajoie–Chang."

"I'm very close to my brother Gilles. I confide in him."

"Say nothing to him."

Madeleine Masson rubbed her shoe, a fine patent leather pump, on the rug then stopped.

"Why?"

"I don't think your husband's death was a hit-and-run accident in the usual sense of an accidental one due to mere carelessness and panic on the part of some anonymous driver. There's a remote, I emphasize a remote possibility that the driver of the car or at least the owner of the car may have known Mr Wilson."

Madeleine Masson said nothing for a moment. I said nothing. The patent leather pump went back and forth on the Chinese rug.

"That's it. That's what unsettles me Mr Knight. You and I are of the same mind. This thought floated over me from near the outset of the police investigation. But I suppressed it. I told myself that it was a delusion. An irrational projection due to my pent up frustration with Clare and our unhappy relationship. A paranoid fantasy. I even subjected myself to self-accusations. Wanted it that way. Made me feel wretched. I felt guilty for Clare's death because I didn't love him anymore because he lied so much to me about his affairs with various women. His constant promiscuity, he used me. I felt used. I thought he only stayed with me so he could have access to my inheritance. That was a depressing thought. A wretched thought. It just made me feel more wretched and more guilty. But you have come to this notion independently and I sensed it. That's why you unsettle me. We're on the same wavelength. Tell me more. What sustains your notion that it was deliberate?"

"Might have been."

"Very well. Might. If you insist on might."

"I don't want to say at this moment. There's a piece of material evidence which I need to investigate further, collect more information regarding it. I am now in the midst of obtaining that information. I need a day or two. The crucial thing is to say nothing to anyone until I can consolidate the information and show it to be relevant evidence. If I can't do that then it is better not to say anything. Did you mention to police your suspicion that there might have been an element of deliberateness or premeditation involved in the accident?"

"No. I was hesitant. Even embarrassed. I told you I was critical of myself, self-accusatory. Then I thought that, even if Clarence did what he did to me, I never wanted to think that someone would do it deliberately. What's more I had nothing of substance to tell the police until I came upon that foolish note. So I thought it was better not to say anything. So I said nothing."

"Did the police ask about your husband's various affairs with other women?"

"Yes. And I told them what I knew. But I did not know about the affair with this young woman, Liz Strachan."

"Did they ask you about your husband's associates?"

"Yes. At times in great detail. Even at times very explicitly. Did he have any enemies. Had he recently had an angry argument with anyone. Had anyone threatened him even in jest. Did he mention that he was afraid of anyone. That sort of thing."

"What did you tell them?"

"Well. I said that Clare had no enemies. And in fact he didn't as far as I know. And he certainly was not afraid of anyone. And if he was he never mentioned anyone. I gave them access to most of his papers. They went through them. But found nothing alarming."

"Did they ever mention Liz Strachan?"

"No. Nobody brought her up until you did. Although they seemed to know that Clarence was promiscuous. They asked about women. Some of whom I knew and others whom I didn't. I told them that I knew Clarence was promiscuous. Why hide it? They'd only find out. And they did find out some things on that score but nothing came of it. But he seems to have been particularly careful concerning this young woman Liz Strachan. None of his friends or associates knew about her. Or if they did they certainly did not say anything to the police investigating Clare's death."

"Fine." I stood up to leave. "It's essential that you say nothing more to Marshall Wilson even if he brings it up. Feign upset. Distress. Tell him you are far too upset to talk about it. Or put him off by saying that you'll seriously think about dropping Lajoie–Chang. Or if you can carry it off without looking phoney, lie outright, tell him that you are fed up with Lajoie–Chang and have taken us off the case. Terminated our services. But if you do that don't do it until after I have had a chance to speak with Marshall Wilson. I'm hoping to contact him today or tomorrow. He'll probably come to you after I've spoken with him but that can't be avoided. Then just tell him you're finished with, done with Lajoie–Chang. Disappointed. Disillusioned with us. I leave you to work out what you're most comfortable with." I smiled.

Madeleine Masson stood up.

"What am I to take this to mean Mr Knight?"

"What? Take it to mean that Georges Lajoie is a careful and thoughtful private investigator. That you deserve to trust yourself, Ms Masson. That those who speak negatively of others often reveal more of themselves than of other people. By the way, can you give me Marshall Wilson's home phone number in case I can't get hold of him at Baldwin Martel Wightman's offices?"

"Certainly." She went to the hallway and got the number from the phone book.

She offered her hand.

"Thank you." There was something comforting in her handshake.

"Mr Knight I don't want you to take what I said or my anxieties at the outset the wrong way."

"I don't. Clients sometimes have reservations and concerns."

"You don't think Norman Burley had something to do with my husband's death do you?"

"No."

"That would be frightening if it were so."

"No. Don't worry about that. The investigation isn't going in that direction."

"I'll see you out."

# EIGHTEEN

I drove back to Bronson. When I came in Cheryl Perron lowered her voice. "That fellow Ed Stanley is here." She gestured towards a conference room. "He insisted on waiting for you."

"What the heck. Jilted lover boys are a speciality."

I looked at my watch, it was after one.

"Don't worry Cheryl, I needed a coffee. No problem. I'll take the lad for a coffee. Just tell him that I'll be with him shortly."

I went in my office and called Marshall Wilson at Baldwin Martel Wightman. They told me he was not in the office today and would not be available until tomorrow. I left my name and number. I called up his home. Marshall Wilson was courteous on the telephone and said it was fine if I dropped by his apartment on Argyle Street.

I went into the client conference room. Ed Stanley looked the worse for wear like he had been getting trashed all night and long into the morning and had not had the calm and relief that comes with either sleep or sex. He looked like stale soiled longjohns piled on a case of twenty-four, coming out of the bush. Not a place I wanted to visit. His Tommy Hilfiger T-shirt was rumpled and saturated with grime and sweat, beyond mere dirty edging towards filthy. He had on a pair of matching designer brand chinos, matching not in the sense of the same brand but rather saturation of filth, the once beige fabric had become so begrimed that it was now turning to khaki. He wore soiled worn Nike shoes without socks. His hair was mussed up. Stanley looked like he was shifting between high anxiety about everything in the world and not giving a tinker's damn about a bloody thing.

"I know you're probably pretty busy Mr Knight but I got to talk to you. You got my messages didn't you?"

"I was intending to call you after lunch. Unfortunately, I'm quite busy just now. However, I should tell you I'm no longer working for the Strachans."

"I figured as much. But look, I need to talk to someone in the know. Liz's parents and sister won't talk to me about what happened. They don't even want to talk to me. For Christ's sakes I am somebody in this situation. I was crazy about the lady. The cops won't tell me anything."

"As the case is under investigation, the police are not saying anything to anyone. Preserve any evidence. So don't feel left out. Probably apart from public relations announcements seeking assistance from the public—you know, TIPS at Crime Stoppers—they won't have anything to say until they make an arrest. That's how it is. Don't take offence, Ed. Don't take it personal. In any event, I or for that matter Lajoie–Chang are no longer involved in the investigation. I was working a missing person file and it has been resolved. Tragically."

"Listen, I still want to talk to you. You got to know what happened."

I glanced at my watch.

"Okay. I'm pretty busy but I need a coffee and could use a bite to eat. You look like you could use a coffee and maybe something to eat as well. So you're welcome to join me." I glanced purposefully at my watch until Stanley acknowledged the gesture with his gaze. "Say fifteen minutes."

"Sure. Sure, Knight. Whatever you say."

"There's a diner down the street. A block or so away. Come on."

I couldn't spare the time but I took the jerk to Saikely's anyway. Hoping to be done with him after listening for fifteen minutes to the litany of self-pity. The me-me factor in any homicide.

We found a quiet corner by a side window. The place was still busy but edging past its busy point. A lot of take-outs on the peg for Albert, he'd be sweating the grill, but the rush had gone past its peak for eat-ins. I noticed their son Anthony was working with him. They seemed to work in good smooth coordination with one another, the minimal exchange of words that so many cooks have when they are in the midst of a rush, get the dishes out without yakking. A quiet respect among the three Saikelys.

I ordered a coffee, tuna sandwich. Stanley asked for a beer. I urged him to order something to eat. He scoffed but finally ordered a plate of fries after I assured him that Al Saikely made the best french fries in the Ottawa valley. I wanted to say forget the beer. But when the beer arrived Stanley placed the bottle under protective custody. His grip on the beer bottle and the way it went to his lips indicated that there was absolutely nothing that I could ever say to the guy that would interfere with his determination and the reach of his strong arm. I knew I would sound so Canadian. I couldn't figure out why no Canadian brewery had yet marketed a brew called Alderman Ale or at least Elbow Bender Lager or Strongarm Stout. So I let Stanley nip on his beer while he smeared ketchup all over Al Saikely's beautiful crisp homemade french fries that had been perfectly blanched then cooled and then fried in the deep fryer a second time and shaken free of the oil. The law of the french fry says only vinegar and salt but the ketchup crime against fries has been going on a long time. As for poutine, it is a massive cover-up. I meditated for a moment: don't let anyone ever tell you that the French don't know what they're doing when it comes to food.

It didn't matter anyway, Stanley mostly ignored the fries. I drank the coffee.

"Man, I can't tell you how much this has devastated me. It's really blown me away. Do you understand? Knight, can you have any idea?"

"I can only begin to imagine, Ed. But to be honest I've never been there. It's beyond my comprehension. I've lived a most fortunate life."

"I mean this is Ottawa. Nobody gets killed in this town. I can't believe it. You never met Liz. She was so beautiful. So incredibly beautiful. You can't hardly believe what a beautiful lady she was."

I sipped the coffee. I picked up a half of the tuna sandwich. Stanley rolled back against the red worn naugahyde bench, his leg bent at an angle, his sneaker resting on the bench. He took a long slug on the beer.

"Knight, you know something."

I took a bite out of the tuna sandwich.

"I can tell." Stanley shifted, lowered his voice and leaned a little towards me. "You know something about what happened to Liz and you're not saying."

Chewing on the tuna I shook my head indicating no, I knew nothing. It can be ever so helpful at times to have your mouth stuffed with food, a courteous tactic for avoiding a response.

"You know something. This thing is gonna wreck me. It's gonna slay me." He was getting blubbery, I didn't want to listen to blubber, it usually leads to useless information, sentimentalism and complaining and I figured Stanley had little more to give. If the big guy did, the cops would shake, rattle and roll it out of him if they figured he had or knew anything of value, this was strictly a freebie feel-sorry-for-me session, and I measured my time running out.

"I can't believe that this woman, this incredibly beautiful woman, so beautiful, that I loved, came to this."

"Believe it, Ed. There's nothing cool about murder."

"Yeah but when you know the person it happened to you don't want to accept it. You want to avoid it. You don't want it to go in here." He gestured towards his heart. "I want to avoid it. The thought of it is killing me."

"You'll have to get past it."

"I can't. I just can't. I need someone. I mean another one. Come on, have one with me."

"Sure. Go ahead. On me." I motioned for May Saikely to bring my friend another beer. "I'll join you where you're at."

Plump May Saikely, who was almost gorgeous, a suave but spiritual figure, with startling black luxurious hair, smooth olive skin and almond eyes, looked at me as if I had gone dim-witted in my soul. When she set down the beers and a pilsener glass, she said only, "Here, Mr Knight. For you and your very good friend."

"It's so fucking fucked up." Stanley slammed his fist on the table.

May Saikely moved away but I could feel the shiver of her flesh. She never swore.

"A guy can't just forget. No way. You can't just pack it all away like goddamn gear in a stinking football locker. I want to get my hands on the guy and kill the bastard."

"Slow down. The police will handle this. They'll get the guy. This is a police matter Ed. Not the sort of thing that people take into their own hands. Understand? There are some top notch detectives on this case. Very good police investigating. There's a lot left behind.

At the scene. The guy was shrewd but there's always something left behind. They'll get him."

"What?" Stanley relaxed for a moment. He started on the second beer. "Tell me what you mean Knight. What's there?"

"Things. All sorts of things. The car itself. Little things. Infinitely small things. Semen. The body being moved. Things being dropped."

"What was dropped there? Something."

"I can't say."

"Did you find anything? I heard you found Liz. Er, I mean someone with you."

"Where'd you hear that?"

"I don't, I don't remember. Some guy over at the university said this big famous private investigator, former Montreal cop found the body. He has a buddy with the police."

"I happened to be in the apartment building at the time but I didn't find the body. No way. I never found a thing. Nothing. It was a fluke discovering her body. Nothing more. A mere accident. Stumbled upon."

"A fluke. How's that? I thought you knew what you were doing."

"The body was found by luck. Luck. Pure and simple luck. Luck always plays a part in an investigation. It was a coincidence really."

"How's that, why a coincidence?"

"Nothing really. The garbagemen mentioned to someone in the building that the garbage really smelt weird."

"Garbage?"

"Yeah. Her body. Never mind, you don't want to hear about it. It's grim." I poured some of the beer into a pilsener glass.

"Yes I do. I have a need to know. I got to know what happened to Liz."

"Well this is just between you and me. You understand. Nobody else."

"Sure. I'm no blabbermouth. I might come from a small city but I'm no gossip."

"Well it could compromise the investigation. The police could get ticked off."

"I won't shout it about."

"Cops don't like it when a private investigator blabs. Meddles in their work. It really pisses them off. I could lose my private investigator's permit."

"This is different. I need to know. I'm like, like one of Liz's family. 'Cause I was so close to Liz."

"How close?"

"What do you mean? I told you. I wanted to marry the lady. You know that. Ask anybody who knew us. We were a number."

"And she wanted to marry you?"

"Yeah. Well kinda. She didn't exactly tell her folks because they'd be pissed off thinking it might not be best for her studies or something. I mean she wanted to finish her education first. I mean we hadn't set the date or anything. And she hadn't told her family or anything 'cause Liz said she had to get her law degree, that was a priority. Anyway I'm being scouted by the pros and I figure I might get a couple of years of pro ball in. She knew I had that. I mean I had a life too. But that was cool with me if she first finished her law degree. So we kinda put off discussion of it. But we were gonna get hitched. That was pretty certain."

"I'm sure it must have been if you say so, I take your word for it. You're a believable kinda guy. Like they say an up-front kinda guy."

"You bet. I'm from a small city in that sort of way. There's some good things still in small places. People down in southwestern Ontario tell you what's on their minds. Up front like you say Knight. None of these head games. I mean I see so many fucking head games. Academic mind games being played over at the U of O. People thinking they're so bloody gawddamn sofuckinisticated. It really makes me sick. Phonies. Makes me want to puke. It's a real screw-up to see the way pretentious people over there screw over other people." He took a long swallow on the beer.

"I suppose it's a drag. I can only imagine it's got worse since I was there."

"Between you and me, I'm not really cut out for that place. I'm a more down to earth kinda guy."

"Salt of the earth."

"I suppose. Yeah. Anyway what's that mean? I hear it back home."

"It means you got your sneakers on the ground. Your feet right down in the soil of this earth. It's some kinda saying coming out of the Bible. High quality. Honest."

"Yeah that's me." He lifted his running shoe, "See that's me. Feet planted on the earth."

I gazed at his big foot.

"I never really understood that expression."

"It means no nonsense. Hardworking. Straightforward. No phoniness. No crap. No crapology. Just honest."

"That sure is my family. We're that way. Straight shooters. We're not farm people anymore, but we go back to the 1840s, we came out with that guy Talbot and cleared the land. Made it work. Soil on our hands. We still got that work in our blood."

"Blood is interesting. Good blood really shows. True blood reveals itself."

"That's right. The earth is in our blood. And our sweat is in the soil. That's what my grandfather used to say. And he said, be proud of it." He stopped talking and drank.

I said nothing. I took up the other half of the tuna sandwich. I told myself eat slow, eating fast is just stress adding to stress.

Then Stanley set the bottle down and said. "But you still haven't told me what you know Knight. What you found. You were saying it was a kinda fluke. How come?"

"'Cause it was. The nose." I set the sandwich down on the plate and tapped my nose and smiled, "The nose tells all. An amazing organ."

Stanley frowned as if I had said something disgusting. I smiled again.

"If the smell wasn't there there would have been no way of knowing that the body was behind the dumpster."

"Behind the dumpster?"

"Yeah. Liz's body was found behind a dumpster. That's what I heard."

"I thought, well, I heard another rumour."

"What's that?"

"That the body was somewhere else."

"Could have been. Could have been moved. That's what I mean, things tell."

He drank hard.

"That's creepy. Really weird stuff. I don't like that. It's like a cat playing with a dead bird. Moving it around. What kinda weirdo goes around moving a dead body?"

"Yeah. I once saw a cat kill a goldfinch on a thistle."

"Thistle? Huh. I don't understand. Where you going. Goldfinch?"

"Goldfinches are shrewd little birds. They eat the seeds of the thistle. And they use the threads from a thistle flower to make their nests. Pretty fine weaving work. There were thistle plants in my backyard and laneway, the goldfinches used to come. The alley cat saw them and killed them. Then like you said it carried the bird's body around and pawed it. Played with it. Here and there. Like it had no intention to eat it. But put it out for show."

"I heard Liz was raped. Is that true?"

"I can't say. But ..."

"Tell me." He finished his beer, he stared at the bottle. He wanted another.

"Not another, Ed, go easy. Okay?"

"I can handle it. This is so confusing, Knight, so friggin' confusing."

"These are confusing times Ed. Black crows and blue jays keeling over from some mysterious tropical disease. Virus. Strange heat waves. Cold spells. Freak ice storms. Massive salt seas in the middle of Asia drying up. Patches of the polar cap that never melted in a billion years melting down. Animals getting sick with the strangest diseases. Subatomic particles drilling through molecules in the brain. Strange wars. Catastrophic diseases. Ebola. HIV-AIDS, never heard about, not twenty-five thirty years ago. And within our lifetime Ed, you and me, wiping out millions and millions and millions of people."

"Sick. Queers spreading it. Sick. Should get rid of them all. Exterminate the whole lot."

"Slow down Ed. Extreme way to eliminate a disease. Not exactly a scientific approach."

"Who cares. Necessary sometimes. Ugh. It makes me sick. Too many of them fucking frog faggots over at U of O. I want to play ball otherwise I wouldn't go there. Where's that fat waitress?"

He motioned towards May Saikely.

"Have this while you're waiting." I motioned towards the half empty bottle. Stanley drank. He seemed reflective for a long moment.

"Was Liz raped? Is that rumour true?"

"I can't say. That's for the coroner to determine. In an autopsy. You know all that fancy forensic handiwork by the coroner, pathologist and the lab, that's their job. Kinda like you see on TV. That's way way out of my league. I'm just a hack on the hustle."

"By me, you're an alright kinda guy. I trust you. I can talk to you. You're up-front."

May Saikely brought the beer. The look of disapproval was lengthening across her lips, it was in her smile. A smile but her lips were thin. But you had to know the changeability of May Saikely's various smiles to detect this aspect of her mood.

"Thank you, May."

Stanley waited for May Saikely to move away before speaking.

"Knight, tell me what you found."

"Well like I told you I actually never found the body. I found nothing. But I talked to a guy who some said found the body or was there when the body was found. It's not exactly clear. You know how it is Ed. Some people exaggerate what they know or what they've seen."

"Who?"

"It doesn't matter. I think he said he had something to do with the building or something. Can't quite recall. With Melgund Corporation, the company that owns the place. But it's a big corporation. He was not exactly definite on that point. He sort of made like he was in the know. He said well the body was naked. All of her clothing was ripped off."

Stanley frowned. "How's that?"

"She had no clothing on. Or at least that's what the guy said he saw."

"Nothing?"

"Nothing except her bra which was tied around her neck. Pretty grim."

"That's crappy. The guy who did it strangled her with her own bra?"

"I can't say. Seems it appeared to be that way. Or at least the killer tried to. But the real cause of death will come out in the autopsy. Sometimes appearances are misleading."

"Can you kill somebody with a bra? I thought that was just weirdo stuff for the movies. To kinda sex things up. Kinky sex."

"It can happen."

"This is really confusing."

"What's confusing?"

"About how it happened."

"Murder is always subject to complex principles."

"Principle?"

"Kinda like a law. A law. Universal law."

"What principle. What law? This sounds like physics or economics." He gazed at me hard and took up the new beer.

"A criminological principle or law. The principle of confusion."

"The principle or law of confusion? I never heard of such a thing. What are you talking about?" He stared at the formica table surface, ran his big hand across it.

"The criminologist not only studies the physical aspects of a crime but also the psychic aspect. It's an obscure principle in criminology. And forensics. But theoretical. The law of confusion is a contradictory law."

"Contradictory law? I thought laws were supposed to straighten things out. Make things clear." He gazed at me.

"It's in criminology. Psychological criminology. You got to study crim. To know about it. It's not exactly common knowledge. It was developed by a criminologist, a specialist in criminal psychology. Guy called Nick Gathel, you probably never heard of the guy. Nobody's ever heard of the guy outside the speciality. It's not layman stuff."

"Tell me, I'm curious. I'm just doing a B.Comm., this kind of weirdo shitfreak psycho stuff is beyond me. I just took psych one hundred. And a required stats course in shrink wrapping. And some breeze biz psych courses on consumer shopping and spending. You know, marketing bullshit, how to shrinkwrap the consumer's brain." Stanley laughed, "This other stuff is way over my head. It sure isn't salt of the earth stuff."

"The thing is, nothing is ever way over the head of the murderer. But the murderer is still subject to this principle of contradiction, this law of confusion, according Nick Gathel. And Gathel interviewed and profiled dozens and dozens, even hundreds of murderers before postulating his principle of confusion. Which says that the killer is always methodical, or thinks he is, in killing but always confused in the act of killing another human being."

"That's heavy. I got to think about that to grasp it." Then Stanley burst into laughter, "Shit. Actually the principle sounds fucked up, confused, if you ask me. This guy Gathel can't be serious. Gathel sounds like numbnuts. It's not exactly a hand-off from the quarterback to the fullback to plunge through the line. How can it be so? I mean how can a person be methodical but confused at the same time? It just doesn't make sense."

"Ruthlessness involves method. Self-preservation involves the methodical so the killer is just careful enough to try to conceal the act. Hide it from everyone else and himself. To escape being caught. Being detected. Get away from it. The instinct after killing, to bury the corpse, the body, the killing. Even from himself. Or at least try. And even thinks, believes, he is doing it even if he actually does a sloppy lousy job of it."

"From himself? How's that. If he did it he's got to know he did it. I mean nasty fuckers like Olson and that way weirdo duo Homolka and Bernardo. I mean I half remember them but from what I've read, heard all about them, they got to know they did it. They just got to. You can't kill somebody and not know it."

"Yes, but the law of confusion for murderers, according to this criminal psychologist Nick Gathel, states that the murderer is confused at the moment, the very instant of killing when governed by the urge, the impulse to kill, the rage to murder, because—" I finished my coffee and motioned for more coffee.

May Saikely brought the coffee urn and poured the coffee into my cup.

"Good coffee today, May."

"That's right, Mr Knight. Water and coffee are staples."

Stanley waited for May to move away.

"Because why? Come on, go on."

"Where was I? Oh yeah, because the murderer is in a state of confusion when deciding to kill. When doing the killing. Because when the murderer is killing another human being—" I paused and sipped the coffee. "Great coffee here, Ed. This is not Starbucks. No way. The real thing. Should try it."

"Go on willya."

"Sure. Now we come to the hard part. The murderers, when they are killing another human being, this is kinda hard to grasp, killing another human, they are not really killing another human being. They're really killing themselves."

Stanley said nothing. He stared out the window then back at me. "That's heavy shit. That's real heavy shit." He burst into laughter again, "This guy Gathel's an idiot. Really. I don't believe it. Between you and me I don't believe that kind of dressed-up crap. It's not there. It's like putting a fucking tuxedo on a corpse. A guy kills somebody else they killed somebody else. Come on. That's the way it is. This other stuff about not killing someone else but really killing themselves, that sounds like a pile of manure. No offence intended Knight. It just does. If you bump into this Doc Gathel tell him I told him so."

"Think about it my friend. Even if you don't believe it. Gathel explains it, tells you why."

"Okay why? Go ahead. But really it sounds like a joke." Stanley was smiling, half laughing.

"According to Nick Gathel it comes out in the denial of emotions. It comes out further in the body. If you've ever seen a murdered person's body, the victim's corpse, you'd believe that the murderer was killing more than the person they were immediately killing. It really comes out when a human being kills with their hands."

"Hands?"

"Hands. Hasn't the advantage of rapid technology, a weapon that puts some distance between himself and the act itself. But has a weapon that's held in the hand like a knife or a bottle or a stone. A weapon or something that requires strenuous force to achieve the fatal end. Then they really go at the body of the victim. Hammering away, hammering the life out of it. Wham wham wham. Oh yeah, especially a knife. Thuugh thuugh thuugh. Or even a bottle. Or a stone. A brick. Kachunk kachunk kachunk. Or twisting a rope or hands around the neck of the victim, urr, urr, urrgh. The murderer exceeding anything necessary to achieve the determined goal of taking another human being's life. Gathel said killers told him about how they went on, and went on, just carried away. In excess of anything that was necessary. Myself, I saw one guy, an old drunk's body in a flophouse, the head just pulverized with a wine bottle if you can believe it by another guy over nothing more than a five dollar bottle of pissola. Horrible. Awful mess. Truly awful mess of the body. Every part of the body raised up to a bruise. Unbelievable. Just unbelievable sight. You can't look at it. It takes your throat away. Demolishes your heart to see. And what the law of confusion tells us is the murderer is murdering himself, murdering the world, murdering his entire world, murdering the world in which he lives because he hates it. Oblivion. Obliteration. Annihilation. Hates himself, hates the world, hates everything that made him what he is. He hates it so much he wants to obliterate it and himself. He thinks killing is the road to freedom. You've got to see a murder victim, the unfortunate corpse to see that. TV can't show this stuff. No movie ever could. Can't come close. TV, well, TV movies just cover it all up. All that talk about guns just covers it up. Guns take the appearance of things out of the law of confusion but the hate still shows itself, the rage, because sometimes the guy keeps firing away at the body. Bahang bahang bahang. Bham bham bham. Then, thunk thunk thunk, bullets sinking into the flesh. Can't stop. Can't take the finger off the trigger. Guns do that. Turns out, it's the same as with the knife in the hand but made distant. Or a guy with his bare hands using all his strength, twisting and turning and choking. He hates himself. Hates the world. He's throttling the world."

"Hates the world? I can't grasp that. I don't understand."

"Yeah. Hates the world. Hates the world in which he lives. Because to kill another human being violates all laws, goes against every human being who ever lived or died on this planet. That's another reason why murder is universally unacceptable. No matter where you go. No matter what society from big to small. From great to little. From old to new civilizations. You name it, Ed. Take your pick. Everyone of them won't allow it. Won't allow murder and killing. They outlaw it. That's universal. The whole universe comes to stand against the murderer and he feels, he knows it. Even all of history. All of humanity. Stands against him. Just imagine what that means when the whole of humanity, the green earth, all of history, the stars, solar system, galaxy, universe, stands against you if you commit the act of murder, just imagine what that means. It's overwhelming. He's got to know it. Can't escape it. Can't escape the opposition rising against him. Even in his own brain. His own head. Can't escape the injunction. The simple injunction." I took a sip of coffee.

"What injunction?"

"The simple injunction: Don't do it. Don't do it. Do not do it. Don't kill."

Stanley said nothing.

"Ed, you should have a cup of this brew."

"Later. Cruelty. Mutilation. Is that what the guy did to Liz? I mean are you suggesting he did something horrible to her body?"

"It was heavy. I heard it was truly heavy. Whoever did it really hates himself."

"Then why didn't he do it to himself? Why didn't he leave Liz alone?" Stanley appeared about to laugh or get angry, I couldn't tell. "I mean she was so beautiful. She was. You just had to see her. No picture tells you. Any guy would do anything to be with a woman as beautiful as Liz."

"Maybe. You could be right. Unfortunately, I never had the good fortune to meet her. But I take your word, Ed. So many people admired Liz."

"It's so." He paused, "Okay let's assume what this guy Gathel says is true. Although I have trouble believing it. But I'm no psychologist. It sounds like a lot of guff to me. But let's assume it is so, if the creep had that much hatred in him, why didn't he just snuff himself?"

"Suicide is in another zone altogether. Way beyond murder. Far out in another galaxy. It's usually not criminal. Well unless it involves hurting or taking another person's life along with your own. Nick Gathel has things to say about suicide although he doesn't really get into it, but it's not linked to murder the way some people are inclined to think. Not anywhere near it. More intricate and complex, not strictly there. Harder, much harder to grasp. In another zone of the mind. Gathel even postulates that suicide–murders, whether familial or mass killings, do not involve suicide. That the killer can't commit suicide. Suicide is another zone."

"Another zone?"

"Yes. Far away. The guy who killed Liz didn't kill himself because he couldn't kill himself. But killing Liz was his way of destroying himself."

"Then why rape and murder Liz?"

"Because unfortunately, like a lot of victims, for the murderer a victim stands in the way of the murderer killing himself. Liz was in this guy's way to killing himself whoever he was."

"In the way? That's beyond me."

"He was a coward." I sipped the coffee.

"Coward? That sounds like crap. He was a weirdo but it took some nerve to kill. The guy wasn't afraid. I'd say he was pretty bold. Kinda scary. I'd stay away from a guy like that."

"No, Ed. Something special about murderers and courage." I sipped the coffee.

"What?"

"Every murderer is a coward. Only cowards murder. Nick Gathel tells us this. They destroy their own humanity. Rather than facing up to their humanity. They're not like everyday guys like you and me. They don't have the courage to face up to their humanity. It takes great courage to get through everyday life without harming other human beings. Great courage. That's why so many everyday people are courageous people. They go through daily life struggling with themselves not to hurt others. That's beautiful. That's the beautiful sum of some peoples' lives. That's a really beautiful thing according to Nick Gathel's theory. In the simplest way we show our courage by showing our kindness to others just day by day. Day in and day out. Getting through troubles. Working through troubles. Instead of getting into trouble. Deep dark trouble. But the murderer doesn't do that. He's afraid to be kind day by day. He's afraid of day to day life. It takes too much courage. He's afraid of himself. Gathel states that the highest emotion is social altruism. That we're programmed for it, not just socialized for it but we need it for our survival. We need others and we know we need others. And we want to be altruistic. And out of altruism comes felicity. Happiness comes from other human beings not just from ourselves. So we got to be altruistic. Don't you?"

"Sure. Sure. I like to be happy. I come from a happy family."

"That's good. You're lucky. But Gathel found that all murderers have one thing, share one thing in common. Arrogance."

"What?"

"They despise social altruism. They see it as weakness. It disgusts them, they think they are giving up part of themselves that is sacred. They refuse to give. They're not like you and me. We want to love and give. Don't you, Ed?"

"Sure. That's why I loved Liz so much. You got to understand that. People have to understand how much I loved the lady. How I thought she was so beautiful. I really really loved that woman."

"I'm sure you did. That's why what happened to her—"

"Get's to me," he interrupted. "Really tears me apart." Stanley's face was upset.

"People who kill aren't like you and me. Isn't that so? You'd have to agree with Gathel on that wouldn't you?"

"I suppose. But listen Knight I wanted to tell you something but it's a little awkward now."

"You're kinda upset "

"Yeah. Kinda."

"I didn't mean to upset you Ed."

"No. No no. Not you. I just can't think straight. I'm so shaken up by Liz's death. It's left me without sleep. Sorta sleepless."

"I suppose you can't remember what you wanted to tell me after all this talking. Sorry I didn't mean to go on."

"That's alright. Kinda heavy stuff. Whoever this Gathel guy is. But it's not that. It's just this place, it's kinda public like. Not the place. No offence, but I don't like this greasy spoon."

"Everybody is overwhelmed by Liz's death. I mean everybody who knew her."

"Yeah."

I glanced at my watch.

"But you want to tell me something, right Ed?"

"Maybe. But not now. Not here. Too many people around. Maybe later."

I glanced at my watch.

"Look I got to go. Busy day."

"Busy day, busy Knight?" He grinned.

"Sure. With the death of someone that intimate to you, it can be pretty devastating. You need someone to help you get over this thing."

"I do. I really do. I'm gonna be okay. It was real good talking with you Knight."

"And it's always better to talk to somebody. Have a friendly ear listening."

"That's right. Someone to shoot the breeze. That's why I called you. I knew I could count on you to be sympathetic."

"And I am, Ed. Guy has to get this off his chest otherwise it will suffocate him. You talk with your friends. Confide in them. Get it off your chest. That's what friends are for. You got plenty of friends. You're a popular guy."

"I can't talk to my buddies. My roomies. I mean I don't feel like it."

"Well if not them, then Bill di Cesare, he seems like a good guy. Sensitive type. I'm sure you could talk with him. And he knew Liz, he'd understand how hard you've taken her death."

"Not really. I mean not really the kind of guy I would—what was the word you used again?"

"Confide?"

"Yeah, I'd never really talk about something like this with him. Truth is he wasn't very friendly to Liz. He kinda despises the people he cheats for on the stats."

"Well if not him, maybe one of Liz's friends. Connie Yonge. She's a good person. And she was close to Liz."

Stanley's face was harsh.

"You don't know that bitch. You really don't. If you knew."

"Tell me. I thought she was a very sympathetic, open kinda person. She really tried to help me in every way."

"She's a lesbo, man. She was trying to hustle Liz. She was always coming on to her."

"But naturally Liz wasn't interested in such stuff."

"No way. No way man. That bitch Yonge, now there's somebody who plays mind games."

"How's that, Ed? Connie Yonge seemed like a pretty straightforward sort of person."

"Talk to Lester Henderson. Poor fucking fucked-up Les Henderson. She really fucked the guy over. Really screwed him around. She had him by the balls. Tickle tickle. Twisting his crown jewels around. What a doorknob." Stanley half laughed.

"Why?"

"She was fucking Les around. Les is married but he likes, you know, to screw around. Get a piece of ass on the side. His old lady is kinda uptight. Somehow he got to know Connie Yonge. And he got hung up on the bitch."

"I don't understand. It doesn't make sense. You just said she was a lesbian."

"You're not listening man. She is. She's a bull dyke but was involved with all these business types. It's a money thing. I can't quite figure it out. She was into freaky things through some hotshot escort service. Doing stuff for money. Into money. She was involved with some weirdos. "

"Who?"

"Ah you don't want to know. I don't give a shit. It's just apartment building gossip. Mattress games. Bedhopping bunch of middle-aged suits who can't get laid without paying. Squad of washed-out relief pitchers from the Viagra bullpen."

"I heard rumours about this but discounted them because Connie Yonge was so cooperative. Helpful."

"Two-faced bitch."

"She really got under your skin, eh Ed?"

"Sort of. You don't know that woman. Maybe it should have been her instead of Liz. The creep in that building got the wrong woman. In the garage. In the garage he should have got that creep Connie. And left Liz alone."

"You don't mean that, Ed."

"Well maybe not. Ah forget it Knight. You don't know the half of it."

"Who else was Yonge involved with? I mean these business guys you heard about. I heard about some guy called Norm or Hurley. A tenant in the building mentioned him."

"That'd be Norm Burley. He's a good buddy of Les Henderson. Hotshot corporate lawyer. Big money."

"And a guy called I think Clark. No Clar—"

"Clarence Wilson. Another hotshot sonuvabitch lawyer. Now that guy was a real bastard."

"Was?"

"Yeah. He got killed. Had it coming to him if you ask me from what I heard about him. Although I never met the guy. Just rumours."

"How's that?"

"I don't want to talk about those old lardy farts. They're way out of my time zone. That guy Wilson is strictly history. It's a drag. Just more bad news. I don't know them except Les. And he's alright. He's a human being. He's okay to me."

"Sure. Anyway I got to go. Good talking to you. I'll grab the bill, don't sweat it, Ed. By the way can you remember what kind of car Liz had? I thought I saw it down in the apartment garage. The cops were checking it. Someone said it was an Olds. But I don't recall that. I think they found some kinda crucial piece of evidence with the car."

"Man, Liz had a Mazda. She had a new Miata. Her old man and old lady shelled out for it. The money for it come out of the accident trust fund."

"Then why do I think it was an Olds, maybe Connie Yonge said it was an Olds."

"I don't know. Beyond me."

"I'll get the bill."

"Thanks. I'm going to finish this one."

"Sure."

I rushed back to the office and told Cheryl Perron to get an agency car and get a surveillance on Les Henderson, shake up Nick Glastonbury if necessary or do it herself and get onto Henderson right away. I checked my watch, I was due at Marshall Wilson's place in twenty minutes.

# NINETEEN

It was a stately apartment building from the 1920s when Ottawa, flush with federal dough, was rolling itself out as fully independent from Britain in international relations. Apartment buildings went up around the city on O'Connor, Metcalfe, Argyle and Elgin, some swell others not so swell, more austere and dreary. A few clung to a certain fashionable display, at times tentative taste for opulence or at least as opulent as Ottawa's architecture would be before the time of Trudeau.

The apartment building that Marshall Wilson lived in was near the Museum of Nature in the Metcalfe loop where some embassies were located. The Museum of Nature was lodged in the Victoria Memorial Building, a hulking edifice in a style dubbed Scottish baronial. A whimsical building constructed from beautiful cut local sandstone with fine stone masonry, jutting turrets and parapets. I'd heard that it had once had a high tower at the front entrance, not unlike the central Peace Tower of the Parliament buildings. But due to either the architect's hubris or engineer's ignorance of mathematics, the tower of the Victoria Memorial proved so bulky and weighty the foundations could not bear the tower's vast mass. It had, in a cruel act of preservation, been chopped down. Ottawa being a former lumber town, we do like to chop. This too was an Ottawa tradition where buildings and institutions are constantly evolving, devolving, being renamed, chopped up or demolished. Continuity is dicey. It was all there before me in the cut stone bulwark of the Museum of Nature.

When I passed by this stone pile of absurdity, errant and roguish images from movie reruns seen on TV that had no connection with this edifice flared up. As a kid, I had watched the reruns on the cheap with my mother who had known them as first fare in her teens, cosy on the couch, feet dangling, chomping on fistfuls of homemade popcorn. The valiant and salacious Vikings Ernest

Borgnine, Tony Curtis and Kirk Douglas, lusting over Janet Leigh in The Vikings. The plucky crusader come home, Charlton Heston, lusting after Rosemary Forsyth in The War Lord, from here the mind may wander where it will, and mine did. But memory has a habit of being out of place, consequently it is a source of either transitory absurd humour or relentless remorse and regret. The battles took place on the home front right there on the parapets of the Victoria Memorial. Queen Victoria had died. The drawbridge of empire and civilization had been pulled up. We were left with the Scottish baronial. All the same I'd had a few madcap memorable moments in the building as a kid on school trips, much to the chagrin of my teachers. There was pleasure getting lost, especially in big buildings with stately staircases, if one lived in a tiny cramped apartment with a single mother struggling on a clerk's paycheque.

The apartment building was more refined and poised, with finer cut granite for the foundations, the corners, window lintels and door frames, and well fired brick for the walls. The casement windows were filled with leaded glass and highlights of stained glass for a richer feeling. The art deco entrance with neo-gothic motifs and four graceful Corinthian columns suggested the opening to a cavern of atavistic rituals. I entered the vestibule of the building lit by a fine bronze lamp in the vaulted ceiling. I thought I had entered a desacralized chamber of some hermetic cult, probably bureaucrats who had become devotees of Tolkien or acolytes of the Matrix or, more pragmatically, disciples of Ayn Rand. As for myself, I was no hobbit, ninja or junk bond dealer, so I did the earthly thing to get upstairs, I rang the buzzer.

A voice that was neither Gandalf nor Morpheus from the Matrix said, "Yes?"

It was one of those avuncular Ottawa valley voices, middle-aged and middle class, confident, assured and momentarily imbued with bureaucracy in its formality.

"Alec Knight from Lajoie–Chang to see Marshall Wilson."

"Come up. Seven twenty-three."

The door emitted an urgent screeching sound and the dead bolt unlocked. I took the old bronze elevator up to the seventh floor and went down the carpeted hallway to Wilson's apartment. It was soon evident that a certain decay had settled into this seemingly esteemed piece of art deco, it permeated the building, first signalled in the crankiness of the door release but apparent throughout in the tarnished brass mailboxes, worn and stiff door handles, the ancient stained paintwork, chipped, bulging and cracked plaster of the corridor walls, the grotty carpets and hairline fractures of the small glass panes in the old bronze lamps with burnt out light bulbs. Clichés were everywhere, made life feel cheap.

A big bluff man opened the oak door. He had a ruddy complexion, good features a little corrupted by puffiness, pale blue eyes and straw red hair going grey. I felt like a bellhop delivering a magnum of champagne, a cigar box of Cubans, a lacquer box of sushi, and a note from a pimp to a former millionaire telling him his credit was rotten and no go in the future.

"Knight?"

"Right."

"Marshall Wilson." He offered his pink speckled beefy hand. It was the sort of handshake that made a fellow feel he was back in grade school visiting the principal's office for the first time because he threw a snowball in the air after the recess bell rang. I had no desire to eat lunch, breakfast or dinner with Marshall Wilson, I had even less desire to meet the guy around the boardroom table and argue with him over a merger. Fat chance of that. My stock market speculations had all remained so hypothetical over the years that they had never gained or lost a cent. I was happily even. Neither a loser nor a winner.

"Come in."

We went into a large high-ceilinged living room. The plasterwork looked original, from a time when it really meant something to do what was called plasterwork, but it was sadly sagging, the ceiling mouldings gave the room a dignified formality, assurance and distinction that was comforting. Fine art deco light sconces graced the walls. But the management had to put some serious money into the joint, otherwise it would begin to crumble. Even the best plaster job lasts only so long. Once stately in the 1920s, the building was now in a decline that exuded disdain. The atmosphere of the place was attractive and repellent, gloomy and unsettling. I felt very uneasy as I sat down in one of the matching red leather wing-chairs.

"What's this about Mr Knight?"

"Your sister-in-law has asked Lajoie–Chang Associates to investigate the death of your brother, Clarence Wilson."

"Right." He took out a cigarette, gave me a glance and offered the silver case.

"No thanks."

Wilson lit up the smoke and puffed and said nothing. I could see it was going to have to come from my side. He relaxed in his red chair. He was not the sort of fellow who could be discomfited into speech through silence. He just sat there in the once nicely upholstered but now somewhat worn chair. He said nothing. Then I knew he wouldn't by the diligent way he smoked.

"I have some leads. But ..." I paused. Marshall Wilson still said nothing, he was the epitome of patience. Like a good solicitor, attentive, diligent and initially keen to listen rather than speak, before taking control of the conversation and the client.

"Well they look good. But I need some time to fill them out. Mr Wilson, have you spoken to the police concerning your brother's unfortunate accident?"

"Yes." And nothing more.

"Have they suggested anything from their end?"

"No. And I wouldn't expect them to unless they had pressed charges against someone. They've made it very clear to Madeleine and myself that they do not wish to discuss the case unless we can provide information or until they are in a position to lay charges. And," he paused and took a drag on the smoke. There was something crass and distasteful in his inhaling of the cigarette, as if he regretted smoking but couldn't abstain and felt this a lack of will power over the habit. But he also seemed to enjoy the moment. More unsettling, his smoking manner seemed to suggest contempt and disdain for who he was speaking with.

"Maybe I'll have one after all." I half smiled and leaned forward. "Been trying to quit but not so good at it. It's a social thing."

"Right."

The man opened the silver cigarette case, offered a smoke, a Sobranie, then held up a matching lighter, silver with a blue sapphire embedded in the metal. I noticed that he wore a blue sapphire ring surrounded by at least six smaller diamonds.

"You were saying something about laying charges."

"Was I? The police's approach is thoroughly understandable. I support it one hundred percent."

"They're trying but don't seem to be making much headway according to your sister-in-law."

Marshall Wilson half smiled, then took another deep drag, as if already exhausted by the conversation.

"Listen, Mr Knight. This event has bowled us over. But Madeleine," he rubbed the edge of his cigarette on the ashtray. I leaned forward and tapped the ash off my smoke, took a drag then let the smoke float away from my hand towards Marshall Wilson. "My sister-in-law Madeleine has taken it especially hard. It is no doubt understandable. But she has—I am not certain how to formulate it, this is a painful subject, not good for a lawyer to be short of words—but let's say she's been a little impatient with the authorities. Which emotionally is entirely understandable, but still. Well. Patience is necessary in such affairs."

"What you say makes sense. But as Clarence Wilson's brother, it must have taken its toll."

"It has. It has Mr Knight. I won't deny it. But it is something I would prefer not to discuss with strangers."

"Entirely understandable, Mr Wilson."

"Regarding the authorities, I'm quite convinced that the authorities are doing their very best to solve the case. Putting out their best effort. Not an easy case to solve. It was a hit-and-run accident on a quiet stretch of a back country road."

"Was it?"

"What do you mean by that?"

"I mean, can one be certain that it was an accident. Accidental that is."

"Why certainly. That's what they indicated."

"The police."

"Yes. It's a tough case. They've as much as said so. What's more, without any eyewitness. Something essential to solving such a crime. And Clarence wasn't found until at least two hours later. So it's a tough one to solve. Very tough indeed. Hit-and-run accidents can be."

"Did your brother have any enemies? Any people he had rubbed the wrong way."

He butted out his smoke. I took one last fake drag and butted out mine.

"This was one of those stupid, grotesque traffic accidents. Careless, reckless driving. And probably involved a panicked driver."

"How can you be so certain?"

"But I'm not. I never said I was. I'm simply going by what the authorities state. As for myself I don't formulate a opinion. I don't have sufficient information to do so."

"Did your brother have anyone he was afraid of?"

"Clare didn't have any enemies. The police investigated that angle and quite thoroughly. It's virtually the first thing they delved into. And they came up with nothing. Zero. That's a Hollywood scenario. Did you know Clarence? Did you have the good fortune to have met my brother?"

"No."

"Well Clare was the very expression of Aristotle's dictum on humanity." He gazed at me with a certain self-assurance and amusement as if the allusion had floated over my head.

"I never read that guy in Latin."

"Greek. Greek my friend. Aristotle wrote in Greek." Marshall Wilson smirked and uttered these phrases with contempt for my ignorance. "Human beings are social animals. Felicity is our highest goal in life. That was Clare. Clare was an immeasurably likeable sort of fellow. Affable. Ask anyone who knew Clarence Wilson. Clare had no enemies. He was too humane, gentle and sociable. Those were his vulnerable traits as well because other people, less generous, cynics, sometimes tried to take advantage of Clare's good Aristotelean nature."

"Not even someone he might have come in contact with in his law practice, for example, a disgruntled client? Or in his capacity as a lawyer, he rubbed someone else the wrong way while working on behalf of his own clients?"

"Amusing. Too much TV, Mr Knight. You've been reading far too much Grisham. The world of corporate law doesn't function that way." The lawyer paused. "It is objectified. An objective realm. It is a world of distant relations. Corporate clients do not take things personally, even if they feel it personally. The world of corporate capitalism would fall apart if it were based on such petty individual emotions. Clarence, who handled corporate litigation, won cases for his clients but there was no malice. Can't we forget all that hogwash? That conspiratorial nonsense of the tired worn-out left. Capitalism is competitive, not destructive like socialism. And it is precisely its competitiveness that makes it so creative for the human spirit. My brother was out for a morning bicycle ride and probably some half asleep hung-over jerk sideswiped Clarence. A truly horrible waste, a wonderful human and a brilliant lawyer."

"Can you tell me anything about a Mr Lester Henderson?"

"'Fraid not." He shook his head and lit another cigarette. "Name means next to nothing to me. I know nothing about him."

"His name has shown up in conjunction with your brother and a fellow lawyer at Baldwin Martel Wightman, Mr Norman Burley."

"Then I guess Norm Burley would be the man to speak to. Better that you ask him."

"I see. Your sister-in-law mentioned Mr Burley and Mr Henderson in conjunction with some business transactions and investments of your brother."

"Could be but I wasn't in the loop. Norm and Clare did some investments together but I wasn't involved."

"Did the investments go well?"

"I haven't a clue, Mr Knight."

"Your sister-in-law seems to think they went badly."

"Madeleine is naive when it comes to the contemporary world of financial investments. The real business world of today. Like so many people who think capital just materializes splendidly because a person craves it. But a person has to work for money. Also Madeleine comes from," he paused and inhaled on the cigarette, "a world of substance based on the past. And has some misconceptions as to how the real world of finance operates today. In the here and now. How investments go good and bad. She's open and generous to a fault but, this is a compliment so don't misconstrue it Mr Knight, innocent. It is one of her appealing qualities. It makes her charming. A charming woman."

"You didn't ever hear of a bad investment in conjunction with your brother?"

"No. Clare wasn't a complainer. You know things weren't exactly handed to us on a silver platter. We worked to get where we are. I damn well wish a few more people would look up the meaning of the word work in the dictionary. We were poor, suffered hardship, but it was instilled in us by our father that the capitalist system is the best system. The system works for those who are willing to work for it. It offers the most to anybody who is willing to make the effort. Clare certainly never complained, that would be whining and let me tell you something, we Wilsons aren't whiners. That's a feature of welfare socialists. People who don't want to work. People who whine and crawl after a welfare cheque. A government handout."

"Liz Strachan. Does that name mean anything to you, Mr Wilson?"

"Frankly, no more than what is currently in the news. In connection with some recent killing. Is that correct?"

"Yes. Did your brother ever mention her to you?"

"No."

"Did Norman Burley?"

Marshall Wilson shook his head and showed a frown on his brow. "Never."

"It appears that your brother had an affair with this young woman."

"I have no knowledge of that."

"Back in April. For maybe a year. Or the better part of a year."

"Can't say as I was aware of it."

"And that he was going to leave his wife Madeleine Masson and be with, possibly marry, Liz Strachan."

"That's amusing if it weren't gossip of the dead. Sounds preposterous. Please don't say that to Madeleine. She has enough to bear."

"How is it preposterous? Why amusing?"

"Where'd that mischievous piece of salacious gossip come from?"

"Not gossip. Your brother's brother-in-law. By way of your sister-in-law."

"Gilles Masson? Interesting. Gilles is Gilles. He not only lacks a sense of humour but a sense of proportion. He's a little excessive in his passions, his pursuits. It would be nice if he followed the maxim of his reputed hero: Reason over passion. A personality on the ponderous side. In his emotions as well as in his politics. Well, let's just say he tends towards the unsustainable. You no doubt know what Gilles does."

"Sort of."

"Well he imagines himself a doctor on a mission to save humanity. But he's got himself mixed up with that outfit that goes a little too far. Gilles is even more naive in some ways than his sister. He takes his inheritance and indulges in these socialist outfits. Do-good do-nothing organizations. Amnesty International. Oxfam. And such. He happens to believe everything Madeleine tells him. As for Madeleine, she was prone to jealousy. If Clare so much as engaged in congenial conversation at a cocktail party, a dinner party, she'd be upset. Get into a state. The Masson family have a clerical bent. Clare was congenial, sociable but Madeleine is inclined to jealousy. I'll tell you this." He tapped away the ash. "Clare was loyal. He didn't screw around. That wasn't his style."

"Right. But apparently Connie Yonge, a friend of Liz Strachan, said Liz told her that they, meaning Clarence Wilson and Elizabeth Strachan, were running off. That Clarence Wilson was going to leave his wife."

"Well I can't comment on that. I don't know either woman. Clare never mentioned any such thing to me."

"Mr Wilson, it seems possible that there might have been another side of your brother's life that you had no knowledge of."

He gave a legal look, as if inspecting a witness on the stand or a difficult witless client, then grinned.

"I'm my brother's keeper but I'm not all knowing. I leave that to a higher authority. But let me make this remark. This observation. As soon as a good person dies all the slanderers have a field day. Now you say, Mr Knight, that you never met my brother. That is correct is it not?"

"Yes."

"Well if you had you would have noted that he was a man of the highest rectitude. I'm not saying that as his brother. And I am my brother's keeper. I guard his reputation. I'm saying that as a lawyer and someone who knew the reputation that Clarence Wilson had obtained as a fine corporate lawyer. Beyond intimidation. Beyond corruption. A man of great probity. A lot more than can be said for some of the politicians in this town."

"But he had affairs."

He gave a stern look.

"Listen, Mr Knight. There is politeness. And then there is being polite. And being politic. Don't be too pressing on this point. It's unproven and distasteful. If there was anything here, the police would have brought it to light. And they certainly did not."

"I suppose."

"No supposing. They dig into every aspect of a victim's life in such a case. And they have made no mention of this. And believe me they have dug." He looked at his watch.

"I was wondering if you have any knowledge of your brother's involvement with the ICCI Bank, the International Canadian–Caribbean Investors Bank?"

"Afraid I can't comment. I am one of the ICCI Bank's solicitors, Mr Knight." He glanced again at his watch.

"Is there anything else?"

"No." I stood up. "Thank you for your time, Mr Wilson."

"No problem. I'll see you to the door."

We went to the hall. I could see that the carpet spread across the marquetry floor was badly worn in patches. Once a very good carpet, it had not been cared for despite its value.

"Mr Knight, one last thing."

I stopped at the door.

"Yes, Mr Wilson."

"I do hope Lajoie–Chang's private investigation in no way compromises the official police investigation. That would not only be improper, but very upsetting to our family."

"We won't. Morrison Chang and Georges Lajoie are former police officers."

"So I've been informed."

"They are careful to do things by the book. I should let you know that we are going to look into every aspect of this case, every aspect. But in no way will we compromise the integrity of the police investigation. And we are at Madeleine Masson's service at all times."

"Admirable. Admirable commitment. That's impressive. But Lajoie–Chang being professionals I'd certainly expect as much. Nothing less."

"Madeleine Masson needs Lajoie–Chang's support. And like any client of ours, she gets our full backing. But we in no way would compromise the authorities' investigation. That's not our style. Our method. We don't go over the line."

"Very good, Mr Knight." He grasped the crystal door handle and opened the apartment door.

"Thanks for your time, Mr Wilson."

"My pleasure."

"It's reassuring to know we can count on your support. Because I am confident that this tragic accident can be solved."

"Good. But how's that, Mr Knight? Why so confident where the police have faced difficulties for several months? Sounds as if you know something. Something the police may have overlooked. Although that hardly seems possible under the circumstances."

"Well in fact, between you and me, although I have said nothing too emphatic, but you being Clarence Wilson's brother and no doubt keen to see the hit-and-run solved, I can tell you I may be very close to obtaining a potentially critical piece of evidence germane to the accident. Between you and me, I may." I began to cough.

"Yes, Mr Knight."

I cleared my throat, "Excuse me, bloody smoking, I really do have to quit. Keep my word to quit. Excuse. I may have a crucial licence number. By this evening, I might have the model and make of a car. And tomorrow. Tomorrow. Well tomorrow, I could perhaps, if things break as I hope, know who drove the vehicle."

"All in the subjunctive as the French say."

"How's that?"

"Well let's say at least it is all conditional. Hypothetical. Unproven states. I presume you have informed the authorities of this possibly important knowledge?"

"In due time. Thanks for your time." I turned away.

"Mr Knight."

I shifted around.

"Yes?"

"Did you happen to tell Madeleine what you've just told me?"

"As you know, as a lawyer, there is a question of client–agency confidentiality. I'm afraid I can't say what I told your sister-in-law, unless she okays it."

"Good day, Mr Knight."

# TWENTY

Back in my car, my cellphone rang. It was Cheryl Perron.

"Alec, I got Henderson coming out of his home going towards Centretown on the 417."

"Keep me posted. Right now I'm over near Argyle and Metcalfe."

I went over near Gilmour Street. I waited for ten minutes. The cellphone did its discount ring. Cheap was its name.

"Alec."

"Cheryl. Alec, I'm parked on O'Connor. Henderson's out of his car and walking up Gilmour towards Bank."

"Stay with him. I'm on Gilmour. He's probably headed towards Parsons' place."

"I'm with him."

I sat in the agency car with my baseball cap down low. I observed the thin wiry warehouseman, a determined, brusque walk like a fighting bantam rooster, very alert, a creature not to be messed with, go to the corner of Bank and Gilmour. Cheryl was on the other side of the street ten paces ahead of Henderson. Henderson turned at Bank in the direction of LTD Escort. I stayed low and waited.

Cheryl came on the line again.

"He went up to LTD."

"Fine. Stick with him. There's a coffee shop across the way."

"Alec, please in the name of our Lady of the Bladder, no coffee." Cheryl laughed.

"Have a doughnut or croissant."

"Why, thank you."

I waited a half hour. The phone rang again.

"He's headed back down Gilmour towards his car."

I waited another ten minutes, when Cheryl called in.

"We're in Hull, he's headed north on Highway 50. Just turned onto avenue Principale towards Farmers Rapids."

"Get ahead of him. If he's been to see Parsons, he's probably going towards Rae and Snoblin's place north of St-Pierre-de-Wakefield. Get ahead of him." I gave Cheryl the directions to Rae and Snoblin's place in the woods.

I took off towards the Outaouais. When I came up the quiet road I found Cheryl's car parked in the high wild shrubs. I parked a hundred feet down the road and walked to her car.

She had her binoculars out and was watching the house through the tree branches.

"What's this?"

"Henderson looked furious. He argued on the porch with a couple of toughs. Or so it seemed. Then went in the cottage with the two bikers. They looked royally pissed off when they came out. He gave them something, looked like money. Then the two guys—"

"Probably Snoblin and Rae."

"Well they took a couple of sledge hammers and crowbars and started whacking the heck out of the old Olds. Smashed the lights in. Take a look."

Cheryl handed me the binoculars. I saw Henderson standing on the porch smoking a cigar while Rae and Snoblin played Laurel and Hardy on the Olds.

"Lovely workmanship. Such handymen. That's it. That's it."

"What?"

"That's the car that probably took down Clarence Wilson."

"You sure, Alec?"

"As sure as I've got long range vision. You get down to the junction and trail Henderson when he heads back to Ottawa. If he goes to Norman Burley's or Marshall Wilson's place let me know right away. I'm going to hang out here with the party boys."

Cheryl turned her car around and took off for the junction. I crawled into the bushes with my binoculars. Ten minutes later Lester Henderson drove off. I sat and waited.

An hour passed by with Rae and Snoblin messing around on their motorcycles and doing things to the Olds under the hood. Quite suddenly the Olds jerked awake as if by remote control. The two bikers were grinning. The Olds rammed into the stonework beside the cottage. It backed up and rammed again. It sputtered, then the motor conked out. The grill and hood were smashed up and the motor smoking and steaming. They went back into the car and played around tearing out components. They sat on the porch for another hour drinking beer and rolling joints and smoking weed.

I heard a vehicle come down the road. It was a wrecker's tow truck. The side panel read Garage Mulroney Gatineau. I noted the name and licence plate.

Rae and Snoblin greeted the tow truck driver. They offered the fellow a beer but he demurred. They gave the guy some money. He counted the cash. They seemed to argue for bit. Then they gave him another bill. He stuffed the bills in his pocket. He rigged up the tow truck and hauled the smashed Olds away. It was getting cool, I moved away and pissed in the woods. I came back and crouched down in the shrubs. Jackie Snoblin was sitting on the porch in a chair tilted back, nibbling on a beer bottle. I waited ten minutes. I felt the quick September chill of the hills descending with the setting sun.

Suddenly, an arm put a choke hold round my neck.

"Merde, don't you get the message?"

The guy's arm was like a vice grip. I could smell the reek of beer and stale rancid smoke in his clothing. I tried to pry the arm free from my neck. I heard feet running towards me and branches thrashing back in front of me. A fist hit me in the stomach. It was Snoblin. He had come off the porch and raced through the woods. He really packed a wallop. He gave me three or four more. I lost count. Rae's arm was cinching and squeezing harder and harder, my neck ached. My breath was passing away. He had my right arm bent back and up my spine. He relaxed a little to adjust the grip.

"Fuck you, you little fuck. Listen. This is two. Two times. You're up here in the woods without a friend. You're on the wrong side of the river. Get it?" He twisted my arm. Snoblin hit me across the face. Snoblin took out a knife and flicked it open.

"See. You come this way again we'll carve some beavertail. Got it?"

There was no point in arguing or agreeing. I closed my eyes and played dead as if fainting. Rae let me slip to the ground. They began to give me a workover with their biker boots. I grabbed Snoblin's boot and twisted his leg. He went over and landed on the knife. It went in his thigh. His head hit a rock and blood smeared out from a gash. It was no triumph of skill and timing. Pure luck and sheer fear. But I'll take that over nothing. Rae lunged at me but I rolled away and jumped up and ran. There was no point in laying around to play at their beaverfest. He'd chew me faster than a wolverine. I dashed through the woods toward the agency car. In his motorcycle boots and leather Rae was not quick on his feet. He thrashed his way through the branches. I dropped my cellphone. I heard it go down into the leaves and branches. I got to the car. The tires were slashed.

In fear, I half limped, half ran down the road like a dog with a bum leg being chased by a bear. There were cottages further down. I hurt all over, my face, neck and guts, my knees and arms. Rae was no longer coming through the woods, although I heard distant curses behind me. The light was dimmer, the woods were gloomy. Aching, I had to slow down, and walked with full caution a half mile until I turned a bend in the road and came to a secluded cottage. I went up the path. The cottage looked benevolent. Even magical. A young woman and a dog were on the porch. The young woman, draped in a shawl, appeared to be nursing a baby. She shifted the shawl to cover the child's face and stared at me.

"Sloan," she called out, then stood up shifting the infant to her shoulder. A young lithe muscular man appeared in the doorway. He wore a carpenter's apron and had a finishing hammer in his hand.

Noting the catch in the woman's voice, I stopped some distance from the verandah.

"I've been hurt, I need some help."

"You look pretty bad, buddy," remarked the carpenter.

"I was assaulted. I lost my cellphone. I was hoping I might use your phone?"

"Who did it?"

"I don't know. I was in the woods and got jumped. My car's tires were slashed." The man and woman gave me a skeptical look.

Then the man said, "Sure come on. Why don't you clean up. Wash yourself in the bath." The guy came down and helped me up the steps. He took me in the cottage and helped me clean myself up.

"They've given you some thrashing but I don't want to know who. Don't want to know why. Leave us out of it. Okay. Here's the phone. Call who you got to call."

"Thanks."

Cheryl Perron came and picked me up. A local garage was sent out to tow the agency vehicle down for repair. Cheryl drove back into the little O and took me to emergency. After the emergency quack had checked me over, he sent me home to bed. I had never seen the doctor before, he was diligent and matter of fact in the treatment but when finished there was something of both amusement and rebuke in his tone. As if an assault was out of place in Ottawa on a tedious Tuesday evening.

The telephone was ringing. So loud. I went to grab it but I heard it still ringing and I couldn't reach it. I picked up the apartment telephone on the little table by the chesterfield in the living room, but the phone kept right on ringing through the darkness. I heard it in the woods, in the leaves and grass. It was my cellphone ringing. I stood up and stared at the floor. And I said, I wish I could reach that bloody phone. Then I heard Inky Baby's voice, he was amused. Lantern, if you'd only leave your cellphone number, we'd call you. Here, talk to Valerie. Who's Valerie? Who's Valerie? Man, I can tell you who Valerie is but to really know Valerie you'd have to meet Valerie, you'd love Valerie if you ever met her. Man, I can tell you. Then Inky Baby was standing in my living room. He wore a pork-pie hat. He picked up my black telephone off the little table, said hello and then said, Lantern, it's for you, it's sweet sweet Valerie. I took the telephone from Inky Baby's tattooed hand and said 'lo. A woman's voice replied, it was that wonderful voice, it gave me a thrill, rich and deep in texture. If voices could have wood textures, hers was like walnut or cherry, with a glow. She said, listen Lantern, I'm down here in the middle of the night at Saikely's with dethead Warnock, we're eating ham and cheese on rye with mustard. Come on over to Bronson and join us. I'm sorry, I said, I don't eat ham and cheese. But don't take it the wrong way, I do like you and I do like rye. I heard a hand muffle the mouthpiece. But I could still hear her voice in the background say, Hey dethead, this Lantern says he doesn't eat ham and cheese on rye. What is he? Tell me is the guy a camel jockey or what? I tell you Valerie that boy is full of wry. He's a regular barrel of cracker jacks. Slap mustard on the sandwich. Maybe he'll eat it. It sounded like Warnock's voice chuckling. Then she was back on the telephone. Standing in my living room by the cheap worn chesterfield my mum had given me, I heard Valerie say the dethead says then eat crow. I said, Huh? Then she said, the dethead says if crow won't do then eat the newspaper, it's got more nutritional content than a box of cereal. Do you mean that literarily or figuratively? She said, listen, Lantern I mean it both ways. I said, then sure, sure. But how do I know you're Valerie if I've never met you, only heard your voice? The woman's voice said, you'll just know. I'd know you anywhere by your beautiful voice. Hey let me talk to Detective Warnock himself. Valerie said, here's himself. Here's Warnock. I heard the policeman's voice come on the telephone line. Hey Knightly, knock, knock. Who's there? War. War who? Warknock of course, ha ha ha, his voice went on and on laughing. Read the newspaper you jerk, my daughter's still missing. I'm counting on you, Knight. I was lying on the chesterfield reading the business pages all about petrodollars this, petroeuros that, petroyuan then. I was getting vertigo following the trail of numbers in the stock market columns. Chaos of numbers all over the page. The canuck dollar is rising says the banque du Canada headline news. I was staring at a green twenty dollar bill and the Queen old Lizzie herself wearing Madeleine Masson's triple string of pearls round her neck muttered, I say now the dollar's rising, straight off the face of a twenty, she said it more animated than an I-idiot on the Internet. Then Warnock said over the telephone line, knock knock. I told you I'm tired of this stuff. Just ask the question Knight. Knock, knock. Okay, who's there? Can. Can who? Canaknuck, how much wood canna Canaknuck chuck if a Canaknuck can chuck wood. Listen you dethead, one more crummy knock knock joke and I'm finished. Warnock barked, you're just a laptop. The newspaper fell on the floor, the distant cellphone was ringing again on the ground in the Gatineau Hills. I told myself, I got to call Inky Baby. I mean Tommy Baby. Tommy who? Not the Who's Tommy. The Canknock Tommy. I bent to pick the cellphone off the ground but a motorcycle boot swiftly kicked it out of reach. You idiot you better call. Just call. Okay. Fine, I said, I'll make the call Lynda if you insist. I hate e-mail. Then just disconnect. Fine.

And the phone was really truly ringing. I awoke and reached over through the bedroom darkness and lifted the receiver. I felt woozy and exhausted. The hurt came back into my body.

"Knight?"

"Right. Johnny."

I shifted on the bed and sat up. My body really hurt as if I was gonna bless the air with my heels. My bones were going through the mattress and floorboards of the bedroom. I stood up to get away from the ache. Standing, I felt better.

"Good to hear your voice," I grunted.

"You okay? You don't sound right."

"Oh yeah. Two guys took me out for a beavertail and poutine banquet. The meal didn't go over so swell."

"Gut ache. Fried food'll get you every time."

"No. Nothing like that. It was a good old Canuck beaver carving, and I was gonna be the carved beaver. I got lucky. It was a Gatineau garden party. Two biker hillbillies."

"This case?"

"Yeah. Looks like it. What you got for me, Olive?"

"I got a match. Four five hours in the wrecker's yard but I found it."

"Good work. Lajoie will be plenty pleased. Send it up. Wrap it as neat as Irish crystal shipped from Waterford. Send it first class courier plenty of insurance."

"I will. No breakage. Watch yourself. Take care of yourself, Alec."

"I will. Thanks Johnny." I hung up and looked out the bedroom window at the alley. It was pitch black.

I thought it must be near ten or eleven o'clock. Neon time clocking in on my brain. Hunger and a horrible thirst ploughed through my flesh, I felt as if I had shed ten pounds in the brawl. I was famished. I went to the kitchen and drank glass after glass of water. I made a meal. Beautiful poached eggs with a dash of vinegar in the rippling water, light rye bread toasted, two thick slices of fresh late summer juicy tomatoes, and on the side a handful of black olives from Nicastro's in the Byward Market. I sat down and ate.

I ate and felt better.

I went through the dream then I sorted through the events. I sat thinking. About Rae and Snoblin and Parsons and Henderson. Tommy MacAlister intruded, followed by another mental sidetrack and I thought about Warnock and Inky Baby. My brain was piled up with confused associations and tumbling thoughts like old bricks on a demolition site. Somebody might want to recycle them but it would take time and labour to sort through them.

I called up Louise Montpetit. She told me that Madeleine Masson had called, and that Cheryl Perron still had Les Henderson under surveillance at his place up near Island Park Drive. I called up Cheryl and told her to call it a night. I sat listening to music, picked up the newspaper that had not been touched and flipped through a brief article on the front page of the city section about Liz Strachan and another one inside concerning Warnock's missing daughter, Laura Cooke. I went on to the sports section, as I read I fell asleep on the couch. When I woke up again, the phone was ringing. The newspaper was crushed and crumpled across my chest. I picked up the phone, it was Madeleine Masson.

"Mr Knight, I apologize for disturbing you at home."

"No problem. I told you to call here if you felt the need."

"I called Lajoie–Chang's office earlier and left a message and waited for your return call."

"I'm sorry Ms Masson. It has been a very full day and I just got the message from the office."

"Mr Knight, you spoke with my brother-in-law, Marshall."

"Yes."

"He called me after your visit."

There was a pounding at the apartment door.

"Ms Masson, could you hold the line. There's someone at the door."

I set the phone down and went to the door. I called through the door, "Who is it?"

"Connie Yonge, it's urgent. I must speak with you, Alec."

"Ms Yonge, please wait a moment."

I went back and picked up the telephone.

"I'm sorry Ms Masson, something has just arisen, I'll call you back later this evening."

"But I need to speak with you."

"Ms Masson, I will definitely be back in touch this evening."

"Please do, it is essential I speak with you."

I got dressed in a plaid shirt, black jeans and moccasins. I pulled back the deadbolt and opened the door with the safety chain still on and peered out. I could see Connie Yonge through the crack standing on the third floor landing, she was dressed in slacks and sweatshirt, her fair face was sleepless and pale, her blue eyes tired. I released the safety chain and opened the door. Anxiety like a thug had hammered her round the block.

"Alec, I really have to talk to you."

"Okay, let's go out for a coffee."

"No. If you don't mind I'd prefer here. I think I am being followed by someone and I'm worried."

"They didn't follow you here did they?"

"I don't think so. I think I might have lost them when I was in the Elgin Street area where I dumped my car."

"Okay come in for a few minutes."

I led her through the vestibule and into the dining room overlooking the alley and fire escape.

"You want something to drink?"

"I could use something. Wine or gin."

"Sorry. I just have the low list menu. Tea, coffee, milk." I went to the kitchen and opened the fridge, "Juice. Mineral water."

"Some mineral water or tea would be fine."

I poured a couple of glasses of mineral water and cut slices of lime. I put the kettle on for tea. I set the glass before the blonde woman. Her eyes gave me a searching look, inspecting my features more thoroughly than she had ever done, this as if to acknowledge the assault that I had taken, but I said nothing even though I discerned she was keen to ask about the bruises.

"Thank you. You're kind." She did not appear to say this in any premeditated way, just as an acknowledgment of a momentary gesture of consideration, or that is the way in which I was prepared to interpret it even if it wasn't so. She hoped for consideration but did not seem to necessarily expect it. It revealed anxiety and distress. Usually Connie Yonge was a brisk and self-confident woman, something had crumbled away.

I made a pot of herbal tea and came back to the table with two small cups.

"Are you upset that I came to your home, Alec?"

"I can't say I'm keen on it. It cuts across Lajoie–Chang policy. But it all depends on the situation. You say it's urgent. Is it?"

"I apologize for barging in like this. It's not my usual style. It's not cool. Actually, it's downright crude."

"I'm sure it isn't your way, Ms Yonge. This is not my usual place to meet people, clients or other people involved in a case. The agency offices would be a better place. This is where I live. I like to keep it separate. How urgent is this?"

"I'm being followed. Or thought I was. I threw the person off down on Elgin and your place was near. I got it out of the phone book. It was a shot in the dark. But I'm worried, I needed someone to turn to but haven't got exactly anyone I could trust for certain."

"I'm a little surprised you want to see me after making it clear a few days ago that you didn't want to speak with me."

"That was my lawyer's advice."

"Who's your lawyer?

"Peter Slowikowsky."

"Figures."

"Why do you say that Alec?"

"Forget it."

"Do you know Peter Slowikowsky?"

"In a passing sort of way. By rumour. But why did you change your mind?"

"I think I could be in danger."

"Why?"

"I know some things I shouldn't know."

"You better go to the police. They can offer the best assistance."

"That might make matters all the worse."

"How so?"

"They questioned me concerning Liz's death. It was inevitable. But it put me at risk. It was after I spoke with the cops that I felt I was being followed. Pete Slowikowsky said the police would protect me but they won't because I'm not an important enough person. Witness."

"Did you ask for protection?"

"No."

"Did you tell them that you thought that you might be in danger?"

"No. That might not be wise. They don't think I'm an important witness."

"How's that?"

"Most of what I told them they insinuated that they knew from other sources. They wanted names of men. And I couldn't furnish any."

"Can you?"
"Only in speculation."
"Did you speculate with the police?"
"No. Never. It would have been really foolish to mention people. At first they were very polite and considerate, then impatient and rude. I was questioned by this Detective Johnpine. She is a very harsh person. I never expected that. Do you know her?" She paused and drank tea, she stared at me.
"I'm sure the police are only doing their job as they see fit."
"Do you know this detective?"
I said nothing, just ignored the question. Instead I poured more tea and offered some to Connie Yonge.
"Sure. Thanks. Alec, I know I was putting you off when you were searching for Liz and I should have been more helpful. I don't know anything about this horrible event. Honestly I thought Liz just skipped out until the situation calmed down."
"What situation?"
"Can I trust you, Alec?"
"Why are you here, Connie?"
"I'm afraid to trust anyone just now. Some of the men I've been involved with have been sleazy, manipulative. I got myself into a situation that is over my head."
"With Joe Parsons?"
"Maybe."
"In connection with LTD Escort?"
"LTD Escort is not what it appears. It's not a dating service, it's not a sex racket. Some of the other women were foolish enough to let some of that happen. It was to protect themselves. Or to get drugs. Can I tell you something?" She smoothed out a small wrinkle on the cotton tablecloth. "You probably know by now. I'm devastated." She rested her head on her arms and wept.
I felt crummy but didn't know why I should. Caught between sympathy and suspicion, I reached around and got a cloth napkin off the wooden hutch.
"Here. Here." I offered it like a little kid.
She lifted her head, her make-up was smeared in tears. She took the napkin and wiped her face. "I loved Liz. Believe me. Things had gone wrong before with these people, but it usually came out right

in the end. We thought this was just another one of those rough patches. Liz thought that. I did too. I loved her."

"I believe you."

"But Liz was bi. And it complicated things. She had a thing with a man."

"Who?"

"I don't want to say. I'm afraid to say. At first I didn't even imagine it although I knew that Liz was bi. I was jealous. I'd never been jealous before. It really hurt me."

"Jealousy is not a natural emotion. It's a false emotion. That's why it's destructive."

"Why do you say that?"

"It's just an observation. Was the guy Ed Stanley?"

"No. That silly boy. Overgrown on steroids. No. Liz had a thing with him a few times. I can't ever figure it out. It was a momentary body thing. Two great bawds. You know, the Hollywood bed thing. Pure appearance.Make it look good. Muscle meets meltdown. Stanley was possessive and obsessive. Not much upstairs. He wouldn't let go. He was clinging. Pathetic. Really a pathetic sloppy creature. Stanley meant nothing to Liz. Liz told me. She dumped him."

"And jealous?"

"Yes. But Liz never loved him. He amused her."

"Who did she love?"

"Me. And this older man. I missed it. I never understood it. He was years older. Old enough to be her father. She completely deceived me."

"Did Liz go with other men?"

"This is sordid. I wish you wouldn't ask." She stared at me. "Hell. No. No. Liz has, had a powerful hold over people. Both sexes. She drew in anybody. But mostly it was just Liz being Liz. Men misconstrued it. Liz, even if she dated them she would not sleep with those creeps but she tried to turn them because we needed something on them to protect ourselves. We had an understanding between ourselves on this."

"How so?"

"This is what I couldn't mention to the police."

"What?"

"They think LTD Escort is a high class prostitution operation but it isn't. There's some sleeping with a client but only if a woman agrees, Joe Parsons doesn't push it. They think that maybe one of the clients is a nut case, it happens, that Liz dated a freak case and he murdered her. That's the side they're investigating. So they got Parsons on the hot seat. They're really drilling him. They want his client list. Parsons is really in trouble. But pushing flesh, that's not LTD's game."

"What is its game?"

"It's a cover. The real thing—big, far bigger money—is money laundering. We were involved with these business guys who were laundering big bucks."

"You and Liz Strachan and the other women at Parsons were mules."

"Yes. It's a crummy word but it fits."

"Did you bring in the cocaine for them as well?"

"Where'd you come by that? Liz and I didn't deal in drugs."

"It doesn't matter."

"If you think that, the police will know it or think it."

"Maybe. Maybe not yet, but probably sooner rather than later. Did you smuggle coke, Connie?"

"No. I didn't."

"That's crap."

Connie Yonge gave me a hard look. Her face looked bleak and harsh.

"I didn't. Don't try to get me to say something that is bullshit. I drew the line on that. I'd be finished with the airline. Muling the money was tough enough. Risky enough."

"You're full of it, Connie. You and Liz Strachan smuggled anything you could."

"Okay. Liz and a few other women, the other women, not Liz, were hooked, they did it three four times. But Liz and I didn't deal the stuff. Some of the other women who were junkies muled the stuff more often because they were really into the snorting and petty dealing themselves. Had debts. They were coerced. You know, debt restructuring."

"Who coerced them?"

"I don't want to mention names. I told you that. It would be dangerous."

"This goes nowhere. It's upside down. I can't help you. In fact I don't even know why you are here. I don't know what or who you need protection from. For all I know they could have sent you here."

"It's heavy, Alec. Believe me. It's too much. I've made a huge mistake. I wanted the money quick. I figured one year and then I'd be set for life but they won't let go. Once I was doing it, they wanted to keep on going."

"Did you have sex with them as part of the bargain?"

"I didn't." A look of disgust passed across her pink lips. "I don't like it with men. If I had wanted to be with a man I would have stayed with my former husband. He was a good guy. He knew I was a lesbian when I married him. He really loved me. We tried to give it a try. But it just didn't work out, if I wanted a man it would be him. None of these sleazoids."

"What about Liz and the other women?"

"Not Liz, I told you we had an understanding. The other women said we should go along and use it on the men. That it could work both ways. It could be used as protection against them."

"It was not just the other women. You did it too."

"Okay so what. It wasn't exactly a choice. A few rare times I was coerced. Anyway the lesbian thing triggers some straight guys. They have no imagination. They were horrible but they wanted it and I accepted it. But in my mind it was temporary. I only wanted the money. And then to get away with Liz. Liz promised me that she would go with me after she got her degree and we saved enough."

"But you never saved enough."

"How do you know?"

"They ripped you off in the dirty money accounts didn't they?"

"Yes."

"Liz tried to force them to put back the mule money, back into your accounts, didn't she?"

"Yes. How do you know?"

"She argued with Norm Burley over it didn't she? So did you argue with Burley."

"Yes. Where did you come by that?"

"Never mind. Did Burley kill Liz?"

"I don't know. I won't ever say that. Even if it is true. Never."

"You're afraid of Burley, aren't you?"

"No."

"He doesn't go to the mattress. He didn't demand something on the side so you had nothing on him, right?"

"Look I didn't come here for this. But it's true. He screwed us out of our share. He wanted to sleep with Liz. Only Liz. But she wouldn't."

"Then she changed her mind and said she would if he would put the money back in the ICCI accounts and got it into clean money accounts off the island, right? That's what they agreed to on the Monday afternoon when you came back from your weekend in the Gatineau, isn't it?"

"No. Liz'd never go with a man like Burley. No woman wants to sleep with a man like him." Connie stopped and stared at me, "Did Pete Slowikowsky tell you all this? Did that creep talk to you? That guy's a bastard too. That two-bit lawyer told you didn't he?"

"No. But it doesn't matter who told me. Is that what you and Liz did up at the cottage, agree that Liz would sleep with Burley so the money would go back in the ICCI and then be rechannelled to clean accounts that you and Liz had access to?"

"No. Yes."

"But then Burley didn't put the money back?"

"That's right."

"So Liz argued with him and he killed her."

"I don't know that. I mean I don't know the last part. You know too much, Alec. This is no good. Burley wouldn't put the money back. Liz wouldn't sleep with him. She phoned me late in the afternoon and told me she couldn't do it. No woman at LTD would sleep with that man. But I don't know if he killed Liz. I heard he could have."

She ran her hand across the tablecloth. She tilted her teacup towards me, I poured more tea.

"What did you hear about Burley?"

"I heard a rumour."

"What rumour?"

Connie had a furtive look like a rat had crawled across the dining room floor behind my chair.

"It's heavy. I shouldn't repeat it."

"What did you hear?"

"It's dangerous even to repeat it. But it came from a good source. A flight attendant from out west said that Burley's a rapist. Burley. He's a rapist. He'd raped a couple of women when he was a Crown attorney. He even raped a young girl. None of us would go near him after we found that out."

"Was Les Henderson in on this scamming of accounts?"

"Who?"

"Lester Henderson?"

"That name means nothing to me."

"Okay. So what of the older guy Liz was hanging out with? What happened to him in the picture with Liz?"

"You know too much. That messed it up. At first I never knew Liz was having that affair with that guy. She completely deceived me. Put it over on me. Later I found out she promised him something, the same as she promised me, that she would go away with him."

"And you found out and killed Liz out of jealousy."

Connie Yonge clenched her fist on the table, furious as if she might hit me across the face.

"You're disgusting." Tears ran down her face. "That's horrible. After I found out, we had a horrible argument over it but that's all. You say disgusting things. It's rotten. Especially after all I told you. You're just like these creeps. I'm going. I've had enough. You know nothing. You just make random accusations. But you're nobody." She got up.

"Connie, think. Think. I know, what I said, that it's crap. I know you didn't but you're going nowhere with all these insinuations and half facts."

"There's something disgusting about you, Alec."

"Sure. Take off. I can manage to get punched out by your boyfriends well enough on my own."

"You don't know. I loved Liz."

"Do you know who did it?"

"Not exactly. But I have a thought."

"Have the tea." I gestured towards the tea. Connie Yonge sat back down.

"Haven't you something stronger than this?"

"Maybe. I'll look. A couple of clients gave me something." I got up and rummaged through the lower hutch and brought out two unopened bottles, Crown Royal Canadian rye and a very old Scotch from the Findhorn.

"The rye." Connie said.

"Straight or on the rocks?"

"Ice please."

I got some ice and poured her a shot.

"Was the older man Lester Henderson?"

She blushed.

"No. I told you that name doesn't mean anything."

"Sure it does. He was a crony of Burley's and you know it."

"Okay. I don't think Liz would have anything to do with him. He's nothing more than a caricature of a man. A worm. A complete worm from end to end."

"But you know him?"

"Yes. I met him a half dozen times. He wanted to sleep with me."

"Did you let him?"

"That's a joke. He's vile. He nearly drools when he looks at a woman."

"Connie, you slept with Lester Henderson."

"Stop it. Yes. I did. Once. I want to forget it completely. I regretted it. But at least he was better than that sadist Burley."

"Who was the guy Liz got stuck on that you were jealous of? Norm Burley?"

"You know that's really disgusting. Especially after what I told you. Why keep bringing his name up?"

"Because it's in the roster of Upper Canada dignified personalities. How well did you know Burley?"

"Only for the transactions. Nothing more. He was cold as ice. Very cold man. He wanted Liz. But it was money turned his nuts on."

"Who was the guy that Liz was smitten with?"

"Liz was very careful never to meet the man when I was in town. I found out that she had her liaisons with the guy when I flew out of town."

"You and Liz had a thing with Pete Slowikowsky?"

"Pete. Are you joking? He's a third rate sleazoid. He found out about us smuggling the money. It was his payment to shut up. He does the Viagra vigil."

"What's that?"

"He's more a voyeur type. Snorts too much coke. It turned him on to watch. Watch and watch and watch. Got more out of just watching than doing it. But no sadism none of that creepy cruel stuff. He liked to watch women masturbate. That's what he wanted. Coke is what turned him on. But the coke ruined him."

"Fine lawyer. Made of sterling stuff."

"Yeah sleazy. But at least not sleavy." Connie half smiled.

"What's that? Sleavy?"

"Our way of saying heavy and sleazy. Burley types. But Pete was better than the rest. At least he did keep his word. He tried to help us. He kept Burley a little under control. But I don't know how he managed that trick."

"What about Henderson. Why'd you sleep with him if he disgusts you so much?"

"They all disgust me. They're all vile creeps. But it's obvious by now, isn't it? He said that he would arrange to have the money put back into our accounts. He'd make Burley do it."

"But it didn't happen."

"No. But I think Henderson did try. He wasn't mean like Burley. Pete said Henderson tried to keep his word and that Burley wouldn't let it happen. Burley was a real brute. You wouldn't want to run up against the guy in a dark alley or a bank vault. Liz wouldn't let the issue go. She kept confronting him. Finally he told her. He didn't need her anymore. And that she was lucky to get away with her panties. That she was useless now. And a risk. But Liz thought she was tough and could take the guy on. She wasn't afraid of him. She stood up to Burley. Liz was no coward. She wasn't afraid of anything. Or anyone. But Henderson told me that Burley would never put the money back. And anyway our share was gone. Henderson said that Burley screwed everyone, that he even screwed Henderson. And Henderson's business was at risk. Burley did everybody except a couple of guys with more clout. And some of the real heavies in the States, who have real political clout with people in a governor's office. Big numbers involved in the savings and loans."

"Who were the Americans in the equation?"

"Are you crazy?" She half smiled. "You do want me killed. That'll never come out. It's way too deep."

"Where'd the money go?"

"To pay off the political guys with muscle in the States and on the islands. The money is all gone. All used up. Channelled off into legit money and speculated on the US and British and Japanese stock markets. Mostly cleaned up. Flushed through the system. And gone into good banks. The rest to buy more armaments. It is untouchable according to Henderson and Slowikowsky. Slowikowsky told me to just drop it all and get on with my life."

"So you ended up with nothing?"

"Looks that way."

"Henderson told you this?"

"Yes."

"Henderson's a liar. So is Slowikowsky, Connie."

"What do you mean?"

"They took yours and Liz's money."

"No." She was livid. Furious. "That's crap. It can't be."

"Ask Slowikowsky and Henderson. And the others."

She stared at the tablecloth for the longest time. Then back up at me.

"Are you sure of that?"

I shrugged my shoulders.

"Connie, I'm running out of names. You better tell me who Liz wanted to run off with."

"I told you already. I don't know."

"You're lying."

"I don't need this."

"Who was the guy?"

"I can't say."

"Why?"

"I loved Liz too much. If I say something it will look bad for her."

"It's not exactly silent knowledge. This is not exactly a silent picture show. The police will come to whoever Liz was having an affair with, including yourself, Connie."

"Maybe. But let them do it on their own. I don't want to be part of it."

"Tell me."

"Fine but only if you keep it between us."

"Sure but I can find out on my own. Couple of names left here. The Family Compact Registry." I pretended to run my finger down an index, "I'll figure it out on my own. Let's see, Marshall Wilson, Alfred Plante ... had to be birds of a feather flew together. Cronies of Burley."

"The man was too much. Too confident. Arrogant. He tried to humiliate me over it."

"But then the guy changed his mind and Liz was angry and now it was her turn to be jealous. Liz was devastated when he dumped her, right?"

Connie knocked off the drink and motioned with the glass for another. I gave her the bottle, she poured a shot. She seemed to assess what I was saying. She was very noncommital.

"This man was more into financial tricks with Burley's boys and just used Liz. Right?"

"Maybe. I don't know. He was something else. Very tricky guy. He was the one guy who had a hold over Liz."

"Say the guy's name."

"Okay since you want to hear it. And you seem to know something. Maybe you even know who he was. Okay. Clarence Wilson. He was a lawyer too. He was in the same law firm as Burley, Baldwin or something. He's not around any more."

"What do you mean, Connie?"

"This guy Wilson's dead now. But Liz didn't— Forget it."

"Forget what? The guy's dead?

"Yeah. He was killed in a hit-and-run accident in the Outaouais."

"So what's it matter then?"

"I thought the police might think Liz or I had something to do with the guy's death."

"Why?"

"Because of a rumour I heard, something about Liz's old car. But that's all I know."

"What and who did you hear the rumour from?"

"Lester Henderson. But he wouldn't say anything much. He just seemed worried."

"And you got to thinking."

"Yes and thinking that maybe Liz was involved in Clarence Wilson's death."

"Why?"

"Because it was hit-and-run. And it was never solved. Wilson was just using Liz. But Liz couldn't see it at the time. She was crazy about the guy. Thought Clarence Wilson was just brilliant. She was jealous that the guy was married. It was completely inexplicable. I couldn't understand it."

"Liz didn't have to kill Clarence Wilson. The rumour was that Wilson was going to leave his wife and go with Liz."

"I can't believe it. Don't say that. Liz loved me. She did. Clarence Wilson was destroying Liz. He was not the sort of man who could love anybody. Nobody. He didn't even love his wife. He just went after her, married her for her money. That's what I heard. She comes from very big Québécois money. Lumber money. Her father was a big judge. Wilson was just a money grubber. Liz finally came to understand that Wilson was incapable of love."

"Believe it, Connie. Wilson was going to leave his wife."

"You're wrong." She said this emphatically. "You don't understand people like him."

"Okay. You don't have to worry. Connie, tell the police what you know. Cooperate with them. They'll protect you. Connie, do it. Believe me it's the best thing you can do."

"I can't talk about the money laundering. I can't. They'll kill me. You don't know the low-lifes that these businessmen hang out with. They make cockroaches look like butterflies. Bikers."

"I've made myself familiar with them. Or maybe I should say they've intro'd themselves. Then we had a moment of improv. Parsons' buddies. Some days of the week there is no difference between a biker suit and a business suit."

"Yeah, Alec you have a point, every jerk unzips his pants the same way."

"That's illuminating."

"You have to see it from where I'm sitting, Alec."

"I guess I can't argue."

"Look, is it too much to ask if I can sleep here tonight? I'm really worried. I'm exhausted. I need a safe place to stay. I know I've said some pretty unpleasant things to you, Alec, but at least I know I can trust you."

"No. Definitely not. Sorry, not here. It wouldn't be wise."

"Alec, I don't know if you've ever found yourself in difficult circumstances with no one to turn to." She reached for the bottle and poured another long shot.

I stared at the bottle of rye. I screwed the cap back on the bottle and put it back on the hutch.

"You don't like drinking?"

"Let's not talk about me. That's not why you're here. You can't stay here. In fact you have to leave, now." I looked at my watch.

"Alec, I'm afraid. How would you feel if you just lost the most important person in your life? I need a safe place."

"Let me see what I can do. Give me a few minutes. But you are not staying here." I got up and went to the bedroom, closed the door part way, and telephoned Georges Lajoie. I explained the situation and he okayed putting Connie Yonge up at the motel room that the agency kept near Constance Bay up the Ottawa River. I thanked Lajoie. I then telephoned the agency and spoke with Louise Montpetit. I asked her to come around, to dress with a scarf over her hair, and glasses and bring clothing for Connie Yonge. Not to park a car in front of my building but around the corner near the laneway entrance and to walk to the building. Connie Yonge laughed when I told her where the motel was.

Louise Montpetit brought a blue dress, black purse, pantyhose, high heels and a dark wig for Connie. She did up Connie's face to make her look tanned. Then Louise drove Connie Yonge to the motel Lajoie kept up the Ottawa River.

# TWENTY-ONE

I left the lights on in my apartment. Put the safety chain on the door, shut the deadbolt and pressed the doorknob lock. Then I went to the dining room and out the fire escape locking the door behind me. I did a quick check for any car parked in front of the apartment building. There was one. I noted it. Then I went by a side street over to Bank Street and hailed a cab.

I sat silent in the back of the cab. I thought of Connie Yonge, at once vulnerable and sullen, defensive, her voice with its range of fluctuations. Louise Montpetit had been almost solicitous of Connie Yonge, not in Louise's character who was often matter of fact, sometimes sharp and quick, but inclined towards quiet. I was indifferent to Connie Yonge but I saw it was a cruel indifference, nothing to do with her love and jealousy for Liz Strachan so much as her evasiveness, but I realized that I had been subjected to insinuations about her —petty insinuations and jealousies—when she had been doing nothing more than a lot of people, trying to grab the big fast buck so as to get away from it all.

More troubling, I couldn't get to the bottom of what she said and it seemed that she was half-heartedly defending Liz Strachan's reputation—like a lover so as to protect not the lover but her own commitments. Even if shallow, there was a faintly admirable loyalty in such a concern for the reputation of a dead lover. Superficially most people would have seen attractive Connie Yonge as a woman trapped by circumstances. But I could not figure out where she was coming from. Her visit had thrown me off. I thought my random accusations were cruel but then I rethought them, out of her presence I wondered, could Connie have killed either Liz Strachan or Clarence Wilson? Probably not. But maybe the police might think Connie Yonge might be connected to Clarence Wilson's death by way of Joe Parsons, possibly that was what Connie Yonge really feared even if she had nothing to do with the hit-and-run. Something lingered from the conversation that I could not shake off. But then I connected all this with one swift blow to the head. As the taxi idled at a stop light, a cat streaked across the road and went under a car wheel. It came out the other side and stared at me from the sidewalk. It was a short-haired white cat. It meowed. I paused. Connie Yonge had reason to be afraid. Snoblin and Rae, Henderson's, Burley's and Parsons' pals were not in need of a flight attendant, they were quick service lads, doers as Lajoie said, not talkers. She was disposable in their equations whether it was over the money laundering or over a killing.

Down in this midnight darkness I thought, Connie Yonge is really on the edge. She has reason. These guys'd take her so far north into a distant forested lake district and drop her into the chilly waters for a midnight skinny dip from which she would not return. The lake could only be bottomless. The taxi pulled up in front of Madeleine Masson's stone house on Keefer near Crichton Street. I paid and got out. I stood in the calm of the midnight hunter green night. Down the block in the distance New Edinburgh Park looked deep green and pastoral, cast in late summer night's shades. In the further distance, I could hear the waters of the Rideau River flowing past Green Island, the rush of the river at the Rideau Falls.

I went up the verandah steps, lifted the cast iron doorknocker and let it fall.

The light went on in the vestibule and Madeleine Masson's half face appeared harlequin-like glancing through the panes of leaded glass alongside the door. She opened the door.

"Thank you for coming by so late, Mr Knight." She paused and took in the bruises. Her facial expression changed, no doubt she was concerned about the bruises, possibly surprised but not so much distressed as suspicious and unsettled, no doubt she was wondering what was the source, maybe even what sort of disturbed personality I was to get myself into such a state. She appeared momentarily reluctant to allow me to enter the house. I said nothing. I tendered no explanation. She seemed on the verge of making some comment.

"Evening, Ms Masson. I think I may have some interesting information." I could see she wanted to ask but I avoided allowing such a conversation. And any mention of Snoblin and Rae. I masked the situation with a superficial stoicism.

"This way, Mr Knight."

We went into the living room with the survey map on the wall.

"As I began to tell you on the phone this evening, Marshall Wilson, Clare's brother, called me after you visited him. He wanted to talk. I put him off. But he said you were bungling the case and compromising the police investigation."

"What did you say to him?"

"I said I preferred not to discuss it."

"Fine."

"But he was pressing. I don't understand what's happening. I do think ..." She paused and scanned my face, I didn't look away, finally she glanced at the survey map. "Never mind. Marshall and I were never close but we were not hostile. He was mostly just indifferent to me. As if I was not essential. In a way I didn't mind that because Marshall can be so sarcastic and condescending should he pay a person any attention. With men he gets close and sort of chummy. But I always found him a bit of a misogynist. That he simply preferred male company. Golfing, fishing, boating. Drinking and smoking with men. And women were a sort of necessary nuisance, accessory, to placate a need. That sort of world but it was all done with superficial politeness."

"Be careful. Tell Marshall that you are fed up with Lajoie–Chang and that you are disappointed with me because I am not competent. Or some such thing. Can you pull that off?"

"I suppose but why would I do that? I'm not a good liar."

"Because Marshall is hunting for information from me through you."

"Why?"

"I'm not certain. Could be mere curiosity. That's not uncommon in such investigations. But suffice to say at this point that it may be something more. He may have knowledge of something that he would prefer I did not have."

"Are you suggesting he knows something about Clare's accident?"

"No. Not at all, I wouldn't go that far. That would be too much. But he may be associated with individuals who wanted to shut your husband up about something. We should be cautious here but not too quick to presume. Or possibly the information might make Marshall Wilson vulnerable on another account that is not connected to the accident itself but something he did with Clarence in his financial dealings and investments that he would prefer to keep private."

"Who?"

"I cannot mention anyone now."

"Very well, Mr Knight." She paused and glanced at me, "But Marshall said you had the licence plate number of a vehicle. Is that so? Why didn't you tell me, Mr Knight?"

"Because nothing is certain until I have a vital piece of information in my hand."

"And do you?"

"Near."

"Then why tell Marshall and not me?"

"Marshall Wilson is a lawyer for a corporation that might be involved in complex financial situations of a dubious character."

"What company?"

"I yet need a little time. In any event, it is essential that you do not discuss this with him."

"Please keep me informed."

"Listen, what is hidden must reveal itself. It is a necessity of the matter. Nothing can ever be completely concealed. I may have solid news for you by tomorrow. But we have to keep your brother-in-law out of the loop. He appears to be hunting for information for other people."

At that moment a tall thin man with a striking resemblance to Madeleine Masson entered the living room, except where she radiated a subdued but attractive sensuality, he was austere, even near to ascetic despite being handsome.

"Mr Knight. This is Doctor Masson my brother. Gilles, Alec Knight."

"A pleasure, Mr Knight. Madeleine mentioned you."

"Right."

We shook hands.

Dr Masson sat down. I did not want to talk in front of him.

"Please continue, Mr Knight. I tell Gilles everything concerning the investigation into Clare's death."

"By all means continue Mr Knight," remarked Gilles Masson.

"Ms Masson, I can return tomorrow."

"No need to. We share everything." Madeleine smiled.

"Fine."

"I was hoping to have the opportunity to talk with you. I'll be direct, Mr Knight, I don't think my brother-in-law died in any accident. I never did. But I was out of the country at the time and had little to say."

"Where were you, Doctor Masson?"

"In Africa working with a medical relief group." Dr Masson mentioned a benevolent group.

"A tough situation, I imagine."

"Yes. But I've been lucky. I've come in contact with so many remarkable, courageous people. Admirable individuals. I've gained a perspective on humanity that I never thought possible."

"I'm afraid I don't know much about the organization you work for."

"It goes without saying that it does good work. Gives some hope where there sometimes isn't much. But this isn't a moment to talk about it."

"Tell me, why do you think Clarence Wilson's death wasn't an accident, Doctor Masson?"

"Because. Because of the ICCI Bank. These sorts of financial institutions are all over the third world. Conduits for money laundering, drug money, black market racketeering, selling weapons to right wing groups, militias and death squads. They are the sinister secret sisters of the two brothers grim, the IMF and World Bank, that work to impoverish nations, by inflicting on them structural adjustment programmes that destroy government subsidies and generate more and more poverty. You'll notice every country that has entered into economic engagement with the IMF and World Bank has these sorts of parasitic banks. From the Caribbean to Southeast Asia. Every nation from Argentina to Zimbabwe tumbles into financial crisis and debt payment problems, bankruptcy. The real agenda of these institutions after the Second World War is to deter developing governments and nations from spending the nation's money on social programs, health and education, and to squander their people's money on military hardware so as to subsidize the military industries in wealthy countries. The money laundering started with countries such as Liberia years ago and continues with island nations where the ICCI Bank is located."

"I thought you were a doctor."

"Certainly, I'm a doctor. But I'm not an economic ostrich. Some countries I've worked in, we can't get any medicine in, any syringes, any band-aids, antibiotics, but you'll find McDonald's, Hondas and BMWs. Hash, heroin and coke. Both versions I might add, Mr Knight."

"We're wandering."

"That's economics, Mr Knight. It's knowledge. Information emulates capital in its wanderings."

"What has the ICCI Bank to do with your brother-in-law?"

"I worked in Haiti. The ICCI Bank was in the Caribbean, it is a well known bank down there, well known as a money laundering institution."

"And?"

"Well regrettably, my brother-in-law Clare was heavily involved with this bank. He was running scared. Just like his brother, Marshall Wilson, is starting to run scared."

I glanced at Madeleine Masson, she had her hands folded in her lap.

"Why?"

"It's these things in the Civic Unity Party. They're in tight with certain political movements in the USA. The savings and loan debacle, it's part of the money laundering scams and schemes. Even possibly the breakdown of big companies like Enron. The financial blowback from the covert wars throughout the region."

"And your brother-in-law?"

"Sadly, a case of poor judgement." Dr Masson paused, "Clare made a huge investment mistake. Polluted water cannot be cleansed with dirty water any more than tainted blood can be purified with dirty blood. Clean water, clean blood are needed. If you follow my metaphor, Mr Knight. So dirty money needs clean capital, legal capital, to purify it, dilute it so the ratio of impurities does not show up so concentrated. Clarence's brother Marshall sucked him down the tube into investing with the ICCI Bank. A channel—I guess a channel. Marshall Wilson was very close to Norman Burley and his American associates."

"What you suggest, this is hard to prove."

"The laws of geometry are hard to prove if parliament passes legislation that the laws of geometry do not exist," Dr Masson chuckled. "Then a consensus coalesces around the accepted statutes even if they are based on false doctrines, premises. We enter a belief cycle. Like the earth is flat because parking lots are flat. But parking lots are only flat because cars need a flat surface. The parking lot goes against the curvature of the earth's surface but we still accept it."

I laughed. Dr Masson laughed. Madeleine Masson laughed. But we all felt uncomfortable. Gilles Masson was in another stratosphere, there was something of a tilted priest in his determined manner.

"Frankly, I need something of substance. I wouldn't dare open that can of worms. Mr Lajoie would think I had emptied my brain into a tin of Brunswick sardines. Don't get me wrong. I like Brunswick sardines. Very Canadian. I ate a lot of them when I was a kid. But something material to link all these rather abstract things, premises, together. What's more the police don't move," I wanted to say by metaphysical speculation as Georges Lajoie might have but I could not utter Lajoie's hypothetical words, "on these cases towards conspiracy or deliberate intent unless proven. Organized crime is a tough sell regardless of what the media pump out. If the police get someone with a car at the scene they'll be content to prove hit-and-run. The Crown will be content to make a manslaughter charge stick. And throw the jerk in the slammer for—"

"—for two years less a day. And suspend his licence for say two years. Five years?" murmured Madeleine Masson.

"Maybe. But the Crown won't go wandering all over the hemisphere trying to make links involving the ICCI Bank. Even the RCMP and CSIS don't dig down that deep. If they dig up a carrot they're happy with a carrot. If a potato, happy with a potato."

"And if a diamond happy with the diamond."

"Yes. But it could be a piece of coal."

"We don't want revenge," said Dr Masson. "We despise harsh justice. Thankfully we don't have Texas law in Canada."

"Not now."

"Yes there's always NAFTA. And who knows what unhappy goblins come out of the closet with such agreements." Dr Masson glanced away as he said this then back at me. "Hopefully not tomorrow. And hopefully the Civic Unity Party will continue to lose the elections.

But Clare's death is complex. It is not the run of the mill car fatality. If the police do not look in this direction, investigate this larger dimension of the situation, the context, they won't find any linkages that will lead to the vehicle and car driver. They will remain grounded in searching only the immediate ground without success. I don't fault them for this but ..."

"Why didn't you tell them this?"

"I tried. But it sounded like," he looked at Madeleine, "well they pooh-poohed it as a conspiracy. I'm afraid they lost interest in what I had to say. And Madeleine was hesitant to present it without substantial financial evidence to corroborate it. And then there is the problem that the authorities might well try to implicate us in it."

"Doctor Masson, did you have anything to do with the ICCI?"

"No. But regrettably Clare did gain access to some of Madeleine's trust accounts. But I put a stop to it. Yet it could look bad."

"A forensic accountant can straighten this out."

"Yes in time. Possibly. But there's no telling where they might go."

"Look," I turned away from Gilles Masson to Madeleine Masson. "Ms Masson, give me something. Anything. How involved was or is Marshall Wilson in the ICCI Bank?"

"I think deeply. He goes to the Caribbean on a regular basis. He was their solicitor. He wanted us to transfer our assets down there. Offered an usually high rate of return."

I noticed that Dr Masson was smiling but saying nothing.

"Did you?"

"No. It would have been folly. ICCI Bank is nothing more than a conduit for money laundering just as Gilles has suggested. They think me naive, especially Marshall, but I am not so naive as that. Our father was a judge. A man of great probity. He was not a grasping sort. He thought we should give something back to the country that had given us so much. Our family has always kept its investments in Canada. Marshall and Clare thought it old-fashioned but I'd never invest outside the country. Never. They disliked that. They saw it as foolish. Ridiculous. Poor investing. They never understood."

I said nothing.

"See, Mr Knight, we're back at the ICCI." Dr Masson half smiled. "It's almost unavoidable."

I glanced at him. I still said nothing. I now understood Lajoie's dictum more than ever. Speech is spam.

"You have to break through Clarence's brother, Marshall Wilson. He knows, he's inside the loop with the ICCI people," Dr Masson remarked.

"If he knows, I have no more hope of breaking through his armour than through the stone walls of this house with a wooden letter opener. Listen to me for a moment." I paused. "I've spoken to a number of people including Marshall Wilson. He's not vulnerable. The ICCI Bank's Miami branch took a beating and even at that the board of directors remained untouched. These people have reserves —legal, political and financial. If Marshall Wilson is connected with them he won't break. He's tough. I interviewed him. If what you speculate is true, then these sorts of people are very good at building distant relations to any crime that could be stuck on them. The regulatory authorities might be the best way to get them but that wouldn't connect anything to the crime and the death of Clarence Wilson. Do you follow me?"

"Go on, Mr Knight."

"These events are hermetically sealed off from one another as crimes. They might as well have occurred on different planets. Even in different galaxies. And the police working on a local hit-and-run investigation up in the Gatineau Hills might well trade or pass on information that would be useful to other police forces but they sure won't go cod fishing when they want to catch a trout. The scale of what you're talking about is too big. It would bring in the RCMP. Possibly even CSIS."

"Everything is linked. And if it isn't, then the person who killed Clare will just go on driving his car."

"No he won't. The local police will get the guy. The police don't like to see this kind of thing go loose. Hit-and-run is hit-and-run. The police want the guy locked up. We're talking a very dangerous creature."

"They're stuck because they started at the wrong joint."

"You mean point."

"No I mean joint. Speaking metaphorically. They're trying to repair a broken bone in the arm when the break is in the leg."

"Well if you couldn't persuade them to take up this case from this perspective it is highly unlikely Lajoie–Chang would be able to. I'd have to get a forensic accountant and much more including co-operation from financial institutions on the case. Someone to work through the ICCI Bank's books and so on and that isn't going to happen. You know it and I know it. Now. Listen." I paused.

Dr Masson gave me a glare that made me feel that I didn't want to be his patient and have him repair my leg. I had lost all moral stature in his eyes if I had ever had any. Madeleine Masson was caught. She wanted to be sympathetic but said nothing. I figured she'd seen her brother, no doubt a good sort after his own fashion, maybe even a top notch physician, dedicated, even a loving brother, give a person the visual shakedown. All this scrutiny probably made him a better doctor especially when he turned his penetrating gaze to the process of diagnostics but I was no patient. And I wasn't about to become his. It came out.

"Dr Masson, I'm no patient. I'm just a private investigator searching for empirical facts. Nothing more. But nothing less."

Madeleine Masson smiled, even gave a pleased light laugh. This seemed genuine. It seemed she wanted us to like one another. I'd seen this before, where one person who likes two people introduces the one much admired person to the other admired person and it is nothing but clash. Finally the dedicated doctor smiled himself, even relented but not so much out of the weight of facts or argument as out of regard for his sister.

"Excuse me, Mr Knight. Sometimes I forget. I'm too used to struggling with, trying to persuade governments, institutions, bureaucracies, even the military to get basic medical things, things for people who have so little and need so much. I apologize Mr Knight. I've spoken far too vehemently."

"Okay. I may have something of substance but it may not sustain the direction which you are going in. But it will potentially at least bring one person, the driver or owner of the vehicle, into the light."

"What?"

I looked at Madeleine Masson.

"Please continue."

"Fine. This piece of information must remain absolutely confidential. Agreed?"

"Certainly. Mr Knight, you have our utter confidence."

"I have a car headlamp from an auto wrecker recycle company in Toronto. Which matches a shard of glass that I picked up in the gravel and grass about thirty feet down the road from the location where the car accident occurred. I have the licence plate number of the car. I have the car. I have the series of ownerships that fills in the gaps."

"And who drove the car on that day?"

"Not yet. More digging and patience. I'm not going to speculate who drove. Such crucial details require positive proof. Possibly Marshall Wilson knows something directly in connection with it. Maybe he knows nothing. I'm not going to presume and I'm not going to allow your notions concerning the ICCI Bank to influence me. I'm not trying to crack a money laundering syndicate with deep or shallow pockets. I'm focussed on what you've asked us."

"Yes. Yes." Madeleine Masson nodded her head in agreement.

"Nevertheless, tell me a little more about the guy."

"This is horrible." Madeleine Masson turned her head away and rested her hand against the right side of her face.

"Look, let's be careful here, will we. I didn't say Marshall Wilson was involved. He simply may have access to some information which implies someone he knows might have been remotely involved. Or has some information that might be instrumental. And other factors come into play."

"Marshall Wilson likes money too much," Gilles Masson remarked.

"Gilles. Please, let me."

He deferred to his sister.

"Marshall was very close to Clare but as I told you they had a falling out over politics and investments."

"How serious?"

"Maybe not too serious in retrospect. But they were not as close as they once were."

"Did he know that you and Clare were going to separate?"

"I don't know. Maybe."

"Did Marshall Wilson know Liz Strachan?"

"I don't know."

"Did he know a woman by the name of Connie Yonge, Constance Yonge?"

"Yes. I've heard that name. Let me think. In fact I met a woman by that name once."

"When?"

"In the Byward Market last fall. At a restaurant. Marshall and she were together."

"What was your impression?"

"I'm not certain. Maybe intimate. But I'm not good at reading those sorts of situations. It was after Marshall's divorce. But I had the impression that it was something more than a mere lunch. But I'm not sure. It was very confusing. I even had the impression that Marshall didn't want me to meet the woman. It was unavoidable so he put a light face on it. He tried to make it appear like some sort of business meeting. It was really quite confusing. The woman was very well dressed. And she seemed to be on maybe a date, somehow she didn't quite come across as a business woman at a luncheon. Although she could have been. I was quite puzzled by it. Later I mentioned it to Clare. And he got sort of flustered and denied knowing anything about the woman or that Marshall was seeing anyone or that it was all news to him. I don't know why Clare got that way. Irritated. It seemed peculiar."

"Did Connie Yonge say anything?"

"Yes."

"What?"

"Nothing of consequence. Something about the food. And the pleasure of meeting me."

"Was she friendly? Hostile? What?"

"She was sort of indifferent. But I detected a little ironic inflection in her voice when we were introduced. When she said it was such a pleasure to meet me. It unsettled me. She seemed a little amused."

"And what about Marshall Wilson?"

"He was sort of jovial but it was a crude joviality. As if he was mocking me. I'd seen that side of him before so it wasn't difficult to detect. He's often that way with people. I've seen him at cocktail parties that way. Made me want to get away from him as quick as possible. Something else at the time. I had a peculiar feeling. I felt, I felt as if they knew Clare was having an affair with another woman. And they were slyly amused that I didn't know."

"Who is Connie Yonge, Mr Knight?" asked Gilles Masson.

I looked at the fine carpet. Chinese carpet with a thick pile of white and blue and pink The pile was dense and even. I thought of little combs and scissors, snipping the threads.

"Who is she?" I replied.

"Yes," said Madeleine Masson.

"Hard to say. Very difficult." I scratched my forehead. "I need to think. It's unexpected that she knew Marshall Wilson in this way." I glanced at Madeleine then her brother.

"Why?"

"Because. She claims that she had a relationship with someone else. Tell me. Let's backtrack a moment. Why did Marshall Wilson divorce his wife?"

"They argued. Constantly. It was a poor relationship. They never got along. They had been separated. In fact they had not lived together in years. The divorce was a legal formality more than anything else. It would have happened earlier except that Marshall fought tooth and nail over a settlement."

"You seem unsettled, Mr Knight, by these revelations concerning Marshall Wilson," remarked Madeleine Masson but with a moderate tone, even comforting.

"I think I better go home and get some sleep. If you don't mind I'll call a cab."

"Certainly. Allow me," said Madeleine Masson.

"I can manage. Please, show me the phone."

"Certainly." She led me out to the hall. As she offered the phone she said, "Mr Knight, are you alright?"

"Sure. Fine."

She went back into the living room.

I called a taxi then returned to the room and Madeleine Masson remarked, "Mr Knight, is this link between Marshall Wilson and Connie Yonge so unsettling?"

"Could be. Could be. It's a high fly ball in left field. I might have to do some fast back pedalling to snag it. But it's still within my range. You better say as little as possible to Marshall Wilson. Avoid this subject. If necessary tell him that you fired Lajoie–Chang. Had a falling out with me personally and are quite fed up and disgusted with me. I'm incompetent or some such thing."

"Does this woman Connie Yonge know anything?"

"I can't say. Some relationships are more complex than a work of origami."

"Let me ask you, Mr Knight." Gilles Masson leaned forward. "We seem to be studiously avoiding something that might be linked. That is in the background of this entire discussion. But we all by an unspoken consensus have studiously avoided it. This is a painful subject for my sister. That Clarence had an affair, even affairs, with women. We all know that Clarence had at one point even spoken of leaving. And according to what Madeleine has told me, this one particular woman, Elizabeth Strachan, was killed as well. Does this young woman's recent death here in Ottawa have anything, even remotely, to do with Clare's hit-and-run?"

"It could. And it could not. It might. Then it might not. But I can't get to the bottom of that. What's more the Ottawa Police Service's major crime unit are on that. "

"But Mr Knight, I understand you were involved in it when it was a missing person case, initially hired by the woman's family, so you may well have seen or found some links. Is that not so?"

"Yes."

"And now?"

"Clearly, I'm no longer involved in any way. It is now a criminal investigation. A homicide case."

"Well tell us this much, was there an appearance of a link?"

"Better to say nothing."

"And this Connie Yonge?"

"I need to check numerous details before I say anything further. And I need a good night's sleep. Give me time and thought. And an opportunity to consult with the people at the agency." I stood up. "I must speak with Mr Lajoie before I say anything further."

"Excuse me, Mr Knight. You're not well." Dr Masson said, "I'm saying that objectively as a doctor. Please let me drive you home."

The door knocker made a solid sound.

"There's the taxi driver. Thanks but no. I can manage. It is better I go home in a taxi."

"I'll see you to the door, Mr Knight."

When we reached the front door, she said, "Mr Knight, I do hope your injuries are not on account of the investigation."

The taxi driver knocked again.

"The taxi." I opened the door. "Good night Ms Masson."

I had the taxi drop me off near the laneway entrance. I did a quick glance around the corner and saw that the same car was still parked out front. I went back down the alleyway and climbed the fire escape.

In the apartment, I crashed on the bed like a pile of bricks knocked off a scaffolding on a hot summer day. My brain clattered down into the dust and rubble. The dust billowed up in a cloud and floated across the construction site. And I was gone. Crashed out. Irrevocably on the other side of the darkness with cawing crows. A dream in black and white and tones of grey as if I had no night vision. Grey without. Grey within. At night, even under subdued moonlight and starlight, colours disappear. Darkness seems eternal, although it is only momentary, because the sun with infinite light is there lurking behind the sheath of the dream. Even inside a dream the sun goes on glowing. The old orb keeps on glowing, even after a moment of death, while the crow's voice sounds so strange and discordant because the wise bird is counting the distance to the sun. Yes, those birds can count across glittering galaxies from star to star. And I slept. A good sleep. Deep and dark.

# TWENTY-TWO

The phone rang. It rang before the alarm went off.

It was Louise Montpetit, her voice sounded like it was coming from inside a wood stove.

"Alec? That you?"

"Yeah. 'Morning. It's me."

"I went back up to Constance Bay to take Connie Yonge a change of clothing and she's gone. No note. No phone call. No word. Nothing."

I sat up on the bed.

"That's a drag. I needed to talk her. Did she say anything on the drive up?"

"Not much. We kept it pretty neutral. Nothing about the investigations. We talked about her family. She grew up in Bancroft. How her family were not there for her. And still aren't. She put herself through university then went to work for the airline. That sort of stuff."

"Nothing about her situation?"

"Nothing. But I'm worried."

"Maybe, maybe we've been suckered, Louise."

"Don't say that. She's worried. I can tell. It is not for nothing. Look what happened to her friend."

"I thought along those lines as well. But I'm not convinced any longer. I needed to talk to her."

"Alec, she's a worried woman. She wouldn't have taken off. I could tell by the way she sat down when we got to the motel. Like it was a great relief."

"Is Georges in yet?"

"No."

"I'll come by. I'll grab something to eat and be by in a half hour."

"We should call the police, Alec, I don't know, maybe file a missing person report. She doesn't have any family except the guy she was married to and divorced."

"Maybe. First we'll talk to Georges. In the meantime you call her apartment and see if she came back into town."

"Alright. But Alec, don't drag your feet."

"Give me a break, Louise. Look I tried to help her. But I don't want to be taken for a sucker. I'll give you more information once I write up the report, okay. It's more complicated than even she led us to believe. Trust me on this. I'm not a callous jerk. I didn't want this. But I did my bit. I could have just turfed her out. If she was up front with the police, you know they might help her."

"Might's a big word under the circumstances, Alec."

"Come on, give me a break Louise. You call her place. And when I get in I'll call her lawyer, Slowikowsky. You know Connie Yonge's not exactly the most reliable person. "

"I understand."

I set the phone down, and just sat on the edge of the bed. I absolved myself of any responsibility. In fact, I didn't want to think about any of them, Liz Strachan and her family, Connie Yonge and her lover and business cronies, Clarence Wilson and his cuff links and suits, not even Madeleine Masson in all her loveliness or her shrewd Jesuitical brother who knew too much about the world and, who knows, was maybe the best and most dedicated doctor that this country had produced since Norman Bethune and Chris Giannou. I didn't want to think about anyone dedicated to love or money, altruism or jealousy. The crows set up crisscross morning caws in cacaphonic counterpoint. Their calls seemed more charming than any human's speech. My mind was down in a moment of longing for Lynda off in Japan. I wondered what I felt for her, but the time had been too brief. She had been good company, no manipulation, confident. A heck of a lot better company than the company I had been keeping over the last week. I smiled. Hey Knight you're lonely, want to crawl back into bed and you're feeling sorry for yourself. You jerk.

The further sound of the crows' complex voices was set off again and drummed on my eardrums. I rested my head in my hands.

Couldn't get my head around the situation. I didn't know Connie Yonge, Marshall Wilson and Norman Burley. I didn't want to know them, they were living somewhere else on another side of the cellphone and snorting off aluminium foil. Fast flights, cautious cellphone calls and dirty money transfers way beyond my wallet, fast beyond my way of living, at another velocity that was so fast it was out of sight.

I got up to go to the bath. From the small hexagonal space between the bath, bedroom, dining room and living room I could see through the living room doorway to the vestibule, my sneakers tossed about, one on its side. I just stood there and stared at the sole of the shoe. Now listening. Caw caw caw. I heard feet running across a slab of concrete. Caw caw caw. Yeah you guys I hear you calling, I hear you calling now. Loud and clear.

I had to talk to Lajoie. I took a bird's bath to the serenade of the wise crows. I still felt grubby. I had a bowl of cereal with toast and peanut butter and an orange. The orange looked simple and wonderful on the table. I typed up the report on the laptop and e-mailed it to Lajoie. When finished I drove to Saikely's. The place was packed with an early morning crowd, business boys in suits yakking investments, scruffy, sleepy young clerks, secretaries well dressed and calm, tired truckers leaning into their grub, garrulous cabbies gabbing in Arabic, city work crews rambling in French, all of them in the know about where to eat. I grabbed a coffee and rolled into Lajoie–Chang's carrying the paper cup.

Cheryl Perron gave me a worried look. She commiserated with me, then was sympathetic and scolding, "Alec get real. Take the day off."

"Georges in yet?"

"Yes."

I knocked on the door. The big man had the Masson file open on his desk. He closed it.

"I read the e-mail." Lajoie got that distant look in his eyes as if I was on the other side of the continent. "Something cunning. Someone charming."

"Very."

"But cunning plus charm equals deceit. Alec, how is it?" Lajoie asked. "You put sugar in your coffee?"

"Come on, you know I drink the stuff stiff and black. I like my coffee pure and keen. What do you take me for? I'm civilized. What's this all about?"

"Balzac. He loved coffee. Anyway let's forget coffee."

"You love non sequiturs." I laughed.

"Non sequiturs are the butter on the bread of language. The garlic and olive oil in the tangled spaghetti of grammar.

"Spaghetti of grammar?"

"Preferably al dente. But you're right there about the coffee."

"Georges, how do you drink the shrewd stuff?"

"You know very well."

"Remind me."

Lajoie smiled. "If French, I like café au lait. As you know. And if not that, cappuccino. Italian. The milk in a nice ratio. One teaspoon of good sugar. Preferably demerara. It cannot be drunk from a take-out cup. Styrofoam taints the taste. Any more than olive oil can be stored in plastic. Coffee can only be drunk from ceramic. And."

"And?"

"And and. Conjunctional non sequitur. Okay. Listen, strictly speaking you probably can't reach Norm Burley. They are discontented gentlemen beyond reach, they've been circumspect. As for these thugs that hang about Parsons, Snoblin and Rae, we'll get those last two and see the police about pressing assault charges against them."

"And Connie Yonge?"

"She was in the equation. But now she's out of it. If she comes around don't do her any favours. She's high risk. But she could also be at high risk. We don't know enough about Connie Yonge. Who knows what she is willing to do for Marshall Wilson if necessity demands. Or if her hand is forced."

"She's in trouble."

"Possibly. Maybe of her own making. You and Louise helped her out but you can't tell her what to do. She's got her own will. What's more the police will want her again for further questioning, sooner or later, concerning Liz Strachan. Or if the Crown cuts deep into the Liz Strachan homicide and there is a link with this money laundering crowd, she'll cut an arrangement with the Crown with help from her lawyer, Pete Slowikowsky. Slowikowsky's good at that game. Maybe if she's got her wits about her she contacted Slowikowsky.

That's beyond us. You've done more than necessary. We've been fair with her."

"She's in danger, Georges."

"No doubt. No doubt. But so young, so cunning, they do not last long in the world of high finance. I believe she went to see a lawyer. She's a bright young woman."

"The greed factor."

"Yes. As soon as the danger subsides she'll be inclined to get back into it. It's a habit now. The usual calculus but the calculator gets used up in a greater sum calculated by a higher calculator. Such equations and sums were beyond her. She made herself expendable because she did not have enough money to stay in the game."

"Or enough charm. Is her life in danger?"

"Only if Liz Strachan's murder is linked to Clarence Wilson's death and both are linked to this money laundering. Which may or may not be the case. I don't think they are but who knows? What is so apparent at one moment from one angle becomes confused from another angle."

"Tell me candidly, do you think Connie Yonge could have been involved in either Clarence Wilson's hit-and-run or the homicide of Liz Strachan?"

Lajoie said nothing. I waited, took up the coffee cup, sipped and glanced over the brim at the photo behind Lajoie's shoulder. Lajoie remained silent, he shuffled through the file, then closed it. He picked up a small paperweight, felt its heft in his hand. Set it down.

"Intuition is not enough. Motive is not enough. How is an anagram of who. But it is not easy to unscramble. Did she have access to Liz Strachan's car? Would she have hit Clarence Wilson using her lover's car? That's improbable, but if she did it, it reveals not only extreme nerve and cunning but utter ruthlessness. But I think not. What was the scale of her jealousy? As for Connie Yonge being involved in Liz Strachan's death? No it seems impossible. What we saw of the poor woman's corpse, that's the work of a man's hands. A very angry man."

"Burley?"

Georges said nothing for a moment, he touched his jade cuff link and readjusted his sleeve.

"That's very troubled territory. Sexual frustration, repression, is a dangerous force. Burley's greed could lead to volcanic anger, and if he felt cheated by Liz Strachan as a mule who withheld money in the transfers it might stimulate his anger. Connie Yonge says Burley wanted to sleep with Liz Strachan, right?"

"Yes."

"Does this seem credible, Alec? Or is Connie Yonge concealing something by saying this?"

"Georges. I got to admit I can't read her character. I could speculate in a thousand different directions, after last night. One thing though," I paused.

"Go ahead."

"Connie Yonge seemed genuinely wretched over Liz Strachan's death. I believe Connie Yonge loved Liz Strachan. And her jealousy was not for someone else but for Liz's interest in Clarence Wilson. Nothing to do with Norman Burley."

"You could confront Burley again, he'd be the link if there ever was one between the two deaths, if there exists one. But a confrontation might result in nothing more than an irritated personality, then again he might say something about Connie Yonge, Henderson, Parsons and his goons or anyone else. But I doubt it."

"It may not be possible. I don't think I could get a foot in Burley's office. Even if I crawled through the bathroom window."

"Yes. Confront him in the street. There's nothing to lose. He is a man, I understand, who is normally of a cool disposition but is reported to have a bad temper if put off. You've seen some of that. He might say something indiscreet if irritated to the point of anger. Confront him with knowledge of his meetings with Liz Strachan and Connie Yonge at the motel in Alfred where he rebuffed them about transferring their percentage for muling."

"Georges, Burley'll go ballistic."

Georges smiled.

"Yes, precisely what you want. Then it's a new game. And there might be something more. Although he probably was not directly involved in Clarence Wilson's death, maybe Burley knows something about it, who was involved in the hit-and-run. If he stays cool then that's it. You'll get nothing out of him."

"And Henderson?"

"Maybe Henderson took a side. Or Henderson and Marshall Wilson sided with Burley against Clarence Wilson strictly over money. Hard to say. Henderson came up the hard way. Knows things. Tough. But probably would arrange something. Another guy with financial troubles. Big transport and warehouse operation, he's got means, access, but he's probably vulnerable. Maybe faced with liquidity or cash flow crisis. Maybe a middle man doing the dirty work for the money laundry crew and not seeing his share. A bonded warehouse and fast trucks are nice things. But Henderson is probably like Burley, he'd be astute enough to put some distance between himself and violence. He's no fool, he'd pass that sort of action on to someone like Parsons to fix. Clarence Wilson's death is very difficult and may be linked to Liz Strachan's but then again that might well be no more than appearance. In any event, Alec, Lajoie–Chang must be careful to stay out of the Liz Strachan case."

"Marshall Wilson?"

"I think it unlikely he'd be directly involved at all in his brother Clarence Wilson's death. Even if they had a falling out over money. Such a killing is rare. Fratricide. Rare. More, he's disoriented. Maybe a man with a bad conscience. More probably, a gentleman with bad investments. A man who lost funds to trusted friends' schemes. Inside information on investments that did not pay out as originally calculated and promised. He's upset. Anxious. What you report sounds like a man with money problems. Then again he's no more than a corporate lawyer who possibly knows too much about corporate clients that he would rather not have any longer. Dealing with privileged information doesn't make one privileged. And a corporate lawyer cannot dismiss a corporate client out of dislike. That sort of legal practice does not work that way. Burley's got clout at Baldwin Martel Wightman because of the corporate clients he pulls in so Marshall Wilson has to stick with him. The Wilsons are creatures at the service of the convenience of money. Lawyers with a technical sense of the law which they can put at the service of corporations but men who at bottom know nothing about investing in their own interest. They are unable to distinguish between being functionaries and being in control. Hence their reputed arrogance. No arrogance like the arrogance of a petty functionary. Particularly Marshall Wilson."

"They like money too much."

"Alec. This is a capitalist society. We all like money too much. Money exterminates some people's consciences. It liquidates other people's health and they still cling to the accumulation of it. But some men can't distinguish between money and capital. In fact most men and women cannot. This is the grand deception of capitalist societies."

"Count me among the deceived. A lot of money is a lot of money."

"But a lot of money is not a lot of capital. A pile of dollar bills is nothing more than a stack of paper. That was Connie Yonge's and Liz Strachan's mistake. Much money needs a medium, needs relations to become capital. Money is just another commodity, bought and sold. Something many people fail to understand."

"Commodity, Georges? I don't understand. I thought money buys things. Gets me what I want."

"Yes, and is itself bought and sold like shoes and shirts and horseshoes, cars and fountain pens and toys. Money is bought and sold like human beings, like Liz Strachan and Connie Yonge, Lester Henderson and Clarence Wilson."

"Like you and me, Georges?"

"Yes. Like you and me. That's what Norman Burley understands so he thieved Liz Strachan and Connie Yonge, Lester Henderson and Clarence Wilson out of their money to make it his capital. Because he knows that a lot of little mounds of dirty money in many little hands is nothing, but united and flushed through the right part of the system it can be turned into a large mound of clean capital. That's what the Massons understand so they tried to keep clear of Burley and his influence over Clarence Wilson. There are those who want to work other people's capital or money to make their own, and then there are those who want to work their own capital to make more capital. A certain amount of clean money is needed to wash a quantity of dirty money."

"You're way over my head, Georges."

"All the petty truisms concerning money conceal the reality of capital. The Wilson boys are competent corporate lawyers but with only a vagrant notion of money and capital. Their father, Hugh Wilson, he was like a kid with a bucket full of water coming back from the well. Splashing money around doesn't make capital. You do not want accountants to run a corporation. They're the worst people. They confuse financial technicalities with productive efficiency. That's the trouble with today's corporations, run by MBAs and accountants. A great law," Georges paused. "Finance capital must not control, dominate and run industrial capital. Never ever. It's a fundamental of capitalism itself. A very dangerous arrangement when the chauffeur thinks driving the car makes him the owner of the vehicle. Two sorts of rich people, Alec."

"How so?"

"The Massons who know the meaning of capital. And the Wilsons who think they know the meaning of money. In between stand the opportunists like Burley. In this town we have few wealthy capitalists and many rich people who imagine themselves wealthy. They are amongst the most confused people around today. But government towns don't breed capitalists, they clone nervous lawyers and ingratiating intriguing mandarins."

"Georges, you won't make yourself popular out at the Corel Centre."

"I watch and applaud the Senators as much as the next fan."

"Which senators?"

"Both. They're all out there and equally entertaining. I know a good performance when I see one. In my book, Martin is the greatest coach the NHL has seen since Toe Blake."

"I think I'll go see Burley. What the heck."

I went back to my office. I phoned Pete Slowikowsky's office but he was busy. I left a message with his assistant requesting he call me. I got out my gear and put on jeans, ball cap and work boots. I drove over to Burley's place and waited. His car sat in the driveway. At ten he finally came out of his home and went towards the car. I got out and approached him.

"Good morning, Mr Burley."

Burley turned to his car, beeper in hand and unlocked the door. The big lawyer glanced at me but said nothing. He seemed to recognize and dismiss me in the same instant. A look of utter contempt without uttering anything contemptible. He opened the door and set his briefcase inside.

"Excuse me, Mr Burley, I was hoping to have a word with you."

"This is neither the time nor the place."

"A few moments might help solve your former law partner Clarence Wilson's unfortunate death."

"Sir. That is strictly a matter for the authorities. I know nothing of that tragedy. I think I have said all I have to say to you. You people are meddlesome."

"The motel is a good place to bed women but not as private a location as it might appear for financial transactions."

Burley gave me a blistering gaze but said nothing. He started to slip into the driver's seat.

"You messed around with Connie Yonge. When you really wanted to sleep with Liz Strachan. It's tough when you can't always have it your way."

He got out of the car.

"You scumbag. Get off my property before I call the police."

"You won't call anybody. After what you did to those two women."

"You've been warned."

"You were driving the car that hit Clarence Wilson."

Burley now gave a smirk, cruel and confident, he said nothing more but got back in the car, slammed the door, and drove off leaving me standing on the sidewalk.

Not cool. Not cool at all Knight, I told myself, you really blew it. I got in my car and drove out of Rockcliffe Park towards Bronson Avenue. Yesterday's dream smoked up in my memory. It was murky. I thought of Inky Baby. I had to find that cellphone. It was ringing in my brain. I drove up into the Gatineau Hills until I came to the road near Rae and Snoblin's cottage. I went through the woods trying to recall the way I had run. I studied the ground and tree branches along the way. Listening carefully for anyone approaching, I searched for twenty minutes. There in the dry leaves rested the cellphone. Untouched. I picked it up and went back to my car. At a depanneur I pulled over and got a bottle of water, drank it and listened to the messages. Two from Inky. Brief, no more than to give him a call. I dialed the number.

"Hello."

"'Lo. Can I speak to Inky?"

"Sure."

"Ah Lantern. Where you been? I thought you wanted me to call you."

"I did Inky. Something came up. You got anything?"

"K. This is no good. K. And I'm not taking any responsibility for the source. I can't give you a name. Outside the question mark. Understand? K?"

"Fine. I won't ask."

"N. Like keep me out of it entirely. Entirely. K?"

"Fine."

"Delete this phone number from your cellphone and your memory. K?"

"Inky."

"I mean it. You gonna do that Lantern?"

"Fine. I'll do it."

"Your person got into a car on Carling Avenue out in the west end after she got off her bus. She was hitchhiking. And the car was late model, white. Drove west. The guy who picked her up is middle-aged, well dressed. Suit suit. Rumour says he's a freakhead. Nothing good here. No good. I'm gone. Bye. Don't call me again on this number. 'Member, delete. Delete. Complete."

"Inky?" The line was dead. I sat in the car drinking from the bottle of water. I deleted the number from the phone. Delete. Delete. I took off my shoe and wrote the cellphone number on the inside of the shoe leather. I drove back into the little O. At Lajoie–Chang I changed back into my suit. Then I telephoned Detective Warnock. He was not available, I left a message that I would be at Saikely's on Bronson for the next hour. I told Cheryl to watch for the parcel sent by Johnny Olive, treat it with extreme courtesy when it arrived, and provide it with the very best and safest accommodations on the premises.

The café was quiet, mid-morning snooze. I ordered a cheese, lettuce and tomato sandwich. May's son was working, doing prep. He gave me a nod of his head and a quick smile in distant recognition as he moved around the prep area. When he had made the sandwich, his mother was serving another customer so he brought it over himself and set it down.

"Thanks."

"Mr Knight? I kinda remember you."

"Do you."

"Yeah. Like sortuv. Face seems familiar."

"Good to see you again. Anthony?"
"Right. 'Joy that san'wich eh."
"I will."
"I betchya will." He winked. "Well I don't mean bet. None of that. Betting causes trouble. Like don't I know it." He laughed. "Last time I was at the casino, they called an ambulance. Guy was having a nervous breakdown, threatening self-demolition. Couple of casino shrinks appeared. Pretty freaky floor show if you know what I mean."
"I heard."
"They call it live entertainment. But you don't necessarily survive the engagement. Back to basics." Anthony Saikely went back to the prep area.
I took a bite. Well not his old man's sandwich but what the heck, you don't learn to turn out a CLT in ten minutes. I'd finished half of it when dighand Warnock rolled in. I stood up.
"Relax Knight, no need to stand in appreciation of my presence."
"If you don't mind Detective Warnock, I'll self-serve." I picked up the plate and went to the back table.
"Gimme a coffee and that hot beef special you people are bragging about in the window. I'll take it back there," Warnock said to May Saikely.
We sat down. I repeated the cellphone conversation for Warnock. When I was finished, May Saikely brought the special. Warnock diligently cut the hot beef into little squares, nice morsels, as he must have done when served at home. He took a bite and chewed. He went on and ate some of the mashed potatoes and peas. Another bite. I finished the other half of the sandwich. Finally he said, "This stinks."
I looked at him, "The kid's learning to cook. Give 'im a break."
"I don't mean the meal. Meal's fine. Better than most. And at half the price. I mean what you bring me."
"I'll keep trying Detective Warnock."
"You don't understand. I want the phone number."
"I don't remember it. I deleted it."
"I want the frigging number. And the airhead that gave it to you, Knight. I told Lajoie. I told 'im. And I told 'im."
"I can't. And you know I can't."
"That's crap." Warnock smouldered.

"Treat it as anonymous. Like Crime Stoppers or TIPS."

"How good do you judge it? There's no twisted stuff in the source? Getting his funnies, chewing on our ears?"

"How good? I'd say quite. Better than ninety-nine percent good. Clean. No money. No nothing. No drugs. No hype. No bragmeister. Nothing. Believe me. It's very neat. And you must know they don't like you, Detective Warnock, but they still want you to know. That means something. Consider that."

"Don't be cute."

"I'm not. These people are worried about your daughter."

"They're junkies, aren't they."

"You're digging for an identity clue but I'm not going to lend you a shovel. I think—"

"What?"

"Nothing."

"Out with it."

"I overstep myself Detective Warnock. It's not for me to suggest anything to the police service. You know what you're doing. I respect your knowledge and abilities."

"Don't be patronizing. Go ahead. Let's hear it. Out with it. Don't be a dignified prick. Leave that for the fucky-fuckfaces on Parliament Hill."

"Okay. I think you better take this as substance. The source is, in my book, an A plus source. Very disinterested person. Person's not a snitch. Not bendable. Very clean."

"Info like that is volatile, could be polluted, radioactive, it's only as good as the source. And we got to verify it. Knight, if I get my hands on your cellphone I'll chew on it."

"I got to go. I try to be polite."

"I'll get your meal."

"I prefer not. You've been rude to me Detective Warnock. I don't like rude people to treat me to a meal. It does not aid the digestion."

"Fuck your etiquette, Knight. You and Lajoie, Mister polite polite. I told him I want the source. You can get your socks tied in knots faster than you can say Harry Houdini. You know that? Eh? Johnpine's really not happy with you people."

The detective's face was flushed and heavily creased, a line of pain across his forehead, rippled lines under his eyes, he looked as if he was going to cry. I know I might have if I were him. But I couldn't comprehend what was going through his nut. He stopped staring at me and just bent over the plate and kept eating, as if eating might help him forget.

I walked down Bronson to the office. When I arrived Cheryl started to tell me that Ed Stanley had called but the telephone interrupted her. It was Tommy MacAlister calling from the shoe store. I went in my office and took the call.

"Hey buddy, sorry to call you so late." He sounded sedately and sheepishly Tommy. "I meant to get back to you earlier but you know how it is when the weather's good. Putting in a lot of cycling. I'm on commission and this is a busy morning."

"Don't sweat it, Tommy."

"All the same. Sorry this took so long. And to be honest I'm not certain if what I got for you is much use. My buddy in sports shoes said that it was kinda tough to tell from the partial print of the sole. But he thought it was a Nike. Well he emphasized that it looked that way but he wouldn't want to swear on it."

"Nike."

"Yes. But not certain."

"What type?"

"Very high end. He mentioned a couple of models. Very expensive sort of sports shoe, top class, professional, but he thought it was really worn. Like that was part of the problem, the sole was so worn even though it was maybe such an expensive one."

"That's a big help Tommy. I really appreciate it. Did he say it could be anything else? Any other type of shoe."

"Yeah. He said it could be one of the others but that was pretty remote. Look, I got to go. Manager just peeked round the corner into this dark corner of the stock room. He's like fifty. I mean what can you do with a dude who's fifty and paying a mortgage?"

"Not much I suppose, except make sales to help with the mortgage payment. Well. You tell your buddy a big thank-you. And that I appreciate it."

"I definitely will. Come by the store some time."

"I will."

"I'm in a rush here, Knight."

"Sure."

"Have a great morning. Make lots of la joie."

"Will."

I sat and stared at the wall. I went elsewhere for a moment. Lajoie and Chang did not give me a nice office. This space had worse dimensions than a shoe box. I didn't rate. That was another thing I was going to talk to those guys about. An office with space. Yes. Definitely. And I don't want to hear nothing about security, seniority, being a partner, an associate. Morrison had space. Lajoie had space. Space. Space. None of that crap on the computer about virtual space. A real physical space. Rated very big in this town. We weren't talking pretentiousness now. We were talking necessity. Head space. For sanity. Self-esteem. Space. A bureaucrat without space is a failure. An absolute zero.

I knew I was evading big thoughts thinking about wanting more space. I picked up the phone. Set it down and paused. Maybe Louise should make this call. I called Louise Montpetit at home.

"Don't be pissed off at me, Louise."

"I'm not. Look, I have a daughter four or five years younger than that woman."

"Okay. Georges had an idea. He thinks Connie Yonge might have connected with Pete Slowikowsky. To put your mind at ease give Plante, Slowikowsky a call."

"Okay. Thanks Alec. You can't do it?"

"Louise I would but I think you'll get more. Maybe even a chance to talk to her. If I called it would be a big fat zero."

"Alec, please call her lawyer."

"I did a while ago and left a message. I'll try again."

"Good."

I dialed Slowikowsky. The conversation was no good. He gave nothing. Understandable, he was all barrister. And I was a nobody with a crummy suit. I set the phone down and stared at it. Big ugly thoughts were growing in my head. A line on the telephone flashed up and blinked at me. It was Cheryl Perron.

"Alec, it's for you. Connie Yonge."

"Thanks. Put her through."

"'Lo, Ms Yonge."

"I want to thank you and Ms Montpetit for being there for me. So generous, last night."

"You took off. You could have let Ms Montpetit know. She drove back up the valley to see about you. You caused Ms Montpetit to be very worried about you. Ms Yonge, you should know that Ms Montpetit is a very caring person."

"I do apologize. Please tell Ms Montpetit, who's a very lovely person, a kind woman, that I am terribly sorry to have put her out. But unfortunately, I had to meet with my lawyer."

"You could have told us. Listen."

"I'm sorry, I am under strict instructions not to speak to anyone."

"Listen. I have something I need to tell you Ms Yonge. Something really important."

"I can't speak with you, Mr Knight. I've been advised by my lawyer to not speak to anyone. I should not have even made this phone call. But I did want to apologize to Ms Montpetit. I'm co-operating with the police. Goodbye."

A big thing, a rhizome, was twisting through my brain.

I set the phone down and then gave Ed Stanley a shout on the phone. He asked if I would come over. I went over straight away.

# TWENTY-THREE

The university student looked as rumpled and tired as the day before. He wasn't drinking but he had the stench of a jock who hadn't stumbled into a shower stall in a week. We sat in his apartment living room while his roommates slept. A young woman came out in a man's bath robe and slipped into the bathroom across the hall.

"Let's get out of here. I can't talk here. Too many earholes in the wall."

"Sure."

We headed down towards the Byward Market. On the way, I suggested something to eat. We talked about baseball and college football, who would win the next game between U of O and Carleton in what might be the last of the Panda games. He talked about his prospects of making it to the CFL. He thought he had a good chance but to play one more year of college ball was probably a mistake especially when there was the prospect of making some real money. He should have gone for a tryout when offered.

We went into a shawarma joint where everyone was speaking Arabic. He had a beef shawarma with the works and I opted for a spicy falafel. We sat on the patio. I said nothing.

"Knight, you know something, I mean I'm worried. Worried 'cause the cops came round again and drilled my head. Again. Last night."

"That's routine. No doubt just to clarify some information. Details."

"Sure. Sure. So you say. But it's kinda awkward."

"It's always awkward. The police understand this situation."

"All the same I'm not crazy about it."

"Just be patient. They'll interview everybody and anybody who knew Liz. In a situation like this they've got to collect as much information as they can about the victim and anyone associated with her, from casual to intimate. It's routine. The police are careful. It's part of the way they operate. Thoroughness, it's part of any good investigation. That's the way it is. The Ottawa police are very good. They'll get the guy who did this. No doubt."

"It put a lot of things on my mind concerning Liz."

I said nothing but nodded.

"They asked all kinds of questions about her that made me feel crummy."

"How so?"

"Crappy questions like who she went out with. Who she slept with. Did I sleep with her. When was the last time. That kinda stuff. It's cruddy."

"Ed, they got to."

"It's slimy, Knight. I don't want to talk about Liz that way. Think about it, I loved her. This is someone I really really loved. A woman I was like really really really crazy about."

"Trust them. They're just doing their job. Some of that stuff, depending where it came from, could be used to corroborate other stuff from the autopsy. The forensic side of things. Accumulate information. Very detailed. Very scrupulous process. Eliminate suspects."

"They wouldn't say it but they seemed to hint that something to do with sex happened to Liz. Was Liz raped? Do you know?"

"I told you I don't know. That's up to the coroner to determine. In the autopsy. Determine the cause of death. Man, not even a detective determines that sort of thing anymore. Everything has gone to specialists."

"I don't want to think about it. But my mind keeps coming back to it. This idea that she was raped."

"Forget about it. It's not so until it's officially stated by the police. You know she might not have been."

"How's that? I don't follow."

"A lot of murderers, even rapists who want to rape can't get it off. They can do it sometimes, but other times, well they get impotent. Can't get it up. They get sexually all mixed up, aroused and confused. Their frustration kills them. Maybe part of the reason. That's why they're doing it in the first place. Using violence. Coercion. If they had any sense they'd see that being kind to a woman would be better, showing affection would be a better way. Better than violence. But they're so mixed up, sexually frustrated. And angry. With themselves. With the world. With women."

Stanley said nothing for a long moment. I looked around the joint.

"Knight. You know what I heard, and it really like freaks me out?"

"Tell me, Ed."

He hesitated. Then he took a big bite of the beef shawarma and chewed in a careless way, some of the shredded lettuce, beets, onions, and tomato spilling from the corner of his mouth and the sauce dribbling on his chin, then he gulped down the half-chewed food.

"I heard a real sleazy rumour that some older guy was hanging out with Liz. Is that true, Knight? Tell me what you heard on that score. Was some older guy screwing around with Liz?"

I set my falafel down. I didn't want to eat, I wasn't really hungry at all. I took a sip of the ginger ale.

"Seems so from what I heard."

"Seems. What do you mean seems? Fucking is not in the fucking category of fucking seeming. Fucking is so or it isn't. Is that what you came up with?"

"Yeah. But Ed, out of consideration, I didn't want to mention it to you seeing as you were so intimate with Liz. I didn't want to violate your, well, your sense of intimacy. And you seemed to have enough to cope with."

"Christ. I can't believe it. And I trusted you." He took another tear at the shawarma and while chewing the food he spoke, "Tell me what you know. I got to know."

"Not much, Ed, to tell the truth."

"I want to know. Don't hold back. You know the way the cops play around. Always looking for information but never telling you anything. It's a head trip. A headbanger. I can't take it. People who play mind games can't be trusted."

"Maybe you should tell them everything that you know."

"I did. I told them everything. I'd never hold back from the police. I've got the highest respect for the guy in uniform. He's a man."

"You're certain Ed?"

"What do you mean?"

"Well you don't want to hold back any information if it would help them solve the crime. That's what you want. That's what we all want."

"I want that. That's important. But I'm not convinced everybody wants that. I think they're dealing with some really creepy people."

"I mean if the police mention a friend or want names, you want to give them to the police. It can look bad if you hold back even out of loyalty to a friend."

"Sure, I see what you mean."

"You know I heard it was—maybe I shouldn't mention names."

"Go ahead. I want to know. You can share it with me."

"Well I heard just a rumour okay. Keep that in mind, no more than a rumour that this older guy who was supposedly getting it on with Liz—" I paused.

"Tell me, I got to know."

"Well it might put you off."

I stared at the remains of the falafel and rolled aluminium foil.

Stanley took a bite of his sandwich, he chewed and then said, "Nothing could put me off. Nothing."

"Well I heard it might be Lester Henderson or one of those guys he hangs out with. That those guys were really hot for Liz Strachan."

"What? That slob. That weasel Henderson. Liz would never go with that greaseball. Never. She liked a guy with a body. She was into that. Liz wanted a guy with something."

"Well you never know. When a guy's got a wallet."

"How's that? Henderson? I thought he was— look, let's forget it."

"Ed, this situation is all inside out and upside down. This is something for the cops to handle. You've just got to get it off your mind. Best thing maybe is to stop thinking all about it. You better tell the police what you know about Henderson. If there is anything to tell."

"I don't know much. We're hometown boys. He's a buddy of my old man but nobody to me. I just work for the turkey." Ed stopped talking.

We ate. But I couldn't finish the falafel.

"I better go. I got things to do."

"Come on, hang out, let's go have a brew."

I looked at my watch.

"Okay but I got a lot of work on my desk. They're going to give me a clerical promotion, make me an inspector of keyboards." I laughed but Stanley didn't. "Better than being an inspector of pavement. You know how it is. A mound of paper. Papershovelling. But if we go for a brew it's got to be just a quick one. I got a boss that I got to explain myself to."

We sat at a pub in one of the historic stone buildings in the Byward Market. There weren't many drinkers. Just the beginning of the lunch trade and some leftover tourists from the summer. And a couple of tables of parents who had driven the kids to Ottawa for the fall term and were taking the bright ones out for lunch before heading back home.

Ed ordered a pitcher of Upper Canada Ale.

We talked about skiing, I made up some longwinded romantic story about how I got stranded on the chair lift in the Laurentians with a beautiful blonde from McGill while her friends waited up top for her. He laughed and talked about the blonde who he never knew and I never knew. Then Ed stopped, and he started back on his own obsession, the beer tended to make him feel worse and then better and then worse. He went in two directions on two horses, he was more contrary than conjunctions in a complex sentence.

He declared with a cosmic profundity, in a tone and expression which the media has bestowed upon my generation, "Life sucks. Don't it."

"Sometimes, but the best thing to do is avoid the vacuum cleaner."

"That's me. That's what happened to me when I got involved with Liz."

"No two ways about it. She may have been devastatingly beautiful but from the sounds of things, she was a complicated woman."

"What do you mean, Knight?"

"Just that she lived a complicated life. She lived in a zone that a lot of people fantasize about but never ever dare visit."

"Yeah. That's true. I'm simple. I'm a simple kinda guy. That was the problem. That was the problem between us. But I don't know how I got here."

"Where?"

"Here in this situation. I mean with all this complication in my life. The closest thing I ever had to do with the police was a speeding ticket."

"Don't worry. It'll pass. And you'll get back to basics."

"No it won't. It stays with me. Dwells on my mind. Fuck it's like a rotten muffler."

"Give it time. Time wipes out everything. Time is next to amnesia."

"I wanted to tell the police something but I couldn't."

"About what?"

"About Lester Henderson."

"What about the guy?"

"It's really crappy. And I'd feel like a snitch. I hate snitches. If anybody ever snitched on me about anything, I'd clobber 'em. Anyway this stuff with Henderson, it's heavy."

"Go ahead, Ed, pass it by me."

"Sure maybe you can tell me if I should tell 'em. I mean the police."

"Especially if it involves a crime. That's not snitching. Ed, it's one thing to be loyal to someone, it's entirely another thing to come clean with the law. If the police want something and they sense you're holding back it really gets their backs up. They won't relax. Tell them. Go ahead. Get it out."

"Well. Les Henderson borrowed Liz's car one time. I mean I borrowed it from Liz and then I lent it to him. I mean, shit it's kinda complicated like you say. Everything to do with Liz was so fucking complicated."

"What car? Her Miata?"

"No. No. The car she had before that. She had an Olds. A 1995 heap. I took it one evening to work. Then I lent it to Les. And he drove it. And brought it back with a busted headlight. Which freaked me. Because it wasn't mine so I had to get it fixed. I didn't want Liz to know. She'd have been pissed off."

"Why'd he take the car?"

"He said his was in the garage getting repaired."

"That's no big deal."

"Well. They kinda asked about Liz's car. If I had ever driven it. And I said no. Liz wouldn't let anyone drive the Miata. Anyway. Well 'cause that was the truth. I had never driven the Mazda."

"Well that's cool, you told them what they wanted to know. They must have been concerned about some evidence in connection with the Miata. The forensic people would be all over that vehicle."

He rubbed his eyebrows.

"Yeah. I guess. But when Les brought the car back he was kinda upset, said I should replace the busted headlamp."

"Did you?'

"Yeah. Problem is I didn't believe the story that Henderson told me."

"What d'you mean?"

"He handed me some cock and bull story about a stone flashing up and cracking the headlight."

"Could happen I suppose."

"Maybe. I got to forget it. It doesn't matter."

"Forget what?"

"What happened."

"Ed, what did happen?"

"You'll never know. Nobody will."

"I guess not if you don't tell me."

"I'll never tell anybody. I can't."

"Maybe some things shouldn't be told."

"That's it, Knight. That's it exactly."

"Some things aren't worth telling."

"Yeah that's it exactly, they aren't worth being talked about."

"Except if you want to be honest with yourself, Ed."

"Honest? That's crap. My old man says the only honest people in the world are in the graveyard."

"Maybe. They're certainly silent enough. But it does not mean that the dead never tell stories, even the dead talk in strange ways. Strange tongues."

"Huh? What do you mean?"

"Nothing much except that the dead are not as silent as they appear. Nothing more, nothing less. Not everybody is a liar. And even liars sometimes tell the truth."

"Man, you should see people on the car lot. People are fucking liars. Everyone talks about the car dealer hustling them but man that's a load of crap, to know the truth you've got to hear the car buyer singing his sob story. They want to sucker the car salesman so bad. So much. Regular crowd of con artists. That crew would swindle you faster than a fox would raid a henhouse. As soon as you put money on the table people start angling 'round it. My old man told me. Some work from under the table, some from behind, some from the side, some on top. You name it everybody's got their way of hustling."

"Cars don't necessarily bring out the best qualities in people. Courage. Honesty. Fairness."

"Christ, you should see them shaking the steering wheel trying to make the car rattle."

"Well you're probably right, Ed. You grew up on the car lot. But all the same you want to be honest. Especially with the police. Like I said before, you don't want to be holding back from the man doing his job."

"What do you mean? I told them everything. I told them everything I know. But," he gulped the beer, the pitcher was empty, "I kinda asked you. I mean I kinda thought you was my buddy. And I don't think you told me everything you know. How come?"

"Ed. Ed, you can trust me one hundred percent. One hundred percent. We're not on the car lot. I'm no shifty car buyer. I know you're a straight shooter. No b-s. I trust you one hundred percent. So you've got to trust me one hundred percent. After all the good honest talks we've had together. Do you think I'd talk to a guy like di Cesare the way I talk with you? Do you? No way. Do you think I'd ever dare talk to Connie Yonge? Absolutely not. Never. But you. I know how you felt about Liz. I'm one of the few people who understands how you felt. I know her parents don't do you justice. And I tell you what I know. 'Cause I can see how you felt for Liz."

"Fucking right. Man, I was loyal. Loyal beyond belief to that lady." He pounded the table. His eyes were red and moist. But he stopped talking, stared at the empty pitcher.

I said nothing.

"Fuck."

"I'll get this. Then I better get back to the office, I can see you could use some time alone. We better go."

"Sure. Wait. Come on back to my place and have a brew." This seemed more than a request. "I wanna tell you something."

I looked at my watch.

"Sure but just a quick one."

He glanced at the full draft glass in front of me.

"You didn't finish your beer."

I felt under the surface of the table to check for the cell in my jacket pocket.

"That's okay. Let's go."

I paid for the pitcher. And while I did, he gulped from my glass.

"Gonna use the can, then we'll go back."

I slipped into the washroom stall and called Cheryl Perron. I gave her Ed Stanley's address and asked if Morrison could come over and watch the place. Just then I heard someone call out.

"Knight, that you in there?"

I snapped the phone off.

"Yeah it's me."

"Sorry about that Knight. I kinda spoke hard. This situation is taking its toll. And I don't like being questioned by the cops." I could hear him pissing into the urinal.

"Nobody does. Perfectly understandable. But you don't have to worry." I flushed the toilet.

He glanced at me over his shoulder when I came out of the stall. I washed my hands and dried them.

We left the pub and headed back towards Stanley's apartment, past the old stone houses and brick shops of the market to the university quarter.

Inside the apartment was sombre and empty.

I sat in a cruddy stuffed chair that was becoming un-upholstered. Stanley cracked open two beers. He slouched down in the couch across from me. His elbows on his knees. He was on edge. I tried to look away.

"Okay. I got to tell you something. Maybe something I should have told the cops. But I figured it might look bad on me. Especially the way they tore into me. Although this has nothing to do with Liz."

"How'd they question you?"

"The first time alright. Who's who. Do you know so and so. That kinda bullshit but last night it was, like more, how do you say it? Up close. In your face. Worse maybe. Where was I. Who was I with. That sort of crap."

"That's not a problem. You've got straightforward answers for that stuff. I can tell. Don't worry. Just answer their questions straight up. No prob. Anyway anyone can see you loved Liz."

"Maybe. But you got to know something. Liz was involved with some pretty sleazy, creepy suits. And Les Henderson and his crew were among them. I didn't say everything that I could to the cops about them. I mean. I mean I've seen things out at the warehouse that maybe I shouldn't have seen. But I'm no snitch. I know Henderson's a hardworking kinda guy, pulled himself up by his own bootstraps like my old man says, but he's got himself involved with some pretty tricky people up here. And things go on in the warehouse that maybe shouldn't. I didn't want to do the guy any damage."

"What didn't you say?"

"I didn't tell 'em about Les Henderson and his buddies. And what I thought he used the car for."

"What did he?"

"Okay. Come on. I'll show you." He set the beer down and stood up. "You want to know. Let's go. I'll show you."

He grabbed his car keys.

We went out.

"Ed, let's take my car. I'll drive," I said. I saw Morrison down the block and gave him the signal to follow.

"No. You don't know the way. Let's go in my car."

"You've laid on a bit, maybe you should let me drive."

"What? I can handle it. I'm driving my car. Don't tell me what to do. I grew up with these things. I was driving cars around the lot as a tot. That was my tot lot, Knight."

"Sure. Whatever you say Ed, you know best."

We took off, flew straight through la petite O like it was a bull's eye, crossed the river and turned in to the Gatineau. We didn't talk much, the car radio was far too loud, blaring into my eardrums. We seemed to be heading in the direction of the stretch of road where Clarence Wilson had been killed. The radio was blasting out some leftover rock'n'roll from the fifties or sixties. I imagined some time warp and my folks at a skating rink or a teen dance, soon they would leave the Teentown dance hall, try to slip down the stairs without being seen to my old man's car, they'd neck in the car. Be momentarily happy but nervous. Go back inside and think they had just experimented and experienced the most wonderful moment in history, back into the teen dance to hear the music, Bobby Avalon, Bobby Curtola, Ronnie Hawkins, Paul Anka. But here I was cruising down the road and that rock'n'roll was nothing in this world but leftover static electricity. And even the electricity was running out. Power shortages were on the way. So much at stake and so little happening. The more music the less people did. The blaring of the radio was ripping off my brain. I could have put up with it if he turned it down, got a little sentimental even, but Stanley was driving through a terrifying time zone, towards a destination that I had no knowledge of. Stanley had the windows down and the wind was blowing across the interior of the car. I caught Morrison tracking us way back.

Stanley flicked off the radio.

"Where we going, Ed? I don't recognize this area."

"You'll see."

We finally came to the quiet stretch with the curve where Clarence Wilson had been taken out on the bike. Stanley pulled the car over.

"You really take me for a no brainer don't you, Knight?"

"No way Ed. I don't think of you that way. I don't know why you'd say such an absurd thing. I'd never think of you that way. In fact I don't think of human beings that way. I work on the assumption that every human being is intelligent. To assume otherwise is to think nothing of oneself. And I think very highly of myself. We only see our intellect in other people's minds."

"Shudup asshole. Put on your real voice. Lock on your real brain, okay. Quit playing child shrink. You are so condescending in your consideration."

"I'll tell you something. Even if you're my buddy I don't like being called an asshole by anybody. Get it. It's not the way we spoke where I come from."

"Get out of the car shitface. We're not where you come from."

"We never listened to that kind of music at breakfast. I told you I don't let anybody swear at me. That's a number one rule with me, Ed. Self-respect. Very important. Okay. Listen to me. I mean it."

He got out and slammed the door.

"I told you get out. You want to know. So get out."

I got out. We stood in the gravel. Stanley came round the car.

"Something rotten happened here." He looked totally focussed on the spot but out of it.

"Just a quiet stretch of road."

"No way. Maybe you don't know what went down here. Nobody knows."

"Tell me."

He looked at me his red eyes glaring.

"Let's go down there." He pointed down the ravine to the grassy area with rocky outcrops. He shoved me on the shoulder to go down. "Go down there. I'll show you. I'll show you life."

We headed down and then across the stones onto the grassy area.

"A guy was killed on this road. Knocked him off his bike. And the guy landed down around here."

"Who?"

"Some big shot lawyer named Wilson who was fucking the ass off Liz. All those sleazy suits want is a piece of ass."

"How do you know this guy Wilson was killed here?"

"'Cause I was in the car when it happened. The Olds rammed the fucker riding his bike."

We were standing in mostly grass. Up ahead rose the high hills covered in red and grey rock, stands of conifers sprinkled with birch trees. The air was wonderfully clear, still and silent. I felt for this land. It went through me, the trees and rock, the air and light. Then I heard from a distant lake a loon call. Across the tree line a blue heron flew.

"Hear that, Ed. See that, Ed. Powerful flight. Isn't that beautiful." I pointed at the heron.

"Who gives a fuck. It's just a crappy bird going nowhere. Did you hear the shit I just told you."

I said nothing.

"Liz's Olds hit that freaky lawyer."

"That for sure?"

"You bet, Knight. As sure as we're standing here."

"Then tell the cops."

"Why should I? The fucker had it coming to him. He was screwing everybody. He was gonna screw Henderson too. In fact he did, according to Les."

"How's that?"

"Never fucking mind."

"Ed, who was really driving the Olds?"

"Fuck you asshole. You're full of shit too, Knight."

I looked at him.

"Yeah I can see you're just another bullshit liar. Small time hustler. Two-bit suit. I see crappy two-bit con artists like you every day on the lot. Haven't two loonies to rub together. Full of 'emselves. From asswipe to assholes."

"I do my thing. Listen, I told you not to talk that way to me. Okay. I won't accept rudeness. I told someone the same at lunch. And he was a far higher authority than you, Ed. And if you knew the man, Ed, you'd understand, that I take this thing pretty serious."

"Which is mostly lying."

"Ed. I'd never lie to a guy like you. Tell me who was really driving the Olds."

"Come on. You're Mister Mighty Bullshit. What's all this crap about Nick Gathel. Criminal psychologist. Blah blah. Blah blah. You really do take me for an illiterate. There's a library over there on U of O campus. No? Isn't there? There's a computer. Yes. I can type. Inspector of keyboards. Imagine that. Gathel. There's no Gathel. It's not even in the New York almighty telephone book. And if it isn't there, it's nowhere. It's only in your head where the law of confusion reigns. I'll tell you something. I don't need anyone to cheat for me. I'm the very top honours student. Highest grades of any graduating class in my high school. Valedictorian. Guys think football, jock. Well any fucking university in this country would have taken me on my academic record alone. I could have even gone to Michigan or Texas. Maybe even Princeton or Yale with my bloody grades and athletic ability. Get it? Do you, fuckface?"

"Sure. I know you're a bright guy, Ed. I never doubted it."

"You are a first class asshole."

"I told you Ed, don't use that sort of language with me. I won't accept it. I accept a lot but not that. I never speak that way to you. I always speak—"

"Shudup asshole, I never raped Liz. I'd never rape Liz. I didn't need to, I could get laid any time I wanted. She was never left behind some crummy dumpster. That's bullshit. You made that all up. You found nothing. You shot a line longer than a fly fisher."

"Come on Ed. I wouldn't crap on you. I tried to tell you what I knew. I wasn't snowing you. I told you I didn't see the body. That it was someone else who did."

"You'll never crap on me again. You crapped all around, all that shit about finding her. Finding Liz."

I shook my head.

"Ed, you want to tell the truth. You're a smart guy. Smart people love to tell the truth. Who did it?"

"Those creeps killed Liz because of the way they treated her. But I would have. I could have. She fucked me over. She fucked around with everybody. She had no loyalty."

"It's not too late to tell the police. Ed why don't you tell them what you did. What you know. They'll understand."

"No. I'm going to illustrate to you how the law of confusion operates. Guys like you think they're so smart. But look where you are mac. Take a look around." He stared at me. I stared back. "Now listen."

"I am."

"I'm going to tell you something. Don't judge by appearances. Don't judge by the way a guy drinks his beer. Don't judge. Okay. If you didn't judge, you wouldn't find yourself here. Today. In this place. Alone. Man you're in a canoe without a paddle, no life jacket, and you're going over Hog's Back."

"You're a smart guy Ed. I've got to admit it. You're a lot smarter than Connie Yonge or Liz Strachan or Les Henderson or Clarence Wilson. The whole lot of them."

"Shudup. Flattery. We get that on the car lot. Just to get a cheaper price. Flattery's the call sign of a chiseller. The cheat. The con. Your fucking brain is flat. Now your head is gonna be."

Stanley charged at me, like a fullback, all two hundred and twenty-five pounds, six three. The way he crossed the distance, I could believe at that instant that he did the hundred yard dash not under ten seconds but in about one second. He drove me across the grass. I counted myself plenty lucky that it was mostly tall grass, I could feel my back and spine skidding and jolting. It was a hell of a rough ride. He landed on my chest. I squirmed and rolled. He was trying to claw up a rock from the grass and soil but couldn't get it loose. He needed both hands to unearth it. As he removed both hands from my chest and tried to pry free a rock, I rolled and shook free.

I scrambled up off my knees and ran up the incline towards the car.

"Morrison," I cried out.

Just as I reached the gravel shoulder and rear of the car I felt a ton of flesh plough into me, I skidded across the gravel onto the roadbed. In the distance I could see Morrison in the agency car come rushing forward. Stanley had a rock. He brought it down aiming for my head. I moved just in time and he hit me on the shoulder. One more and I was kneaded dough. I squirmed. A car door was flung open. And Morrison Chang cried out.

"Drop it mac. I'll blow your head off." I heard Morrison throw his whole body into Stanley and knock him into the gravel.

Morrison gave him five or six solid karate whacks on the head and neck with his foot. Stanley tried to stagger up. Morrison hit Stanley again at the neck with everything he had, then nailed him with one swift kick to the jaw, and the big guy crumpled out on the gravel, his mouth and nose bleeding.

I gave Morrison a wonderful smile. He yanked me up off the ground.

"My friend. Your suit is soiled. Torn. I really don't know what Georges is going to say. He doesn't approve of our employees being poorly dressed. Suits not properly pressed. You know Lajoie himself sets a very high standard and a fine example."

"Yeah and my spine is out of line. I won't screw for six months and Lajoie–Chang is going to pay disability for a year."

"And this guy? Call the cops or call the doctor?"

"Stanley. Call the cops. I figure he killed Liz Strachan. And maybe even Clarence Wilson, or at least knows who trashed Wilson."

Morrison slipped off his belt, rolled Stanley over and wrapped the big fullback's wrists with the belt. Morrison flicked out his cellphone and called the police.

When he got off the phone I asked, "Morrison, do I get a raise?"

"My man, did I not just raise you up? What's more this is clearly neither the time nor the place to discuss wages. Company policy."

"Come on, give me a break. This guy near broke every beautiful bone in my beautiful body."

"You must always use discretion when pursuing a case especially one that may potentially involve a criminal suspect. Common sense says as much. And Lajoie–Chang Associates employee policy clearly states that during an investigation an employee must never put himself or others at risk or in harm's way. You've violated company policy. But I'll overlook it on this occasion and speak to Georges Lajoie on your behalf, see what I can do to mitigate his disapproval."

"Do I get a nice office with space?"

"Be reasonable."

A siren wailed.